I0593794

A
NECESSARY
GARDEN

A
NECESSARY
GARDEN

A NOVEL

ARLENE MACLEOD

❧W❧
WEYMOUTH PRESS

A NECESSARY GARDEN. Copyright © 2018 by Arlene MacLeod

All rights reserved. Printed in the United States of America. No part of this book may be used or reproduced in any manner whatsoever without written permission except in the case of brief quotations in critical articles and reviews. For information, contact Weymouth Press.

FIRST EDITION

Quotation from "Summer" by Dafydd ap Gwilym, translated by Richard Morgan Loomis, in *Dafydd ap Gwilym: the poems*, Center for Medieval and Early Renaissance Studies, Binghamton, New York, 1982, page 91.

Quotation from *Brut Y Tywysogion: The Chronicle of the Princes of Wales*, edited by The Rev. John Williams Ab Ithel, Longman, Green, Longman, and Roberts, London, 1860, pages 201 and 203.

Library of Congress Control Number: 2017914856

ISBN 978-0-9978010-0-2 Hardcover Edition
ISBN 978-0-9978010-1-9 Paperback Editions
ISBN 978-0-9978010-2-6 E-Book Editions

For my family,
Bruce, Morgan, Hannah, and now Simon

A
NECESSARY
GARDEN

"A girl pale as foam I love

Under the twigs, and her rashness is summer."

Dafydd ap Gwilym

…the king led his army into the mountain of Berwyn, and there the king encamped, with his advanced troops, in the mountains of Berwyn. And after remaining there a few days, he was overtaken by a dreadful tempest of the sky, and extraordinary torrents of rain. And when provisions had failed him, he removed his tents and his army to the open plains of England; and, full of extreme rage, he ordered the hostages, who had been previously long imprisoned by him, to be blinded…

Brut Y Tywysogion: The Chronicle of the Princes

WALES
12th Century

CHESTER

GWYNEDD
CAER YN ARFON

OSWESTRY

BERWYN
Mountains   Shrewsbury

POWYS

LUDELAVE

YStrad Flur   THE
BORDERS

CEREDIGION

ABERTEIFI   Hereford
CILGERRAN
RIVER TEIFI
NEWYDD ADPAR DINEFWR LLANDOVERY
EMLYN

River Wye

DEHEUBARTH

MYNYW   STRIGUIL
TENBY PEMBRY KIDWELLY
FOREST
GWYR

THE SEVERN

BRISTOL

N
W   E
S

Ilfracombe

PART I

CHAPTER ONE

Ceredigion, the Western Coast of Wales, 1151

IN THE GENTLE SPRING MORNING, in the endless forest outside the wandering stone walls hedging in the market town of Aberteifi, Tanwen walked alone. Her fingertips trailed along the uneven velvet tips of the high ferns crowding the path. A stream accompanied her way, gurgling loud as it rushed over tumbled stones. Damp air curled her heavy hair and pressed against her cheeks and bare neck, smelling of disturbed earth, lush growing, and the sharp scent of water. The path twined through ancient oaks, and as she walked, Tanwen hummed a broken song.

Above the trees, a red kite swooped and screamed. Tanwen stopped, listening, until the hunting bird beat away and the silence passed and the creaking, twittering hum of the forest resumed. She walked on. Reaching a horseshoe bend in the rushing stream, she shoved her skirts through the braided belt at her hips and yanked off her stiff boots. She crossed the water, never slipping on the green-slimed stones, smooth with endless rolling. On the far side, her feet squelched in thick mud and moss. She pushed aside feathery lady ferns, water sprinkling her forearms, searching. She'd planted roots here last Martinmas, when summer died and animals were slaughtered and dark gathered early under the trees. Now green shoots thrust like tiny fans from the moss and a single cloud-purple iris bloomed. She touched the stamens. Ochre dust smeared her fingertip. But where were the rest? She'd planted one for each passing season; the pattern was incomplete.

"Tanwen, whatever are you doing?"

Tanwen's foot skidded off a wet stone. Her skirts tumbled from her belt and swirled into the water.

"You truly are the most trying child." Aunt Agatha loomed on the far bank, a gloved hand gripping a slender birch, which arched under her weight. Agatha retreated. "Come back over here, this very moment."

Before answering, Tanwen ruffled the ferns into place over the single flower and waded back across the stream. "You know I've passed fifteen summers," she said then, and bent to wring out her skirts.

"We've no time for your ways now." Agatha's eyes searched the spaces between the trees. "Pull on your boots. You're right. You're not a child, so listen well to me now."

Tanwen hiked her skirts above her knees and shoved her boots onto her wet feet. Her aunt grasped her elbow before she'd finished and rushed her down the forest path. Tanwen darted a look behind them, but the path was empty and the forest peaceful, new leaves shiny and limp as the morning breeze faltered. "What's happening?" she asked. Aunt never came after her into the forest, outside the town walls. She was shocked Agatha had even found her here, in what she'd thought was her own secret place. No doubt Daron, her younger cousin, had showed Agatha the way. And a narrow hank of grey hair was falling from Agatha's always tight-wound bun.

"Men have come." Her aunt's voice cracked.

"To Aberteifi? What men? What do you mean?"

"We've no time to waste."

Was that fear in Agatha's voice? A tightness tingled between Tanwen's shoulder blades, so that she almost turned around again. Something was happening, disrupting the drab routines, the drawing of water, weeding onions, scrubbing stairs, cleaning and cleaning, waiting and waiting for life to begin. A pair of woodlarks darted between the high branches with a whir of wings, singing.

"Quickly now." Agatha was walking fast, her skirts dust-streaked and snapping with each step. They turned onto the wide path that led to the town fields.

"Aren't we going into Aberteifi?"

"Hush," said her aunt, "this is no game. It's bad enough you're out here alone."

Tanwen let herself be tugged along, her mind tumbling over the possibilities. They walked so fast even her breath quickened and aunt's face grew white and sheened with sweat. They pushed through the honeysuckle bushes, entered the orchard, and emerged into the fields. Swallows swooped over their heads, but the wide strips of new barley were empty of the workers who should be weeding the shoots and watering.

"Where is Daron?" asked Tanwen, staring at the fields.

"Where she ought to be." Her aunt's voice was hoarse. "At home. Dugald is with her."

Dugald was their day worker, clever, but prone to fits of anger. Once, in the barn, he'd clutched his head and roared, swaying, so frightening Daron that she fell over a bale of hay as she tried to get away.

They plunged into the hot sun and crossed the still field, Tanwen's wet skirts slapping at her ankles. At the far edge, Agatha stopped in the shade and wiped her forehead with her sleeve. Then she turned east and they stumbled along a rutted path, spiraling up. At the top, Agatha closed her eyes, her chest rising and falling. Small finches piped in the high grass, but no other sounds floated up from the town. Tanwen examined the treetops and the strips of barley arranged below them. The quiet was eerie.

Agatha hustled her down a grass-choked path Tanwen hadn't even known existed, so fast she stumbled over the splayed tree roots. "Pay attention," said her aunt. They reached the bottom, coming out behind their house and ran, hand in hand, up the narrow lane that skirted the back garden. Dugald swung the door open. Tanwen turned to look behind her, but Dugald yanked her through the door and pulled in the latch.

"I was coming," said Tanwen.

"Enough." Agatha dipped a handkerchief in the water bucket and wiped her forehead and cheeks, then her palms and each one of fingers. "The doors and shutters?"

"Bolted," said Dugald. "I'll watch from upstairs." He ducked his head under the doorway to the sitting room and Tanwen listened to his boots clomp up the stairs.

"Sit yourself down, Tanwen," said Agatha. She wet her fingers and smoothed her hair back into its precise bun. "It's time we talked."

Tanwen grabbed a stool. "Who has come? Who are these men you speak of?"

Her aunt regarded her for a long moment, her dark eyes distant, hardly seeming to notice her snarled hair or mud-streaked skirts as she usually would. "Soldiers. Armed men," said Agatha.

"Whose men?" Tanwen jumped to her feet. "Are they Normans? Northmen?"

Her aunt pushed her down on the seat. "Whether from the borders or the mountains, 'tis one and the same. They be armed men. Such as can bring only trouble."

This was a long speech for Agatha. Tanwen drew in a breath, her mind flickering with images of bold strangers armed with deadly tasseled spears. She knew the harsh stories, but the last armed men who had come to Aberteifi departed years ago, long before she came here to live.

"So we must talk of your future," said her aunt.

Tanwen stopped twirling the cloth of her skirt in her fingers.

Agatha stretched her hands out to the cold hearth as though they could be warmed. "You have two choices. I thought to pose them to you at midsummer, and let you ponder them well, then make your choice by harvest. Time has run on too fast."

Tanwen stared at her aunt's face, but in the shuttered room she could see only dark eyebrows and the stark line of a long nose. She started to speak, but her aunt held up a hand.

"Listen well. I've put much thought into your future, and Daron's too of course. But it's you who needs to think. It's not my life we speak of."

Tanwen swallowed. This was not the kind of conversation she ever held with her aunt. "These men will go, surely, after a few days, and things will go back as they were." She smiled up at Agatha.

Her aunt did not smile back. "Your grandmother was a healer."

Tanwen straightened her back. Agatha never spoke of Ceridwen, nor of Sorcha, her mother, and Agatha's only sister, and Tanwen had learned, when she first came to Aberteifi and her aunt's house, that she must never speak their names aloud either.

"Do you wish to follow that path?"

"I haven't thought," Tanwen whispered.

"Exactly," said Agatha. "And yet no time is left. You must decide, before a fortnight passes."

"So few days?" Tanwen stood up, but her aunt pushed her down again.

"War is coming, violence and blood. I'll have Daron and you both well out of it." Agatha stopped pacing and cracked the shutter to peer outside.

A shaft of bright sunlight struck the floor and gleamed orange. It was hard to believe in violence, with a hot May sun shining down on the garden outside and beating a circle of light on her aunt's smooth hair.

"It will come. If not in a few days or weeks, then in a few more." Her aunt's voice cracked. "There is no help for it; men will always fight. And after..." Agatha touched her forehead with one finger, as though it ached. "If you do not wish to turn to healing, you must marry, and soon."

"Surely not. Whatever is the need for such haste?" This conversation was so extraordinary. "And who would I marry?"

"I've sent word to a distant cousin. They'll be here in days." Her aunt paused, and now her eyes took in Tanwen's crumpled skirts and muddied feet. "She has a son."

"But how can they get into the town, if these soldiers are so dangerous?"

"He's a good prospect for you, far better than you could expect. You'll have a good home, clothing, food."

"But what about Daron?"

"She'll marry Rhodri."

"She has agreed?" Daron always said Rhodri, the weaver's eldest son, was stuck up, and his shoulders were bent already from leaning over his work.

"I haven't told her yet. But of course she will do as I say. I would do my best for you too, as my dead sister's child. The only question is, do you wish to marry at all, or will you be a healer?"

Tanwen frowned. "My grandmother married."

"You would need to go to the convent to learn."

"No!"

Her aunt sighed. "I do not force you Tanwen. The decision is yours to make." A shout from the street drew Agatha back to the window. Tanwen tried to see around her. Strangers in brown leather, armed with longbows, streamed down the lane between the houses. Agatha edged the shutter closed. "Do not leave the house. I will go to Lally's for news." She opened the door a crack, peered out, then slipped through.

Tanwen flung open the shutter. But the soldiers were gone. Her aunt, grey shawl flapping, disappeared into Lally's at the end of the lane. High purple clouds raced across the sky, plunging the empty passage and silent houses both into shadow.

CHAPTER TWO

TWELVE IS THE YEAR when one becomes a person. Her grandmother had said that to her, in a musing voice, as they sat, knees touching, by a stream one brilliant day in May. Not this stream in her secret place, so fast moving and cold, but another, far from here, a warm and wandering stream of slow green water, near the home she'd lost. And not this May. For Ceridwen was long since dead.

Tanwen lay back on the damp ground, let the sun warm her nose and neck, and tried to think, her fingers scratching up the cold dirt under the moss. Was she a true person yet? Ceridwen had meant it was time to choose a path. A person shouldn't meander like a stream.

She squinted into the hot brightness between the branches and sighed. Agatha was after her, all moments of the day. Even this morning, as she stirred her oats with honey, swirling them into the spiraling pattern she liked, her aunt had gripped her shoulder. "If you do not choose, Tanwen, I shall do it for you." Yet the soldiers had retreated from the town square to a noisy camp outside the gates, surely proving Agatha had overreacted. In the market square, boys tossed sticks and woman gossiped as always again, but Agatha just repeated in her toneless voice, "They'll be back." Her aunt let her work in the kitchen garden and let Daron make cheeses in the dairy, but kept them confined beyond that. Today was the first time she'd even managed to slip away. And all day long the litany--choose, choose.

Grandmother would have taught her healing, for that had been her path. Tanwen plucked a strand of grass and wound it round her finger. The villagers had feared Ceridwen, but came to her with broken bones, cracked skin, or strange lumps in their bellies. Ceridwen cured some and helped many. She had learned much, trailing after grandmother in the woods, but when that fierce autumn came and the ground froze and ice glazed the stream, Ceridwen had caught a chill, and by morning she was coughing deep, coughing day after day until her chest gurgled and her lips cracked dry and her finger tips turned blue.

Tanwen got to her feet. She had to get home, before Agatha realized she'd escaped. The sun sent streamers of warm yellow light spinning down through the trees and the woods were noisy with the songs of mating finches. Yet Agatha was always gloomy, harking back to the old days when soldiers had come and Aberteifi burned. Her own mother had died in those bad times, struck with the fever that took a third of the town when the soldiers left. Bodies had choked the river and it had run black for days with blood. Or so all the old women said. Still, all that was so very long ago; her aunt could never be cheerful or free of dread.

Tanwen began to run. She'd be missed, or Daron would tattle. In a convent, how harsh it would be, never to feel fresh air blowing on uncovered skin. So many kneeling prayers, dim chapels, and cold rock floors, and did she even want to be a healer? Plants she loved and the growing of them, searching out herbs and rare leaves in deep woods and marshes—but not the illness of people, old men with swollen legs, boys with bloody wounds and frightened eyes, frail mothers and frailer children. It was what she should do, she sometimes thought. To honor Ceridwen and live a life of purpose. But how awful to spend her days bound to the beds of the sick. She felt her stomach tighten and turn, like she was a twisting leaf captured in a shaft of wind, whirling until her vision blurred grey and she couldn't see which way to go.

She turned down their lane, sweating in the heat, and found the front door ajar. Men trudged in and out, red-faced and loaded down with wooden crates. Daron, in her blue gown trimmed with lace, appeared in the doorway, beckoned to one of the men as though in charge, and disappeared back inside.

Her aunt came to the door and Tanwen stepped back into the

tree shadows, but she'd been seen. Agatha waved impatiently. Tanwen sighed as she headed for the door, but in truth, she was curious. She paused on the doorstep. Inside, the dim chamber seemed over full, the guests clustered in the darkness, like a gathering of spiders.

"Come, Tanwen." Her aunt's voice held an edge of something odd.

But there was only a young man with dark hair. He sat on the bench and beside him perched a skinny girl, her hair all wispy curls, silvery white, under a white cap. Beyond them, in the shadows, sat a woman, straight-backed in aunt's chair. She wore flowing midnight wool, warm for this weather, but very fine. Her head was covered in a cap of linen trimmed in looped silk ribbons, pale, like moths fluttering around a lantern.

"Your mother was Sorcha." The woman spoke in a deep, musical voice.

Tanwen looked at her aunt. Agatha nodded, without meeting her eyes. "Yes, Sorcha was my mother." Saying the words out loud made her feel light, as though her mother had been swallowed up in darkness and now spilled free.

"What think you, Pennar?" said the woman.

The man stirred; his eyes met Tanwen's for the first time. They were the brown of a new walnut, secrets enclosed tight. "As you wish, mother."

Tanwen frowned and turned to her aunt.

"Pennar, take your sister outside, but do not stray from the garden. We shall not be delayed long," said the woman.

Man and girl slipped, soundless, from the room.

"Aunt, you haven't introduced me to your guest," said Tanwen. It was rude. But Agatha just fluttered her hands in an unusual way.

"I am Angharad," answered the woman. She did not smile, though her dark eyes were assessing rather than cold. "We have journeyed from the north, from Caer yn Arfon, to conduct our business, the shipping of wines. My son is learning the trade for he will take over one day." She turned back to Agatha.

"Wait," said Tanwen. "Excuse me, but I mean, why are you here now?"

Angharad tapped a gleaming boot twice on the stone floor. "My husband was cousin to your aunt's husband. You look intelligent and healthy. I want someone who can help Pennar with the books and you have been educated. I also want grandchildren and you should do for that as well." She spoke to Agatha. "Shall we settle the details now?"

Marriage, they spoke of marriage. "But I have not yet considered," said Tanwen, her voice strangled and too loud. She stepped backward, hitting the stool and the tray of spice cakes, which clattered onto the floor.

Tanwen stared at the scattered cakes, then rushed past the two women, out the door. She plunged across the road and on into the bright fields, running. I do not agree. I do not agree. The words darted and crackled in her head. She reached the woods, ducked under the tangled oak branches and ran on, until a stitch stabbed her side so insistently she had to slow.

Breath coming fast, she huddled in a quavering spot of sunshine, and let the sweat dry on her forehead. She wrapped her arms around her knees. She was no longer a child. Aunt was only doing her duty in finding her a husband. And there were those soldiers, milling around beyond the village walls, stealing chickens, trampling fields, waiting. Waiting, for the time being, but for how long and for what, everyone wondered and no one knew.

Her mother had loved a stranger, a wanderer who appeared in Aberteifi one brilliant summer day. Ceridwen had told her that her father was tall and had the bluest of eyes. But he had disappeared one day and never returned, though her mother had waited long days, and months, and then years. Did he wander off to a new life or a new woman? Or had he been killed somewhere, by a wolf, or a thief, or a Norman?

Her mother was dreamy, until love made her crazed. Ceridwen had been talkative and practical, using her skills to help others. But what did all that matter? The question was, who was she?

Her aunt offered her a new start, in this far off Caer yn Arfon. She'd learn the wine business from Angharad, who would be difficult to please, she thought, but probably fair. But why was Angharad willing to gamble on her? Why not find Pennar a wife closer to home? Tanwen tried to conjure up an image of Pennar, but he was a blur. Only dark Angharad glowed before her eyes, in her midnight gown.

A week later, Tanwen dug in the kitchen garden, her wool skirt glistening with oval drops of water from the sprinkle of rain just past. She thrust her trowel into the dirt. Already she'd put in green onions, leeks, beans. Now she was planting flowers. Her aunt did not approve, so she nestled ox-eye daisies and cow parsley in among the useful vegetables, keeping an eye toward the house. Dirt crept up her arms and her fingernails were earth-filled crescents. She hiked her gown over her knees and worked, not finishing until the sun, a glowing white ball behind the mist, sank beyond the hills. Sitting on her heels in the twilight, she made small pies of mud and listened to the sociable green finches in the three apple trees.

After awhile, she drew water from the well, rinsed her arms and splashed more onto her neck, careless of the way it dripped. For the thousandth time, she thought of Angharad and Pennar, turning the choice this way and that in her mind. Marry or be a healer. She wished, almost, that Agatha had decided for her.

Her aunt had said nothing more. But the soldiers could be heard every day now, thudding arrows into the timber fence they'd erected, practicing their killing games. Some said they came from the North and would kill them all as they slept. Others said they came from farther off, across the eastern mountains or even the sea. Who led them and what would they do next? None of the merchants or farmers knew. Time was racing away. She would have to choose soon. Her head ached day and night and she wanted only a deep unbroken sleep.

Voices floated from the house as she crossed the muddy yard and nudged open the door. On the bench by the fire, with Daron at his side, sat Pennar. An entirely different Pennar surely. He wore a tunic of marigold cloth, gleaming like the summer feathers of the finches that flew to her hand when she tossed crumbs. Handsome deerskin gloves lay on his lap and a wool cap topped with curling feathers tilted on his head. He was laughing, head thrown back, at something

Daron had just said, and then he touched her hand. Daron blushed and looked away, but she didn't move her fingers from his.

Tanwen banged the door shut. The kitchen maid jumped and the goblets tilted on her tray. Pennar leaped up and bowed. "Mistress Tanwen, how pleased I am to be in your presence again." His words were too formal. How ridiculous she was, standing before him in her dirt-smudged gown and mud-crusted feet. Daron was dressed in her best, and the crocus yellow set off her dark hair, shining loose to her waist from under a lacy linen cap. Her own hair was a mad tangle, in a mass atop her head, and long strands, wet with well water, clung to her neck.

Agatha entered and gestured to the maid to stop gawking and set out the dishes of nuts and sausage. "We've been honored by an unexpected visit, Tanwen. Do ready yourself and then join us." She turned to Pennar, comfortably settled again on the bench. "Won't you let Daron serve you some ginger biscuits with the fine wine you brought?"

Tanwen backed out of the room. She climbed to the attic chamber she shared with Daron, her cheeks flaming. She yanked her gown off and pulled her best chemise from the chest against the wall and dragged it on, the cloth catching on her damp skin. She forced a comb through her tangled hair. How Pennar's brown eyes had sparkled when he'd whispered in Daron's pink ear. Daron was too young for marriage, and promised besides, to Rhodri.

Tanwen paused in lacing up her gown. It seemed she'd best choose soon or she'd have no choice at all. Pennar was a good match, despite the distance to his home, or maybe, if she were honest, because of it. No more women nattering behind her back about her mother's waywardness or her grandmother's frightening skills. She could begin anew, be a normal woman and wife.

She must draw this man to her, make him hers. She'd have to outshine Daron, who was everything she was not, so small and neat, with her gleaming dark hair and perfect white skin. She swung around to the mirror dangling from a leather cord on the wall. Her grey eyes, wide and wild, stared back.

She braided her thick hair and coiled it once round her head and let the waving ends fall in a thick copper sweep down her back. She laced her gown tighter, to show her form. She doused her neck with lavender water and a big splash of the rich rosewater she'd made last summer. She laced on soft shoes, a gift from grandfather, before he'd forgotten her, gone strange with Ceridwen's death. She examined herself. Her face was strained and pink. Her hair escaped her braid and curled at her neck, but she was neat enough. She ran a finger along her dark brows to tame them, and took a long breath.

When she descended the narrow steps, she found the sitting room silent and empty. Then she heard their voices, outside. She followed, lifting her skirts high to avoid the mud. Her new home would have stone pavings everywhere. No mud, and masses of useless brilliant flowers.

She threw open the garden gate, and stepped into the garden she had just planted, transformed in the dusk, lit by lanterns in Agatha and Daron's hands. Pennar's eyes flickered over her.

"You have returned sooner than expected to our town," Tanwen said. "Have you more business to conduct?"

"It is my hope," Pennar said and moved toward her.

"Do the soldiers buy your wines?" Tanwen pulled some mint leaves and shredded them in her fingers, lifting them to catch the scent.

His eyes followed her fingers. "Shall we return inside, and I will offer you some of the Gascony wine?"

His eyes locked with hers in an alarming way. Tanwen looked away and took a shaky breath, then deliberately met his gaze and smiled.

They all trailed her back inside. She settled herself on the bench, and let him sit beside her, leaving no room for Daron. His eyes traced her wrist as she reached for a goblet of his dark wine. It was round and full and richly spicy on her tongue.

She held the goblet out to Pennar for more. Firelight flickered amber patterns on her bare forearm. He was staring. Amazing. One had only to tighten one's gown and comb one's hair. Tanwen bit into one of her aunt's sausages and flicked a crumb from her skirts. Being the wife of a wine merchant might be fine indeed.

The grey morning light threw harsh shadows on her aunt's face. Agatha beckoned, and Tanwen, shivering, threw back her blanket and followed her down the creaky stairs. Daron did not stir.

Agatha poured herb tea into two cups and set them steaming on the table. She sat, her back to the fire, which crackled with an armful of apple wood. "A worthy performance last night."

Tanwen shoved her hair from her eyes and shrugged.

Agatha's mouth twitched. "You haven't done badly, you've won him. He agreed to the betrothal before he left."

"He's gone?" It all seemed like a dream.

"He's eager. And Angharad approves. We'll hold the feast next week, Wednesday, I think. You'll marry two days after. Midsummer he goes to Gascony for the harvest."

Stated in Agatha's flat voice it sounded so final. Marriage. Still, it was what she wanted. Needed. A new start in a new land.

"I'm not sorry Daron will stay here with me, she's young yet. Though it would have been a good match, even for her." Her aunt repositioned her cap on her head, and considered Tanwen, her fingers tapping. "You've got your mother's ways after all, though you haven't shown it until now. Just so she looked when she was after your father."

"You knew my father?"

Agatha picked up her tea. "This man will not be disappearing on you. Use those gifts of yours to bind him, and you'll never know want. You're my sister's child, and I've done the best I can for you." She drained her cup and left the room.

Tanwen wandered to the window and drew back the shutter. Weak sun fell on her face. She should feel glad, but instead she felt empty, like a hollowed out tree, and cold in the exact center of her chest, as on that November day when she'd first walked, alone, into Agatha's town.

CHAPTER THREE

T HE MAY WEEK before her marriage swept by, fleeting, enchanting. Tanwen rose early and did her weeding, then wandered with a sack of dried pears or apples through the forest, sitting in the ferny shade until violet shadows and evening cold drove her home. The soldiers seemed occupied in their camp north of town and something like normal life in the town had resumed. Aunt did not chastise her about unwashed dishes or plucking geese, but let her go. Tanwen felt only that she must keep moving, out among the trees, or she'd not be able to breathe.

Her aunt bothered her with only one thing, fittings for a wedding gown, which delighted her for the gown was green, made of fine wool the color of new leaves. She loved how her red-gold hair hung brilliant against its mossy depths.

Daron stopped following her around and kept up a sullen silence rather than filling the air with her usual chatter. Tanwen was bothered, more than she would have expected. But Daron would marry Rhodri and spend her life here in Aberteifi, and they would see each other rarely, if at all. Tanwen felt numb when she thought of this, and rose ever earlier to avoid her cousin's silences.

The day before Angharad and Pennar were due back in Aberteifi, Tanwen lay on her pallet after another wakeful night. Daron snored lightly beside her. The first birdcalls seemed to insist she come out. She tossed back the blanket and fled down the stairs. A shifting veil of mist surrounded the stones of the garden wall and turned the slate path slick and black. She laced the sides of her gown and shivered. If she went back for her cloak, Daron would not wake, but Agatha might.

As she hesitated, the door creaked open and Daron slipped out. Her hair was already neatly braided and a thick cloak pinned tight at her neck. "Where are you going?" she said in an accusing voice.

Tanwen shrugged. "Just for a walk."

"It's freezing out here."

"Then go back inside." It was disconcerting to have Daron stare at her with open hostility, though they had always argued, ever since her first night in Agatha's home.

"I'll come with you." Daron fingered her brooch as she spoke.

"You never like walking in the woods."

"You know Mama dislikes it. Why do you go?"

Tanwen waved a hand, cutting off the flow of words. "She will not know this time. Unless you tell her." Which was unlikely, for Daron was ever jealous of her mother's attentions, good or ill. Tanwen brushed her loose hair from her eyes and looked toward the forest. "Come, if you like." She decided on the path that headed up to the hills. After a moment, Daron stumbled along behind her. Why had she let her come? Still, she turned to wait.

They walked side by side until they reached a clearing, brightened by a pool. Daron gave a hesitant smile, though her cloak was spotted from the dripping trees. Tanwen sat down on a flat stone and stared at the silver water.

Daron, arms folded over her chest, stared at the water too. "Aren't you getting hungry, shouldn't we turn around?"

Tanwen shook her head. Breezes were sweeping away the mist and the sky was turning a delicate blue.

"Tanwen, did you hear me? Aren't you hungry? I could eat a whole platter of venison, or a giant bowl of porridge."

"I heard you, of course I did."

"So say something in return."

"You invited yourself. I didn't come to talk."

"But Tanwen." Daron sat, folding her skirt under her knees. "Aren't you excited? You'll dress in rich clothes everyday and drink wine that's never sour. And Pennar is very fine."

Tanwen laughed, disconcerted at this picture of such a strange life. "I'll learn the wine business."

"Don't be ridiculous. Angharad will never let you see her accounts. She barely lets Pennar do anything. You'll be idle all the morning and feasting in the afternoons. On swan and sugared grapes." Daron turned her eyes to the pool. "And have you thought of what it will be like."

"What are you talking about?"

"Lying with Pennar, have you thought of it?"

Tanwen stood up and looked to the east. She'd always wanted to walk all the way to the head of the Teifi, walk until she reached the deep pools where they said the river began.

"Tanwen! Are you listening?"

"I'm going on."

Daron looked alarmed. "We can't go further. Mama will be very angry."

Tanwen started walking.

"Tanwen!" Daron trailed behind. "Don't go. What about the soldiers, it's not safe."

"It's fine."

"Stop, Tanwen, I'm not going any further." Daron's voice rose shrill, frightening the birds.

"Don't then." Tanwen walked faster.

"Mama is right," Daron yelled after her. "You're naught but trouble, and crazed like your mother!"

Tanwen's eyes burned. She knew Daron gossiped with the other girls about her, but she'd never said such words out loud. She glanced back at Daron's face, white and abashed, then began to run, leaving her cousin's anxious calls fading behind. She'd spend the whole day out in the forests. Soon she'd be a wife, dressed in fine wools, encased in closed rooms. But not today.

She ran until heat flooded her chest and warmed her palms. Then she slowed to a walk and kept on. In life, one could not have all one wanted. The empty garden of her childhood home, after Ceridwen died and the flooding rains came and the crops failed in a sea of icy mud, flashed through her mind and she drove it away, as she always did. Unlike her mother, she would be sensible. But not today.

The sun was a warm band of gold encircling her head. She followed the river's edge, on the narrow path trod flat by red deer. First she walked fast, striding along, admiring how quickly she covered the ground. Later, she strolled and hummed, as sun heated the woods and the air stilled. She could hardly get lost if she followed the river. She tried to think about nothing. How angry Agatha would be when she returned, but in a few days, whatever Agatha thought and Daron said would be nothing to her anymore.

When the sun poured straight down through the high oaks, she stopped. She should turn back. Too bad she'd never reach the deep pools where the river began. They were rumored to be a strange place, haunted even, ringed by dark firs and filled with black water that people claimed could tell your future. She leaned against an oak and waved at a cloud of gnats. She tried but could not imagine her own future, in the frozen north with its snow-peaked mountains and green ice sea. Pennar would come on the morrow, and the marriage would take place, and she would go away with him.

She sat down on a flat rock and opened the pouch hanging from her belt. She placed dried apples on bread in a precise circle like a flower. Feeling calmer, she ate. The chirps of robins and rustling of leaves was all she could hear, and in the distance the tumbling rush of the river. She unsnarled her hair with her fingers, thinking. This would be her last chance, maybe ever, to wander like this in the forest. Neither Pennar nor Angharad would tolerate that, it was certain. And she meant to be a good wife, her part of the bargain. She picked at a loose thread on her skirt, until she'd made a tiny hole, and pressed her fingernail into her white thigh. Her last day of freedom. She picked up her bundle and tucked up her skirts. She'd have to walk quickly now, though the days were at their summer longest, to make it up the Teifi and home before dark.

She must have slept, her body felt heavy, languorous. She stretched, the earth warm underneath her, yawned, and sat up. Afternoon light spilled through the trees. She should be worried about getting home, but she felt content and calm instead. She pulled up her skirts and let the sun pour heat onto her white legs. Her bare toes clutched the dark earth, as though she too were a plant, joyous at the start of endless summer. She laughed at her fancy and got to her feet. Her legs ached in a pleasant way. Moss grew soft tassels that tickled as she walked and the faint scent of garlic wafted from whorls of star ransoms. To be alive on such a day! How glad she was she'd kept on.

She stretched her arms above her head and began to hum a dancing song; it had been circling in her head all this fortnight, since some minstrels with a lute had come to play. She had stepped forward to join Daron and the other girls who danced in the market square, but Agatha had dragged her away. Why not dance here? Today was too lovely for dark memories, the sun too caressing, the woods too scented with sweet violets and the scent of the river flowing dark under the sun.

She tried a few hesitant steps, humming. Her voice sounded loud in the clearing and she stopped. But there was no one here. She started again, switching to words, recalling the melody as she went along, until the notes echoed like songbirds calling from the trees. She reached the end and laughed when she realized she'd silenced the real birds. She walked to the center of the clearing, her feet sinking in lush grass, closed her eyes and started again at the beginning, twirling like a real dancer, sun and shadow crossing her face as she whirled. Her eyelids lit up with warm redness and blackened and she sang, any melody she could remember or invent, her hair flying in a circle. She wished she had on her wedding gown so she'd match the ferns, but her old skirts, bleached linen, gleamed like new wheat. Her feet beat out the intricate steps, which she knew by heart, though Agatha forbade it, saying she'd remind the villagers of her mother. She danced around the scattered boulders and tiny clustered firs, danced until her body heated and her legs tired and her song was interspersed with gasps. She whirled, and whirled more, breathing in sharp fir, crushed grass, and spicy damp earth.

A clank of metal sounded. Tanwen stopped, her skirts wrapping around her knees.

A man in a bright mustard cape, and behind him more, hovering in the shadows at the wood's edge. Tanwen grabbed up her skirts and ran. She heard a shout and more men stepped out from the trees in front of her. She darted to her right, but one grabbed her waist, another took her wrist, they encircled her. So many, and she so foolishly alone.

The man in the bright cape approached and the others fell back. He lifted an arm and the grip around her waist loosened. But there was nowhere to run. "What village do you come from?"

Tanwen played his words over in her mind, for his speech, though Welsh, had the strange intonations of the nobility. He was young, his hair a mass of chestnut waves, gleaming clean. They were of a height, for she was tall for a woman. His shirt was made of the finest tucked linen, his red tunic belted in silver and hung with a green-jeweled dagger.

She drew her bare toe in under her skirt. "I am Tanwen, of Aberteifi." Her voice came out as a whisper.

The stranger smiled, a friendly smile of even white teeth. "And I am Owain ap Macsen, of Adpar." He took a step towards her. "Will you do me the favor of sharing a meal with me?"

"I must return to the village. They expect me back."

"You are quite safe, here with me; surely you have time for a small repast."

Tanwen bit her lip.

"Do you only sing and dance, and not speak, like a wood sprite?"

Tanwen felt herself smile.

Owain took off his glove and thrust it in his belt, and slowly reached a hand toward her, as though she were a bird who would flit away. "Just a meal, there can be no harm in that."

His eyes were warm amber and looked at her as though nothing mattered more than having her agree. She hesitated. But it was a magical day, her last day ever of true freedom, and this strangeness seemed but part of the whole. She examined the ring of men behind him, dressed alike in dark tunics.

Owain touched her hand.

"Have you a cook here in the woods then?"

"Indeed yes," said Owain, and she laughed. But a small man saluted her and started giving orders. Soon the clearing was transformed. They erected an open tent of gleaming red cloth and set two folding stools beside a table. Evidently they had carried all this on an extra packhorse. Even sullen Daron's face would light up when she told her of this wondrous encounter!

Owain seated her, as though she were a fine lady and gestured to his man, who brought a skin of wine and poured it into a carved wooden cup. He held it out to her. She took the cup and her fingers brushed his. She sipped the wine, golden like the day, full and round and sweet.

Owain talked, telling small stories of the hunt, putting her at ease. He turned a commonplace stalking of deer into a fine adventure, laughing often. When the meal came, remarkably soon, it was roasted venison, stewed turnips mixed with apples spiced with fragrant cinnamon and biting pepper, and fresh picked greens coated with vinegar and honey. They drank another wine, red and dry, heated with cinnamon, stronger than she was used to. As they talked, and laughed, Owain's men melted away, leaving the two of them alone in the circle of the red cloth, sheltered from wind, bathed in the sun's slanting rays.

She tried not to look too amazed as she tasted the luxurious food, while Owain told her amusing stories of his home, a place named Adpar. He asked her no questions. She let the talk flow around her, enveloping her in a new world. He talked much of his horses, each one special and beloved as a person. As he described his manor home, she stared at the firs ringing the clearing, trying to imagine a timbered hall surrounded by high walls, and kitchens built of logs long covered with ivy. A permanent place, a true home.

She examined him too, when she could. His face was browned by sun, though it was yet earliest summer, and unlined except near his eyes, where the skin crinkled each time he smiled. His hands were whiter than hers. She pulled her bare feet in further under her skirts and pleated the linen in her fingers to cover the hole at her thigh. But Owain was looking out across the meadow, to the circle of his men, laughing at some joke. He smiled, a slow smile, then caught her staring. Heat rushed to her cheeks. She tried to breathe. She couldn't draw her eyes away.

His smile widened, and he reached across the table and lifted her hand to his mouth. His breath ruffled warm over her fingertips. He kissed her palm, his lips slightly rough. She tugged her hand back. But it had not been unpleasant.

"Tanwen," he said, then waited as his man gathered up the dishes and carted off their table. "Come away with me."

She laughed, and glanced at his men, who were collecting belongings scattered across the clearing. It was time to end this enchanted day.

"I do not jest." His voice was serious. "What would hold you in Aberteifi?"

She got to her feet.

"I find you…" A puzzled look came to his eyes. He didn't finish, just shook his head and looked away, into the trees.

She looked where he gazed, but there was nothing there, only shadows gathering.

"I would have you near me," he said.

"I am to marry."

"No. I want you with me." His voice was fierce. "Tanwen." He traced a finger, hardly touching, along her chin and down her neck. "You must come with me. I have met no one like you, ever." He backed away, frowning.

She felt a sharp longing to be touched so, just once more.

"How would we live?" She shook her head and turned away. Had she said that? She did not know him at all. It was fantastical and so strange, but never had anyone seemed to so desire her smiles and words. Never had it been easy to wile away hours speaking of anything and everything. And she had found him here, in her woods.

She did not know Pennar, either. And this man was no merchant of wine in the far north, but a lord, with servants, and lands, a manor house, silver-plate and coin. A life she knew nothing of, nothing at all. No, it was all crazy, a whirling dream of the forest. And evening was hastening on, the shadows long across the grass. "I must go."

Owain gestured to his men, who moved to their horses; the tent and the stools they had seated themselves on were already stowed away. "From now on, you will be safe, with me. We will have many days, just like this. And more." Owain placed a solemn kiss on her brow, and led her to his horse.

She touched the spot on her forehead. Something seemed to have been decided. Had she said yes? She hardly knew; she felt so odd from strong wines and strange longed for emotions, beckoning her on.

CHAPTER FOUR

LYR GETHIN, a stranger in Aberteifi, leaned against a shed on the outskirts of town, ignoring the smell of sheep and hoping he looked inconspicuous. Aberteifi was crowded for the Saturday market, so perhaps he'd escape notice. But he was taller than the men here and his short black hair and shaved face drew stares. These men were bearded, like all the upland Welsh, but he'd long ago adopted the Norman style. Though he was not Norman. He belonged nowhere, which made him useful to Rhys, younger brother of the princes of Ceredigion.

A whiff of frying sausage floated by and his stomach rumbled. For weeks now they'd traveled hard, Rhys and his band of men, one night here, three nights there. He hadn't slept a full night for so long he wondered what it would be like, to sink into that oblivion, not for a few short hours but for something like eternity.

Five nights past, the barn they'd sheltered in had shot up in flames. Luck was with them, the hay gone, so they'd stumbled out coughing smoke and watched as flames flared and heat cracked the oak beams and the whole glowing skeleton crashed to the ground, coals flying into the night like crazed stars.

Gethin's eyes floated over a group of farmers passing just in front of him. No threat, just farmers with turnips headed to market. He joined the throng and sauntered along with them, as though shopping for greens and ham for his supper. Market day meant the chance to observe and listen, which was why Rhys had sent him on ahead.

After that fire, Rhys' men had muttered about carelessness, but Rhys, one of the six sons of Gruffydd, former lord of Ceredigion, never made a mistake like that. He knew someone had tried to kill them. Life had made Rhys wary, with both parents murdered and an elder brother already dead. The prince had ordered them mounted even as the barns still smoldered and they'd not halted longer than a few snatched hours since. Rhys had the stamina of five men and the persistence of ten, and he wanted the men who'd kindled those fires. Gethin studied the families streaming around him. The men eyed him too, then looked away, or at the ground, and hastened on.

In a fury or not, Rhys had no match at drawing men to him. And that was the other intention here, as in all the towns and hamlets they'd passed through, Rhys threatening and charming men to his side, because in the end he meant to have it all back, everything his grandfather had lost and his father had died to regain, the whole kingdom of Ceredigion. Which meant driving out the Northmen and Normans both.

Gethin eyed a pile of hay in an empty stall and yawned, but kept his feet moving and his eyes scanning the crowd, the market square, and the hills beyond the town walls. Already this morning he'd combed those hills, looking for anything unusual. He'd found Northmen camped in the forest, bored and violent like soldiers everywhere, but nothing else.

A glint of silver on one of the hills caught Gethin's eye and he stopped walking. But it was a gull, not sun on swords, only grey feathers sparking. He studied the green hills, shadowing to violet as they rolled to the horizon off to the east. The river he'd seen this morning would be there, winding through the grass like a dark snake. He itched to trace its path as far as it went. But his job was to scout the town, or as necessary, spy.

A stir made him swing around. Rhys was riding in with his teulu crowded behind, dressed in matched tunics of leather and carrying bright spears to impress the town. He waved a gloved hand to the throng, his black hair gleaming and his brows drawn together in a fierce frown, making him look older than his nineteen years. A huge intertwining brooch of silver fastened his crimson cloak.

"Lyr Gethin!"

Gethin frowned at the slap on his shoulder.

"A fine greeting," said Huw, a jovial newcomer to Rhys' teulu.

Gethin turned back to Rhys. His men were too careless, sure their handsome young lord was invincible.

"Come on. We've only a few hours. Rhys is safe as a babe here and you're not his bodyguard anyway." Curiosity lit Huw's square face, but Gethin offered nothing.

Huw surveyed the crowds with a delighted smile. "There's bound to be women somewhere."

Gethin let Huw drag him forward. They wandered past the market stalls and his stomach cramped with the smells of honey and just baked wheat bread. Mostly the stalls held piles of fresh greens, new onions, and wheels of white cheese, but one was piled with bolts of wool, blues and browns. There was the occasional bolt of finer fabric, dyed brilliant red or saffron.

He stopped to pass the time with the merchant, a tall man with an air of adventure, though his hair was grey and he limped. "Fine wares," the man said. "Are you in the market for some fabric for a gown perhaps, for a lady back at home?"

The innocent query stabbed somewhere deep in his chest.

The merchant studied his face. "Perhaps a look at some sturdy wool then, for a tunic; a man needs something heavy on the coast. Will you be here long?"

Gethin relaxed at the man's unabashed search for information. "I'm with Rhys, and how long we stay only he knows."

The man pulled a bolt of sturdy brown wool forward. "Warm, this," he said.

"But dull," said Gethin.

The man pulled down another bolt, without hurry, this one a midnight color, not black but deepest blue.

"I'm not in the market for buying," said Gethin.

"No harm done in looking." The merchant spread the wool out and his hand, white in the sun, was lit by an unusual ring, intricately etched and set with a square red stone.

"Have you traveled far," Gethin asked, "looking for these wools?"

"Used to," said the man. "Now my nephew does the trading; he's in Constantinople. Supposed to bring back some of those embroidered silks and some brilliant wools from Venezia."

"There's a market, for such, here?"

"More than you'd imagine," said the merchant. "Norman fashion sweeps the valleys."

"What's it like, traveling to such places?"

"Wondrous," said the man, a smile igniting his blue eyes. "Commotion, colors, horrible and delicious smells, intense heat." He grinned. "And yet for all that, it's just like here, violence and love, different people but all the same. They all need clothes."

Gethin wandered away, a package of wool wrapped in oiled cloth under his arm. It would make a fine tunic, though he'd have to find someone to make it for him. Gethin lifted the packet the merchant had given him to his nose, a tiny pillow filled with shavings of sandalwood. "The smell of the East," he'd said. The scent tingled in his nose.

A boy bumped into him and sped on. People were pointing. Gethin turned, expecting to see Rhys but it was another man, expensively mounted and dressed, whose bodyguard crowded the lane. He grabbed the elbow of a youth passing by. "Who's that?"

"Owain ap Macsen, from up the Teifi." The boy tried to pull free of his grasp. "Look at his dagger!"

Gethin let the boy go. Owain, a flashy but useless dagger strung from his wide silver-linked belt, wasn't alone. Behind him was a woman. She was ignoring the whispers, her eyes on the forested hills he'd examined earlier. He turned to ask who she was, but the boy was gone.

The small procession passed him. He trailed along after with the rest of the curious townspeople. Owain and his men dismounted outside a house with a spill of gold flowers in a pot near the door. He lifted the woman off the horse and sent a man to pound on the door. For a long time no one answered. Then a woman of middle years, dressed in a dark gown, stepped out onto the step. She stood still, her hands laced together, facing the men.

Gethin drew in closer. The light was fading. But he could see the woman's face was solemn and her eyes too bright. She ignored the men and spoke only to the young woman. "I should have expected no less from you." Her voice was so quiet the crowd jostled in closer to hear.

The young woman nearly took a step back. Then she straightened her shoulders and spoke up, her voice carrying. "I am sorry, truly, Aunt. But I am going with Lord Owain."

"Lord Owain, is it now," said the older woman, turning to the man with the flashy dagger. "And where are your lands, sir?"

Owain made her a small bow, and said, "To the east." He gestured vaguely. "I will take Tanwen there and she will be well cared for."

The aunt's mouth tightened. She looked past him to the young woman. "You have a chance, Tanwen. You can turn your back on the past."

The girl flushed and her eyes filled, but she lifted her chin and said nothing.

The older woman watched her without blinking. Then she swallowed, her face creased with holding in her emotions. "As you wish," she said, so quietly the crowd leaned in to hear. "But hear me. You were born in a hard year. A time of turmoil and black blood flowing. I see you now. You'll live a tumultuous life, with nothing easeful or easy." She waited, in the silence, looking not at the girl but down toward the glinting harbor, then she turned her back, entered her house and silently shut the door.

The young woman stared at the closed door. The crowd hesitated, then started only slowly to move and speak, as though released from a spell.

Owain leaned over and whispered something in the young woman's ear. She shook her head slowly, then met his eyes and smiled at him, and the sinking sun sent a last gleaming ray down to set her copper hair ablaze.

Gethin frowned and backed out of the gossiping crowd. He leaned against a garden wall, the granite rough and cold against his shoulder. A strand of wayward ivy curled against his neck and he brushed it away.

Owain seated the woman behind him on a bay charger with

feathered legs and they passed quite close, walking, so close Gethin could see her pale forehead and her lips pressed tight, but she did not turn her head his way. She sat very straight. Not touching Owain, not looking back.

CHAPTER FIVE

A Hunting Lodge North of Adpar, 1151

TANWEN WOKE with a start. She stared at the fluttering linen ties on the bed hangings and remembered where she was. Owain's side of the huge bed felt cold. Sun streamed through the open shutter across the room, marking a golden triangle on the tumbled blanket. She thrust her head under the covers. They smelled of wool and lovemaking.

Her face grew hot, but she smiled and stretched, just to feel the scratch of blanket against her bare skin. She'd been here, with Owain, for one month, an early summer month of long days and too short nights. She never slept enough, though she hardly cared.

She tossed back the covers and crossed to the window. Warm air ruffled her hair, tickling her neck. Another lovely summer day. She peeked out, but the men were long gone, traipsing off to hunt before dawn. The packed earth yard of Owain's lodge was silent. A long day stretched ahead, unfamiliar, strange, and wonderful.

She picked up a new robe of sheer linen and swung it over her shoulders. Owain was generous and she so wanted to make him happy. Last night, he'd come up from the stables late, after she'd fallen asleep. He'd awakened her body with feather-like strokes, twining her hair around his fingers. She felt herself blush and she crossed to the oak chest, where a basin of water and a bowl of rose scented soap waited. She tossed water on her hot face and ran her fingers through her hair. She should be downstairs long since. Though this was but Owain's summer residence, it was formidable, with a dining hall, their timber chamber above, stables large as their living quarters for Owain's pampered horses, and a kitchen and several sheds. How would she learn what she must if she rose every morning when the sun was high? Owain liked to drink far into the night, coming to bed long after she had fallen asleep at the table, her head in her arms. Then he was still wide awake, and wanted her to prepare a bath in the wood tub by the fire, unlace his clothes. He would tell her stories of the hunt, or of a fine hawk he saw climbing the currents up into a purple sky. In bed he was gentle, insistent, and once satisfied rolled off her and plunged into sleep. He seemed never to dream, but slept silent, sticking to his side of the bed.

Tanwen picked up a gown and laced up the silk ribbons, tying bows at her hips. The dairy girl's flirty laugh floated up through the window, sounding for a moment like her cousin. What was Daron doing now, back in Aberteifi? She almost missed her incessant chatter. Tanwen leaned out the window and watched Cook cross the yard below, long loaves of the fine white bread Owain favored stacked in her arms. After fastening the shutter against the day's heat, she sat on the bed, releasing the sharp scent of lavender. Owain's chamber was square, symmetrical, and so quiet. Set apart. As she was, for she was now Owain's leman. Special to him, his lark, he called her sometimes, in the night. But no longer someone Angharad would ever consider as a suitable wife for her precious Pennar.

Where had that silly thought come from? Tanwen jumped up, grabbed a ribbon and wound her heavy hair up off her neck, and sped down the uneven stairs.

Elise waited, slumped at the bottom, her freckled face glum. Tanwen halted halfway down. She should have called the girl, but it was strange to ask for help throwing on a gown. Owain had presented her with Elise as her maid after that first enchanted night. But it wasn't like that, some sort of crude payment. And it wasn't just words, though words flowed so eloquently from Owain. He loved her. She could feel in the touch of his square-tipped fingers on her neck.

Elise coughed and stood up. She was tall, taller even than Tanwen. "I'll see to the chamber then, mistress." She climbed the stairs, her back stiff, lifted skirts showing bare feet and red-earth smudged ankles. The oak door stuck, but she shoved it open with one arm.

Tanwen stared up the empty stairwell. She should go after her. She hesitated on the bottom step, considering, then yanked open the outside door. Tomorrow, she would do better. She'd rise early and let Elise tug her gown over her head and untangle her wild hair with a birch wood comb.

Outside, warm wind rustled the leaves of the three oaks shading the yard. Tanwen stared at the trees, wondering where to go today. In Agatha's town, she'd forever been the outsider, the strange girl who'd walked in one day, feet blue with cold, seeking an aunt she'd never seen. But here she had a chance of a new life, in Owain's home. It was wonderful, but also daunting. She ran across the wet grass and pushed open the swinging door to the kitchen.

Cook and three girls clustered around a table, peeling last year's apples. Fresh greens and small onions with dirt clinging to their plump sides were piled in a basket on the floor. Their voices halted and the girls stared. Though she'd been at the hunting lodge a month, she'd never intruded here.

Cook put her knife down and studied her. "A good day to you, mistress. Will ye be having something to break your fast?"

"No, it's so late. I meant to get up…"

One of the maids elbowed another. Tanwen felt her cheeks flush.

Cook scowled at the girls. "Get yourself to work, those apples nor the onions won't be peeling themselves. Come this way," she added to Tanwen. "Don't you be minding these muddle heads." She drew Tanwen to a windowed nook with a table and bench. It was a pleasant kitchen, not large, but built with a high ceiling so the smoke could coil away and scrubbed very clean. Cook brought her a tin cup of watered ale and some brown bread and soft cheese, then stood by the table, arms folded over her broad chest.

Tanwen took a bite. "This cheese is very good."

Cook just stared until Tanwen felt like squirming. "We haven't seen you here before."

"It's very quiet in the hall, alone." Tanwen put the cheese down.

It was sticking in her throat.

"He's happier, since you came."

Tanwen looked up. "Is he?"

"I've known him all his life. I've been here, in this very kitchen mind, since he was a wee child." Cook pointed to the cheese. "It's not good?"

Tanwen put a chunk on some bread and took a bite.

"The question is," Cook said, "what are you going to do with yourself?"

Tanwen swallowed the cheese. Cook seemed an odd sort of servant. She ordered everyone in the lodge about, even Owain's men. Tanwen pulled a strand of hair from her mouth and leaned forward. "That's just what I was thinking. I need to have something to do. Something, I mean, that is mine."

The older woman pulled a heavy bowl toward her and picked up a knife and an apple. "What are you good at then?"

Tanwen shrugged. "Laundry, soap-making, sewing."

"Same as anyone," said Cook. Her fingers twirled the apple, sending a spiraling peel onto the table and even slices into the bowl.

Tanwen twisted the silk lacing of her gown round her thumb. "I can do some healing, though I don't have a proper gift for it." She frowned. Why had she even said that?

Cook narrowed her eyes. "We have old Fiala down by the pond and she could use some help, truth be told, but she's not likely to want any competition. How about herbs, do you know anything of them?"

"I know how to find them in the forest and which ones heal. I know what plants need, to grow." Tanwen looked out the window, where a flock of sparrows dashed among the swaying oak branches. "I love best to walk in the forest."

Cook finished slicing the apples into her bowl. "Not a very useful activity."

Tanwen flinched. A leman hardly needed a useful activity.

"No doubt you'll find your way in time." Cook tossed a handful of flour and a generous pinch of cinnamon onto the piled fruit.

"But what am I to do, now?"

"Put those onions in a pot on the fire with some of that butter and wine," Cook called to the girls. "I can't tell you that," she said, turning back to Tanwen. "But you've asked the question, which is a start. And if you're asking it of me, I'd say start with that you love." She pursed her lips. "My name's Alica. Come earlier on the morrow."

Alica set the girls to sorting mushrooms. Tanwen watched as she finished her meal. Alica was old, near as old as her grandmother had been, but she was big where Ceridwen had been tiny, and solid, not feather-light. She piled more cheese on a piece of bread and went out.

Whatever did Alica mean about doing what she loved? It seemed exactly like something Ceridwen would have said, one of those odd things that made no sense but lodged in your throat. Tanwen frowned at two orange butterflies frolicking by the door. She couldn't just wander among the plants or linger in the kitchen garden with its rows of twining peas all the day. Her aunt had forever been after her to come in from the forest, spend the long dreaming summer afternoons scrubbing or sewing at the table or weeding, at least, among the vegetables. Duty, she talked of duty, day and night. And Daron was always so responsible, happy to embroider and chatter in the kitchen even when the sun streamed in and demanded that one come out into the day.

Tanwen headed back to the dim hall, which would smell of damp and cold ashes from last night's fire. Everyone, it seemed, had a place, somewhere to go, something to do. Only she had been launched and drifted, without direction, untethered.

Another month passed, a month of light-filled days. One afternoon, Tanwen crouched by a stream in the forest beyond the hunting lodge and drank deep. Her loose hair dragged in the current. She gazed at the green rocks under the water and enjoyed the feeling of her hair dripping cool down her back. The day was humid and low clouds hovered over the trees, weighing down the leaves. It would storm. She should be getting back. Instead, she sank onto the cushiony moss. She didn't mind if the water did seep through her gown. She had a pile of gowns now, tended by stern Elise, folded with cedar sprigs in two wooden chests.

Home was out here in the forests, it sometimes seemed. She cupped water in her palm and let it spill out through her fingers. Most days, when she got up, Owain was already off hunting. She visited the kitchens for oats and hot tea, mostly to talk with Alica, if she weren't too busy ordering the girls around and kneading dough for the loaves she baked twice weekly. Alica always had something unusual to say. But Alica would go back to her work, and Tanwen tired of the shadowy hall, and one day she had just walked until she was deep in the woods.

The forest here fluttered with delicate birches and shivering on branches of hemlock and it was crisscrossed with narrow wandering paths. She would walk all day and into the long evening, and arrive back just before Owain rode in with a flurry of stomping horses and shouts to the servants, impatient for hot food. She'd sit beside him and share a goblet of wine. One day, he'd brought back lengths of green linen, bought from a passing merchant. Tanwen fingered the soft cloth she wore today, peacock with palest green ribbons sewn down the sleeves by the clever Elise. She couldn't have been finer dressed, even if she'd married Pennar, and he'd brought her cloth from Gascony along with his barrels of wine. Angharad would have held those purse strings tight. But Owain answered to no one. His father had died in the fighting years back and his mother took a fever and followed soon after. Owain was alone and did as he liked.

Tanwen glanced at the sky, where clouds crowded in, anvil-topped. Mist dampened her face and thunder rumbled over the hills. She started homeward and when rain began to fall, she ran, following a path the deer had worn away. Thunder cracked, near overhead now. She couldn't outrun the storm, she'd have to wait it out. An oak with outstretched limbs towered above her, branches creaking. Further on, a nursery of young firs crowded the edge of a clearing. That would be safer. She slipped under the wet branches. Cold water rolled down the back of her neck. Thunder cracked again and lightning arced in the purple sky. The silver-spangled branch above her shivered in the jagged light and dark twisting shadows.

Tanwen hugged her knees and rubbed her dripping nose. Wind plastered her drenched sleeves to her arms. Thunder rumbled and rolled again and again, and finally, rumbled farther away. She stood up and the branches showered her. Her wet gown clung to her calves. It was late. She was careful, always, to be back to the lodge before Owain. She hauled her soaked skirts up and started walking, feet sloshing through the puddles.

The only sound was the thrumming rain. With the storm, dark had come on fast. But soon the single strip of planted field attached to the hunting lodge stretched in front of her, a mass of sticky red mud and barley shoots. She hesitated, her gown would be ruined, but it would take too long if she went around. She slogged across the field, imagining the hot bath she'd have Elise draw. Surely Owain would be delayed by the storm too. She could almost feel the hot bath water lapping over her shoulders. She'd wash her gown in the water after and dry it by the kitchen fire, and no one the wiser. Owain had never been angry with her, but once he'd slashed the stable boy with his whip when he learned one of his horses had broken a leg. She crossed the yard, dark in the slanting rain.

She slipped through the door and stopped, water streaming down her legs.

Owain and a cluster of his men stood by the hearth, blazing with a hot fire that leaped high as their heads. They all turned and stared. Three strangers stood among them, arrayed in fine bright tunics. Tanwen drew herself to her full height, and smiled at the men, as though she were properly dressed to greet guests. "Good sirs, it is a true pleasure to welcome you to our hearth."

Owain's face reddened. He crossed the room in a few steps and spoke through clenched teeth. "Upstairs now."

Alica appeared from the shadows and beckoned. Tanwen ignored her. "Owain?"

"Now I say." Owain glared and returned to the men.

Alica grasped her elbow. "Come, before you do more damage."

Tanwen watched Owain, until she caught the laughing malicious eyes of one of the strangers. Suddenly conscious of her drenched gown clinging to her thighs, she climbed the stairs.

"I told you not to cross him." Alica gestured to Elise, already lifting a gown from the chest. "He's been spoiled all his days."

"He embarrassed me, in front of guests."

"I'd say you did that yourself." Alica went to the door. "Get her ready Elise, I must see to the meal. Put a cap over that red hair of yours and you might last."

"What do you mean?"

"How do you think the last girl went? And if he knew how you spend your days…"

"What's wrong with walking in the woods?"

Alica just shook her head impatiently and went out.

Last girl? Cold wind seemed to circle round within her chest. Was she just one in a line of mistresses? Her chemise tore as she yanked it down around her knees. She grabbed her comb and ripped it through the dripping hanks of hair.

"Stop that. Let me." Elise pried the comb from her cold hand with strong fingers. She braided Tanwen's hair in two neat plaits with blue ribbons, straightened the pleats in her chemise, and laced up her gown.

Soft shoes on her feet, Tanwen stood by the unlit hearth. Her throat felt tight and her head ached. Surely Owain truly loved her, and didn't she truly love him too? She must go down, face him and their guests. It was as though summer had been a long winding dream of hot nights and warm breezes, and she hadn't thought, hadn't wanted to think. She was the leman of Owain ap Macsen. What did that truly mean?

She slipped away from Elise's fingers and descended the stairs.

Owain's men clustered at a long table lit by beeswax candles. Owain had given one of the guests her seat, but she ignored that and smiled at Luke, holding a pitcher of wine. "I'll serve our guests."

She turned to one of the strangers, a short man, hair cropped to his chin like a Norman. She poured him wine and served him the best slice of venison when the platter arrived. Owain and the stranger with the mean laughing eyes conversed, ignoring everyone else, heads close together. The Norman beside her didn't seem to care for the meat, though the spicy smell of rosemary spiraled up from the trencher and made her stomach grumble. "How was the hunt?" she asked.

He shrugged. "What we hunted got away."

She tried a new topic. "Do you hear news of Aberteifi and the castle there?"

"Cilgerran will hold. The princes will never take it back. That's a strange question for a woman to ask." He stopped picking through the stew of apples, onions, and mushrooms, and stared at her.

"It's only that I come from Aberteifi. The next town over," she said when he stared at her blankly. She glanced at Owain, who had an arm around the stranger's shoulder now. When she turned back to the Norman beside her, he was staring at her neck. He smiled and downed another cup of wine.

She stood to signal Luke to bring more.

The Norman snaked an arm around her waist.

"Let go." She pushed at him. But he held her tight with one arm and chewed on a chicken wing, slowly, staring at her breasts. She tried to edge away, without making a scene, but he tightened his grip. Her eyes met Owain's. His flared with anger, and she thought he'd come free her, but he looked away. One of the boys brought in a new skin of wine and the Norman grabbed for it. She mumbled something and ran from the hall.

Outside, the yard was a gleaming square of water in the moonlight. She slipped off her expensive shoes and held her skirts high and picked her way along the cold stones to the kitchen. Inside, it smelled of cinnamon and smoke. Alica gave a harried nod but returned to stuffing a goose with plums and shouting orders. Tanwen sank down on a stool by the roaring fire. Two boys tried to maneuver a heavy skewer loaded with pigeons around her. She was in the way.

She went out again into the night. She could hear the men laughing indoors and the twang of lute strings. She walked around the lodge, heading for a seldom-used door hidden behind some firs. She turned the corner and stopped. A man loomed before her, wearing black, blending into the night. He was tall, and wearing a scarf over his face. Before she could step back, before she could run, he grabbed her shoulders. She threw herself to the side and together they crashed to the ground.

He covered her mouth with a heavy palm. "Silent," he ordered in a curt whisper.

She bit his hand and tried to roll away, but he tightened his hold. A sharp rock bit into her shoulder. She tried not to panic and concentrated on sucking air in through her nose. Through the heavy fir scent, she smelled smoke and sweat and something else, something like ink. She tried to shove him off her and this time, he almost let her, his attention drawn away. Then she heard it too. The fast clump of hoofs on wet turf. She opened her mouth, but he clamped his hand down hard and mouthed, "Be still, if you would live." Their eyes met. He looked away immediately. His eyes were dark, blue like a desolate lake on a winter night.

The rider was close. The man pressed her down harder, hurting her shoulder. Should she try to scream? Who was the rider at this late hour? It could be one of the lawless who dwelled in the forests, who stole and raped and murdered. Or a soldier, far from his camp. Or worse, a Northman.

She could feel the man stop breathing. The rider passed by just beyond the oak tree stretching over the kitchen shed. Then the thud of hoofs faded and there was just the sound of pattering rain.

The man yanked her to her feet and took his hand from her mouth. She gasped in air. He kept hold of her arms. "Tell no one, if you value your life."

She tried to wrest her arms away. "How dare you hold me? I'll have Lord Owain after you, he'll tie you to that oak and let you rot of hunger."

He hesitated, then made an annoyed sound and released her, so she almost fell.

She ran, her skirts crushed in her fists, thrust through the firs and the overgrown holly bush, thorns scratching her arms, yanked open the heavy door and closed it tight behind her. She found the wooden latch and locked the door and waited, listening. But she could hear only rain. Inside, it was very dark, the air thick and cold. A cobweb trailed over her cheek. She inched forward, trailing her fingers along the wall until she found the stairs and climbed to her room. Or Owain's room. She had her belongings in it too, but now she realized she hadn't suggested any changes. The hearth was cold, no one expected for hours.

She could call Elise, but she didn't want to talk. Who was that stranger? She got a blaze going, tugged off her wet gown and pulled on a robe lined with grey rabbit fur. Another gift from Owain. She must look the thing head on. Everything she had was a gift from him. But what of it? A leman was more than a mistress, nearly a wife.

Still, that Norman downstairs clearly thought she was his for the asking. He'd paid her none of the respect a wife was due. Did Owain think she wanted that man to touch her? How angry he'd seemed. Tanwen paced the chamber. What were Normans doing at Owain's table anyway? Though he kept such matters from her, she knew he met with the Northmen, secretly, an old alliance left over from his father's time. But all knew the Normans were dangerous and bitter enemies of the Northmen besides. And who was that man out alone in the dark, and who had ridden by? Was he with the Normans too, keeping watch? Or was he the one they hunted?

The fire burned down to coals. She piled on birch logs, though it was wasteful, but she couldn't stop worrying, and she couldn't get warm. Soon, Owain would come and she'd explain everything. Alica had warned her, said Owain was one to be jealous. She should have been home before him. But shouldn't he believe in her too? Her eyes ached so much she had to close them. She climbed into the high bed and pulled up the scratchy blanket.

Much later, when she awoke, her mouth was dry and the room too warm. Owain was not beside her. She listened but she could hear no voices from the hall. It was very late, or early. She crossed to the window. Yes, there was a faint grey sliver on the horizon. It was dawn, and for the first time, Owain had not come at all.

The long August days stretched out and grey light late into the night made sleeping hard. For a fortnight, Owain hunted and feasted with the Normans. Tanwen stayed away from the ornate dinners and Owain slept in the hall with the men. Tanwen tried to ask Alica for advice, but the older woman had little time, so she fretted, waiting out the endless days indoors.

One night, Owain walked in the bedroom door, startling her as she stared out the window. "I didn't expect you," she said.

He sat down by the fire. "Why not?"

She hesitated, then unlaced his tunic, unpinned his silver brooch, and slid the cloth off his shoulders.

He caught her hair, tied back in a long braid, and lifted it to his lips. "Loosen it." He watched as she unbraided her hair and shoved her playfully to the bed. They fell onto the mattress, laughing, and Owain stopped, suddenly, and stared down at her. She put her hands on his shoulders. He made love to her then, and was gone, as always, when she woke. By this, she knew she was forgiven, or needed. She wanted to talk with him, she wanted to understand, but she felt the wall of silence he built around himself, and she couldn't decide anyway what it was she wanted to ask or say.

One morning, a sharp wind rattled the shutter, drawing Tanwen to the window. The wind blew from a new direction.

Elise entered, a steaming bowl in her hands. "Summer is over." She plunked the bowl down, nudged Tanwen out of the way, and fastened the shutter. "What gown do you want today, mistress?"

"I wish you'd call me Tanwen."

"It wouldn't be proper." Elise looked down at her, dark brows drawn together over hostile eyes.

Tanwen cracked the shutter again and looked out. The day sparkled blue, like the colors had been moistened with water and darkened and deepened overnight. She glanced at Elise, pulling up the blankets on the rumpled bed. "Do you never wish to have a day off, a day all to yourself?"

"Why do you ask that?" Elise clutched the blanket to her chest.

Tanwen stopped drinking her tea. "I only meant...do you have family you'd like to visit?"

Elise went back to straightening the bedding. "I'm fine as I am."

Tanwen sighed. Elise combed her hair, washed her gowns, even bathed her, but rejected all overtures. "Bring the blue gown and dark blue ribbon for my hair. And my boots."

Elise set out the clothes and gathered Tanwen's hair in her strong hands. Tanwen wanted to wince when the wood comb caught but she did not, she just looked out at the clouds, flat and lavender, flying fast.

On a day late in autumn, Tanwen strolled into the kitchen garden behind the lodge. The earth felt cold under her bare feet but sun lit the rows of plants, glossy leaves upturned. She balanced a watering can in her hands, beaded with glittering drops. After trickling water near the base of each plant, she sat on the paving stones set between the plants. Clusters of hanging beans tickled her knees. She'd planted leeks and also violets she'd come upon in the forest.

She'd been impulsive, choosing Owain, she could see that now, thinking only of the strange draw of his eyes and the appealing way he smiled and how wonderful the sound when he laughed out loud. Pennar and ambitious Angharad would have been safer.

But Owain pulled at her. He desired her, in some mysterious way she still needed to understand. That afternoon when they met in the forest, the light had glowed golden and she had felt something magical and strong, something hopeful, something that might grow.

She plucked a curving bean and took a bite and put a hand on her belly, warm in the sun. He gave her everything she needed. In the long autumn nights, they'd forged a bond, a connection that was strong now surely, and unbreakable. She touched her belly again, not yet rounded, but it had begun. A lime songbird flitted by her knee, searching for seed heads, or a mate. She didn't know its name. She watched as it swooped low over the grass and winged on.

CHAPTER SIX

Aberteifi, 1151

LYR GETHIN LEANED over the cliff edge and studied the crescent of pebbled beach lapped by grey sea below. Men jostled and shouted, lugging crates unloaded from a small boat now serenely headed toward the mouth of the bay, leaving a triangle wake behind in the evening water.

Rhys walked among the men, encouraging, shouting, shoving like the rest. Gethin watched, as in a silent play, as the men clustered around Rhys, who gripped one fellow's tunic and plunged his fist into the man's face. Rhys had a temper and suffered fools not at all, yet they all loved him. The man crumpled, blood running from his nose. The others began laughing, and getting back to work, lifting crates. The man on the ground put his head in his hands.

Gethin rubbed his knee. Mist, which shrouded the beach in floating silver, threatened to turn into outright rain. They had been camped in this damp spot near a fortnight, taking on supplies. He watched as Rhys clapped another man hard on the back and laughed, his head thrown back. Good, he needed Rhys in fine humor. Tonight he would definitely approach him.

"Lyr Gethin ap William." A tall man with spindly legs bundled in extra leggings, wound with leather ties, peered at him from a spot in the evergreens.

"Iowerth," Gethin answered, omitting the ap Bleddyn as he knew it would annoy the man. Sure enough Iowerth frowned, pale brows touching over his thin nose. "Is Cadell here then too?" Gethin asked, fearing the answer.

"He comes tomorrow early."

"Indeed." Gethin kept his voice neutral, but Rhys and his older brother would clash leaving Rhys in foul temper for days.

Iowerth studied him with eyes leached too pale, like his hair. "We have not always gotten along, yet we have much in common."

Gethin turned back to Rhys, still laughing by the fire. Iowerth scouted for Cadell, and he was right, Gethin was Rhys' spy, but he hated the word and the life. Irritated for letting Iowerth get under his skin, he turned to reply. But Iowerth had slithered back into the woods like the salamander he resembled, his message delivered. Gethin ran a hand through his damp hair. Now he must tell Rhys his brother was coming.

Gethin headed down the steep path to the beach. Whatever his older brothers thought, Rhys was a formidable leader. Already half of Ceredigion was firm in the princes' hands and soon even Gwynedd, leader of the Northmen, would have to concede that Ceredigion belonged to the house of Deheubarth again. But the closer the brothers came to their goal, the more they worried and argued. Should he wait to approach Rhys? But he was always waiting.

After a meal of lumpy barley and too many onions, the men scattered, some bedding down for the night in the woods and some on watch. Rhys was finally alone, staring into the fire. Gethin took a deep breath and entered the circle of light.

"Have you ever wondered why the fire leaps from one branch to another," said Rhys, his voice quiet and his eyes on the flames.

Gethin had wondered that, but they needed to talk of other matters. "Your brother comes in the morning."

"I see." Rhys' dark eyes glittered in the firelight. "Cadell comes to tell me I must take Ystrad Meurig within the fortnight. And to issue the usual warnings and cautions."

Gethin kicked a log back into the fire. "Can you do it, take the keep?"

"For certain, but should I?" Rhys spoke as though he talked of wandering out to feed the cattle in the barn.

"Cadell is your older brother." And in command supposedly. But for all their jostling rivalry, the brothers had an unusual understanding. Nothing seemed to stop most Welsh princes from murdering kin. Maiming a cousin or a brother was nearly a duty. But the sons of Gruffydd were different. When the eldest, Anarawd, was murdered, the brothers had drawn together, not apart.

"I'll take the castle. As ordered. But now I want you to find someone for me. His lands touch on my caput at Dinefwr. Therefore, I need him." Rhys smiled, his teeth gleaming sharp and white. "He hasn't been to any of the gatherings I've called. I fear he's cozy in bed with the grizzled Northmen, maybe even the Normans, or both. But perhaps he can yet be persuaded away."

Gethin tossed a stick on the fire. "Who is it?"

"Owain ap Macsen."

"And how will I persuade him?"

"Just bring him to me."

"To talk?"

Rhys frowned. "Yes, talk. Haven't I said so? For now." He yanked out his eating knife and stabbed a chunk of venison from the pot. "I know your qualms."

Gethin looked away from the fire into the dark woods. "You know what I want." The words rushed out, not as he'd rehearsed. "Give me a ship. To map the coast, off Mynyw, and all the way up to Aberystwyth, and beyond." Gethin's hands dropped to his sides. "I would need only weeks, a summer perhaps. It would be a model, of what could be done, a true map of all the coast."

Rhys shrugged. "A ship is valuable."

"Maps such as these would be valuable. There would be nothing like them here. Even the maps in the abbey, they are not the same." But Rhys was looking away.

"Get me this Owain, get him to meet with me at Dinefwr, and we'll discuss this journey of yours."

"You'll fund a voyage?"

Rhys tossed a heavy cape around his shoulders. "I'll consider it."

Though Gethin woke early the next morning, already Cadell and Maredudd hovered by a roaring fire with their younger brother Rhys, resplendent in a crimson robe with a fur hood. Gethin threw off his blanket. He hadn't slept well, dreams of voyages waking him.

"Rhys is more handsome than those two put together," said Catrin, Rhys' latest woman, plunking herself down beside him, her eyes on the brothers. "Why are they here?"

Gethin shrugged.

"They envy him."

Catrin's voice was vehement. Gethin turned to examine her. Catrin was dark haired, her heart shaped face the exact color of new cream, unmarred by a single line. And very young. But then Rhys was not even of age. Still, the girl should not be here, enduring endless nights in a damp tent.

Maredudd and Cadell mounted their horses, leaving Rhys alone at the fire.

"Where are they going? Won't they stay with him?" Catrin's voice was high with worry.

"It's just another battle," said Gethin, "no need." Rhys was in danger every day, in battle or out.

The girl chewed on a fingernail, gazing at her lover. "Will you go with him?"

Gethin frowned. "Only if I must."

"Why won't you fight for him?" Her voice was fierce.

Gethin kicked at a rock. "It's not my battle."

"You will draw your maps then, like a priest?"

Gethin swung back to stare at her.

She shrugged her shoulders and her shawl slipped down. "I listen, of course."

He frowned. When had he even talked of his dream, except to Rhys? Did Rhys confide in this girl?

Catrin touched her earrings, twisted gold like water drops in a cage, tangled in her black hair. "Will he let you go?"

"I'm not sure." Even he could hear how surly that sounded.

"What will he make you do for him first?" She stared at him with deep blue eyes and smiled.

Gethin noted that smile, with its tiny white teeth and red lips. He'd underestimated Catrin. Pity Rhys if he did so as well. "Just another meeting to be arranged."

She moved closer and whispered. "Easy, compared to what you must have done."

Gethin inched his arm away. "We all do what we must."

Catrin drew her shawl tight under her chin. She stalked away, down the hill, toward Rhys.

A fortnight later, Gethin placed the delicate stems of charcoal back in the box he'd made to house the bent sticks. He looked at the map he'd drawn on a scrap of rough sheepskin. It showed the keep and the winding paths of the village near Ystrad Meurig - the strips of field and fallow land, the river, and the hills surrounding. It was accurate as he could make it, having trudged each of the lanes and fields and hills and forest paths strewn with yellowing fall leaves himself. It would smudge when he rolled it up. He wished he had time to take it to the monks at Ystrad Fflur. They'd draw the map in brown and green inks on fine smooth parchment. He thought of Cynan, his boyhood friend turned monk. It would be good to see his honest face now.

He had no friends in Rhys' camp. Right now, the men were looting the village lanes winding around Ystrad Meurig, for Rhys and Maredudd had captured the gate and tower with little bloodshed early this morning. He had no taste for taking sour ale and tattered blankets from wretched villagers, and less for dragging young women into the forest. It drew a line between him and Rhys' men.

Gethin drew three sea-smoothed pebbles from his pouch, oval as songbird eggs and mottled grey. A ship was worth a small fortune. Buying a share in one, like a normal merchant, wouldn't serve his purpose. So he was here, for the time being. He'd have to get this Owain to meet with Rhys. Rhys had promised not to harm the man, but the dark truth was, for the chance to draw his maps, Gethin knew he might persuade himself to do almost anything.

Weeks passed; Ystrad Meurig's walls were rebuilt. Rhys was already arguing with his brothers that they should be off to the next fight. So Gethin was being sent south to scout once more, accompanied by two wiry Welshmen, who knew the forest paths that twisted through the thick-wooded hills. They were taciturn though. Not that he minded, he wasn't much of a talker himself. And so they rode, in silence, putting in as many hours as they could.

Their days started when grey dawn lit the hills and ended only when the dim shadows of dusk made going hard. Nights were long and he slept badly. His guides ate their oat bread and chewed on dried herrings and rolled up in their blankets to sleep. But he peered up between the bare branches, through the ever-dividing twigs, to the stars. He wondered, some nights, if that's where she was, Julianna. And if she were lonely too. How sad that would be. Mostly he thought about his maps though. Like the great map he'd seen with Cynan, at the monastery a day's ride from Bristol. Nearly a man's height and just as wide, the map showed the continents of Europa, Africa, and Asia, and the location of Paradise. Jerusalem glowed at the very center. The snowy sheepskin let the inks shine dark and rich. And in the corners fearsome beasts roared.

A fine map. It showed the idea of the world, or the idea the church wanted men to have, of the continents here and Paradise beyond, but he wanted to do something different. Show the actual world. Perhaps Paradise was there, where they said, but no man could find it and come home to tell. He wanted to make something sailors could take when they went out of the port and merchants could use to bring their goods home. He wanted to make something that showed the earth as it was. Use and beauty combined. He'd draw it in black ink and glowing colors on the finest skins and it would tell a truth, something solid to be counted on in the churning roil that seemed to be life. He rolled over, feeling each hard root under the thin blanket. Perhaps God would strike him down for such thoughts. But God had already struck at him, had he not; he could do him no worse.

In the mornings, the three men shook the silver drops of water from their blankets, snuffed out the smoky fire and wolfed down toasted bread and more fish. Though he'd only been traveling a few days, Gethin felt like he'd entered a silent purgatory in these woods. He might never emerge again. It wasn't clear it mattered. To anyone but him, or to anyone, perhaps. Rhys would ask questions. He didn't like to lose his men, weeping if one he thought lost was returned to him unharmed. But that was nothing personal. No, Gethin decided, looking at the cold, clear stars, there was no one to care and that was as it should be. A man could exist, unencumbered, and silently do his work. And so his mind circled round again to his maps, always his maps, until he slept in tangled dreams of twisting coastlines drawn in vermillion, and emerald seas of lapis lazuli, and mossy forests in the deepest brown of oak galls.

Eventually, they came out of the woods. It happened suddenly, as he dozed on his horse, plodding along the twisting path, barely awake enough to duck his head when a branch hung too low. They walked out into the bright sun of midday and his head ached with the sudden light and the harsh shouts, for it seemed to be market day. His guides gave him a salute, regarding their job as done. Rhys had paid them and clearly they meant to spend the silver coin in the market that very hour. They rode off, but Gethin waited, near the shadowy wood, letting his eyes get accustomed to the light, and his mind to the idea of men.

His meat pie was tasty, the pork falling apart before he stuck in his knife and the crust flaky and seasoned with salt and something else, he didn't know the name but it gave the pie flavor. Gethin mopped up the gravy with bread and drank the spicy hot wine.

The matron of the inn came to his table, solid arms folded over a sturdy chest covered in a linen apron, clean and stiff.

"It's wonderful." His sincerity must have been come through, and she unbent enough to nod at him.

"You've been in the forests," she stated.

"I have and worked up an appetite salt fish couldn't cure."

She smiled then. "I have an apple pastry, if you'd like something to follow your meal."

"I would, and some more wine too, if you have it."

She nodded. "Will you need a room for the night, not that I have much, with the market on."

"I'll sleep outside." A bed packed with five other travelers, farmers, fishermen, and their smells of ale and sweat, made him grimace.

The matron bustled off before he could ask her about Owain ap Macsen. He looked around the chamber, enjoying the feeling of a full belly. It was too close to Norman territory here, but it wasn't like he was Welsh, and no one here knew he worked for Rhys. There was a table of farm folk, and another of sailors, getting boisterous off the ale. And in the corner another sole traveler. He wore a tunic of clean wool, with neatly tied leggings. His beard was growing in and his short hair was covered by a red cap. A Norman, trying to blend in.

Gethin grabbed the flask of wine and the pie from the matron. He crossed to the man's table and set the pastry down. "Share a drink?"

The man looked up from his stew. "Why not?" he said, "especially as I see you've brought some pastry from this magnificent cook." He winked at the matron, who blushed scarlet and hurried off. The man laughed, too loudly. "I'm Raoul." He waved at the bench opposite him.

Gethin sliced the apple pastry down the middle and shoved the platter toward the other man.

Raoul ate with a satisfied smile, then drank deep of the wine. He wiped a few red drops from his chin with the tablecloth. "That's better eating than I've had in some days."

"Where've you been then?"

"To the land of sea and monks."

Gethin polished his eating knife on the cloth. "You'll have to speak plainer than that."

"Plainer I can't speak. The monks disdain a fine table, at least while I sat with them, though they were thin scarecrows, so I believe they truly didn't have pastries and hams stored away for my departure. But the sea, silver lights and glittering waves everywhere."

You've been to Mynyw?"

"I see you take my meaning after all. Perhaps you're not slow as you seem." Raoul grinned.

Gethin ran a hand through his hair. This Raoul was out of place in a simple inn, his posture more that of a soldier than a merchant. "Who do you serve that sends a gourmand like you to the monks, and out of season too?"

"Myself, obviously." Raoul pushed back from the table with a theatrical sigh. The matron appeared. "My congratulations on a delicious meal. But I'm wondering if you have a bed, with deep feathers and snowy linen to match."

The matron laughed. "I've a bed of straw and four fellows to share it with, or you can try your luck in the barns with this good fellow."

"Ah." Raoul frowned, obviously not used to his charm failing him. "Well, to be sure, I'm off again early. Can a good breakfast be found before dawn?"

"Of course," said the woman. "And do you head back to Lord Owain? If you do, I'd take it kindly if you'd bring a packet to my daughter, who works in his kitchens." She paused. "You keep away from her though, she's bound to a fellow here once they've enough for setting up."

"I'll bring the packet," said Raoul with a yawn. "I'm off to bed."

"Why not share another goblet with me?" said Gethin. "I've been in the forests myself and could use the sound of another voice." Gethin ordered more wine and the matron rustled away.

"You've heard the news, of course," said Raoul.

"I've been in the woods these past days, I've heard nothing but rain drops and branch cracks."

"Delightful, I'm sure." Raoul drew his brows together but his lips curved into a smile he couldn't contain. "Cadell, ruler of these parts, he's been injured, near unto death."

Gethin tried to keep shock from his face. The Norman watched him with narrowed eyes. "Cadell of Deheubarth?" Gethin said, buying time.

"What other?" Raoul said, "though some would have named him King of South Wales." He smiled as though sharing a fine joke.

"Who has done this?" Gethin noticed his fingers tapping on the table and stilled them. He forced himself to pick up his wine.

"The Flemish, it's rumored, though who knows. Set upon him while he was hunting, left him battered and dead, so they thought. But he lives yet, or he did yesterday, for I had word from a merchant, who'd traveled this way selling horses."

"Battles and strife always," said Gethin, striving to sound disapproving but nonchalant. He was supposed to be a merchant himself. What would such a man say? "A man isn't safe on the roads nor in the towns anymore. Fine protection the English offer here." He frowned. "Think you it will be safe on the morrow?"

"Where do you go?" The Norman traced a stain on the tablecloth with his finger, but his voice betrayed his interest.

"Carmarthen. I've business there with some of the cloth sellers." Gethin babbled on then about bolts of silk and wool, until he could see he'd thoroughly bored the Norman. He wanted more information, but this Raoul was too clever, nosing about for his Norman masters. But what would happen to Rhys now? His mind rushed back and forth but he kept his eyes blank.

Raoul rose to his feet and brushed the pastry crumbs from his tunic. "I'm to bed. It may have four friends in it, but in these times I'm not one for sleeping alone."

Gethin called for another skin of wine. Let the Norman think he drank the night away. The chamber was emptying out as men wandered to their beds. His head ached behind his eyeballs. He wanted to rush back to Rhys, but Rhys would have heard the news already. And Rhys wanted this Owain. He'd not welcome delay, no matter the reason.

Gethin nursed his drink until the candles burnt down to smoking stubs. When he lay down on a hard bench with his head on his elbow and dozed, he was troubled by dreams of black blood flowing and men shouting and Rhys in an eerie dance behind Anarawd and Cadell, and finally, in the silent hour before true morning, he dreamed of Julianna's waxen face, lit by a rosy dawn.

The matron clattered around, but Gethin pretended to sleep on in a wine stupor. She let him sleep, distracted by getting a packet off to her daughter. After Raoul left, Gethin sat up, running his fingers through his stiff hair. A swim would be heaven. But outside, cold rain drummed down and wind pummeled the trees.

He left the spilt wine and sweat smells of the tavern and went out into the wind. The Norman, bundled in fur, was just riding out of the inn yard. A barelegged Welsh guide rode a black pony in the lead. Gethin marked the path they took, went back inside and ordered a hot breakfast of ham and porridge, then asked the matron the news.

"Lord Cadell, poor soul, is like to die, they say." The woman paused her clattering of dishes as she cleared a table. Would Ceredigion fall back into the hands of Gwynedd of the North? Or worse, fall to the Normans? She speculated, and he encouraged her, until she'd told him all the gossip. He told her his story, that he was a merchant of cloth going to trade with the English at Carmarthen.

"To stay in business, we all do as we must," she sighed.

He felt a twinge at her sympathy. How easy it was to deceive. How troublingly good he was at it. If only he could be out on that silver-lit sea, aboard a fine oak boat. He sighed. If Rhys fell into more troubles, the timing would be terrible to wrest a ship from him. Christ's bones, but the battles went on and on, and all for what?

He found his pony standing patiently, blinking its eyelashes against the rain. Gethin paid the matron and she tucked the silver coin in her bodice and turned to a new group of customers riding into the muddy yard. He headed off in the direction of Carmarthen. Once he'd cleared the fields he led the pony through the woods, in the direction the Norman had taken. He found their track, for they weren't worried about anyone following, and mounted again. It was noon, light breaking through the clouds and shadows falling suddenly. Later, rain pelted down again. He tied his cape tight around his neck and kept on.

The Welsh guide's body lay across the path, the arms stiff, fingers sticking out from the drifted oak leaves, seeming to point the way. Gethin brushed rusty leaves from the man's face. He had no mark on his throat so he rolled him over. Black blood pooled over the moss, trailing from a slit in the man's back.

He let the body roll back. The man's eyes, brown and surprised, seemed to follow him. Branches cracked in the wind high up in the oaks. Gethin broke off evergreen fronds, wandering far to find them, and piled them over the body and last over the man's face. He wondered who would wait for this man, for long days, until she knew he would not come home again.

His pony nudged him in the thigh and Gethin started, then looked around. Was jovial Raoul hidden under more leaves nearby? Or had he been the one who stabbed the Welshman in the back? Gethin mounted the pony, stared at the pile of green branches, and turned north. Cadell and now this nameless man. The rolling hills of Wales flowed with blood and more blood.

He rode under the silent trees for a time, his mood dark, then shrugged. Death stalks us all, he murmured out loud. The pony quirked whiskery gray ears back to him, and lurched into a rocky trot. Gethin hunched his shoulders against the stiffening wind and let the pony charge on.

A warm fire crackled in the hearth of Owain's kitchen at Adpar. Gethin downed the hot chicken broth the maid plunked before him. The hour was early for Owain himself to be up, but the kitchen maids were preparing the day's meal. A roast drizzled fat into the fire.

He'd traveled two days to get here and spent another two nights lurking in the cold woods, watching the manor. The promised storm had arrived and wind lashed the trees and cold rain poured down. He'd almost given up, decided Raoul had been left murdered in the woods, when the grooms brought round a fine chestnut horse. Raoul had come from the hall, talking genially with another man, who must, by his dress, be Owain. Raoul had ridden away, despite the rain, accompanied by three of Owain's men. Presumably they'd not receive a knife in the back for their pains.

Gethin frowned at his empty bowl, thinking of the convoluted alliances of the English borders.

"Cook wants to know if you be wanting more." A soft voice

interrupted his reverie.

Gethin handed the bowl to the maid. "If you'd be so kind."

"It's my mother's recipe, though all soup's good when you come in from the rain." She pointed a ladle at the door.

"You've had a visitor here lately."

The maid tossed her loose hair over her shoulder. "We have visitors near every day."

Gethin waited, but she said no more, and nothing about a murdered Welsh guide. It seemed Raoul hid the murder then, or was the murderer himself.

"What business have you here in Lord Owain's lands?" It was the cook, not the maid, who stood over him now. Sharp eyes swept over his rumpled tunic.

Gethin sat up straighter. The cook, an older woman, was silent, but did not go away. He ran a hand through his hair. "I could use a bath." This was a strange household. It was unspeakably rude to ask a stranger his business.

"No doubt." The cook signaled to one of the girls to heat some water.

"I must speak with Lord Owain," he said, "at the request of Rhys of Deheubarth."

Her eyes betrayed surprise, a flash that disappeared like a trout poking his head out in a stream. She considered a moment and sniffed. "Definitely a bath first and give me those clothes. I'll have them brushed clean for you. Lord Owain's one to respect a man who dresses fine. If you want to be heard, that is."

"I may as well, since I have come." Gethin gulped down the last of the soup and a maid beckoned him to the corner, where they'd set a tub of water and a screen.

But Owain kept him waiting. Four days passed, and still Owain had not granted him an audience. Gethin punched at a fat chicken leg with his eating knife and watched the clear juices stream out. The hall was smoky, full of men eating and laughing. Boys rushed between the two long tables, carting round bread loaves and pitchers of wine. A fine meal and Owain wasn't even here. It bent all the laws of hospitality to leave a guest alone and deny him a prompt hearing. How long should he wait? How angered would Rhys be if he returned without even meeting this Owain?

Gethin shouldered his way out of the crowded hall. Even as he observed the courtyard, silvery with a hard frost, a shout from the gates signaled Owain's return. Ten men rode in, hoofs clattering. Gethin strode forward, stopping right in front of Owain's dappled horse, dancing still, playing with the boy trying to catch the reins. Owain, muddy from the hunt to his thighs, jumped down.

"I seek the favor of some words with you." Gethin spoke loudly and bowed, but not deep as he might.

Owain's men fell silent. Owain handed his reins to the boy and went into extensive directions for feeding and rubbing down the animal. Finally, he turned back to Gethin. "Of course," he said, as though it were the first day and not nearly a sennight that he'd been at Adpar waiting on him. He gestured not to the hall, but to a timber stairway leading up to the top of the gatehouse. "Go in and eat," he called to his men. "I won't be long."

They climbed the steep stairs in silence. At the top, Owain looked out over the dark forests surrounding his home, so Gethin looked too, but the winter forest was nothing he hadn't seen already. A few dark purple clouds streaked the grey sky and the air felt sharp in his chest. Owain didn't seem to be about to speak. Gethin finally plunged into a polite speech.

Owain stopped him mid-sentence. "What is it you're here for, truly?"

Gethin hesitated. "Rhys of Deheubarth wants to meet with you."

Owain said nothing. Then he sighed. "And why should I meet with him?"

Gethin frowned. Most jostled for the chance to meet Rhys. "He wants to meet with you, isn't that enough?"

"So you have indicated." Owain pulled off his heavy gloves, sat on a bench and crossed his legs. "Did you know that in my grandfather's day, Adpar stretched far along the river, nearly to its very source?"

Ambition drove him then, though hidden well. "Your lands are rich and productive. Rhys too seeks to regain lands his grandfather lost."

"My father always said a good hunt and a fine dinner and a comfortable woman were all a man should want."

Gethin waited, but Owain added no more. "And do you agree, lord, or do you want something more?"

Owain frowned, and turned away from the cold woods and the black river to meet his eyes. "I don't know."

The stable boy bridled the pony, fat and sleek, one of Owain's on loan. Gethin took the red leather reins. Once he reached the woods he looked back at Adpar, the house surrounded by low fences, hardly enough to defend the place. The clearing, dusted with new snow, glowed in late afternoon sun. Above, streaky clouds scattered before a wind, curling streams of cream and lavender. The low murmur of the river floated over the quiet fields. Lovely and far from strife, but not for long. For Owain had agreed at last to meet with Rhys, agreed with an odd eagerness mixed with reluctance.

CHAPTER SEVEN

The Hunting Lodge, 1152

TANWEN FOLDED the gold silk of the finest gown Owain had given her yet. It fell in shimmering folds, or it would, when she could wear it again. She stroked the soft material, then placed it in the carved chest Owain had sent a week past. He'd sent a message too, a sheaf of delicate snowdrops tied up with a green ribbon, and a note asking her to come to Adpar. His men would come for her by midday.

Her clothes layered in the chest, she added some packets, wrapped tight against the damp. Seeds she'd gathered in the meadows, bright orange-yellow daisies, deep blue bellflowers, delicate lavender sweet peas. And tiny bulb clusters of wild garlic, which she loved for its bursts of star-like flowers, brightening the shade under the oaks in this hopeful time of the year.

Winter had been long and dark. She'd spent the dreary weeks here, alone but for Elise and several servants and two of Owain's men. It wasn't safe, Owain had said, for her to be at Adpar. And indeed the times were frightening. Death and murder stalking the land. She had to protect the child, so she'd reluctantly accepted the parting.

Owain had come often, as he'd promised, but there had been two long times, nearly a fortnight each, when heavy snows prevented him. And when the snows fell, and the air grew deeply cold, the winter days had seemed so dark and she'd begun to fancy she'd be left abandoned.

Nonsense of course. She climbed onto the window seat into the shaft of sunlight. Warmth and light. That was what Owain was to her. He'd arrived one morning, after a snowfall, with ten of his men, all laughing and shouting, and after they'd eaten venison and fruits, and drunk a cask of wine, finally she'd been able to draw him apart, into the house, into their room.

"You cannot wait for me," he'd proclaimed, with a grin, and she'd loved him in that moment, the sureness of him, the confidence that he was Owain of Adpar, beloved. Surely some of that confidence was hers now by right.

"Owain," she'd whispered.

He pulled her close. "I have missed you, and would have come but for the snow and the matter of securing our borders. So much unrest, Teilo never leaves me alone, he is always after me to fix fences and… but no matter, I'm here now, sweet." He kissed her. "Come." He drew her toward the bed.

"Owain," she said, "I have something to tell you."

He smiled, pulling her beside him, until she gazed into his brown eyes, his fingers undoing her laces.

She took a deep breath. "I am with child." She watched his eyes go completely still, like a pond you gazed into, so deep sunlight itself could not penetrate and you saw only light dappling the surface. "Owain?" She bit her lip. "Are you pleased?"

"Pleased?" He kissed her forehead, then her cheeks, then her lips. "Yes, sweet one, I am pleased." He tucked her head to his chest but she saw what he was hiding. His eyes were wet.

"Will she be as beautiful as her mother?" He fingered the ends of her hair.

"I think it will be a he."

"Do you?" He sat up abruptly and looked out the small window, toward the hills. When he turned around again he was smiling.

A shout outside startled Tanwen from her thoughts. She thrust open the shutter. Owain's men, dressed in his brown and green colors, milled about below her. She walked carefully down the uneven stairs and Teilo, Owain's steward and Alica's husband, came forward. He greeted her, his wrinkled face screwed into a smile and a shock of grey hair standing up on his head. "Are you ready to travel?"

"I thought Owain might come?"

Teilo shook his head. "Busy times, mistress, my lord had visitors and a delegation of merchants as well." He took a pouch from his belt. "He did send you this." He handed her a packet and recited, turning red, "Come soon and safely, my own Tanwen."

"Thank you," she said, feeling her own cheeks flush. "Would your men care to eat before we depart?"

"We'll leave now, if it suits, and use the daylight as we can. Owain says we're not to travel hard, and you're to tell me straight away if you're tiring."

"I'll be fine." She went back into the lodge and looked around the dark hall. She had been content here, much of the time, sleepy with pregnancy and winter dark. And no one was happy always. That breathless idyllic first summer, such a time could hardly last. She turned the packet from Owain over in her fingers and opened it. Inside a pouch of silk she found a brooch, made of silver surely, its twining spirals forming a delicate flower with leaves encircling its center. It sparkled in her palm. She was going to Adpar, finally; she would be acknowledged, no longer hidden away in the forests.

She walked out of the lodge. Teilo assisted her in mounting a fat, cream pony with a waving mane, bells on his red bridle. Elise scrambled up behind one of Owain's men, clutching her bag, her blue eyes wide. Tanwen smiled at her and Elise hesitated, then smiled back. They left winter and the lodge behind.

Tanwen woke as rosy light flickered on the whitewashed walls. Owain slept on beside her. She tilted her head to watch him. His face was relaxed, his hair a tangle of chestnut waves against the linen bedding. A shout below made him stir. She willed him to sleep on. When day commenced he turned away from her, but nights he was hers alone. These first days at Adpar had been thrilling, with the wonder of admiring its huge hall and seven chambers above stairs, each with multi-colored hangings and silver candleholders. Their chamber was warmed with a fire day and night, and smelled of the mint and rosemary mixed in the rushes and the Yule boughs still hung on the walls. Yet the pattern of her days had changed little.

Violence had erupted anew in Ceredigion. The Welsh princes Maredudd and Rhys raided castles every fortnight, driving the fierce Northmen or Normans out. All manner of thieves and malcontents and deserting soldiers wandered the land. Owain was often closeted with mysterious men, or drawn off by Teilo to attend to the estate. He never spoke with her about these meetings, though she questioned him, evenings by the fire. He laughed and teased her, and told her it was not her concern. And with the baby coming, her curiosity was blunted. He needed her here, with him, and he'd brought her to his true home. Nothing else mattered.

She felt a flutter and then another slow and deep in her belly. Owain opened his eyes and smiled. Then he looked away, out the open window, thinking already of the day to come. She looked out the window too, at the blue sky and the slate line of migrating birds. How longing and contentment were mixed, though what she longed for was a puzzle, for she had what she had always wanted. He turned back to her and she smiled. He looked surprised, almost, that she was there, but then he drew her to him.

When she woke a second time, Owain was gone. Wagon wheels creaked down in the courtyard. She stretched, enjoying the soft linen, warmed by their bodies. Again she felt that fragile fierce fluttering within. A wave of protectiveness and love swept over her, surprising her with its intensity. What was he like, this child?

The door squeaked open and Elise peered in, arms laden with folded linens. "I knew you'd be wanting a bath, so I've got water heated." She twitched the bed curtains shut and Tanwen heard the men lug pails of steaming water to the tub.

"Hurry or the water will cool," called Elise.

Tanwen laughed as she climbed down from the bed. How strange life was! Only last year she'd bathed in a stream.

"Shall we do your hair?" Elise lifted a strand and ran it through her fingers.

Tanwen tugged her hair away. But she let Elise dry her off with a strip of linen and dress her. Her polished chest sat against one of the walls, as though it belonged.

Owain never mentioned, but Tanwen heard gossip from the servants. Ceredigion was engulfed in war and merchants stayed home, their wares buried in stone cellars. Teilo made Owain plant more barley against the winter. But she was so heavy with her pregnancy now, and sleepy all the time, as though someone had poured poppy into her wine and left her unable to lift her eyelids, lace her gowns, think about making a garden or even stay up evenings waiting for Owain. He left her earlier than ever in the mornings, off to hunt most days and when cajoled by Teilo, oversee the work of the manor; she had the long day to fill before they ate dinner together, she yawning until he laughed and sent her to their bed.

One afternoon Elise shook her awake from a nap, slumped in the window seat. "A visitor is coming. You must dress." She pulled Tanwen up the stairs, sat her down on a stool, and rearranged her braids. She dampened a cloth in rosewater. Tanwen yanked it from her and scrubbed her own face.

Elise looked hurt, so Tanwen handed back the cloth. "Who is coming?" She pressed her fingers to her temples. She, always so quick, was so slow these days.

"I don't know." Elise drew the comb through her hair, finding a snarl. "I'm sorry," said Elise, her fingers clenched around the comb. Alica said Elise feared being sent back to her stepfather, who used her to haul water and worse.

Tanwen put a hand over Elise's. "You need not fear me. We're friends now, aren't we? I'll not send you away."

Elise pressed her lips together. "If you say so, mistress." She clipped a necklace of gold set with a single giant pearl around Tanwen's neck. The pearl dangled between her breasts, creamy apricot, catching sunlight in its depths. Elise stared at the pearl, then threaded a green ribbon in Tanwen's braid.

Tanwen followed her, clumsy and slow, down the circular stairs to the hall, and out to the courtyard. A rider was already inside the gates. A woman, surrounded by four of Owain's men, hardly able to stand on her own, as if exhausted or ill. Tanwen put a hand on her belly.

The woman stumbled toward her. "Tanwen."

"Daron, is that really you?" Daron's face was strained and white and her beautiful dark hair hung in limp tangles under a dingy cap.

Daron stared at her with eyes void of expression.

"You've been ill, cousin?" Tanwen reached out a hand.

Daron looked at Tanwen's belly, flushed scarlet, and took a step back. "The whole of Ceredigion has been ill, but you haven't been touched here I see."

Tanwen swallowed, irritated at a surge of guilt, for how often had she thought of her smaller cousin, or her aunt? "I've missed you," she said after a pause. "How do you come to be here? Are you alone? Has aunt not come with you?"

Daron turned away. "No."

Tanwen hesitated, then because Daron looked like she might fall, she linked her arm with her cousin's and drew her into the hall. "Owain sent for you to keep me company?"

"No, but I am come. He does not know." Daron clutched her arm with sudden energy. "Do not turn me away Tanwen. I have nowhere else to go."

"Whatever do you mean?"

"Can you not guess? Are you so enchanted here, so high above it all, away from all threat of illness, or ... Mother is dead, Tanwen. Everyone is dead or dying. In every house, fever. And I am turned out by the guild head; he says she owes coin on the house and I have no way to fight him." Daron stared at her, a defiant gleam in her eyes, but she swayed, and her eyes were ringed by purple circles.

Tanwen swallowed hard. Agatha dead? That hardly seemed possible. For a moment, the hall seemed to tilt. She led Daron to the stool by the hearth. "Do not fear. Of course you will stay with me. Owain will see to it." Tanwen bit her lip, unsure what else to say. Her cousin's lively ways and endless chatter were swept away and this unsettling stranger slumped by the fire. She gestured to Elise, who hovered by the door. "Fetch some of that cooked chicken and the strong wine. And prepare the chamber at the top of the stairs for my cousin." Tanwen blinked back tears. "It will be good, truly, to have you with me."

A week after Daron arrived, Owain dressed in the morning dark. Tanwen watched him slip on his tunic and belt, trying to still the jingling noise. "I'm awake," she said.

He turned, silhouetted against the dim light from the shuttered window. "I hoped to let you sleep."

"I cannot sleep nights, then I'm tired all the day."

"It will not be long." He smiled at her complaint, lighted an oil lamp, and stirred the fire in the hearth.

He could call a servant for every task, but he did these things himself. She liked that. She turned over in the bed. The child moved and she sighed. How she longed to see this child, but she dreaded the birth. There was no escape from this body of hers now, she must see this through. A truth no man could fully understand.

Owain sat gingerly on the side of the bed. He touched her hair. "I'm off for a few days, perhaps a sennight."

She bit her lip and didn't let the words spill from her-- don't go, don't go.

"I'll be hunting." He twisted a strand of her hair around his finger and gazed at it, but seemed not to truly see her. "And I go to see which way the wind blows."

His brows were drawn together in an unusual knot. He referred to the horrible news that had reached them yesterday morning. Lord Cadell had been near murdered back in winter. Realizing he'd never recover fully nor be able to rule, he'd handed Ceredigion over to his two younger brothers and though the brothers had cooperated before, all feared violence would flare up now.

Tanwen touched his shoulder. He didn't like to talk of these matters with her. He must be worried indeed. "Must you go?" The words tumbled from her.

"You're yet a fortnight from your time, I talked with the midwife." He stroked her forehead. "I'll be back well before then and you have Daron here now."

"Of course." But Daron had been utterly quiet and kept to her chamber, pleading illness. Tanwen hauled herself up against the pillows.

"You're everything to me, sweeting, you know it."

"Is it so?" She pressed her lips together. Never would she say it, but she had hoped he'd marry her before the child's birth. A dream only.

"Of course." But his voice held an edge now; he was anxious to be out in the world.

"I will lie here a little longer and plan a day for Daron and myself."

"You must not tire yourself."

"I am never tired," she said.

He grinned and strode out, the door thudding shut.

So quickly he wished to be away. Tears blurred her eyes. If only he weren't always so busy, if only the times were not so terrible. But she shouldn't even think so, she who was so very fortunate.

Elise slipped in as Owain left. She crossed to the bed and stood over Tanwen, frowning. She reached down, slowly, and put her arms around Tanwen's shoulders and hugged her carefully, as though she might break. They stared at each other.

"All men are so," said Elise.

Tanwen swallowed the lump in her throat. She tossed back the covers.

Elise flushed and looked away. "I'll get your gown."

"The green one. I'm thinking I'll go walking."

Elise tugged her gown from the chest. "Don't walk far."

"Will it storm?" Tanwen looked out, but sun was climbing over the trees.

"No. But you need to take great care." Elise dropped the gown over her head, laced the sides, and clumped off down the stairs.

Tanwen sought out Daron in her chamber and found her standing at the tall window. She was leaning out, watching something or someone intently. Her dress was blue with pleats and her black hair bundled under a comely cap of sheer linen. Daron had magic in her fingers and she'd made fast work of the lengths of cloth Tanwen had given her when she realized Daron had come from Aberteifi with only one torn gown.

"What is it like, Tanwen, to live with a lord?" Daron flicked her a hostile glance.

The maid cleaning the hearth sat back on her heels, with a delighted smile.

Tanwen frowned. "I've come to see if you'd like to go walking. It's a lovely day."

Daron shrugged.

"The gardens are full of flowers. Do come out with me," said Tanwen.

"If you require it."

"Why do you talk so? I'm asking you, inviting you, to come." Tanwen took her cousin's arm. "I know you grieve for Agatha, but it would be good for you…"

Daron shook off her hand. "Don't speak of Mama, you have no right." She grabbed a shawl and threw it on. "I've said I'll come."

They descended the stairs in silence. In the kitchens, Alica gave them cheese and dried pears. She frowned at Tanwen and handed the food to Daron to carry. "It's foolishness to overtire yourself."

"Don't fuss," said Tanwen, with a smile. "Truly Alica, I feel fine, very good in fact today."

"That's what worries me." Alica stared at Tanwen with a crease in her brow.

"Are we going?" said Daron.

Alica muttered something and turned away.

Daron and Tanwen strolled through the gardens. The plot closest to the house was a rectangle of primroses and pansies she'd planted herself. But the gardens further on were neglected, tangled weeds and broken stone. Tanwen imagined them scented with red roses and spangled with marguerites. So much to be done, and she had no energy, though Alica said she'd regain it with the child.

The stream at the edge of the gardens was flowing strong, for it had been wet for days. The lush grass and thick leaves seemed to glow like Owain's emerald-jeweled dagger. "Let's go on, it's so lovely," urged Tanwen.

By midmorning they had walked far, staying by the stream as it wandered toward the river. Tanwen rested at the top of a rise, her back beginning to ache. She rubbed it and thought about turning around. She hadn't gone so far in weeks, what with the terrible news of Cadell's near murder and the child coming. But it was a glorious day, the sun beating down. She felt strong and full of energy. And Daron was with her, even if she still trudged along in silence.

"Perhaps we should turn back?" said Daron.

"It's early yet."

"We should be heading back soon though."

Tanwen examined her cousin's thin face. "You are so quiet these days. Can't you tell me what's wrong?"

Daron met her eyes, then turned away.

"Daron?" Tanwen was startled by the hostility she'd seen.

"My mother is dead."

Tanwen frowned. "I know," she murmured, but it was more. Daron was transformed. No longer vivacious, instead she was silent and ominous. Tanwen stood up, too quickly. The child was making her fanciful.

"Shall we go back then?" said Daron after a long moment.

"Not yet."

Daron shook her head. "You'll never change."

"What do you mean?"

"Why did you throw Pennar over? Why didn't you marry him?"

Daron's voice was so low she could hardly hear. Tanwen hesitated. What should she say to keep Daron talking? "It was such a strange day, and I met Owain…"

"Mama was so angry, and Angharad was furious, when she and Pennar arrived. And you left me alone to deal with it all." Daron stopped.

"I thought," Tanwen said, "that you might marry Pennar. Would you wish that still, I can talk to Owain."

"Marry Pennar?" Daron's voice cracked. "You say that to me now! Angharad would have none of us, after you rejected her precious son.

Humiliated him in front of all."

Tanwen grimaced. "I didn't reject Pennar, more I chose Owain. Do you love him?"

"What does it matter? He is gone back north with his mother, who vowed to have no more to do with us, and you can be sure she's not one to change her mind. My chances are gone, the house is gone, Mama is dead. I am ruined."

"Why ruined? What about Rhodri?"

"That was Mama's plan, never mine! What is to happen to me now? You have done this!"

Tanwen stared at Daron. "To you and your mother everything is always my fault!"

"You killed mama! Of course it is your fault!" Daron threw off her shawl.

Tanwen tried to keep her voice even. "That's unreasonable. The fever…"

"And will your Owain marry you, do you think, when you have had this child?"

Tanwen took a step back, then turned about and walked away. Daron was a shrew, always jealous, first of her mother's meager attentions to her, now of her happiness with Owain. She walked fast over the rock-strewn path. She must not listen, Daron was angry and bitter, it would harm the child. After a time she stopped under an elm, rubbed her back, and wiped her forehead. It was so humid.

She heard the crack of twigs and knew Daron followed. She didn't wait. Eventually she reached the river. She stared down at the dark water. All that water, always rushing by. Never returning. The ache in her back had traveled down her legs. It would be a long trudge home.

Daron came up behind her, but did not speak. There was only the dull roar of the river. Then the clink of metal hitting stone. Daron stifled a scream. Tanwen turned around and saw a man, sword in hand, in the path. She gasped and teetered on the riverbank. Daron grabbed her elbow.

"What are you women doing here?" said the giant man, his voice menacing.

Tanwen took a deep breath. "What are you doing here, on Lord Owain's lands?" She made her voice as commanding as she could.

The man frowned. "Foolish woman." He took a step toward them.

"Run Daron!" Tanwen shouted.

Daron gripped her arm even tighter. "I'll not leave you."

The man lowered his sword. "I'll not be hurting you." He sounded annoyed. "Who sent his women to do his spying?"

"We're not spying," said Tanwen, "and what is there to see?" She twisted to stare at the river, but it flowed as before, the sound of bees in thick clover filling the warm air.

"What the devil?" Another man burst from the woods. His voice was sharp and she couldn't see his face, for he wore a steel helmet with a nose piece, battered and unpolished.

"Two women. I found them peering over the edge," said the big man.

The man turned his masked face their way and Tanwen felt the eyes she couldn't see running over her. He raised a hand, and more men emerged from the woods. Daron huddled closer to her side.

The giant grasped her wrist and Daron's. Should she tell them they were from Owain's household? But that could be worse, for they'd certainly hold them for ransom. Owain would have to pay dearly and he would be angry, nothing made him angrier than money troubles and Teilo had been after him so often about expenses.

Tanwen's fingers twitched, but she restrained the urge to tug her arm away from the giant. Just then, she felt a stabbing pain, deep in her stomach. She nearly cried out. Her back had been aching all day, but she couldn't be having the baby now.

Without speaking, the men seemed to have reached some conclusion. The man in the helmet snapped his fingers and another bounded up, leading a pony. "Get on, and ride away from here, fast. Do not look back and do not come back whatever you do."

Tanwen frowned. "But who are you? What are you doing here?" She stared at his face, trying to see through his helmet.

"If you choose not to listen, I cannot save you." He turned on his heel and disappeared again into the trees, his men disappearing after him, as though by black magic. Only the giant remained, clutching the pony's reins.

Daron tugged at her gown. "Come Tanwen, while we still can."

Tanwen tried to move, but Daron's voice seemed to come from far away. She put a hand on the pony's neck, and another pain struck her.

"What is it? Tanwen!"

"I'm just tired. We have walked far. It's good we have this pony to see us home." She tried to keep her voice even. "You can go," she said to the big man. "I'll loose the pony so you can find him later."

"I'll see you home and return with the pony."

"As you will." She had no strength to argue, and pulled herself onto the pony. Daron clambered up behind. Tanwen wound the rough black mane around her palms. The huge man plodded ahead of them, holding the reins. They threaded through the trees, then onto a different path than the one they'd followed earlier. Tanwen held in another gasp as pain bit into her back.

Daron clutched her belt. "What is wrong," she whispered, dread in her voice. "Tanwen?"

Tanwen shook her head and Daron subsided, but her fingers were too tight around her waist. Still, the pony's smooth gait lulled her, and though she waited for the next pain, it did not come. Gradually she felt her muscles relax and her breathing return to normal. A passing false labor, brought on by walking over far, and fear. She closed her eyes, exhausted in every bone and muscle. She listened to the whispering leaves as they plodded on and must have dozed, leaning against Daron, for there was suddenly a jolt and they were stopped. The sky had darkened from azure to a purple haze of roiling clouds and soft rain was falling.

"We must have shelter," she heard Daron call to the soldier. The voice seemed an echo, so far away. She wanted to snuggle down into her blankets. "Help," she heard Daron call. She wondered what was wrong and then felt herself slipping and tried to grasp the pony's mane tighter, but her fingers wouldn't work.

When she awoke, she was on the ground, tree boughs piled beneath her to make an uneven pallet and a half constructed lean-to of fir over her head.

Daron crouched over her. "Blessed Mary, you're awake."

"Did I fall asleep? What is happening?" Her head felt tight; she closed her eyes against the flickering bright lights.

"Lie still, don't move a muscle. Are you cold?"

"I'm tired, I want to sleep."

Daron shook her gently. "Tanwen!"

She grimaced and opened her eyes again. The back of her legs ached down to her ankles. She struggled to sit up but couldn't seem to manage it. And then a pain ripped at her, harsh and long. She groaned.

Daron touched her forehead. "Lie still," she whispered. "Don't move."

She heard Daron shouting, her voice frightened and too loud. So be it. She was having the baby, not in Owain's warm chamber, but here in the forest, where she belonged. Her fingers scrabbled in the piled maple leaves until they touched dirt, damp and cold.

Daron wanted to weep. Where was that horrible man, now she needed him? She darted up the path and there he was, behind a tree, slashing boughs from a fir with his sword. She rushed up, gasping so it was difficult to speak. "She's having the baby."

He looked up, then down to his sword, which he cleaned with a wad of grass and put into its sheath. "Yes," he said, "I think you are right."

"Of course I'm right! Is that all you have to say! She's having her baby!" Daron put her face in her hands. "Here in the woods, and no midwife and no..." Her voice trailed off at the enormity of what they lacked. "You must do something." Daron drew herself up to her full height.

He took a step back. "I know naught of women's business. I'm a soldier."

"She is the leman of Owain of Adpar. This is his child."

The man twisted his big shoulders and peered off into the darkening shadows toward Tanwen's lean-to, then back at her. "Still, she must have the child as all women do."

"We need..." Daron stopped. Her voice was a disconcerting wail. "We need..."

Abruptly, the big soldier pulled her to him. She cried out, but he enveloped her in an embrace, a strangely comforting embrace. And held her there. She could hear nothing but the slow, loud beat of his heart. His smell of sweat and horse surrounded her. Gradually her own heart slowed and her back relaxed.

He pushed her out to arm's length and examined her face. "Now, what is it you need?"

"What is your name?"

He shook his head and looked away. But after a long moment, he met her eyes and said, "I am Huw ap Math."

"I need to help her." Daron clenched her fist. Tanwen, always so proud. She had never accepted sympathy. Even when she'd first come to Aberteifi, collarbones sticking out and hair so matted mama had to cut it all away. And later, months later, when she was clean and no longer starved, they could see her white skin and grey eyes that sometimes turned green like the sea, that's when the village women began to gossip about her mother and grandmother. Tanwen always raised her chin in the air and went her own way. Once, only once, she'd heard her crying in the night. She'd wanted to turn on the pallet and comfort her, but she hadn't dared. Tanwen would so hate anyone to see her weep.

But Tanwen needed her now. Tanwen, who had ruined her chances with Pennar, ruined her life. It was torture to watch her with Owain every evening as they climbed to their chamber together while her own life was over, cut off, before it had begun.

Huw was looking at her. Whatever Tanwen was or what she'd done, she must help, of course she must. "We need a fire," Daron said, "some pot to heat water in. We need a sharp knife." She chewed on a fingernail. Once she'd watched a birth of a neighbor's child, and that time the baby had died.

Huw stood before her, waiting.

"After that, you must ride for help. You must fetch the midwife from Adpar."

Huw nodded and bent to gather firewood.

Daron hurried back to Tanwen. Her cousin's face was flushed and she was biting her lips, holding in her groans.

Tanwen opened her eyes. "I'm having the child here, now."

"Yes," said Daron, making her voice calm, "you are. But no matter, here or inside, a baby comes just the same. You are strong and this child will be strong too, like his mother."

"And generous, like his father," murmured Tanwen.

"Yes," said Daron, though she thought Owain self-centered and vain. Always tossing those chestnut curls around and looking about to see the effect. And he hadn't married her yet, nor would he.

Huw set a cup of water on the ground. "I've got a fire going." He pointed to a clearing she could glimpse through the trees. "There's a spring on the north side. I've put water in my helmet by the fire, it will warm some but the hot will have to wait until I return. I'll bring pots."

Daron nodded, realizing he was leaving, feeling panic return.

He met her eyes. "You can do it," he said, "you've the strength."

With that surprising statement, he urged the pony out of the clearing. What if he didn't go to the manor? What if he just returned to his men and whatever foul business it was they conducted out there in the woods? Daron put her face in her hands.

Tanwen stifled a gasp.

Daron looked up to see Tanwen staring at her, eyes huge in a white face. She knelt down by the rough pallet, made herself smile, and stroked Tanwen's hair, streaked dark with sweat. "That soldier's gone for the midwife and we've a fire and water. Would you like some to drink?" She gave Tanwen a sip, then set the cup down. "Let me help you up, I've heard it's best to walk." She grasped Tanwen, heavy with the child and always bigger than she, and half dragged her to the clearing. "Now walk," she said and they walked up and down, stopping as the pains hit and Tanwen grunted and doubled over. Up and down, holding her cousin upright, until her arm and back muscles screamed. Up and down, as rain sprinkled and then pelted down, warm rain luckily but soaking their clothes and hair. Making Tanwen even heavier. Night came on so gradually, one moment she looked around and realized it was late, past midnight, and stars began to dot the sky between the clouds. A wind puffed up, pushing the last clouds away, but making it cold. She stripped the wet clothes off Tanwen and tried to dry them by the fire. And still she listened for the sound of hoof beats. He must come back. What if he did not?

When they came she hardly heard them, for Tanwen was back on the pallet, screaming, and she was gripping her hands, and then Huw was pulling her aside and the midwife was poking around and saying, "Exactly so mistress, you're doing wonderful here. You'll have this child by morn, and that's not too far off, is it." Daron let Huw drag her back to the fire. She sank down and fell into sleep, lying on Tanwen's drenched gown.

CHAPTER EIGHT

Aberteifi, 1153

GETHIN EXAMINED the fog and imagined green waves splashing against an oak hull. The land seemed to clutch at him, like the red mud stuck to his boots.

"Where should we unload, master?" asked a short man, his hairy legs red with cold.

"There, you'll find a small cove." Gethin pointed. Rhys had given him the dangerous job of getting supplies off the Irish ships and into the hill caves. Gethin followed the man back down the winding path, ignoring the cliff that dropped to black rocks and foaming sea.

At the bottom, a stranger waited, grey hair standing up in tufts when he pulled off his cap. "Teilo Fawr," he said, "I come from Owain of Adpar, with messages for Lord Rhys."

Gethin held out a hand.

"For Rhys," insisted Teilo.

"I am to arrange the meeting, so I need to see those missives."

Teilo indicated the path to the village. "Why not come with me, there's an inn and the woman serves fine ale."

Gethin sighed. He'd been trying to arrange this meeting with Owain for months. First Cadell's grievous injuries, and the subsequent retreat of Maredudd and Rhys to their caput at Dinefwr, had intervened. Then Gwynedd of the North launched a clutch of raids, and once they were pushed back, the ceremony making Rhys and Maredudd officially co-princes and the injured Cadell's departure on pilgrimage to Rome, made it impossible. Always obstructions. To be fair, these weren't all Owain's doing, but Owain had been evasive.

Gethin shouted to the men unloading the skiff. No doubt some barrels would disappear if he went to this inn, but they would disappear anyway. He stretched a smile on his face and added a few gracious words as they trudged down the muddy path. Might as well get Rhys the information he wanted and secure this meeting at last.

At the inn, two tables stuck under a thatched roof with driftwood logs for seats, they ordered ale. The hefty brewer brought the cups herself, and also a loaf of new bread, steaming still. Gethin gave the woman a real smile. She smiled back and turned with a swish of her large hips. They drank the ale and stretched their legs in the feeble sun burning through the fog. After he judged a reasonable time had passed, Gethin said, "So, will your lord meet with Rhys?"

Teilo wiped his mouth with a sleeve. "He'll do it." They watched a hawk soar upward, with its terrible cry. "As who would not?"

Gethin stifled the urge to ask what had taken Owain so long to arrange.

"But not on his own lands, he wants to come here, near Aberteifi."

"Why?" Gethin drummed his fingers on the table.

Teilo shrugged. "I don't know everything he thinks, of course."

Gethin noted that Teilo turned his eyes back to the sky as he spoke, though the bird was gone. No doubt Teilo did know; he probably devised the plan. It was clever. With any luck, the Northmen would never know Owain talked with the enemy. Nor would the ambitious Normans who frequented Owain's keep. Owain would be free to make deals on both sides, and whoever eventually won would reward him. "Tell your lord that Rhys agrees."

Teilo looked surprised.

"Tell him also, the meeting must be within the month, or there will be no meeting at all." That was his own addition, a good one judging by Teilo's expression. He grinned. "More ale?"

The grin seemed to unsettle Teilo. But he placed a coin on the table. "Agreed."

A fortnight later, Gethin scouted the clearing for Rhys, who was taking no chances. Morning sun was clearing the treetops and dew shimmered on the grass spears. Owain was a small lordling, but his lands covered a strategic pass through the hills, and joined with Rhys' lands at Dinefwr, making Rhys vulnerable and the vacillating Owain, in the recent reshuffling of alliances, valuable. Gethin waited, fingering a periwinkle shell he carried in his pouch.

After a time, he heard a distant jangle, echoing off the ridge. Owain hadn't silenced the horses' bridles. Not expecting trouble, or not sufficiently careful. Gethin ducked under a fir tree with sweeping low branches. If Owain said anything worth hearing, he was to report to Rhys before the meeting even began.

The jingle grew louder until Owain and three men appeared. Teilo trailed behind, a cautious fourth, surveying the clearing. The rest were laughing, mounted on well-fed ponies. Owain was attired in a tunic edged with gold silk. Fitted lambskin gloves covered his hands. Gethin flexed his own cold fingers. A shower of droplets landed on his head, so he stilled and tried to pick up the thread of conversation.

It didn't really seem to be about anything. Hunting, some hounds, a woman. Nothing to raise eyebrows. Perhaps this Owain was just what he seemed, a petty noble with petty tastes. Except in women. Gethin fingered the shell, tracing the smoothed edges and whirling ridges, remembering the green scent of her. She'd been fierce, even though afraid, when he'd encountered her outside Owain's hunting lodge in the dark. It had been a long time since a woman appealed to him. He'd been startled, when he saw her again, in the woods that day with Huw. They'd been preparing an ambush on the Northmen for Rhys when two women had wandered into the middle, disrupting everything. She hadn't recognized him, with his face masked, but he'd faded back into the woods, afraid of her observant eyes. She'd been preoccupied, pregnant and fearful. Why did Owain let such a woman wander unescorted in the woods? He should take greater care.

Owain's men idled in the clearing, tossing a stick in some sort of game. Owain still sat his pony with its scarlet saddlecloth, making a fine picture. Cold water seeped into Gethin's left boot, where the leather had split.

Suddenly, silently, Rhys appeared at the edge of the clearing. Owain whirled his pony around. Rhys, a silk tunic of bright blue thrown over his hauberk, stood in a spot of cold sunlight. "Welcome Owain ap Macsen," he said, making himself the host. He raised his arm in greeting and two wide armbands of gold flashed.

Owain's face stiffened, but he slid off the pony and gave a graceful bow, his reply lost to the ground.

Rhys drew him away from the others, putting his head close to Owain, talking, an arm around his shoulders. Gethin sighed. Few could resist Rhys when he sought to charm. Owain said something, his voice loud. Gethin caught the name Maredudd. Rhys had anticipated Owain would question him about who truly ruled Ceredigion, but it would rankle.

Rhys' men produced bread, a roast of venison, a wheel of orange cheese and wineskins. The scent floated to Gethin and his stomach rumbled. Rhys and Owain resumed talking as the men ate, apart from the others. Or Rhys was talking, gesturing, pointing north and east, one moment serious, the next laughing.

Gethin wondered what Rhys would have to say, to convince this Owain that he should make his lands available, house and feed soldiers, provide horses, and set ambushes for Normans and Northmen both. It would cost coin and foodstuffs and it meant danger and new enemies–from Gwynedd of the North and from the Normans who harried the hills. What could Rhys offer that would make Owain spend his resources and take those risks? He didn't know and in truth he didn't have to worry. That was Rhys' job and he was doing it well, it seemed, for Owain was doing the talking now, his face alight with some new vigor and drive. Rhys had that effect. Gethin flexed his numbed fingers. Else why was he here, crouching drenched under a creaking cedar?

He watched as Rhys and Owain moved to the center of the clearing and embraced. The men on both sides paused, chunks of meat in their greasy fingers, uneasy, unsure what their new role as allies entailed.

Rhys waved an arm and mounted his horse. His men shoved the meat in their mouths and melted into the woods. Owain stood alone where they left him, transfixed it seemed, in the center of the clearing. Gethin watched Owain's eyes fix on the clouds and the pale sky between the clouds and beyond, and he wondered what vision it was that Owain saw.

Tanwen laughed and pulled small Bryn to his unsteady feet. He clutched her hand with his sturdy fingers. Such a happy child and healthy, for which she breathed thanks every night, staring at the far sky over the purple hills. She wasn't sure who or what she prayed to, the God Owain's priest worshipped or the spirits of the forest her grandmother left offerings for, small gifts of rosemary and onions. Bryn was growing so fast she kept her fingers pricked sewing for him every night. Days she chased after him, for once he walked he was always running. She could have charged Elise with his care, but she preferred tending her child herself.

She'd even made headway with the women of the manor. Elise laughed with her each morning as she dressed and Alica would call her in for a mug of steaming tea and a chat. Still, at times she longed for her own mother, that strange flitting figure, always singing. Perhaps they could have talked, about those things that truly matter. Like how Bryn loved to fish but grew silent when he saw a fish knocked into stillness. Or how she felt when he had first fluttered in her womb, and she knew that they were linked, for all this life. How could she put words to the way she loved him, and who to say such words to?

Elise ran up the uneven stairs of the garden, her skirts yanked up to her knees. "Mistress!"

"What's happened?" But she didn't worry, Bryn was examining a bug in the grass only an arm's length away, his chubby knee gleaming.

"Lord Owain is back, you told me to tell you right away."

"Your da is home." Tanwen swooped Bryn up in her arms.

Bryn laughed. "Da, da." His brown eyes crinkled at the sides, just like Owain's.

"Come!" Tanwen grabbed his hand and pulled him along, though his fat legs couldn't go that fast. They reached the edge of the gardens as Owain cantered through the gate. So handsome he looked, chestnut hair covered by a blue cap she hadn't seen before. Sun gleamed off the rippling muscles of his horse, the exact shade of his hair. She picked Bryn up, and he was silent in her arms, absorbed in the spectacle. "See da," she whispered.

"Da," he repeated.

It seemed Owain had been away forever, and it had been long weeks. The times were tense; he had responsibilities she knew nothing of. Sometimes he still seemed a stranger, magical, who had swept her from her old life into this enchanted manor with its gardens. She hugged Bryn. He wriggled in her arms. "I'm sorry, little walnut," she laughed, loosening her grip. She stepped out of the shadow of the garden gate and walked toward Owain, glad she was wearing her new gown, blue like the summery sea. Bryn looked the tiny lord he was, his waving hair long still, lighter than Owain's, and his tunic cut short so he could run.

Teilo saw her and nodded, grave as always, and spoke to Owain, who turned her way. But Owain didn't stride toward her, sweeping her up, whispering that he'd missed her unbearably. He shouted an order to his men. The grooms led the tired horses toward the stable, leaving Teilo and Owain together, arguing.

Owain turned away abruptly, without meeting her eyes, and entered the hall, his men scattered behind.

"Da." Bryn still waved his fat arm and clamored to be put down.

Teilo came up. "Mistress, perhaps a word."

Without speaking, they strolled to the far end of the garden, flanked by tall roses, on the path meant to be enjoyed as dusk faded into blue evening, white flowers looming up like the ghosts of loved ones. A garden to stroll in with a lover. She'd imagined this garden, dug the earth, planted the bushes, laid the stones. To walk in with him. And so they had, sometimes. She swung around to Teilo. "What has happened?"

"He has met someone."

"A woman," she whispered, putting Bryn down on the trimmed grass.

"A man, but not just a man. Owain met with Rhys."

"What has he to do with a prince?" She took a stone from Bryn's fist. "What if the Northmen or the Normans hear of this?"

"There is danger aplenty," agreed Teilo, drawing his shaggy eyebrows together. "Gwynedd of the North must never hear of this."

"You think I would betray him?"

"I am cautioning you. It is a difficult time we live in," Teilo said sadly. "Owain has been sworn to the Northmen all his years and his father before him. But meet he does with the Normans, as all know. And meet he did with Rhys, and when they came back my lord was like a man bewitched…in his eyes a light, something akin to a strange fever." Teilo poked at a tuft of moss, uprooting it, releasing the scent of dirt into the air.

"When?" asked Tanwen. "Who else knows?"

"Before winter set in deep. There are many who know. Owain is not discreet, and the times are full of danger, people watching and whispering."

Tanwen felt her heart pounding. That loyal Teilo would say all this meant he was worried indeed.

Things had changed. Small things only she would notice. Even Teilo seemed reassured, now Owain was home and the strange light faded from his eyes. But Owain never played with Bryn. No longer ruffled Bryn's hair, or sat him on his horse. Nor did Owain seek her out for conversation. She had the feeling when they were making love that he was thinking of something else entirely. Was it another woman? She didn't think so. Yet something had him in its grip. Owain had been hers, all hers, and now he was not.

She spent time with Alica, learning to bake breads with wheat and rye flours. She made puddings of pears and apples, mixed with costly cinnamon and ginger and honey. She tried to fill up her time and Bryn was there, licking the wooden spoon, sticking his fist deep into the bread dough and laughing with that funny laugh deep in his belly. Yet loving a child is like carrying a deep well of fear inside always.

"Owain," she said one morning, as they ate. "Must you go hunting today?"

"Of course I must." He shoved away from the table and paced, gazing out the open window.

"You look tired, that is all." She seemed to be always placating him these days. "What troubles you, can't you speak of it to me, can't I help?"

Owain frowned at the door, open to the next chamber where the servants could be heard cleaning the hearth. "This is no place for private conversation," he said, and strode out before she could say more.

One day, Tanwen stripped off her shoes and dangled her feet in the pond she'd had dug in the center of the gardens. Bryn splashed by her feet. Daron, a pale shadow of the girl she'd been, laughed out loud at his antics. She continued to avoid Tanwen, but helping in Bryn's birth had made her fond of the child.

Tanwen yanked the linen scarf from her head, impatient to feel sun beat on her hair. She laughed at Daron's reproachful look. "I might stop wearing it altogether."

"People would say you're a …" Daron stopped, cheeks red.

Tanwen tossed a pebble into the middle of the pond. "They'd say I'm Owain's leman." Bryn looked up at her changed tone, then went back to building a twig barn for his wooden cows in the flattened grass.

Daron avoided her gaze.

"I am. Why not say so out loud? In fact, I refuse to cover my hair from this time on." She balled up the scarf and threw it into the pond. Bryn watched it sink and looked back to her with an uncertain smile.

"Don't aggravate people so, Tanwen. No one talks of you badly." Daron handed Bryn a handful of straw to feed his wood cows.

Tanwen fixed her eyes on the far edge of the pool, where birch trees trailed green leaves. Bryn tossed a toy cow in the water and when it bobbed up he started to cry.

Daron hoisted Bryn on her shoulder and jiggled him, singing a gentle tune, as she fished the toy from the water.

Tanwen tried to ignore the prickling at the back of her eyes. She was mistress to a lord, an important man. Even the prince Rhys talked with her Owain. Since Teilo told her of the secret meeting, she'd kept her ears open, and she knew frequent messages passed from Adpar to

Rhys' seat at Dinefwr. Only the Normans made a fuss about marriage anyway, with their anxious priests and cold-eyed lawyers. And what did any of them know, about a woman and her heart?

Daron put Bryn down on a blanket in the shade, covering him gently as if he were hers. Then she stood over Tanwen. "I meant nothing."

Tanwen shrugged and shredded a daisy.

Daron sat down by her side. "I do think you are right to be concerned."

"Why? What have you heard?"

Daron bit her fingernail. "Nothing sure. But there is talk."

Tanwen pulled at a thread on her skirt until the fine cloth ripped. "Wherever I go, there is always talk. I hoped Owain would marry me, once Bryn came."

Daron touched her sleeve.

"My pardons." A deep voice startled them. A big man, in a dull silver hauberk stood in the path.

Daron jumped to her feet.

"Who are you?" said Tanwen. But as she spoke she recognized the soldier. It was Huw. "How did you get in here?"

Huw bowed. "I've come to prepare for a journey, mistress."

"What journey?"

"I serve the prince Rhys, and Lord Owain meets with him soon, at his castle, Dinefwr."

Tanwen examined his face, but Huw was looking at Daron.

"We'll speak later," said Daron to her in a low voice. Face pink, she walked with Huw down the path that led to the outer fields.

Tanwen stared after them. Daron had never mentioned this Huw. And why had she spoken to Daron about Owain? She should never have confessed her deepest fears to her cousin. She'd talked to Daron as though they were true sisters. Yet in Daron's eyes there was no warmth for her, only for her son. Bryn whimpered and she hoisted him up, his body heavy and smelling of pond water. She brushed rough grains of sand from his silky skin.

A few days later, Tanwen was weeding onions when Daron, in her newest blue gown, swished up.

"I want to talk with you," said Daron.

Tanwen straightened up. Seeing Daron's dark hair gleaming did nothing to improve her mood. "I'm busy." She yanked another dandelion. "Where are you going in that fancy gown?"

"You sound like mama," said Daron. "Don't, I have something to ask. Something important. Listen to me, Tanwen."

"I can hear you fine." Tanwen started to cut onion shoots to season the stew Alica was making for dinner.

"Tanwen!" Daron came closer, skirts lifted above the dirt. "I can't yell it out for all to hear."

Tanwen sighed and wiped her knife on her apron. "What then?"

Daron glanced around as though she were in a play. "Owain is going to go to Dinefwr, Rhys' caput."

Tanwen pressed her lips together.

"You must get him to take you."

"How could I? I can't leave Bryn."

"I've thought of everything. We can take Elise to care for him."

Tanwen pricked her fingertip on the knife blade. She glared at Daron. "We?"

Daron reddened. "I must come with you too, it wouldn't be respectable otherwise."

"Respectable?" Tanwen gave a low laugh. "I'm Owain's leman remember."

"Don't be ridiculous," said Daron, "you're good as married in the eyes of anyone Welsh and that certainly includes Rhys."

"Perhaps."

"Persuade Owain. Tanwen, think! It would be so exciting." Daron whirled around, her skirts flying out around her ankles.

Tanwen rubbed her arm where a bug had left an itchy bite. She felt a thousand years older than her cousin.

"Say you'll do it," said Daron, leaning over her.

The truth was she doubted her ability to persuade Owain, but she wouldn't admit that to Daron. "I'll try," she said, her voice unconvincing, even to her own ear.

"Owain will fall in love with you all over again, in a new setting," said Daron, and she was gone, skirts flying above white ankles.

CHAPTER NINE

Dinefwr, 1155

GETHIN TRIED to jiggle his leg without seeming bored. Rhys had finally called him to his bedchamber before dawn, then busied himself with messengers and ignored him. He wanted breakfast, a cup of boiling tea and a chunk of venison or some cold chicken in a ginger spiced sauce. Rhys and his advisors clustered by the fire, peering at a writ, one more squabble over lands. Normans loved to argue over some legal quibble and the Welsh seemed no better. Lately, he'd been finding himself in a dark mood, angry with everyone around him, needing to drink more of that sour French wine every night to find some hours of sleep.

Gethin stood up, his stool toppling over with a thud. Rhys and his men looked over, disapproval on their faces at the disruption. Rhys muttered a few terse words and the lawyers scattered, clutching their precious papers. Gethin felt his throat tighten. Rhys, he must remember, could have him put to the sword and none of his teulu would think twice about carrying out the order. After all, who was he? A foreigner, useful to gather intelligence, too quiet to make friends, too involved in secrets to be welcome as a drinking companion. Now the time was here, he was tongue-tied. "Maps," he said finally.

Rhys sat on a chair by the fire and stretched his long legs out to the warmth.

"You need maps of the coast. Why keep me here! I kick my heels all day at your beck and call, but anyone could accomplish these tasks. I could serve you better."

Rhys stared at him, his eyes focused inward. One finger traced a pattern on the dragon-carved arm of his chair. "Maps of the coast will be of little use to me or my brothers if we don't secure these lands now."

"A prince must think ahead."

Anger sparked in Rhys' eyes.

Take care, Gethin warned himself, but where had that gotten him, all these months and years? "It's time for you to plan for when you have gained all Ceredigion," he said.

Rhys smiled, like a cat about to leap. "There is one more task I need first."

"There is always one more," burst out Gethin.

Rhys gazed out the window, where a dark sky loomed over the hills. "Go to Adpar and fetch this Owain. Bring him here to Dinefwr."

"He doesn't need a nursemaid. He is coming; he has agreed."

"He might change his mind and that would be a disaster now. Bring him. When his visit is over we will talk of the future."

The next week, Gethin passed through Adpar's gates with little trouble, for the place was in an uproar. Men carted bundles wrapped in oiled cloth, women scurried across the courtyard, carrying a skin of wine or a platter of food, or wooden boxes filled with spices. Children were screeching and getting in everyone's way. Gethin surveyed the commotion with a frown.

Inside he found more chaos, but a kitchen maid told him the lord was going to see a great king. Gethin smiled grimly. At least Owain was not likely to change his mind. He wandered the halls, looking for someone to bring him to Owain, and eventually located Owain's chamber himself.

Owain stood in the center of the room, being fitted for a new tunic of rich red. Gethin bowed. "Rhys sends greetings and bids me accompany you on your journey to his caput."

Owain assessed him as the tailor fussed with the length of his tunic. Gethin realized he should have stopped to bathe and be shaved.

"A kind gesture," said Owain.

Gethin set himself the task of shunting Owain's suspicions away. After a welter of tiresome compliments, he convinced Owain to leave two days earlier than planned.

Gethin descended to the hall, bent on getting outdoors to breathe some air before a long evening. He rounded a corner, and came upon two figures pulling apart. The woman rushed away.

"Lyr Gethin," said Huw, his square face flushing.

"What are you doing here?" said Gethin.

Huw played with the sword at his belt. "I might ask you the same."

"Rhys sent you?"

Huw shrugged. "Of course."

"You've found a fine way to pass the time."

Huw's face drew into a dark frown. "Say no more."

"As you will. Where can I get a cup of ale here?"

Huw continued frowning, then said in an unfriendly voice, "Come with me." Some time later, they lounged at a rough table in a hut housing the village brewery, emptied cups before them. Huw folded his arms over his chest. "Why did Rhys send you? Where is the danger?"

"No danger he thought fit to tell me," said Gethin, "which doesn't mean there isn't plenty. Gwynedd and his Northmen would love to stop this alliance if they heard of it. And it's hardly likely to remain a secret with all these preparations. He has men spying for him here."

"There was no stopping Owain once he'd started preparing. And now with the women coming."

"What women?" Gethin dropped the pebble he fingered on the table.

"Owain's leman and the child and her cousin. Daron that is." Huw dropped his eyes. "She's the lady…"

"They weren't included in the invitation."

"They're coming nonetheless." Huw stuck his booted feet up on the table.

"We'll be riding slow," Gethin said, "we'd best gather more men. If the Northmen hear of this, they're bound to try an ambush. We'll leave at first light."

Tanwen sang as she sewed. She admired her stitches, the gold of coreopsis in a midsummer field, brilliant against the moss linen of her gown. She would look a fine lady, the sort Owain would be proud to claim as his own. And Bryn would look perfect. She'd already finished a tunic for him; he looked so grown up when he'd tried it on tears rushed to her eyes.

It hadn't been hard to convince Owain, after all. She'd told him what a fine lord he'd look with ladies accompanying him. They'd be gone some weeks, so she'd given Alica instructions about digging the new garden she'd planned for the spring, if the ground thawed. Elise would come along, to help with Bryn.

Daron swirled into the room. It was the word, for she never merely walked any more. It was that Huw. "Is your gown ready?" Tanwen asked.

"I finished attaching the trim last night."

"And have you worn it yet?" Tanwen kept an innocent expression on her face, and laughed when Daron gave her an annoyed glance.

Daron looked out the window, and whirled out of the room.

Tanwen put her sewing down. She opened the big door and waited, blinking in the bright sun. She couldn't see Daron or Huw but she strolled toward the stables, trying to think up a plausible excuse about why she would be there. She just didn't want Daron harmed. Huw had helped when Bryn was born, but men were unpredictable, and what did they truly know about him?

She slipped in the door and stepped around a pile of hay and stopped, hearing their voices.

"You misunderstand," Huw said.

"I understand you too well," said Daron, sounding close to tears.

"I do love you, Daron, you must believe me," said Huw.

"How could you suggest such a thing?"

Tanwen edged away. She didn't want to hear this.

"Your cousin…"

"Exactly," said Daron, "she clings to Owain for any crumb. I'll never be like her."

Tanwen froze, then fled out the door, down the path through the winter garden, where dried flower heads bent in fantastical shapes, through the far meadows, fled until she reached the forest edge. She sat on a fallen log and listened to the quiet and the snow buntings. Dusk gathered and deepened and her fingers and toes grew numb. Finally, in the dark, she trudged back to the manor.

Daron met her at the door. "Tanwen, what have you been doing? Your gown is filthy."

"Garden work."

"Now? Never mind, you must come right away. We're to leave early. Is your gown finished? You've certainly ruined that one."

Tanwen lifted her stiff muddy skirt and stared at the stained hem. She rubbed her frozen hands together. "I'll miss my gardens."

Daron tugged her up the stairs. "We're going to Dinefwr, high court of the prince. I'm in a dream!"

Four days later, they approached Rhys' castle at Dinefwr. Tanwen tried to ignore the skipping of her heart and the sick feeling in her stomach. They'd ridden hard, Rhys' men pushing them on until full dark. This morning, in the cramped tent, she'd shaken the wrinkles out of her second best gown and pinned the swirling silver brooch Owain had given her onto her cloak. She'd put on polished leather boots, but the effect was ruined by the rough wood pattens strapped to the bottoms to keep her from the mud. When she'd come out of the tent, she'd found a clear breezy morning, the wind smelling of cold fir, but now clouds had gathered and dusk had come early.

Owain rode toward the front, handsome in his new tunic, sitting the horse as though he and the dancing stallion were one. She rode toward the back, clutching the high pommel of her saddle, though they'd given her the safest nag, who plodded along, eyes half shut, never breaking into a trot. And her throat was scratchy. If only she didn't catch a miserable cold.

Elise had Bryn before her on a dun pony. Tanwen wished Bryn could be riding with his father. She'd asked Owain to take Bryn with him last night as they'd eaten dinner, stew gulped standing by the fire. Owain stared away from her, as he always did when he was going to say no. "I can't approach Rhys with a babe in my arms," he'd said.

They rounded a bend in the river, winding black against the wet earth. "Dinefwr!" cried Daron. The castle loomed over them, part stone, part timber, surrounded by high walls on its near side, built right into red cliffs on the other. A place where gods would live, not people. Tanwen's nag chose that moment to pick up her head and walk faster. She clutched the reins and tried to relax as Owain had taught her but the horse shook her head, jingling the bridle. The other horses danced too as the scouts shouted and galloped ahead, hailing the soldiers at the gate.

They waited in the sudden quiet. The only sound was the river, snow-swollen and rushing on. The huge gate swung open with a grinding screech and they rode into Rhys' enormous paved courtyard. Dinefwr, ancient seat of the princes of Deheubarth.

Inside people swarmed everywhere, more people than she had seen even on market day back in Aberteifi. Some stared at the newcomers, but most ignored them, shouting to each other, lugging barrels or leading horses. Owain's men dismounted.

"What should we do?" called Daron. Her voice was gay and she was twisting around, looking at everything at once.

Tanwen's horse snuffed at the muddy pavers, looking for grass. Owain didn't come to lift her down. He was talking with his men. The double oak doors to the great hall opened and a score of men dressed alike in green wool filed out and greeted Owain, bowing and gesturing to the hall.

Forgetting her fear of the nag, Tanwen managed to climb down. She handed the reins to a stable boy. Owain was nearly to the hall and she wanted to hurry after him, but she had to get Bryn. She found Elise, Bryn clinging to her knees.

"'Tis glad I am to see you, mistress."

Bryn peered at her from Elise's skirts and flung himself on her legs.

"I am here," said Tanwen, speaking calmly as she picked him up. His head was hot and he snuggled his face into her chest, wiping his tears on her gown. She hugged him tighter.

Daron danced up. "Huw says we must go, right away, else we'll lose Owain." They followed Huw without trouble, for the crowd was melting away. But at the door, soldiers gathered, blocking their way, and already one of the big doors was swinging shut. Teilo's serious face appeared, peering around the carved door. He beckoned them into the echoing hall and found them a bench.

"Thank you," said Tanwen. "I was feeling out of place. It was kind of Owain to send you."

Teilo blinked, and turned away. "Will you be comfortable here? I will send for food and drink."

"We're fine." Already Bryn had dropped asleep in her lap despite the clamor of voices that rose up to the high ceiling, where smoke coiled about dark beams.

Teilo left, followed by Huw, leaving Daron staring at his broad back, pink-cheeked. Clearly they had made up after their quarrel. Tanwen studied Bryn's relaxed fingers splayed on her arm as he slept. Daron was right to hold out for marriage. But it was different for her. Not only because Owain was a lord, but because he loved her, of course he loved her, as she loved him.

They sat for some time, as men flowed in and out of the hall, and cold air rushed in the opened doors to swirl around their ankles. Owain was seated already at the high table, beside a man with dark hair. "Is it Rhys do you think?" Tanwen whispered to Daron. There was something about him, despite his plain clothing.

They watched Teilo approach Owain and whisper in his ear. Owain met her eyes, turned back to Rhys, and said a few words. The prince focused his dark gaze on her, unsmiling, for a long time. Tanwen felt her cheeks flush hot. Rhys said something to Owain, and swept from the room, servants and lords and soldiers jostling to get out the door behind his back. Owain stayed seated at the table, frowning, and finally wove through the crowded hall toward them.

"What is it?" Tanwen asked, examining his taut face.

Owain glanced at Bryn, still asleep. "Accommodations are tight and there are so many here to house."

"Yes," she said, "but we will stay with you, won't we?"

"Of course." Owain fiddled with his belt, his eyes on the door.

"Go with Teilo."

"Where are you going?" But Owain was already out the door. Teilo gestured to the wide stairway and Tanwen got up slowly, but Bryn woke anyway. They left the hall accompanied by his angry wail.

Daron and Tanwen huddled over the brazier in the chamber allotted to Owain. The weather had stayed cold all week, with rain that promised to endure. Smoke circled above their heads and Tanwen thought with longing of the fine hearth with its high ceilings and chimney hole back home. Daron coughed and Bryn looked up from where he crawled on the floor, musty rushes caught in his curly hair.

"I might go for a walk soon," said Daron.

Tanwen examined Daron's flushed cheeks. "You hate to get wet."

Daron laughed. "Yes, I promised to meet Huw."

"Why don't you see him at dinner?" Tanwen winced at her own motherly tone.

Daron flicked her hair behind her shoulder. "Rhys doesn't like his men to consort with Owain's household. He demands complete loyalty." Daron peered out the window.

"Can't you close that shutter? Why does he say that? Owain is not Rhys' enemy."

Daron threw a blue cloak on. "How do I look?"

"You know you are quite beautiful!" Tanwen held her reddened hands to the fire.

Daron stopped whirling her skirts and put a hand on Tanwen's knee. "You need not worry. I am careful." She fiddled with the pink-jeweled brooch at her neck, one of the few things she had of Agatha's. "You'll be invited to the hall to dine today, you and I both. The men have been occupied with all their talk, but this afternoon, I heard, is to be an elaborate dinner!"

"Of course," agreed Tanwen. How odd that Daron was attempting to make her feel better. Everyone here treated her strangely, like some servant Owain had brought along, instead of his leman. Bryn had been completely ignored. He was a child, but he was Owain's heir. And she'd hardly seen Owain.

Daron peeked out the door, then, with a rustle of skirts, she was gone. Bryn called out, "Auntie," in an outraged voice, but went back to the deer she'd fashioned out of rushes. Tanwen went to the narrow window. Rain streamed down, blackening the granite walls.

The door creaked open. "You're back," Tanwen said, but it was Owain, his hair dark with water and slicked back from his forehead.

"It's wetter than the ocean out there." He stripped off his soaked clothing. "You're right, it wasn't my idea. Rhys wanted to know about the boundary of my lands and nothing would do but that we go out ourselves this morning and ride the lines."

"Let me," Tanwen said. "You'll catch a chill, come to the fire." She pulled the linen sheet from the bed and toweled him dry.

"He's beyond energetic, that man, never stops. Always harping on the same things, boundaries, strategy, lands." Owain looked at her. "You look pale. Are you well?"

"Just a small cold." She pulled a dry tunic and leggings from the chest. "Just a tiny bit cooped up."

"It's not what you expected. I agree. I told Rhys we needed to have some fun. He looked at me like he didn't know the word." Owain yanked on his tunic. "Then he ordered a feast and minstrels for this afternoon. Just like that. I think he truly didn't think of it before. The man works himself to death."

"What does he want from you?" Tanwen untangled his hair and dried the dripping ends.

Owain shrugged. "He needs me and my lands. It's an opportunity. But enough, what do you say to dining in the hall, sweetheart?" He swung her around. Bryn dropped his deer and laughed.

"I say it's grand," said Tanwen. "Am I truly invited?"

"No doubt," said Owain, buckling his belt. "I'll send Teilo to fetch you."

"And Bryn?"

"Leave him with Elise."

The decorated hall was the most incredible chamber Tanwen had ever seen, but for a dream. The brilliant tunics of the men and their silver armbands dazzled, and the aroma of roasting meats mixed with smoke curling up from the central hearth. The noise of so many people talking was deafening. Tanwen hesitated at the door; it hardly seemed they could squeeze in. Then Teilo appeared, slipping under the arm of a big soldier. He bowed low and Daron giggled.

Tanwen gave Teilo a grateful smile and took the arm he offered. He elbowed men away and led them to a table out of the drafts. They sat on a wide bench, Daron covering her nervousness by arranging her skirts. Tanwen gazed around in awe. At the high table, men conversed, and in the center Rhys himself surveyed the hall, resplendent in crimson edged with dark fur, three gold armbands glinting. Even his black hair reflected light, there were so many beeswax candles burning.

"Maredudd is there too," Daron whispered. "Huw pointed him out to me earlier." Tanwen shifted her gaze to Rhys' elder brother. He was smiling in a genial way, but he didn't draw the eye as Rhys did.

Owain was seated directly beside Rhys. With a twinge of worry, Tanwen wondered once again, why all this attention? Owain was drinking the flattery in like ambrosia. Rhys laughed and flung his arms about and the very air around him seemed to radiate. Everyone hung on his words.

"Don't be sad." Daron touched Tanwen's hand. "Don't they all look fine?"

Daron's eyes weren't on the high table, but on the shadows by the door, where Huw, dressed in a stiff blue tunic, joked with his companions. Tanwen looked away, and pushed away also the memory of that dreadful conversation she'd overheard. That Daron could be right was a dark thought for the hours when night met morning. Tanwen sat up straighter and deliberately curved her lips into a smile. Owain would come sit by her, after the food, and they'd laugh as they always used to and everyone would see that she was his. Her thoughts were interrupted by the rumble of a deep voice.

Daron extended her gloved hand, like a fine lady. Huw took Daron's hand and turned to Tanwen. "Are you enjoying this food and drink?"

"It's magnificent. Never have I seen the like," Tanwen said.

"Rhys seldom takes the time to put on a feast. The cooks have been in a whirl all day," said Huw. He turned back to Daron, so Tanwen conversed with the quiet woman to her left, a widow beholden to Rhys, but anxious to get home to her three children. Rhys planned to marry her off again, and she waited for the arrangements to be concluded.

"Do you ever think of just going home to your children?" asked Tanwen.

The woman stopped eating, her knife halfway to her mouth. "I will do as the prince wishes," she murmured.

Tanwen gazed around the crowded hall, thinking how she would describe it all to Bryn in the morning. He would be outraged he'd missed the giant roasts of venison and plates of goose with current stuffing and long silver fishes whole on huge platters. And he always loved to hear about knives and swords. But tonight the weapons were piled by the doors.

"Who is that?" Daron asked.

Two ladies stood poised to enter the hall, prolonging the effect by pretending to arrange their gowns. They were dressed in silk, oddly styled, with long sweeping sleeves, no doubt the latest of fashions. Tanwen fingered her own new gown, which suddenly seemed dull. One of the women had the golden hair the poets were always praising, and an ivory gown that rippled and gleamed in the candlelight. The other was brown-haired, her gown cut low, deep red striped with blue. A shining silver circlet wound through her thick braid and sparkled as she tipped her head to speak.

"Who are they?" repeated Daron.

Huw glanced in the women's direction. "The golden-haired one is Gwenllian and she's whispered to be Maredudd's intended wife. She's the daughter of Madog of Powys and very grand, never speaks to the like of us." He shrugged. "And why would she? The other I don't know, some companion no doubt."

The ladies were escorted to the high table, where the men ceased their talk. The golden-haired Gwenllian sat next to Maredudd. Rhys placed the dark woman between him and Owain.

Tanwen picked up her silver goblet. Owain bent to speak to the woman, and Tanwen felt her cheeks grew hot; she felt uncomfortable, as though she were some sort of spy. She turned to the two men opposite her. She must be sensible. Of course Owain had to talk with Rhys' guest.

Servants entered, trailing scents of rosemary and roasted meat. The men talked of hunting in the deep forests nearby. Tanwen answered their questions with smiles and appropriate words. They offered her the best pieces from the platter of venison. But through it all, she stole glances. Owain was enjoying himself, paying more attention than necessary, surely, to the woman with the sparkling circlet. The golden-haired woman was always laughing, her hands sketching pictures in the air, and men circled around her as though she were a jar of amber honey, but the dark one talked only to Owain.

"Who is she, that dark lady?" Tanwen bit her lip at the escaped words.

"Never seen her in these parts before," said the young man seated across from her.

The older man swallowed his mouthful of roast. "I know who she is," he announced, "and more even, why she's here." He took a gulp of wine. His son tried to take his cup, but did not succeed. "She's Lady Susanna, from Gwyr way, brought in special like."

The younger man frowned. "Here's the sweets," he said. "I am wondering what specialties the cook has managed for us tonight."

A wonderful sugared swan was being paraded around the room and platters with yellow cakes, sparkling with expensive sugar, were set on the tables with bowls of golden wine. The young man ladled some in her cup and Tanwen rolled the spicy sweetness on her tongue. Owain had his hand on the dark woman's elbow now, laughing, and the woman laughed as well. He dropped a swift kiss on the woman's cheek.

Tanwen examined the table, where a blotch of gravy darkened the ivory cloth. Her fingers felt suddenly cold and stiff.

"Good wine," said the older man, leaning back, nearly toppling off the bench. His son righted him. "She's from Gwyr," continued the elder, "which as I say is on the sea and has a fine port town, which I've visited many a day." He stopped to swallow more wine. "She's daughter to William, who serves Henry by holding the castle there. One of the daughters, heard tell he has four, but she's the eldest. Maredudd captured all four girls. Rhys plans to marry her off to that Owain there, make a claim to her father's lands and tie them all up tight with his."

The son made a noise like a snort and tried again to nab the wine goblet.

"A perfect screen against the Normans," continued the father, "cut them off so to speak with a fence of Welsh lands, a pathway for his soldiers from Dinefwr straight to the sea. And from there, to anywhere. He's a good soldier is Rhys. No question about that."

Tanwen's fingers clutched the tablecloth. Her goblet teetered and fell, splashing wine over the cakes. The son gazed at her, pity in his blue eyes. She heard herself murmur, "I must have air." She heard the young man scolding, "now you've done it father, chased that lovely lady away." She skirted the tables of laughing men, gorging on the cakes. Tears blurred her vision; the door was so very far away.

She tripped over a man's leg, and would have fallen, but a hand caught her elbow and a voice said, "This way."

She escaped the hall, laughter trailing her into the twilight. Cold air bit into her uncovered neck. Afternoon had turned to blue night. "Thank you," she said and freed her arm. But the man didn't go away. She walked blindly, tears in her eyes. He grabbed her arm again, as she stumbled over an icy rut. He led her up stone stairs to the top of the castle walls and pulled her around a corner, out of the gusty wind. He pushed her down on a granite bench.

"You need not stay," she said. "I am fine."

He undid his cloak and tucked it over her shoulders. It smelled of hay and damp earth and it was soft with rabbit fur warm from his body. "The stars are brilliant tonight," he said, and sat down beside her.

She looked at him for the first time, into dark blue eyes. "Rhys' spy, is it not?"

His face froze. "As you say. We've never been properly introduced. My name is Lyr Gethin."

Tanwen frowned, her fingers picking at the ties of his cloak. "I saw you at Adpar. It was you who persuaded Owain to meet with Rhys."

Gethin took a knife from his pouch and scraped the blade on the stone.

She winced.

"Sorry." He put the knife away and clasped his hands around his knee. "I must be always fiddling."

"I must go," she said, getting to her feet.

"Shall I escort you back to the hall?"

"No."

He frowned. "You could get a wrap and it will seem you were chilled and went to get something warm to wear."

"In that overheated hall?"

He shrugged. "I don't know. You went to get whatever it is women go to get."

"Why should I return?"

"It's not often you get to attend such a feast, is it?"

She pulled his cloak tighter around her neck and closed her eyes.

"If you don't return, Rhys' ploy will certainly succeed."

"What do you mean?"

Gethin paced in front of her, his boots clunking on the stones. "You know he has plans for Owain." He ran a hand through his hair, leaving it disturbed.

"And if he does, why would you tell me?"

He frowned and looked up again at the stars.

"You think I don't know you but I do. It was you outside the hunting lodge that night, doing your spying."

"Rhys' plans are nothing to do with what I want." Gethin's voice was sharp.

"But you do the bidding of Rhys, whatever he says, do you not? You are his."

"Do you want to return to the hall or not?"

"I'm sorry to have delayed you." Tanwen took off the cloak and held it out to him. "I'm sure you have somewhere else to be."

"Rhys has many plans. Or call them ambitions. To the great, marriage is about alliances, never emotions. Certainly not love."

Tanwen shook her head.

"He acts as he will. The great are like that," Gethin said.

"They shouldn't be, and you don't approve, yet you don't stop him." Gethin said nothing.

"What does he want from Owain? Why can't he leave us alone?"

"You cannot stop Rhys; he's a force of nature," said Gethin. "He's a prince."

Tanwen stood up and headed toward the stairs.

He grabbed her arm. "You can't go down there and scold Owain like a child."

"It's Rhys I'll have words with," she said. "Or his older brother, surely he will talk sense into him."

"Especially not his brother. Are you crazed? If you want to outwit Rhys you'll have to do it with your brain. You need some plan."

"Rhys can never take Owain away," Tanwen said, "what does he have, after all, that Owain wants. He wants only me, and our son."

"All men have their price, or their dreams."

"Not Owain." She yanked her hand from his grip. "Owain is mine. You could not understand."

He released her arm. "No," he said. "I bid you good evening then."

Tanwen hesitated, but he was back to looking at the sweep of stars.

The next morning, Tanwen tugged at the fingers of her gloves and slapped them down on the chest by the bed she and Owain had shared only once since they'd come to Dinefwr. Daron stirred on her pallet. "Wake up Daron."

"It's early yet," said Daron, opening her small mouth to yawn.

She even yawned beautifully, thought Tanwen. "Wake up now. We need to…" What? The anger and hurt swept in again and tears spilled down her cheeks.

Daron blinked at her, then sat up. "Are you crying Tanwen? What has happened?"

Tanwen shook her head. "I'm not crying."

"Tanwen, dear Tanwen." Daron slipped an awkward arm around her shoulder. "What happened last night? You rushed out."

"What do you care, you hate me. I've seen it in your eyes." Tanwen walked to the window and breathed in the cold air.

"No." Daron touched her shoulder. "Or not anymore."

Tanwen wiped her face with her sleeve. Her anger was gone, but she was so tired. "Why not?"

"I'm not sure." Daron twined her hair and pinned it up. "I have Huw now. Perhaps I understand better, perhaps I've grown up."

Tanwen clutched the windowsill. Fresh tears filled her eyes.

"It was Owain. The way he talked with that woman." Daron picked up a ribbon. "Don't worry so Tanwen. It cannot last."

Tanwen rubbed the tears off her cheeks. When she'd gathered all her courage and returned to the noisy hall last night, Owain and the dark haired woman both were gone and though she looked everywhere in the boisterous hall, and waited in the shadows by the door, they had not returned.

"What will you do?" asked Daron.

"Do?"

"To get him back."

"How easy for you, the expert on love!" Tanwen threw open the chest and rifled through her gowns and boots. "It's not some game." She dropped her gowns on the bed and went back to the window. "Never would I believe he could be so cruel," she whispered. She stared at the folded purple hills and imagined her own forests. How homesick she was. She wasn't meant to be away. She began to throw gowns into a traveling basket.

"What are you doing?"

Tanwen tossed in her cloak and the few bits of jewelry she'd brought; how excited she'd been to come to a real court, the home of a prince.

"You can't just leave."

"Because you want to stay?"

Daron looked hurt, then mad. "No. Because you need to lure

him back."

Tanwen laced her gown. "I've been away from home too long."

"Home?" said Daron. "You have no home; it's Owain's."

Tanwen glared at her. "Then, neither do you. Yet it is my home, and I am Owain's leman, and mother to his son. My place is there."

"So you'll leave Owain here, to do as he will."

"This is Rhys' home. His castle. His caput. I can't fight a prince."

Daron shook her head. "It's wrong. You must tell him so."

"Not everything happens in words." Tanwen found a sleepy Bryn, cuddled up with Elise, who smiled when she learned they were leaving. What did Daron know of the weight of a sleeping child, or a husband's leg thrown over you in the night? She would wait, if that was required. But not here. They expected her to stay, all of them, but she would not.

CHAPTER TEN

Weeks passed. Winter lost its hold on the valleys and then the slopes. Toward the end of Lent, thrushes twittered and green leaves sprouted from fat fuzzy buds. The path Gethin rode was muddy and his horse plodded along. Still the feathery breezes promised spring. He'd been sent north for information. He'd traveled a long month through steep passes in the high mountains, still and deep with blue shadows and white snow. He was returning to Dinefwr now, sifting through the troubling things he'd learned, wondering what to tell Rhys.

He found Dinefwr's gates shut. Gethin yelled up to the soldiers and after a wait, the iron door creaked open. Inside, donkeys hauled carts loaded with round stones and longbows. Boys rushed back and forth carrying arrows. Huw, strapping a sword to his belt, strode by. Gethin grabbed his arm.

"Where in hell's chambers have you been?" said Huw.

"What's happening?" Gethin watched three kitchen maids struggle by with heaped baskets of cheeses and sausage.

"Maredudd is dead."

"What?" Gethin turned aside as tears knifed the back of his eyes. "How?"

Huw shrugged and took his shield from one of the boys. "How else? Killed. Murdered. By poachers maybe. Or more likely the English killed him, or that bastard from the North."

Gethin cursed. Maredudd had been fun loving, and a good soldier, even if Rhys did chafe against his older brother's restraints. "Where do you go?"

Huw eyed him. "No business of yours, is it? Always asking questions."

Over the day, Dinefwr's inhabitants calmed and the defenses were shored up. At nightfall, Gethin was summoned to Rhys' chamber where a conference was in progress. Rhys' face was tight and lined, like a man twice his age. "We will avenge him," he said, his voice raw.

The men around him nodded, staring at the floor. Nearly all the brothers murdered now. That Rhys would be next was etched on all their faces.

Rhys jumped to his feet. "By God's fist, are you men? He's been murdered and we'll have our revenge. You think we're done for. We're not, I say. We'll carry on. I shall carry on, and I will win." He glared into the men's faces.

"Rhys, and Ceredigion!" shouted one. The others leaped to their feet, arms in the air, yelling curses.

Rhys spent the night hours muttering terse orders and signing parchments. He sent men to the far villages and castles of all Ceredigion to pull together their defenses. He didn't have to say how important their arms and persuasive words would be in keeping the kingdom intact in the coming harsh months. The men left, eyes glowing.

Gethin fell in with the last as they filed out through the double oak doors. As he passed, Rhys gestured to him. The heavy doors shut with a dismal echo. The room was dark but for the flickering fire.

After long moments, Rhys said, "he did not deserve it."

"No." Gethin wanted to touch the chess pieces on the table in front of him, but he stuck his hands behind his back.

"I must make it right."

Gethin swallowed. "Sometimes, one cannot."

Rhys stared into the fire, seeming to forget he was there. But when he turned to slip away, Rhys said quietly, "I'll give you that ship you're after."

Gethin tried to speak but his throat felt strangled.

"We attack, straight away. Gwynedd of the North won't tarry when he hears this news, if he's not in fact responsible and knows it well already. We need to let him know it won't be easy." Rhys grasped a parchment from the table.

It was his own rough map of Ceredigion, Gethin saw, with Dinefwr drawn in as a castle in bright red, the whole map bordered with a leafy edge of gold and green, Rhys' colors.

"Here, on the Dyfi, we'll raise a new castle. Timber, with stone walls. To keep Gwynedd penned up in the north." Rhys pointed to the spot where his land and Gwynedd's met. "I need you to organize it. Plan the routes for bringing in materials, workers, supplies. Oversee the work."

"I'm not a castle builder," said Gethin. "It could take years."

"I have someone to do the actual building. A Norman. One of King Stephen's men, but now, Stephen is finally dead." Rhys smiled grimly.

Gethin frowned. He'd heard the news from across the border, but Stephen's death raised new problems, for now Henry was not just king of England in name, but in fact. He was occupied still in Normandy, but he would cross the channel, soon. And by reputation Henry was nothing like the late indecisive Stephen. He would deal with the troublesome Welsh borders without hesitation or mercy. No longer would the English be occupied with their own strife; the era of their inattention was over.

"You can map the river and the castle defenses and the surrounding terrain while you're there." Rhys dropped the map back on the table.

Gethin took a deep breath. Even if Rhys kept his promise of a ship, it would take months, years even. Always the goal was dangled just out of reach.

"Ask questions," Rhys was saying, "You have an uncanny way of sucking information out of men."

Gethin opened his mouth. But with Maredudd dead, his body stiffening even now in the great hall, he could find no way to say no.

Two long years passed and still Gethin labored on for Rhys, building a castle and high wall along the Dyfi against the Northmen, who gathered in plain sight some mornings, or raided for horses in the night, but never actually invaded as Rhys had feared.

Gethin cursed as his horse stumbled over the muddy rocks. The only sounds were the steady pouring of rainwater on leaves and his horse's hoofs as they sucked in the mud. He was headed to Carmarthen for supplies. The promised castle builder had never arrived and while the Northmen never fully attacked, skirmishes were a weekly affair, which kept the soldiers occupied but caused setbacks in the building. Rhys himself had come by twice only in two years, spending his time fighting further south. He was altered since Maredudd's death, his face grim and laughter gone. The change had stopped the words in Gethin's mouth. He couldn't add to Rhys' burden and so he stayed, building and waiting, dreaming of escaping this dank inland river only at night, as he lay unsleeping on his pallet, listening to the shouts and snores and garbled murmurings of the men.

His horse's head jerked up. Nearly unseated, Gethin grabbed its mane and the horse reared and danced sideways. Gethin clung on and cursed, then he smelled it too. Something burning. He pulled the shivering horse to a stop and listened. No doubt another hut or whole village. It seemed to him sometimes that all of Wales was ablaze. He tried to decide which way to go to avoid the conflict. Smoke swirled from all directions in the fitful wind, but he heard no shouts, no clang of metal weapons. Then he heard a cry, unearthly and desolate in the rain soaked forest. He should turn away, now. Instead he found himself wheeling the horse in the direction of the wail.

The cry did not come again. He urged the horse over a muddy rise and looked down on a valley, with a clearing barely open to sky between tall oaks, sodden leaves hanging down. The hut was destroyed, charred and collapsing, black smoke pouring up from its center. He couldn't see anyone. He kicked the horse and they slid through mud and stones down the hill.

When he got closer, he saw that they were all dead. Hacked apart, so it was hard to see how many they had been. A man, and another, and women, two or maybe three. They'd cut the hair off the third and hung it on a branch. It draped, darkened by the rain and curling where the ends swept the ground. He felt his stomach clench and heave. He climbed off the horse and tied the twitchy animal to a bush. His throat burned with smoke and vomit. He wiped his face and walked closer, avoiding the pooled black blood.

When he saw the small boy, he wasn't sure he was alive. He was sitting up though, his head in his hands, staring at the house, his back to the bodies. Gethin approached the stiff back. "Boy?"

The child didn't answer or even move.

"Boy." Gethin walked around him, reached out a hand, and pulled it back. The boy's face stopped him, his wide eyes, staring at something only he could see hovering in the air. Gethin swallowed and a branch cracked and he looked around. But the clearing was empty. "What's your name?"

The child just stared and Gethin realized he was not even blinking.

A raven flew in and cawed and landed by one of the dead women. Gethin grabbed a branch and swung at the bird. The raven flew to a nearby branch and screeched again, and more birds answered.

The boy just sat. Gethin ran both hands through his wet hair. He picked up one of the bodies and lugged it to the burning house. One by one, he carried the two men and three women. He stopped, twice, to get sick, choking and heaving. When he was done, he piled wood on top of the bodies. It would hold the birds back for a time, and maybe the fire would pick up, though the rain still poured down. He went and stood by the boy, who made no sign.

Gethin picked up the boy and carried him to his horse, stuck him on the saddle and swung up behind. The child's skin was icy. He wrapped his cloak around them both and turned the horse away. As they left the valley, the boy made a small gulping noise. Gethin pulled the horse to a stop, but the boy said nothing more, nor did he move, so after a moment, Gethin kicked the horse and they pushed forward, rain slanting down silver, the trees black wraiths.

The boy stayed mute. Gethin named him Sam and the boy followed him, refusing to be separated, so that Gethin became accustomed to having him around, whether cajoling the stonemasons into fixing a crack in one of the walls or studying sketches of possible improvements to the castle with the builder, who had finally arrived. Sam ate well, and played with the other children in the ditch by the walls, but he never shouted or screamed as they did. He didn't seem to remember his old name, or old life, or if he did, he never spoke, and Gethin didn't press him.

One day, Gethin and Sam walked a narrow path through tall beeches, Gethin holding the branches away from the boy behind him. The air was summer humid. Gethin wiped the sweat from his face with his sleeve. "We need a new plan." He'd grown used to talking with no response. Sam dashed his own sweaty blonde hair from his forehead and waited. They walked on to the storehouse, where Gethin assessed the building materials piled within. Stone, iron, timber. He thought about the mountain of work still to be accomplished before the castle could be called done.

That night, Gethin lay awake, thinking on Sam's tendency to imitate everything he did, like an ever present looking glass reflecting your every action or expression.

In the morning, Gethin packed his bag, and Sam's, and told the new builder the improvements now were up to him. The man shouted and threatened, but Gethin ignored him and he and the boy set off with sun streaming onto their heads and sweat trickling down their foreheads, though it was not yet noon.

A week later, toward dusk, Gethin sent an encouraging grin to Sam. "See if you can find anything that will burn in these wretched woods." There was no sense going further today. They'd lost time every day this week, with pouring rains, flooded streams to ford, and always this unearthly heat. The packhorse was tired with mildewed feed and Gethin was exhausted with not sleeping nights. Sam slept like a tree log and grabbed his bread like a normal child in the mornings. But it seemed to Gethin that with this new journey, he had taken on the child's misery. His own nights were troubled with choking smoke and gulping flames and blood boiling in deep puddles in the heat. He'd lost the knack of sleep.

Stomachs tight with oats and a cheery small fire burning, they sat in companionable silence. Sam poked at the fire with a long stick.

Gethin spoke to the boy as though he'd speak back. "We're going to Adpar first." He lay back on his damp blanket, elbows behind his head. "A Welsh lord named Owain lives there. I've a message for him from Rhys."

Sam continued to poke at the coals.

"A secret message, for Owain's ears only."

Sam looked up, then poked the fire again. Encouraged, Gethin laughed. "I know. Still doing work for Rhys." Then he frowned at the echo of his laugh in the steaming woods. The hills were crawling with violent men, some Northmen, some Norman spies, and some deserters from Rhys, loose and angry and outside all law. Gethin rolled over and tried to meet Sam's eyes. "I must do this one last job. Then I will be done and free of him."

Sam said nothing, just curled up in his blanket and fell into sleep.

"One last job only, then I'm free," said Gethin out loud, testing the thought. He lay awake, thinking of Rhys who was still fighting, but soon, it was said, he'd be hiding in the deep forests beyond Dinefwr from this new English king. It wasn't that Rhys might be a fugitive now, he just wanted no part in all of this anymore. Something in him had shifted. Perhaps it was the coming of Sam, or maybe just the passing seasons and years.

Gethin adjusted the blanket over the boy and lay back again. His clothes were stiff with sweat and mildew and his head ached. Tomorrow he'd shove into Adpar, deliver this last message for Rhys, then he was done with him and the scouting, spying life that went with him. He'd head toward Ilfracombe, with Sam, where he planned to sign onto a cargo ship as a common sailor. The dream of gaining his own ship was officially over.

A soft rain pattered down on his face. The boy had shifted his reliance from his dead family to Gethin with horrifying innocence. That was another problem. He couldn't take Sam to sea. He'd leave him with Julianna's sister in Ilfracombe, but Sam didn't know that yet. Gethin stared at the treetops until the swaying finally sent him into a fitful sleep. He dreamed of dry paths winding though sand dunes and twisted palms tossing in a gusty sea breeze, as in the stories sailors told when he'd haunted the Ilfracombe docks as a boy.

Owain was enraged. Tanwen could see his red face and rigid back from across the great hall. Dropping her mending on the window seat, she reached the men as Owain slammed his fist on the table, toppling the wine, which dribbled red over the edge. A man, dressed in black, and a boy, skinny and poorly clothed, stood in front of him. They were both dripping, hair plastered dark to their necks. This was no way to treat guests, no matter what they might have done.

"Please come by the fire and dry yourselves and I'll have some food and drink prepared." Tanwen glanced at Owain, who glared at the ground but didn't protest.

"I thank you," said the man and untied the leather belt holding his soaked cloak together.

Tanwen dropped her eyes, startled. It was Lyr Gethin, Rhys' spy. She hadn't seen him since the night she left Dinefwr so long ago, but it was certainly him. She turned away, flustered, hoping he didn't remember her and busied herself seeing to the food and drink, and having the fire built up.

Owain paced by the windows, then stood before the guests, glowering. "You left him alone, and didn't stay with him to fight?" He was shouting and he raised an arm and lunged.

Gethin stepped between Owain and the boy, a hand on the knife at his belt.

Owain choked out, "You bastard!" But he stepped back, breathing hard and pointed to the bench opposite him.

Gethin stood for a moment, then pushed the boy behind the bench and sat. Owain sat opposite him, both men glaring at the other. The boy waited, eyes huge.

Tanwen hated to leave, but the men would say nothing important until after they'd been served. She rushed to the kitchen. "Hurry, bring ale and some of that bread and chicken, and …"

Alica frowned at her. "I think I know what best to serve guests." She gathered up sausages and chicken, added a hunk of cheese, and garnished the platter with small pears. "Come then, if you're so anxious. You can serve it, but do fix your hair, Tanwen."

Tanwen hurried back to the hall and offered the food. The men still sat silent but the guests took something. Gethin, some bread and cheese, to be polite, but the boy took chicken and bread, and when she smiled at him, a pear and a sausage. Tanwen thrust the tray into Elise's hands and stood in the shadows as they ate. She beckoned to the boy. He shot a glance at Gethin, and wandered over to her. "What is your name?" she asked.

The boy made no reply.

"Well, are you far from home?"

He eyed the bowl in her hands.

She held it out and he selected a pear. "Take two," she said, and he thrust the second into the pouch on his belt. "Take care it doesn't bruise."

He bit into the pear. Juice ran down his chin and he wiped it with his sleeve.

"What do the men speak of?" she asked. When he wouldn't reply, she added, "I know they're speaking of Rhys. Has Henry of England taken Rhys' lands already?" She knew Rhys had retreated into the forests beyond Dinefwr and King Henry had crossed the border and penetrated deep into Wales, searching for him. Thus far, no one had betrayed the young prince. The forests were deep; he might never be found. The boy took a last bite of the pear and licked his fingers. Tanwen imagined this boy, nearly the age of her child Bryn, caught in battle and winced at the painful thought. "Is Gethin your father?" she asked.

The boy ignored her and wandered back to the men.

Frustrated, Tanwen followed on the pretext of pouring ale. Gethin might recognize her, but knowing what was happening mattered much more. Owain frowned as she approached, but didn't motion her away. It was her duty as hostess, after all.

"You must see you cannot leave him now," Owain was saying in a strained voice. "In his hour of need."

"I'm not sworn to Rhys. I've worked for him freely, and now I choose to go. He makes his own trouble, and it's not my life."

Gethin's face was pale.

"You're a coward," said Owain, leaping to his feet. Tanwen gasped, grateful the table separated the men.

Gethin got to his feet. "You have an interesting way of treating guests."

Owain's face contorted. "I repeat, you're a coward," he spat out.

"Owain," said Tanwen, but he was past hearing her.

"Rhys is worth five hundred of you and you dare leave him?"

Gethin narrowed his eyes. "I don't see you at his side."

"I will be there as soon as my responsibilities here permit, but you…"

"That's easy to say, but I have responsibilities too."

"Such as what, spying and drinking…"

Tanwen laid a hand on Owain's arm. "You must not…" He shook her off. She stumbled back and tripped over her skirts. Owain stormed out.

Gethin reached out an arm to help her up. "Are you hurt?"

She stared at the open door and got to her feet, ignoring his hand. "You are leaving Rhys' service?"

"So it appears." Gethin gave her an enigmatic look, and started toward the door.

"Where do you go?" she asked, wanting to stop him though she knew he'd tell her no more about his message to Owain.

He looked like he might not answer at all, but then he said, "South, to the Mediterranean."

She thought on that a moment. "Is it quite beautiful there, all blue and gold as the Crusaders say?"

A smile lit his face and disappeared. "I intend to find out."

"How marvelous to venture off on such a grand plan," she said. "How I'd love to see something of this world."

Gethin's face held a puzzled expression. "Get Owain to take you."

"It is not his dream."

"Does that matter?"

"You know it does." She frowned. "Surely Rhys deserves your support in his time of need? He has a great plan to unite all of South

Wales."

"Ah, the great plan, I've heard much of that."

"Don't you believe in kicking the Northmen out?"

"The Northmen are no longer the problem. It's Henry of England who will take Wales, and there is no one, even Rhys, who can stop him. And these endless battles won't grow crops or feed children." He picked up his cloak and bundle and nodded to the boy. "I wish you well, Mistress Tanwen." He bowed, then paused, staring at the ground. "You will be well here?"

"What message is it that you have you brought to Owain?"

He considered her in silence and then shook his head. "You should take great care." He gestured to the boy, who bounded after him without a backward look, a pear in his hand.

Gethin and Sam traveled swiftly on ponies he purchased in the next market town and they arrived in a fortnight, without trouble, at the coast. They slept in an inn for one night and ate a meal of hot stew and traveled further, taking a barge across the water with the patient ponies, and then riding on. They entered Ilfracombe at dusk, Sam twisting in the saddle and staring, and found Enid, Julianna's older sister, still snug in the same house.

Enid welcomed him as though he'd been gone a week and not eight years. She welcomed Sam too, handing him a huge biscuit covered with honey and then carting him off to a bath. David, her husband, was hospitable in his own quiet way and as there were two young daughters now, Sam slipped into place. He worked with David in his woodshop most afternoons and helped Enid with stacking firewood and as a taster for her baking. He played running games with the girls in the back garden and they seemed to accept his silent ways.

Gethin studied Sam one evening, as he sat at Enid's feet, her girls already asleep. Enid wound blue wool onto a spool and told the boy a story of a giant troll who lived in the west mountains. When Sam had been hustled off to bed, Gethin asked, "Would you take the boy? For good I mean, he needs a home."

"Yes," Enid said, "but it would help him, I'm thinking, if I knew what he'd been through, for it's clear he's lost much." She stood at the trestle table David had built, kneading bread dough. The room was filled with gold light from the flickering fire and the warm smell of yeast.

Gethin hesitated, not liking to bring such news into this warm place. "I found him near his dead family. His home burned. He was alone. Dazed, just staring."

Enid frowned. "You've been to some trouble-strewn places."

Gethin flicked a raisin into the fire. "Yes."

Enid's plump hands patted the dough into a perfect ball. "And how do you fare, Gethin?"

"The same."

She put a hand on his arm, leaving a dusting of white flour on his dark sleeve.

The next afternoon, Gethin told Sam he would be staying with Enid. "She loves you already, like her own. Someday you'll come with me, I promise. If you still wish it. But it's early days yet. She'd have my head if I took you now!" Sam looked away, and Gethin hoped he understood.

Within the week, Gethin signed on to a ship, replacing another who couldn't get over the seasickness. He threw his belongings into his oiled bag. "Hold this for my return." He handed Sam a long knife in a leather case. Sam's eyes grew huge and he hung the knife on his belt with a length of twine.

"Can you not stay in one place?" Enid's eyes brimmed. "Does it still hurt so?" Gethin stiffened and she threw up her arms. "I'm sorry, dear Gethin, you know I cannot stay quiet about anything. How I shall miss you!"

"And I you." He hugged her, drawing in the scent of warm dough and roses.

"Could you not find someone again, have a family? Must you go to such dangerous lands?"

He picked up his bag. "That's over for me."

On the ship, Gethin looked back to shore where Enid and David waved and felt an unexpected burst of loneliness. Sam wasn't on the pier. He found himself wishing the boy stood beside Enid. At first, it had been troublesome to look after the silent boy, but he'd grown accustomed to having him around. Still, he'd have a real home here.

Gethin turned his face to the deep water. Salt wind ruffled and cracked the sails as they cleared the bay. He had forgotten nothing. The blue water tossed whitecaps, seabirds skimmed and called, and soon he could see no land, only sea. He felt his spirits bob up, like the seaweed on waves, floating, finally free.

CHAPTER ELEVEN

Tanwen pulled weeds in the central octagon of her rose garden. Bryn shrieked and flourished a sword made of sticks, pretending to be a crusader, like the pair who had stopped in their journey home last month. He had grown tall this winter, having reached his sixth year. The sword game no longer seemed innocent. So many men, heading off to far lands to fight, or failing that, fighting close to home.

The news was all battles and blood. In gaining the English crown, Henry had finally ended a full generation of civil war within England. After acquiring his wife Eleanor's territories in Aquitaine and securing his own base in Normandy, Henry had returned to England to enlarge, it was said, his own kingdom. He'd invaded the north of Wales forcing Gwynedd to look to his own survival, which at least kept the Northmen out of Ceredigion.

Tanwen rocked back on her heels, savoring the heat of the sun on her face and neck. Owain had left soon after Lyr Gethin and the boy had come and gone, and he had not returned to Adpar in months, except for short stays of a day or even hours, preferring to stay with Rhys. As King Henry had been occupied over the channel, Rhys had been able to resume living in his castle and he'd resumed raiding too, harrying the Normans and stealing from English merchants. It was only a matter of time before Henry would have to come to deal with him again.

Owain sent her messengers with directives for the lands of his estate, and from time to time, a gift. She had two new brooches of silver, set with colored stones, and once he had sent plants, roots wrapped in moss, which grew deep pink flowers scented of spice and cloves. That had been a lovely surprise. But no words for her ears alone. He had never chastised her for leaving Dinefwr without him, nor even mentioned it when he came home, weeks later. And he had not agreed to Rhys' plans for marriage either. Or perhaps the plans had been set aside with Maredudd's death and the looming threat of war. Whatever the reason, she was glad. Yet something had come between them and nothing was as it had been before.

"Mama, who is that?" Bryn swung his play sword in a circle over his head.

Tanwen brushed dirt from her skirts. Men were pouring through the outer gates, usually kept tight shut these days. She glimpsed Owain's shining hair. Without thinking, she stepped back behind the roses, stabbing her arm with a thorn.

Owain tossed the reins to a groom and passed into the hall. Tanwen realized she was holding her breath. The smell of grass mixed with the dusty scent of gravel in the noon sun. Larks swooped overhead. Bryn had run to the garden's far edge, where he was climbing the rope swing. Owain would be busy for hours with petitions. Already, villagers gathered and Teilo formed a straggling noisy line across the courtyard up to the hall door. Bryn swung back and forth, flinging himself too high. She should call to him, tell him to take care.

Evening fell, and Tanwen dressed with care. She went to tuck Bryn into his pallet, though he was getting old for her visit, and sometimes pretended to be asleep already. Tonight he stared up at her with bright eyes. "Is it my father come home to stay?"

"He has come," Tanwen answered. "Tomorrow he will speak with you, I'm sure."

"Will he like to see my sword? Or how I ride my pony?"

"Perhaps. We'll talk of it over breakfast."

Bryn turned over on his pallet, away from her.

Tanwen wanted to touch his shoulder, but she just watched him, breathing in and out, and then went up the stairs, which seemed steep and tiring. In her chamber, she examined herself in the mirror and could see only her eyes, huge and anxious.

A tap sounded on the door. Elise swung it open. "Teilo, it's lovely to see you in good health. Alica must be so pleased to have you home," said Tanwen.

Teilo nodded, with an embarrassed grin. "Fine way she shows it. She's whipping up a spice pudding and ordering the kitchen boys about. I've not a chance to even speak with her." He paused. "And you, mistress, you look to be in health."

"Yes," she said. "As is Bryn."

"The child, yes, that's good." Teilo fiddled with the clasp of his belt.

"Have you come to tell me something?"

"Alica sent me, though I would have come myself, make no mistake." Teilo took his cap off and put it back on. "Have you heard the latest news? The English king, he's coming again."

"I heard that Henry encircled Gwynedd in the North last year."

"Now he plans to march here."

"Here?" She motioned him into the room and closed the door. "Henry is coming here, to Adpar?"

"He means to come to South Wales and put Rhys in his place. He will do it too, he's got mercenaries from Flanders and coin from his marriage to pay them and he wants it done." Teilo shook his head. "Rhys is over young yet, he has only his courage. Men follow him anywhere, but they are too few." He scratched his chin. "There is much danger."

"I see," she said, imagining Bryn asleep on his pallet.

"Not to you, nor the child, but great danger to Rhys, and any he associates with."

"You mean Owain." A chill wind from the window shook the shutter and ruffled her gauzy sleeves.

Teilo sighed. "I got him away from Dinefwr, but it took weeks to persuade him."

Tanwen frowned. "Is it true then, what they say?"

"There's no doubt Henry will invade. Even now, his men assemble on the borders. He can travel quickly. He could be here in weeks."

"No." She pleated the cloth of her skirt between her fingers. "About Owain I mean. Will he marry?"

Teilo looked away. "All is on hold. Rhys has other troubles."

"She is lovely."

"Owain thinks of nothing these days but Rhys. He is convinced absolutely of Rhys' cause."

Tanwen pushed her hair off her face. "Owain has never been one to take sides, or be vehement about anything."

"You're right, and wrong. Because he does now. He has changed." Teilo's face flushed and his eyebrows drew together. "And what about? What is this thing they fight for, Wales? Someone else's cause, and like to bring this manor and its people to ruin."

"Surely not."

"Owain is reborn as Rhys' man through and through. He is possessed. I'd never think a man could change so much." Teilo shook his head.

She touched his sleeve. "We all have cause to thank you then. For bringing him home to Adpar."

"You're to come to dinner."

"Did Owain say so?"

"Haven't I said Owain thinks of nothing now, nothing but Rhys and his plan of an independent Wales, some grand idea, fantastical." He let out a ragged breath. "But you must come. He wants you, or he will when he sees you."

"Has it come to that?"

"You need him, for your son. The estate needs him here, to protect the people and see to the planting. You must help him remember his place." Teilo went to the door. "Perhaps we can all yet escape."

Tanwen flexed cold fingers and put a hand to the door. She entered the great hall, into the mass of men and raised voices. Owain, laughing, raised a bright goblet at the high table. Her skirt caught on a splinter in the doorway, and she paused to free it, with a rush of heat to her chest. How dare Owain make her feel the stranger in her own home? He'd barely spent a dozen days here in the last year, while she had taken over all his duties, managing the fields and trading the crops, as well as running the household of forty. All so he could be with his precious Rhys.

Teilo, bending close to Owain, whispered in his ear. Owain looked her way, then stood, unsmiling, but holding out a hand. She lifted her head high like a grand lady. He was beautiful, as always, and she felt a needle of pain in her chest.

She walked toward him, as though pulled on the skein of yarns she used for weaving. She walked and ignored the men's comments as she passed by. Owain's eyes met hers, as though they'd never been apart. How could he? But she took his hand and sat beside him.

"You are looking very lovely tonight." His breath wafted through her hair.

"You too look well, my lord."

"Tanwen mine, such formality." He touched her arm. "I am Owain, always, to you." He said this softly in her ear. And then blew slightly, causing a frisson to run down her back, as he knew it would.

Tears rushed to her eyes. She was so glad to see him, glad to smell him, far too glad. Her finger touched his thigh. As he sucked in a breath, she gathered her confidence.

"Lovely Tanwen, how I've missed you." His voice held a note of surprise, as though he'd just realized his feelings. "I have been gone long, too long."

A platter of Alica's stewed lamb and pears, with the scent of cloves and pepper, was placed in front of them. Owain served them both and ate as though starved, drinking deep of the wine. She ate too, and the food tasted delicious as food had not for days, months even. After the platters were taken away, the boys brought in a custard topped with crystals of sugar and ground walnuts.

Owain motioned Teilo closer. "Tell Alica she has prepared a dinner better than any I ate at Dinefwr."

Teilo's rare smile crossed his face, chasing the wrinkles of worry away. Petitioners approached, but Owain waved them away. "Let us go."

"Now?" Tanwen asked.

"Why not."

She felt her face heat again and put her eating knife in its case.

Owain just laughed. "I want you." He drew her from the hall, up to his chamber. It had been long since she'd been there, she'd avoided it since he'd gone, but the smells were the same, smoky fire, the sharp berry scent of wine, and the musk of furs on the bed. The window let in damp air. Owain tossed logs on the fire. Tanwen stood in the center of the room, her feelings a tangle.

Owain dipped a finger in the goblet of wine and drew it down her neck to the top of her bodice, laced tight. She felt herself quiver and knew he felt it too.

"Lovely Tanwen," he said, "you are always so clear like a mountain stream, on a day in the summer when there is naught to do but picnic in the woods."

"The world is dangerous these days," she said.

His eyes sparked with a sudden light. "Dark days are here, but there is hope for a new future, hope for Wales."

She shook her head.

"Never mind. Tonight is not for the world outside, only for you and me. I've missed you."

He tugged off her clothes piece by piece and it was like the very first time they'd lain together, seven summers past, when she'd been a young girl and felt little but awe. Though they'd been apart, her body knew him. She found herself opening to him, moving with him, and she wanted to ask questions, let the hurt escape from her heart. But she buried her head in his warm shoulder and moaned only at the end as he drove into her one last time.

Daron tossed the pillow she was embroidering on the floor. "Everything is working out for you. You have Bryn, and even Owain back in your bed."

"You must not speak so."

"Why not? I'll always be alone."

Daron's shoulders were rigid. Tanwen reached out, then withdrew her hand. "Now Owain is back, I'll bring it up with him. There are many young men…"

"How can you say such a thing. Just because you compromise…"

Tanwen looked at the floor, surprised at how much Daron could still hurt her.

"Life is passing me by and all I can do is wait." Daron rubbed her nose with a square of embroidered cloth.

"Have you heard from Huw?"

"He's forgotten me."

"You will hear from him soon. It's the times; everything is awry."

Daron shredded the tassels of her belt. "He says he cannot marry me."

"You have talked of it?"

"Of course we talked of it. He loves me. And I love him."

"What can stand in the way? Owain will certainly allow it."

"Huw will not. Because of Rhys."

"What has he to do with this?" Tanwen's voice was sharp. She was tired of hearing about Rhys at every turn. Owain never spoke ten words without calling on the man's name and his conversations twisted and twirled around Rhys and Wales, Wales and Rhys until she was dizzy with worry. "Rhys is a prince, surely he doesn't care one way or another how you or Huw marry."

"He controls everything and everyone. Huw is his soldier, sworn to seven more years service."

"Seven years is a long time. Would you think of waiting?"

"I'll be an old woman." Daron collapsed onto the window seat.

"Let's go down to dinner," Tanwen said, to distract her, though the last thing she wanted was to spend a long evening at table. Owain had men here, he was always inviting men here now. Rhys had retreated deep into the forests once more. Henry had come, crossing with ease into southern Wales and speeding through, stopping only to secure castle after castle. In truth, Rhys had lost everything in the last two months, his entire kingdom but one cantref, where his castle of Dinefwr sat. In one stroke, Henry had taken it all, the blood and murders of twenty years spilled for nothing, just as Teilo had predicted. Friends and supporters of Rhys mobbed their hall, and Owain was never happier than when they were all drinking and strategizing. The wild enthusiasm of the caged men made her uneasy.

Late autumn light set the orange lilies glowing at the edge of the garden and a bee buzzed around the spires of larkspur. Tanwen stretched her arms out and settled herself on a square of stone set in the bed of silvery rosemary. Her fingers fiddled with a ripe seed head of wheat. She drew the tassel along the skin of her neck.

"I know you're in there." Daron crowded in beside her, arranging her skirts to dirty them as little as possible.

Daron's hair was arranged into intricate looped braids, and she looked full of news. "What have you heard? Has Huw told you something?" asked Tanwen.

"Rhys is fighting again. He's attacking up and down the river."

Tanwen stroked the wheat tassel along her bare foot, thinking. For weeks Owain had fumed and schemed over Rhys' predicament. She'd learned from a passing peddler that Rhys feuded with the border lord Clifford, provoking the English king. Henry's men had chased Rhys back into the thick forests beyond Dinefwr and finally Rhys had surrendered, his men hungry and surrounded.

With that news, Owain had been impossible to please. But only a week past, how suddenly happy he'd become. She'd hoped he was over his dangerous infatuation with Rhys. How could she have been so stupid? "Huw told you this?"

"He says there's been a truce and Henry has sailed back across the Channel. Rhys is uncaged again. Already he's sent out word for his men to assemble. He intends to fight again."

Tanwen drew in a deep breath, thinking of the violence beginning once more. "What of the truce?" But even as she said it, she knew it would not hold.

"Also, Huw wants to marry me, so he says." Daron's voice was casual, but her fingers fiddled with a loose thread trailing from her embroidered belt.

"That's wonderful! I thought he was tied to Rhys for years yet?"

"Rhys freed him, for his services fighting Henry."

"I'm so glad for you!" She pulled Daron close. Her hair smelled of warm roses and sun.

News of fighting filtered to them sporadically and Daron always heard it first, for Huw called in regularly to Adpar. Owain was irritable. Tanwen wanted to ask him what he intended to do, but the right time never seemed to appear. Owain thought of nothing, talked of nothing, but going to fight with Rhys. At dinner every day he argued with Teilo. Teilo would tell him he must stay, that everyone depended on him, his responsibility was here at Adpar, but Owain was restive. At night, he poured out his frustration in long sessions of lovemaking. Some nights she was bruised, but she was glad he needed her, for now.

One morning, Daron told her Huw had left, in the night. Henry had demanded coin and many horses, all to be sent on to Normandy as part of the truce. Huw would deliver the horses to the coast, to pacify the English king, then winter with Rhys at Dinefwr. Now Daron was irritable too.

November passed in uneasy days, and winter came on. They passed a warm December, the grass still green and rain falling. After the Yule, the manor stilled, asleep in this darkest time of the year. Tanwen's gardens were bleak with rain and drooping branches arched over dead stalks and scattered leaves.

Alica woke her late one night. "Can you come, Tanwen, and bring some fever herbs."

Tanwen stirred. "Fever?" Though she did some healing when absolutely necessary, she far preferred to leave it to widow Fiala, down in the village. But this was Alica, who never asked for anything. Owain, beside her, did not wake. She slipped on a wool tunic and ran down the dark stairs. "Who is ill?"

"Teilo." Alica's voice quavered.

Tanwen squeezed Alica's hand. "What happened?"

"He stayed out too late in the fields two weeks past," she said, "getting in the last of the barley. It was a raw night with rain, you'll recall." She left the rest unspoken, that Teilo was out there because Owain was not. "He's not been right since, but he's worsened, and so hot."

Teilo was awake and coughing when she entered. "I'm that sorry to be causing trouble." His voice was gravelly.

"We'll have you well in no time." But he was scarlet-cheeked with fever, his eyes like the glazed surface of an early morning lake. "Sit with him, Alica, keep him comfortable. I'll brew something for that fever."

Tanwen stirred up the fire, woke the kitchen girls and put them to work making thin porridge. She went to the herb room and stared at the dusty boxes. It was frightening to have Teilo ill. How much she'd come to depend on his steady competence and good humor, especially with Owain. And how much Alica handled, the streams of hungry people who came each day to the kitchen door, their houses burned and men disappeared or dead.

She opened a box, crumbled some handfuls of the dried plants into a pot, and added pinches of other herbs, her fingers remembering her grandmother's recipe. She brewed a large pot, swirling the herbs around. She brought the hot drink to Alica, then piled blankets on Teilo, who shivered with deep chills.

Alica urged Teilo to sip the tea all day. His fever did not drop nor did it rise, but he tired from the incessant coughing and he would not eat.

Tanwen appealed to Owain to send for a physician, but he snarled at her. And where would he get a doctor and how would he convince one to come here? Fiala came, but had nothing more to offer, though she made a fuss over the tea and concocted her own brew, her long grey hair trailing into the bowl. Tanwen let the woman try. Then there was nothing to do, only wait and hope Teilo's body was strong enough to outlast the gurgling sickness in his lungs. Alica's eyes were deep wells and her face seemed to wrinkle overnight. Tanwen tried to relieve her, but Alica would not hear of it. She could only get her to sleep a few hours in the afternoons while Teilo slept too.

Days passed into a fortnight and Teilo clung on, but did not improve. Owain spent his days seeing to the necessary manor and farm work. When she came to bed he was asleep, their intimacy a distant memory.

Teilo died in the early morning as Alica sat with him. Tanwen entered the kitchens and found Alica crouched by a cold fire. She sat down across from her friend. Alica stared at the slate floor and said, "I have in mind a simple burial." That afternoon, as raw winds tore the last oak leaves from the trees, they carried it out as she wished. After, Alica stood alone by the grave for a long time, oblivious to the spitting icy rain.

When Alica finally returned to the hall, she stood before Owain, her hands clasped tight over her apron. "I'll be leaving Adpar."

"No Alica," said Tanwen, jumping up. "Where would you go? You know you always have work and a home here."

Alica turned her gaze to Owain. Tanwen lifted her eyes to him too, and saw him tug impatiently at his cloak, as though the heavy brooch bit into his neck. The words were Owain's to say, but he was silent as the grave they'd just left.

"I can't stay here, not with him gone." Alica sighed. "But I'll say this and no more, in his place. Even now, Lord Owain, you could save Adpar, if you wished."

Owain made a choked sound.

Alica turned to Tanwen. "I can't find the strength to stay and help. For that I'm sorry." She was gone the next day, with only her clothes and the silver coins Tanwen had emptied from her savings pouch. She saw Owain stop her at the gate and hand her a pouch as well. He was still generous. But he wasn't unhappy Alica would be gone. She and Teilo had managed the estate, but she chided Owain too often, seeing in the man the child she had once known.

Winter gripped Adpar then, with harsh winds and ice in the water bucket every morning. Spring seemed an impossible dream. Owain worked day and night. He didn't mention Rhys or the dream of Wales at all. Tanwen watched him, unsure whether to be troubled or encouraged. If only he'd forget his obsession and spend his thoughts and vigor on his manor and people.

"I've found a new steward," Owain said one night as he threw off his shirt and climbed into the bed.

"Have you?" She felt a pang, thinking how soon people were replaced, but that was unfair, Owain had been working too hard. A steward would take on the routine tasks. George Fychan came the next afternoon, and he seemed competent enough, but cold. She did not like him overmuch. Because he took Teilo's place. But also, he treated her with a strange taint of insolence.

Summer came on them again, with scarcely a spring at all, and the scent of lush grass and warm earth floated on the breezes. Tanwen woke one morning, happier than she'd been in some time. Owain had come to her in the night and made love eagerly. She touched his face.

He was not sleeping, as usual, but turned to her. "Tanwen."

How serious his brown eyes were.

"There's silver coin in the chest."

Her fingers halted as they stroked his face. She drew her hand away and tucked it under her breast.

"If you need anything, you must use it as you see fit."

"But you're here to see to me and Bryn."

He sat up, his back to her. "I am leaving. To go to Rhys at Dinefwr."

She swung her legs from the bed and stood in front of him. "Owain, you cannot, the manor needs you. The people need you. As do I, and your son."

"I am going." His voice was flat. He pointed across the room. "There's coin, and you can always send word to me, if you have need." She shook her head to clear it of his words. "You can stay here, you and Bryn, for as long as you wish."

"You are not coming back at all?" she whispered.

He shrugged. "It is my home. But there will be war. For many seasons, before Wales is free. It's coming, here, to this valley even."

"Then how can you go and leave us all unprotected!" She dropped to her knees in front of him, and grabbed his legs. "Owain, you cannot."

"I don't leave you unprotected. The men know their duties, I'm leaving six here to defend the place, and George Fychan is here to run the fields and keep the accounts. Don't look at me like that." His voice was cold. "I've waited far too long."

"We need you."

Owain tugged on his tunic. "Try to understand, Tanwen. Rhys will defeat the English. He'll unite Ceredigion, even all of Wales. I must be part of that!"

"Must you?" But he was already calling his manservant, tying on leggings. He shouted out the window to his men. "We leave within the hour." He kissed her, but it felt like their lips did not touch. The men called to each other in the yard, and hoofs clattered loud on stones, and the iron gate screeched shut after they rode off down the road.

CHAPTER TWELVE

Adpar, 1163

TANWEN LAUGHED at Daron's joking. "The children will hear; you must stop." They were standing at the giant oak table in the kitchen.

"Always so serious," said Daron.

Tanwen shook her head. She poured batter from the heavy pitcher onto an iron skillet set over the fire and waited as it bubbled up and browned. Daron giggled with Bryn and helped him sneak some apple slices from the table. Tanwen flipped the oatcake over and gazed out the open door into the brightness, thinking again of Alica, who taught her to make these cinnamon cakes, to be piled high, layered with honey. A new cook had come to take Alica's place, a cousin of George Fychan, and like him, cold and efficient.

Noon sun spilled in the door, lighting up the tin spoons and copper pots, brightening the hair of Elise's small niece Celi. Bryn entertained the girl with a bit of hard soap and a knife, fashioning tiny animals. He was approaching eleven years now and often too serious. But he was laughing with Celi, and the animals were perfect replicas, a goat and a cow, their faces with wide eyes gazing surprised and generous laughing mouths.

They enjoyed the sticky treats in silence. Tanwen made the children wash their hands in the slate sink, where she'd had a pipe installed, flowing with water from the spring uphill. The children ran out the door, hands dripping.

A shadow fell over Tanwen's hands as she rinsed them. "Good day,

George. There are griddle cakes if you'd like, just made."

"I've eaten long past," he said.

Tanwen suppressed a sigh. There'd be no Mayday celebrations at all if he had his way. Still, the men who worked the fields had no quarrel with him and Owain trusted him. But that was convenient for Owain. "What is it then?"

"A messenger waits in the hall, he asks for you."

"Why didn't you say," she called, rushing out the door. Surely it was one of Owain's men with some word. Owain himself had come home for three short weeks last summer, but stayed away since the fighting began with Rhys. And though she'd showed Owain her new gardens and the orderly fields and the repairs to the hall roof, he had no place in his mind for the needs of the field workers or repairs to their cottages, no thought for the beauty or utility of the rows of onions and nodding purple chives, no room in his head for anything but Rhys and Wales. She'd tried to talk to him, of how she'd grown to love the manor and its lands through her work, how she'd grown and changed these past years while they'd been apart, but always he'd changed the subject or walked from the room.

Tanwen stopped short of the hall door and thrust her unruly hair behind her shoulders.

Daron came up behind her. "Has Owain come then?"

"He's sent a messenger. Perhaps there will be word of Huw as well." Though Daron and Huw were betrothed, their wedding, like everything it seemed, waited on the end of the fighting. Tanwen pulled Daron with her into the hall. The messenger stood by the fire, still wearing his dusty cloak, and others waited at the door.

The man snatched off his cap. "Good morrow." I am come with a message from Lord Owain for the ears of Mistress Tanwen alone."

"I am Tanwen."

The man looked at Daron, who slipped her hand from Tanwen's. Tanwen shook her head. "Whatever you have to say can be said in front of my cousin."

The man nodded, but hesitated still.

Tanwen felt a twinge of uneasiness. Through the wide open doors, the sun cast shifting patterns of gold on the new rushes of the hall floor. "Owain, he is in good health?"

"Yes, perfect health."

She felt her stomach relax and gestured to the messenger to sit.

He remained standing. "Owain is with Lord Rhys and they celebrated the truce and recovery of Llandovery Castle with a grand feast…" The man trailed off as Tanwen's smile faded.

She hadn't heard the fighting had ended. Owain hadn't thought to send word, and she'd thought too that she would be invited to that celebration, when it came, something to wipe out the memory of that past dismal visit to Dinefwr. It seemed the feast had happened without her. She wondered what heiress Rhys had thrown at Owain this time. "What is the message?" she asked quietly.

The man fixed his eyes on his boots. "Owain requests his son be brought to Dinefwr."

Tanwen blinked. The hall was silent. Far off, from the kitchen, she could hear the maids laughing. When she spoke, her mouth felt stiff. "Do you mean that Owain wishes us to come to him at Dinefwr?"

The man shifted his cap from one hand to the other. "His son only. He sends for his son."

Boys were taken from their mothers and raised in foster homes, it was the way of the nobility. And Bryn was a lord's son. But Owain had promised her it wouldn't happen yet, not until the fighting ended and it was safe. "Tell Lord Owain that we will be glad to come to him if he sends suitable escort in the autumn, assuming the fighting has truly reached a conclusion."

The man sighed, but did not turn to go.

"Come Daron." Tanwen picked up her skirts.

The messenger looked up from the floor to stare into her eyes. His were brown and full of dismay. The soldiers moved toward her and more crowded in the door, blocking the light. "I am sorry. But I have my orders. From Lord Owain, and from Lord Rhys himself, who is my master. I am to bring the boy to Dinefwr. I'll see him there safely, never fear."

Daron's hand pulled out of hers. "Huw?"

One of the soldiers lurking by the door stepped forward. "Yes, Daron, it is me."

"What is the meaning of this?" Daron's voice shook.

"Owain wants his son."

"But Owain has shown no interest in his son whatsoever for most of his ten years, why send for him now?" Daron asked.

Huw shifted uncomfortably. "There is reason," he said in a low voice. "Don't make this harder."

Another soldier stepped forward. "Where is the boy?"

"I don't understand," said Tanwen. "Is Owain fostering him out? To who?"

The messenger studied the ground and the soldiers shifted uneasily, their swords clanking.

"He's not going with you, not unless I know where he's going," said Tanwen.

The messenger put on his cap and beckoned to one the soldiers behind him.

"I won't tell you where he is," gasped Tanwen. She took a step forward, glaring at the soldier.

"We will find him, of course," said the soldier, his face hard. "You can gather his things and send him off with us, or we will simply take him. It is your choice." The soldier signaled to a maid listening by the door. "Bring food and drink. We're starved and ride again within the hour."

Tanwen shook her head, which felt full and heavy. "Why does Owain want Bryn now? What has changed?"

Huw stepped forward. "Tanwen, think. The boy will be frightened needlessly."

"Rhys is behind this. Why does Rhys want my Bryn?" Tanwen stared up into Huw's eyes. "You must tell me. You were there, at Bryn's birth. Why does Owain only remember his son now?"

Huw took a breath and turned away.

Daron put a hand on his elbow. "Huw, where is he sending Bryn? I am asking you."

"Daron," Huw said, shaking his head. There was a long silence.

"Rhys sends the sons of many lords from all of Ceredigion to King Henry of England, as that king demands. They go as hostages to ensure Rhys' adherence to the new truce, for the safety of Henry's kingdom."

Tanwen stared at Huw's muddy boots. The floor seemed to waver under his feet. She played Huw's recited words back over in her mind. "A hostage, to that monster Henry," she whispered, "my Bryn?" Surely this was a horrible dream; she must awaken.

"Nearly twenty youths will go, including two of Rhys' own sons."

"But to Henry," she stopped, unable to even voice the thoughts.

Daron broke in. "Huw, you must stop this. Henry could do anything, anything, to the boys if he chose and no one to stop him. He is rumored to be insane, he falls into rages, he hates the Welsh, he might…"

"You cannot have him." Tanwen grabbed her skirts and ran out the door, her mind leaping ahead; she must get to Bryn, who must be playing even now with Celi, somewhere in the gardens, and they must escape, somehow, get away, far away.

Daron called her name, but she kept running.

Steps sounded behind and Huw whirled her around. "Tanwen, think, do not frighten the boy unnecessarily."

"Unnecessarily," she gasped. She hit his chest with both fists.

Daron rushed up and gathered Tanwen in her arms. "I hold you personally responsible," she shouted, glaring at Huw.

"I had no part in the decision." He took a step back, his hands up.

"You carry it out."

"It's my duty. There is no choice, it is Owain's right. Bryn is his son."

"And he has only just remembered this. He sends the boy to his…" Daron stopped at Tanwen's choked cry.

George Fychan entered the hall, with Bryn by his side, a packet of oiled cloth in his hand. Tanwen struggled free of Daron's arms.

"Mama!" Bryn ran to her, then slowed to a walk as he saw the other men. His face was pale. "George says I am called to my father."

Tanwen found she couldn't breathe. "Yes," she managed to say in an even voice. "Your father wishes you to be with him at Dinefwr."

"Are you coming too, mama," whispered Bryn.

She swallowed. "Not right now, dearest," she whispered back. "Owain is busy with men's work now, and it's right you join your father." She heard the men shuffle behind her, but she sank to her knees and stared into Bryn's serious eyes. "You are the son of a lord, my son, and you will be called on to do men's work, for the country faces war."

"Yes," he said, "I know. I'm to be a hostage."

For once she felt grateful to George. "Yes, but remember, a hostage is not a common prisoner. You'll be treated honorably and you must be very brave. I will make sure you come home as quickly as may be and your father will too."

"We must go or the light will fail." The soldier's voice was harsh behind her.

Tanwen hugged Bryn to her, and for a moment he snuggled into her as he had always done, but then he remembered his new position and straightened. "Have no worry about me, Mama. I will give your good wishes to my father." He pulled away.

Her throat burned. She got to her feet. She must try to give him the adult leave taking he wished. Her darling child, so tall but his hair still tousled and fingers sticky with honey. She unpinned her silver brooch, the one she wore always, and handed it to him.

Bryn's eyes widened and he closed his fist around the disk of swirling silver.

Huw thrust forward. "Master Bryn, let us be on our way; perhaps you'd like to ride with me."

"Yes, Huw," whispered Bryn.

"Do you go with him, to England?" asked Tanwen, forcing out the words.

"If I can, I will. It is all I can offer."

"I thank you," Tanwen said.

"She may thank you, but I never will," hissed Daron. "How can she be grateful for such a crumb. You are dead to me, Huw, from this time on." Huw's mouth tightened and he grabbed Bryn's hand. They walked out the door.

Tanwen ran after them, calling Bryn's name, but Daron caught her around the waist. They tumbled together to the floor. Sharp rushes jabbed her cheek. Her mind spun like a swirling ball of wool, round and round. She couldn't see, only hear. Horses' hoofs clattered on the courtyard stones. There were shouts and the gate creaked shut. Crows cawed as the soldiers reached the forest. Tears wouldn't come, only stabbing and misery deep in her chest.

Tanwen knew she had survived the terrible months after her grandmother died. When rain beat the garden into mud and there was no food to eat and no voice in the empty hut to console her, only her mad grandfather staring silent into the fire. But nothing approached the desolate grey days after Bryn was taken.

At first, Tanwen locked herself in her chamber and stared into the fire, cold, right to the bone. The second week, she'd been ill with fever. She shook with chills and tossed hot on the bed far into the night. The third week, she lay on her bed, recovered but listless. Mist swirled in the open window to mix with the smoke of her fire. She had told Bryn to be brave, that he would be treated well, but she knew how hostages could be dealt with. Women hung naked in wood cages, children locked in towers and starved, men thrown in deep holes where rats chewed their frozen feet while they slept. She lay, half awake, in a world of nightmares.

One morning she looked around the darkened chamber. The shutters were closed. Clothes strewn on the floor. Dust layered with ashes covered her wooden chest. She pulled a clean gown from the chest and threw open the shutter. A cold rain slanted down. The flowers on the apple tree were tight buds dripping silver.

She opened the door, startling the boy sleeping on the stairs. "Why are you here?" He stammered that the lady asked him to sit by the door. Daron, meddling again. She'd been hovering these weeks, always with advice. When Tanwen reached the hall, Elise jumped up. "Oh mistress, I'm that glad to see you up."

"Where is Daron, I need to talk with her."

"She's in the gardens."

Daron was shelling peas, mud on her gown, water dribbling down her neck. Tanwen felt a lump in her throat. Daron hated to get wet, but she had tried to keep the garden for her. Silently, she started in weeding. She could feel her cousin looking at her, but Daron returned to pulling weeds as well. They worked side by side. The sun was peeking in and out of the clouds, and wispy strands wandered across the sky. After an hour, peas heaped in a basket, they rested in the lee of the stone wall, where sun heated their faces. Daron pulled off the rough gloves she wore to keep her hands fine.

"I have been thinking," said Tanwen, picking at a thread on her skirt. "I can wait here no longer. I have to get Owain to change his mind. He cannot send Bryn to Henry. His son. His only son."

"Owain has never liked his orders questioned."

"I know," said Tanwen. "But this time, I must."

Daron touched her hand. "He might turn you out."

"I know that." Tanwen swallowed. "I must do it. Though it may mean your home too."

Daron nodded. "I've made you two gowns, to take with you to Dinefwr, so you won't be ashamed in front of those grand ladies."

Tanwen looked up.

"I had to do something while I watched over you. I knew you'd go to Owain. "

"Already I've wasted time."

"You're strong, Tanwen. No doubt they're still at Dinefwr and you'll persuade Owain."

"I wish Alica were here."

"What would you ask her?"

"Does she still miss her child?"

Daron sighed. "She told me they were so beautiful, her two little ones. They sickened and coughed and in two days they died. It was hard to accept. But she had Teilo."

Tanwen put her face in her hands, pressing her eyes hard so she would not cry again. "Owain sends him into terrible danger. He's obsessed with Rhys' dreams and blinded. Henry of England is near a madman, they say; in a rage he will do any violence."

Daron patted her arm. "Yet Rhys has sent his own sons. He'd do nothing that would put them at true risk surely."

Tanwen pressed her lips together. "I think that Rhys would risk anything, even his own sons' lives. He won't stop fighting; he won't hold to this truce, or any other. All for some vision of a Wales we'll never see."

"Huw said he would try to go with the boys. Surely Owain will go too."

Tanwen shook her head. "Owain will not leave Rhys. Not for anything, nor anyone."

Three days later, Tanwen was ready. She'd prepared everything she could think of, and George was here, he'd deal with Owain's interests. Which was good. The manor would be Bryn's home and lands one day. She didn't know how long she'd be gone, but she thought the full summer, to go to Owain at Dinefwr, convince him, and return with her son, their son, to Adpar. How she would convince Owain or outwit Rhys, or what she'd do if she failed, these things she did not think of at all.

Her bag was packed with the two new gowns and a warm hooded cloak and food. She would take two of Owain's men. George would not like that, but she had no choice. She went to bed too early, light still in the sky, hoping to leave before dawn.

She was awakened by the door creaking open. She fingered the blanket, confused. The room was dark and the heavy step not that of Elise. The intruder tipped over the small table by the hearth and cursed when it crashed. "Owain?"

"You're awake then," he said. "What is strewn all about the room? Light a candle."

Tanwen fumbled for a candle. "Owain, you're back, have you brought Bryn?" She thrust a candle in the coals of the fire and stuck it in the holder. "Where is he, how is he? I want to see him right away."

"A fine welcome from you indeed," said Owain, his voice slurred.

"Of course I'm glad to see you, so glad you've come home." She threw herself into his arms and he stumbled back.

"Tanwen, mine." He pulled her with him, back to the bed.

"Just let me go take a peek at Bryn first; I'll just be a moment." She tried to slip from his arms, but he tightened his grip, and sat heavily on the bed. His eyes were hidden in shadows. The smells of soured wine and sweat mingled.

Owain shook his head. "He's not down there." He yanked her robe off her shoulders.

She pushed him away gently and spoke, trying to sound calm. "What do you mean, he's not down there?"

Owain got to his feet, swaying. He pulled his tunic over his head and she saw his familiar chest, brushed with brown curls that glinted gold in the hearth light. He bent over her, pulled her robe off her shoulders again.

"Owain?"

"He's with Rhys, or more like, headed off with the other boys to Henry."

Her heart seemed to stop, then start up again, skipping uneven in her chest. She grabbed his shoulders. "How could you not go with him! You can't have let him go alone!"

"He's not alone," said Owain, shoving her away. "He's with twenty others, by God, and ten of Henry's men. He's safe enough."

Icy fear clutched her stomach. "How could you send him away, your only son a hostage!" She grasped at his hands. "I was coming, to see you at Dinefwr, to tell you. Or talk with you," she said, seeing his face stiffen.

"Rhys is gone," he said. "He is not at Dinefwr."

"Gone where?"

"England." Owain put his hands up to cover his face. "Henry has gone back on his word. The truce is finished. He's taken Rhys himself prisoner."

Tanwen tried to think, what it meant for Bryn.

"All our plans for Ceredigion," Owain said heavily.

"Never mind that," she snapped, then bit her tongue. She needed to cajole, not argue. "Owain," she pulled him closer, so his chest touched the tips of her breasts. "Owain," she whispered. "He is our son, yours and mine, your heir."

"He's my son," said Owain, "but a bastard."

She snatched her hands away, as though burned. "That's a Norman word," she whispered.

"We're not married, are we?" Owain found the wineskin and drained it. "Well, are we?" His voice was harsh. "The world is changing, can you not see it? He is illegitimate."

She lifted her chin. "You could marry me Owain," she said softly. "Then he would be your heir and naught the Normans could say."

Owain stared at her, his mouth working, but no words coming. He stretched out a finger and touched her cheek. "Oh Tanwen mine," he said and turned away.

She bit her lip until she tasted blood.

"There's more involved than me or you or our wishes." He was shouting now. "More, you can't understand."

"Make me understand," she said, moving so he had to look into her face. "Owain, what could be so important, what could matter so, that you send your only son away as a hostage?"

"A vision. A future for Wales." His face hardened. "You're a woman. You can't understand."

"Is that what Rhys says?" Fear and anger clogged her throat, but she moved towards him, somehow she must reach him. She threaded her hands in his hair. "Owain, Owain mine." She kissed him slowly, placed a hand on his chest, and whispered, "We could go after him."

He kissed her back, lifted her onto the bed and sank his weight on hers. For a moment, she wanted to feel nothing, only his arms wrapped around her in longing. "Owain," she murmured and tightened her arms. She wrapped her legs around him, making him hers and only hers, willing him to remember. He thrust into her and called her name, sank his familiar weight onto her, his eyes closing already into sleep. "Owain," she whispered, "let us be together. You and me and Bryn. Be as we were."

"Leave off, Tanwen, it's not to be." He turned on his stomach.

She pulled herself from the tangle of sheets. "You cannot mean that. He is in danger."

"Go to sleep Tanwen. It's done."

Anger and fear seemed to flame from her chest, down her arms, into her fingers. She pounded on his back with her fists.

"Curse you, woman!" Owain shook her hard, and thrust her away. Her head cracked against the stone wall. She fell against the rough granite, scraping her bare shoulder. She heard herself cry out and she felt blood on her fingers, warm and strange.

Owain stormed out. She heard him stomp down the stairs and slam the outer door. He was gone, perhaps to the hall, or the kitchen, or the stables, it didn't matter. Nothing mattered, nothing. She shivered and looked down to see blood dripping, down her arm, onto the white linens of the tumbled bed. She wound the sheets around her. Cold air rattled the loose shutter until it cracked hard against the stone wall and she imagined she heard Bryn calling out for her, as he did, in his sleep.

Dawn come in the gradual graying of the dark, until the bloom of sun filled the room with an uneasy orange light. The back of her head hurt and when she closed her eyes it felt like flames radiated from the center of the ache. Blood was crusted in her hair.

She got out of the bed and threw all the wood in the box onto the fire. When it was roaring, she gathered up the sheets from the bed and thrust them onto the flames. It was horribly wasteful, but she didn't care. The flames roared up, nearly touching the ceiling and she backed off to the edge of the room and watched.

Her shoulder throbbed and ached and burned. When the flames died down, she managed to pull on a loose chemise and a gown, but she couldn't do the laces, she'd have to wake Elise. She heard a step on the stairs.

"Mistress, whatever are you..." Elise halted at the door, her mouth gaping.

"Can you lace my gown?" said Tanwen. It was as though she spoke from very far away.

Elise took the laces from her stiff fingers and pulled them snug, her fingers gentle. "I see Lord Owain is back."

"Where is he?"

"Sleeping in the hall. I put a blanket over him."

Tanwen nodded and winced. "I'll be back late, not until evening."

"Where are you going? I mean, I could come along?" Elise's voice faded.

"I must be alone," said Tanwen.

Elise frowned. "Please, let me help." She stared at the mess of burned sheets and the overturned stool. "You don't have to stay here, you know that. You could leave him." Elise's words came out in a rush.

"What do you mean?"

"I've been thinking, since you came back from that Dinefwr. For so long now, I mean, you've been unhappy. But I knew you'd never leave Bryn."

Tanwen frowned. "Unhappy?" she said and looked down the stairs.

"The convent, at St. Anne's, my aunt is there, we could be happy." Elise sniffed. A tear streaked down her cheek. "I can't bear to see you distressed. I could work in the kitchen and you could train to be a healer, like your grandmother."

Tanwen put a hand on the door, to hold herself up. "I don't understand you," she whispered.

"We could be together there, you and I, free of Owain." Elise touched her arm. Her round blue eyes were wide. She pulled Tanwen slowly into her arms.

Tanwen rested her head on Elise's muscular shoulder, so solid and warm. She felt Elise breathing, in and out. "I cannot."

Elise's eyes brimmed over. "But he has hurt you. We could be happy."

Tanwen wound her sleeve around her bleeding arm. "Tell no one." Elise knotted the linen, but her pale face told Tanwen she'd go to Daron anyway.

Tanwen walked down the stairs, steadying herself against the rock walls, past the hall. Owain still slept by the hearth. She unlatched the door, and closed it behind her. The grass was wet with dew and her skirts were soon soaked and slapped against her legs. She passed through the outer gate.

Under the dark trees she breathed more easily. She walked until she reached the pond where she and Owain had sometimes slipped away to make love, their own private spot, where he'd drop his mask of manor lord and be just Owain, as he'd been that first day in the forest. She entered the clearing and found the sky soft like a sea pearl overhead and the trees dripping silver. The pond was streaked with brown and silver reflections, and green leaves floated serenely on the top, like boats with fanciful curled hulls.

She pulled out the long knife she kept in her boot. At the pond edge, she sank to her knees and leaned over, peering into the water. Usually you could see down to the bottom, to the tiny swirls of sand, the occasional burgundy leaf, crystallized and suspended in the depths. But today the waters were murky, stirred by last night's winds.

She washed her hands and walked to the granite stone in the center of the clearing and managed to pull herself up onto it with her good arm, though she slipped once and cut her finger where she gripped the knife. Blood welled up around the slit in her finger.

She closed her eyes, feeling the wind on her face, lifting strands of her long hair. She grasped a handful, thick and curling, alive in the damp air, and sawed at it with the knife. It was harder than she'd thought, not a quick slice but a rough hacking through. Still, in moments, it was done. The hair lay in a long dead hank on the granite. She grabbed another handful and a third. Sun glimmered from between the clouds and lit up the coils of hair, scattering fiery highlights, like the flames she'd watch through lowered eyelids when Owain sank into her, calling her name. Racing purple clouds covered up the sun. A cold wind lifted and shifted the strands of hair. Tanwen turned in a slow circle, letting all fly away in the winds.

Daron rushed to meet her. "Where have you been, you're soaked Tanwen, you'll catch your death." She pulled Tanwen in the kitchen and shooed the girls away from the fire. Rain was pouring down in sheets now. "You've been gone all day."

Tanwen shrugged and her hood fell back.

Daron's eyes widened. "What have you done?"

"Where is Owain?" said Tanwen.

Daron pulled the drenched cloak off. "Get water for a hot bath and warm some towels by the hearth," she ordered. The girls hurried away, silent for once. Daron grabbed the cloth from the table and wrapped it around Tanwen's shoulders. "He is gone. Hunting, he said. He took five men and enough food for a fortnight at least. I think he goes back to be with Rhys' men."

"Good."

Two girls lugged a tub into the room and draped sheets around it. Behind the screen, Daron unwound the tablecloth and peeled off Tanwen's drenched gown. She stared at the raw skin and dark bruises. "He did this to you?"

"It doesn't matter." Tanwen sank into the hot water, and let Daron bathe her, her mind cold and empty. As the heat flowed into her, her toes and fingers burned and ached, but the heat did not reach her chest or her heart. "Cheese, oatcakes, oats, ale, a warm cloak."

"What?" Daron paused, soap dripping from her fingers.

"That's what I'll need."

Daron touched her face gently, and lathered the soap, fragrant with last summer's spicy gillyflowers, through her shorn hair. "For what?"

"To go after Bryn."

Daron's hands stopped. "But Owain said Rhys is taken prisoner, he's already on his way to England. Bryn has been taken on to the borders too; he won't be at Dinefwr."

"I'm going to find him."

"What? Are you crazed?"

"No. Now I see what I must do."

Daron said nothing for a long time. The dribbling sound of water filled the room. "You cannot," she said finally, "you're a woman, alone." She touched Tanwen's arm. "To go with Owain's men to Dinefwr, that was one thing, but to go to England, by yourself…"

Tanwen closed her eyes. Her head ached so much. Perhaps she'd hoped Daron would offer to come with her. But she and her cousin had an uneasy truce, nothing more.

"Thieves and soldiers are everywhere; only the evil are on the roads.

And where will you go, how will you even find him?"

"I don't know." Tanwen spread her two hands out before her and stared at her wrinkled fingers and walled off her mind. She must not think of all the difficulties or she'd never go, and she must; her life was nothing if she did not. Owain had betrayed her, absolutely. But she would find Bryn. She would find her child and she would bring him home.

PART II

CHAPTER THIRTEEN

The Forests, 1163

TANWEN FELT SPRAY on her face, soft like the touch of a lover. She licked salt from her lips. How she had longed to see the ocean, hear waves pounding up the sand, feel sun baking the smoothed rocks and wind tossing and tangling her hair. She dove beneath the water, down below umber drifting seaweed, where a current traveled fierce and cold. Strangely, she could breathe, though it hurt, and she swam naked, with no way to hide. Her hair tugged at her head, fanning exuberant into the green water. When she broke the surface of the water and gasped into the soft air, a breeze fluttered like moth wings against her cheeks and dawn spilled pink and brilliant on a distant shore. She swam, longing to touch the rippling gold sand, perfect as the absolutely smooth skin of a baby, like her Bryn. Pain caught her up, but she held on. She walked out of the waves onto the crescent of empty beach. Gulls called and sea waves sang. She reached out her arms, but her fingers hit rock, rough and icy, and she woke alone, tears running down her face.

Tanwen shivered and sat up, tugging wet leaves from her hair, still caught in her dream. The air was sharp and slate clouds covered the sky. A dismal whine sounded high in the fir trees. She closed her eyes and tried to hold onto the sun and pink light a moment longer, but they were gone.

At least the tall boulder behind her blocked some wind. She needed a fire and hot food, but she didn't dare light one. She'd been walking four full days since she'd left Adpar. She'd walked far and fast that first day, treading paths she knew well until dusk gathered under the elms. The second day, she'd traveled a path less smooth and unfamiliar. Yet she'd walked with ease, glad her body was strong. On the third day, the sun hid and wind tossed the branches, and her boots rubbed blisters on her heels. Yesterday, she'd trudged down a twisting path, through empty hills, rough with rocks and roots. Her legs aching, she'd dropped into sleep, leaves heaped around her against the unseasonable cold. With a sigh, she got to her feet and went on, munching on her last apple.

By the seventh day, Tanwen's tired legs had stiffened, jarring her with every step. She stopped to rest, swatting gnats, and assessed the sky. Would the flat clouds spit rain or blow apart and let the sun shine? It was summer, after all, and she was headed south, toward the coast and its ports, where she'd surely pick up the trail of the hostages. The forest around her was a maze of scrubby oaks, twisted with wind. No people seemed to live here. The desolate cry of a hunting hawk and the drip of water were the only sounds. She should have reached the wide route to the coast by now. She plodded on, while day faded and the mist thickened, until her eyelashes dripped.

She came to a split in the path, both ways covered with undisturbed leaves. The treetops had disappeared, shrouded in fog. Tanwen leaned against a stump, telling herself not to panic. She simply had to wait out the night and the aggravating mist. In daylight, she could navigate again. She made a bed of damp leaves but she didn't sleep. She kept hearing voices, almost, and she was cold. She tried to keep her mind blank. When thoughts crept in, of Bryn being chased by a wolf or wild boar, or falling sick in this cold smoky mist, or getting lost in the endless hills, she shoved them away. Morning came slow, leaving her exhausted. She picked one path at random and walked on. By mid-morning, there was no avoiding the awful truth. She was lost.

She couldn't stand to go back, so she went forward and the slippery path wandered, but never quite dwindled away, though she lost it twice and had to retrace her steps. Her skirts were sodden to the knees and she was so tired the ground shivered under her feet. By nightfall, as the light shifted from pewter to darker grey, she could hardly move. She huddled in her wet cloak and listened to the wind moan in the firs.

She woke to sun pouring bright onto her face and a brisk breeze tossing leaves above her, sending a volley of drops onto her head. She could hear laughter, coming in fits on the wind. The sound of human voices was irresistible. She moved closer, stepping with care. Finally, peering around the trunk of an oak, she saw two boys seated on a felled log in a clearing, goats butting at their knees. The smaller wore a grey tunic with a straggling hem, hanging off thin shoulders. The other had wild black hair tamed by a faded blue cap. They were eating hunks of bread.

Tanwen stepped out into the field.

The boys gaped and exchanged glances and the goats clustered in close, their strange oval eyes staring, gold-centered black.

"What is this place?" Tanwen asked.

The older boy stared, no longer chewing, and didn't answer. She repeated her question slowly, wondering if he spoke another tongue, and made a circle with her arm to indicate the clearing.

He mouthed, "Crazed." The younger boy's eyes opened wide and he jumped to his feet. The older grabbed his loose tunic and shouted, "Stay away! If she's a woman at all, and not some demon."

Tanwen glanced at her skirts, drenched and mud-streaked. She'd forgotten her shorn hair was uncovered, sticking out in all directions and threaded with twigs. She called out, "I'm but a woman, and no wood spirit. Answer me, if you would. What is this place?"

"Barri Math." The younger boy spoke up, his eyes still unconvinced. The older one cuffed him.

Tanwen's throat tightened, as though a hand gripped her neck. The boys were herding the goats together, disappearing down a path on the far side of the field. Barri Math, mound of the bear. She could see the green high grass waving on top of the mound on a bright morning in early spring, when she and Owain had walked together, and he'd told her stories of the bears that lived in these dark woods, back in the days of Arthur. Barri Math, barely a day's ride from Adpar and near, quite near, to Owain's hunting lodge. Tanwen dropped to her knees in the wet grass. She'd come in a circle. Seven long days lost. It seemed even the forests had turned against her.

The boys stopped at the wood's edge, then growing brave, they yelled and ran toward her, their goats scattering and bleating. Tanwen ducked into the brush and flew back along the twisting path. Their voices faded, but still she ran, their shouts of crazed and witch woman echoing. She ran until her ribs stabbed and she tripped over a snaking root and fell, knocking the breath from her chest. She lay, her face in the wet leaves, moss in her fingers, wet and smelling of worms.

A long time later, Tanwen pulled herself up. Sun had heated the woods and steam rose in spirals from the rocks. She examined her scratched ankles and scraped knee and thought about her chamber in the hunting lodge, so near, the linen covered bed with its curtains hanging in soft white folds, a rectangle of gold light spilling over the planked floor, Owain sleeping warm beside her. How happy they had been there, that first summer. And how she wanted a hot bath, steam rising from the deep tub with its scent of cedar and mingled rose and lavender in the creamy soap. The longing rose in her so strong she felt her eyes burn.

But she couldn't go back. The chamber was there, with its wide window and warm hearth and huge bed heaped with blankets and furs. But the room would be empty and cold; it would smell of old ashes. And Bryn's high voice floating up from the courtyard, that too would be gone.

The next afternoon, Tanwen reached a stream, clear and deep. Surely somebody lived along its banks, taking advantage of the easy water, and if she followed, she'd be able to get directions. She had to keep her head, stop wandering blind. She headed downstream until the light failed, scanning the sky for smoke that might signal someone's home. Her wet boots rubbed her blisters raw, so she tugged them off and trudged in the mud by the stream's edge. The water burbled along in miniature falls and shallow whirlpools through woods that felt empty, where the high wail of wind put her on edge.

She thought of her mother as she walked, how the village boys called Sorcha crazed. How she'd run to Ceridwen, crying, when her mother tried to hold her hand. What did it mean to be crazed? What she felt right now was emptied, exhausted, and alone.

A stone shifted under her foot. She stumbled, her legs stiff, and fell, her mind still gripped with her mother's face. She landed on her side, gasping at the icy water. When she tried to stand, her ankle stabbed. She hauled her skirts out of the water and thrust her throbbing ankle back into the stream. She was shivering already, her soaked skirts clinging to her hip and thigh. Her sleeve had ripped and her arm burned, where it was scraped and bleeding.

She waited until her ankle was numbed by the cold, then she dragged herself up the stream bank, towards some clustered hemlocks. She yanked branches off, piled leaves and twigs, and struck a spark. Even with scraped palms and shaking fingers, she got a fire going. "See," she chided herself aloud, her teeth chattering, "just a sore ankle. I can stay here, even a whole day if needs be, then go on." Her voice wavered and disappeared among the silent grey trees. And what if her fire attracted wolves? She forced this thought away. She had Ceridwen's charm after all. She pulled the chain from the neck of her gown and stroked the warm curves of polished amber. She had Owain's pearl too, strung on a second chain. She cupped it in her palm. Lavender reflections glimmered from its wavering surface. She closed her fingers tight around the heavy pearl, as though holding the sea in her hand.

CHAPTER FOURTEEN

WHEN TANWEN OPENED her eyes, wincing at the throbbing in her ankle, a man bent over her, eyes dark under thick brows. "I see you're finally seeing fit to wake up. I was ready to wake you, I need help, and can't be waiting longer."

Tanwen sat up, clutching her cloak to her neck. "Who are you?"

The man eyed a hawk winging over. He was bulky in his striped wool tunic and the hair under his cap was grey. "Who are you is more the question. Everyone in these parts knows well who I am, but you we don't know." He was gripping his arm tight to his side.

"What's wrong with you?"

"I took an arrow. In my shoulder."

Tanwen looked around but the woods loomed still and empty. "Who shot you?"

The man shrugged. "What does it matter?" He swayed and sat down, hard, on the ground in front of her.

"I can't help you," she said.

"Needs to be pulled. I can't reach it myself."

Tanwen glanced at the sun, already cresting the hills. She needed to push on. But she could feel Ceridwen pressing on her shoulders. "Show me." She rinsed her hands in the stream.

The man tried to pull his tunic from his shoulder and grunted.

"Let me. I'll have to tear it." She ripped the cloth, and folded it out of the way. The arrow, broken off, was lodged deep in his muscles. "This will hurt."

"Don't I know it," he said. "Do your worst."

Tanwen examined the shoulder, bruised and trailing dried blood.

She wanted to look away but she took hold of the arrow and wiggled it, almost freeing the tip.

The man sucked in a breath.

She yanked it out.

"Holy Mary!" He bit his tongue and made no more noise.

She soaked a wad of moss in the stream and washed the wound until the blood stopped seeping. Then she packed it with clean moss and took her belt and wrapped it tight, strapped awkwardly across his broad chest. "You must get honey," she said, "and onions and make a poultice of them and pack it on with clean moss. Change it every other day for a fortnight."

He nodded. He was breathing hard and his face was grey under his beard.

"Are you all right?" she asked, but he wasn't. Sweat beaded on his forehead. "Where do you live?"

"Downstream."

"Rest a moment more," she said. "I'll bring you home."

The man dropped his head between his knees. She wound her shawl onto her ankle tight as she could and gathered her things.

He struggled to his feet and, leaning on her shoulder, they stumbled downstream. Her ankle stabbed, but the wrapping held. They walked until the stream flowed into a pond and they entered a clearing, with a thatched hut slung between two huge oaks.

The plank door creaked open and a woman appeared, dressed in brown, except for a bright blue cap over graying hair. "Dai, whatever has happened to you?" Her eyes took everything in. "Look at the pair of you; don't worry, we'll have you both to rights in no time." She grasped Dai's arm and they half-carried him into the house and laid him on the pallet in the corner.

Tanwen hobbled to the bench by the fire, so thankful to sit tears welled up in her eyes.

The woman inspected Dai's shoulder. "You know something of healing I see."

"I lacked honey."

"I have enough. I'll dress it, and brew some tea." She fluffed a wool throw over his shoulders.

"Don't fuss," he said and fell asleep.

The woman shook her head, and turned to Tanwen. "Don't you worry about anything now. I can see you're done in." She set a pot of water to heat, as though strange women appeared at her doorstep every day. She pulled linen strips from a chest and bound Dai's wound, then gave Tanwen a bowl of steaming tea and set a pot of chopped mushrooms and greens to stew on the fire, and another of honey, wine, and onions.

"You're very kind. It's lovely to have something hot," Tanwen said. Her throat scratched when she swallowed and she was chilled from sweating as she half carried the man.

The woman draped Tanwen's cloak to dry by the fire and pulled up a stool. Dai was snoring. "So," she said, "I suspect I know what he was doing to catch an arrow. But now you can tell me what a young woman like you is doing wandering about in the woods." The woman picked up some yarn. "I'm called May," she added.

Tanwen shifted the hot cup to her other hand and stared at the earth floor, swept clean. "I'm searching for my son."

The woman took up some pointed sticks and set to work, so Tanwen swallowed some tea and went on. When she had no more to say, the room was quiet, with only the click of May's knitting sticks and the crackle of the fire. A comfortable silence, nothing like the dank emptiness of the woods. "What are you doing with that wool?" asked Tanwen.

"A new kind of fancy work. I learned from my cousin. Her husband's been on that crusade." May spread out her work so she could see the pattern, brilliant triangles of gold on grey.

May took the pot with the honey poultice off the fire. "When he wakes, it will be just cooled," she said. "Crazy old man."

Dai stirred on the bed and opened his eyes, which met May's for a long moment. May leaned over him and tugged at his whiskers. "What was it this time?"

"Deserters, from the Norman king's forces. Didn't see them in time, but they saw me."

May shook her head and held a cup to his lips.

"Perhaps you have seen travelers, a large group, soldiers and boys?" Tanwen asked.

Dai frowned. "I've seen nothing."

May gave him a sharp look. He took a gulp of tea.

Tanwen sighed. They could have passed anywhere, but it was good to think Bryn might have been here and May might have handed him a bowl of hot soup. "I'll keep asking." She cleared her throat, wincing. "Thank you for the tea."

"Dai." May's voice was sharp.

Dai shrugged. "I've seen nothing, only heard rumors."

"Tell her," said May.

Dai shrugged again. "When her ankle heals I'll take her to those that might know." He raised his brows. "Now can a man have something to eat?"

"To Lily's." May frowned as she ladled stew into a bowl.

"It's where men come, and where they often do talk." Dai winked, but his face was pale.

Four days later, after Dai fed the cow, Dai and Tanwen left the cozy cottage. A few hours slow walking took them to a house, set alongside a road. Tanwen studied the shuttered house. "I thought it was a tavern?"

Dai avoided her gaze. "Wait here."

Tanwen waited as Dai went to the door. Below the closed shutters, window boxes trailed white flowers to the ground and in the kitchen garden, peas were twining up their strings.

Dai pounded on the door. A woman leaned out from the upper story, black hair loose on her shoulders. Her green gown was cut low over full breasts. Tanwen stared, then remembered it was rude and looked away.

"Dai, is that you?" The woman banged the shutter closed and they heard her calling as she descended. She flung open the door and enveloped Dai in a hug.

Dai reddened and tried to push her away. "Now Lily, here you are, looking just the same."

"Not at all, you old liar," she said, "but I've done well. Yes, I have at that." Lily put her hands on her hips and surveyed the clearing behind the house with satisfaction. It was peaceful, scattered with daisies, and smelled of ripe grass. She glanced at Tanwen. "What are you up to? Where's May?"

"May's at home," he said. "How about a drink then Lily, we've had a long walk, and Tanwen could use a sit down, for her ankle's wrenched up."

"Sissie," Lily called into the house, "bring a couple of benches out here, and some of that plum juice. The trees are early this year," she said, gesturing to the tiny orchard beyond the kitchen garden. "Sure sign of November snow." She sighed. "Still, early winters is good for business, that's my view on it."

They sat down. Tanwen felt lightheaded with excitement and worry. Would this Lily know something of Bryn? Dai was taking forever to ask.

Sissie brought the food and Dai ate, then looked up from his trencher and grinned. "You do set a fine table, always did."

"Get on with you," Lily said, but her cheeks turned pink. "And so…" she said.

"Yes, I've a reason to be here this day." Dai pointed at Tanwen with a honey-smeared finger. "Her son's gone. Taken to that Norman king, madman that he is." He lifted his shoulder. "She yanked an arrow out of me. So I'm wondering if you might be knowing if these men have passed on by."

Tanwen examined Lily's face. Once Lily had been very pretty and she was yet handsome, with high cheekbones and dark brows. Her hands were white, like a lady's.

"It's dangerous times we're living in." Lily flicked a crumb from her skirt.

"We all know that," said Dai. He put a large hand over Lily's and held it there. "Can you help her?"

Lily stared at his hand, then extracted her fingers. "For old times." She sniffed, then laughed. "But she can't go to the English dressed that way."

"Why not?" Tanwen felt her cheeks redden and she got to her feet.

"You'll never catch a man's eye." Lily untied the laces of Tanwen's cloak with long elegant fingers.

Tanwen stepped back. "I don't want to."

Lily sighed extravagantly. "Do you want my help?"

"Yes," said Tanwen hesitantly. "Yes."

"Dai, be off with you."

"Whatever you say, Lily dear. Knew I'd brought her to the right place." Dai nodded to Tanwen. "You'll be fine in Lily's hands, don't worry." He plunged into the woods and was gone, even the sound of his footsteps swallowed.

Tanwen stared into the thick leaves. When she turned back, Lily was examining her, tapping her upper lip. "We've got to make some changes."

"What sort?"

Lily laughed. "The sort that turn a man's mind to thinking."

Tanwen shook her head. "I'm afraid you don't understand."

"Answer me this. Why else is a lone woman traipsing about the woods, far from her home? Will you tell the Normans you're trailing your son? Will you tell everyone you're alone and unprotected?" Lily crossed her arms over her chest. "You'd do better to just stay here with me."

"I must go after my son."

"If you must, then you must." Lily's eyes sharpened. "What have you for payment?"

Tanwen swallowed. "A few silver pennies."

"You'll need those on the road. Have you anything else?"

Tanwen hesitated. But why else had she brought it? She pulled the heavy pearl out of its warm hiding place between her breasts and took the chain from her neck. "I have this." Lily took the coiled chain and the heavy pearl dangled, swinging, reflecting sunlight. She cupped it in one palm, weighing it. Then she nodded and dropped Owain's necklace into the pouch at her waist.

Tanwen felt a stab. The spot between her breasts felt bare.

"Good. Let us begin." Lily snatched the cap from Tanwen's head and tossed it on the table. Her eyes narrowed. "Who did this to you?"

"No one," said Tanwen. "I did it."

Lily walked around her, examining her from all angles. "Sissie, bring a knife."

"Leave it," said Tanwen.

"Dai asked for my help." Lily took the knife from a yawning Sissie, who disappeared back inside. "Sit down, so I can reach your head. Times are hard. Men are hard. If you want to see your son again, do as I say."

A week later, Tanwen waved to Lily from the edge of the clearing. Lily's girls weren't up, but she'd bid them goodbye the night before. Whatever would Aunt Agatha say about her now? She glanced at her burnished boots with tassels decorating the tops. Her skirts ended well above her ankles, the cloth a wool of brightest blue. A hood covered her head. Lily had cut her hair to an even length, then washed it in lavender soap, all the way from Aquitaine she'd said, and rinsed it in clear water to make it shine. She'd tousled the ends until it curled instead of standing out in ragged tufts. A fake silver ring decorated her index finger.

More important were all the clues they'd drummed into her, how to lead a man on without actually stumbling into his bed. Lily said she wasn't ready. But the cottage made her uncomfortable. Nights were loud and unpredictable. One night a man barged into her corner of the attic, stumbling over her legs and falling by her feet. She'd escaped only because he was far gone in drink. Lily had shrugged it off. But after that she'd had Tanwen sleep with her. Sometimes she woke to Lily's fingers skimming over her hips.

In the mornings she had to gather her courage just to start a new day. She repeated Bryn's name over and over, like a charm. She knew Lily thought she'd never find Bryn, never reach the coast untouched, or perhaps at all. The road was used by merchants, who kept the thieves at bay, but it was not the season for trading. She'd find herself alone, at best. And if not alone, did she want to play a loose woman? In Agatha's village, the gossips had called her mother a whore, though she'd never been that, merely strange. And the Normans at Owain's table, they'd thought her no better, though she'd gone to Owain for love, or the bright hope of it, never for his coin or position. Tanwen shook her head, to shake the doubts away. She'd have to be clever as she traveled, and more clever still once she reached the coast. Dressed this way, men will see you as a harlot, Lily had counseled, they'll think they understand you and they'll underestimate you. Be a woman of business first. Always smarter than they.

The morning was dry and warm, mocking her fears, and as Tanwen walked her worries floated off into the sunshine streaking the path. She headed south, toward the village of Tenby, only a few short days' travel away, where she was to go straight to Lily's younger sister. Afta would know all the news of the busy port. She had friends, important friends and connections, Lily had said. Afta would send her from one friend to the next, and the next, all the way to the borders, all the way to Bryn. Tanwen imagined a chain of smiling women with dark serious eyes, all reaching out, pulling her along by her fingertips, one after the other.

In the sunshine, it seemed possible. She'd made it through unfamiliar forests, been lost and found again, and found people and they'd been kind, not villains as in the terrible tales of robbers and murderers Teilo loved to tell on winter nights. How long ago those winter evenings seemed, curled by the fire in Owain's hall, something from another life. Had that been her? Or was this new person her? She examined the bright green stockings, gartered under her knees with a ribbon of scarlet. She quite liked them, though they were, of course, shocking.

When Tanwen reached Tenby, it was later than she'd hoped and her ankle, bound in linen under the green stocking, ached to her knee. She saw a hut, and a boy herding three cows, and beyond, two men worked, forking manure. She paused under a leafy horse chestnut, her cloak clutched around her neck until the men finished and went inside. Only then did she walk into the port town. Houses clustered around a crescent bay, some leaning, and all with timber doors and shutters wedged tight. The smell of slops mixed with the scent of onions stewing and brisk salt wind. There were shouts, and the hum of conversations, and Tanwen thought of Alica's warm kitchen smelling of roast apples. Further along the muddy lane, a woman was singing a lullaby. Tanwen paused to listen to the melody, unfamiliar yet comforting. It must be a good omen, a sign that she would find Bryn soon, and he'd be safe, just as the words of the song said, warm and snug as a songbird in a high tree nest.

At the end of the winding cluster of cottages, Tanwen found a solid timber house of two stories, just as Lily had described. She struck out on a footpath toward the sea. The wind picked up as she crossed the meadow, the mineral sea-scent mixing with ripe grass smells. She felt her grandmother striding beside her. How often they'd walked in the summer fields, gathering marjoram leaves or mint. Wasn't that a light, off to the far edge of the field? That must be where Lily's sister could be found. As she neared, shouts and male laughter floated on the night air. She slowed. Her ankle had delayed her. Should she wait till morning? Her fingernails pressed into her palms.

"What have we here?" She whirled around, too late. A man laughed and caught her around the waist. "One of Afta's best, I'm thinking, free for the taking."

Of course there were men here. She must not act the panicked girl. She forced herself to relax back into his arms. "You caught me now. Afta sent me out here. To meet you."

"She did?" Another man, taller, less drunk, came out of the dark.

The first shrugged, but kept hold of her. "A prime start to the evening, perhaps we'll go in, have a drink or two?" As he talked to his friend, the man ran a heavy hand over her breasts. She managed not to stiffen. He smelled of fish and sharp sweat. "After we take her, of course." He laughed. His beard was dark and stiff with salt and ale.

The second man tipped her chin up, then tugged at the curl escaping her hood. He shoved a lantern close to her nose. "A redhead, though lad or wench I'm not sure."

"She's a wench sure enough." The man gave her breast another squeeze, then he belched and pushed her away. "I've had enough of red-headed women to last me." He strode off into the dark, muttering.

The other man laughed. "Don't worry girl, I've nothing against copper heads." He put the lantern down on a rock and moved toward her.

She backed away. "Come inside sir, do, it's far too chilly out here to be comfortable." The man edged closer. She felt her stomach clench, but she gave him a wide smile, and flipped her cloak open, letting him glimpse her breasts above the low cut gown. Then she strolled toward Afta's. She heard him swear, but he picked up the lantern and followed. She walked faster, her muscles tight, and reached the door. She shoved it, but the door stuck.

The man crowded against her, pinning her to the heavy door. "I'm thinking here's a fine spot, and the drink can come after." She smiled wide, fumbling for the door latch behind her back. At last the door flew open behind her and she tumbled backward into the room.

"Hey!" the man grunted and swayed above her in the doorway, his eyes mean.

The brightness of dozens of candles and the roar of voices and the sweet hot smells of wax and sweat and perfumes stunned her.

"Shut the door, what's wrong with you," bellowed a fleshy man wearing leggings but no tunic.

Tanwen scrambled to her feet and banged the door shut and inched away along the wall. The first man had forgotten her already. His fist clutched a mug of ale and his arm encircled a plump blonde woman with black brows.

Tanwen edged along, her back against the wall. Men argued and laughed in noisy groups. Women, garbed in vivid blues and greens, offered ale and draped themselves around the men. She wanted to back out, her breath was coming too fast, and sweat trickled down her back. Too many men blocked her way to the door. And she had to find Lily's sister, of course she did. What else was she here for?

She put a hand on the bare arm of the closest woman. "Where is Afta?"

The woman looked her over with an unsmiling face, then jerked her head to a dark woman sitting alone on an ornate carved bench by the hearth.

Tanwen struck out across the room. The woman watched her weave between the clusters of men with no change of expression on her white face.

"Afta? Are you Lily's sister Afta?"

The woman, deep set blue eyes framed by black brows, hair in long braids tipped with polished brass clasps, said nothing.

"I come from Lily," Tanwen said.

"Do you?" said the woman. "Why?"

Tanwen glanced around the crowded room, suffused with the biting smell of sweaty men and ale. Was she really supposed to talk here? But Afta didn't offer anywhere else. "My son has been taken, hostage to the Norman king."

Afta snapped the tasseled fan in her lap open and waved it in the humid air. "Forgive me, but I'm puzzled. Why exactly are you here, and dressed as you are?"

"Because…" This was so much harder than it had seemed when Lily explained the plan. "Lily said if anyone could help me, you could. She said that you had a child too, once."

The woman's eyes flicked to the window and she frowned. Tanwen took a step back. The smell of perfume and smoke swirled under her nose. Someone was tuning a lute. The discordant notes mixed with the harsh laughter of drunken men.

Afta looked back at her, her eyes steady and empty. "Lily has been lost in the woods too long. She knows nothing of what it takes to run a business here. I cannot help you."

Tanwen's mouth went dry.

"Unless," said Afta, "you actually want a job. In that case," she looked her over again, "you'll get your food and a place to sleep and two pennies a month. If you work out. On a trial basis."

Tanwen gaped. "But I'm not…"

The woman shrugged. "Then I suggest you leave here, quickly. Not all my customers will be so easily distracted as Will." Afta gestured to the black-eyed man she'd evaded at the door. He was tugging the gown from the shoulders of a bored looking woman.

"You have to help me," Tanwen said. "You know what losing a child means."

"I was a mother," said Afta. She examined her white hand. "And costly it was in emotions. I won't make that mistake again. Lily was wrong to send you. I cannot help you. Or I will not. It's all the same." She rose and pushed Will and the woman toward a curtained alcove in the side of the room. "An extra penny Will, but she'll make it worth your while."

Tanwen felt hot panic rising from her stomach to her chest. She grabbed Afta's costly red sleeve. "You don't understand, I have coin." She reached toward the pouch under her skirts.

Afta grasped her hand. Her fingers were strong and moved up to circle her wrist. "Don't be a fool. Would you show your coin in here? You'll be rid of it in moments." Afta pointed to the door. "You'd best go, and now."

Tanwen stared, mouth open. She must find the right words. But her mind was empty and Afta turned away.

"Hey honey, over here," said a man, a sailor from his ragged salt-stained tunic. He reached out a hand, with filthy broken fingernails, trembling from drink.

Tanwen backed away. Her fingers fumbled with the door. Her eyes burned from cheap candle smoke. She slipped out and hesitated on the step. Voices, carrying on the wind, as more men hiked up a path from the sea. A ship must be in. Tanwen drew up her cloak to cover her face and stepped down into the shadows. A group of men sauntered past and she stumbled away from the house.

The whinny of a horse sounded nearby. Not all sailors then. Men from town too. She crouched in the high grass, put her head in her hands, pressed hard on her temples. Her only plan had been to reach Afta. She'd never imagined Afta wouldn't help. She'd paid Lily and put up with the strangeness of her home, her brothel it was, in truth. Tanwen swallowed a cry. The comforting chain of understanding women Lily had promised seemed to glimmer in front of her, but she couldn't reach the fingers of the first outstretched hand.

The horse whinnied again. A man rode into the amber light of

Afta's porch and tied the horse to a bush. He gave the animal a loud thwack on the neck and entered the noisy house. The light from the opened door gleamed on the horse's chestnut sides, then the door swung shut with a thud.

A horse. Tanwen stared at its mane fluttering silver, its muscles moving over big shoulders, its wide eye staring right at her. With a horse she could get away from here. Ride somewhere, anywhere where she could get word of Bryn.

But a horse. She didn't actually know how to ride. She'd done it, of course, with Owain. They'd ridden all the way to Dinefwr and back. But a boy had held a leading rein and walked in front and the horse had been a lazy nag, no taller than she.

She stood up. This was a real horse. Seeing her move, it tossed its head and snorted. But it wasn't sidling about like Owain's hunters, or rearing like the fierce beasts the crusaders rode. Could she get on? The horse dropped its head and cropped grass and stamped its back hoof. Tanwen hesitated, watching its large bared teeth yank out the grass. It was stealing. She'd be flogged with a split cane on her bare back or hanged by her neck, if she were caught. There would be no going back.

She wouldn't be caught, that was all. She scanned the field, tucked her skirts into her hip belt, keeping an eye on the door, hoping the man wouldn't come out, hoping he was planning to drink sour ale and wench all night. The sky was dusky blue, littered by a scattering of stars and streaky clouds. But soon it would lighten, starting another long August day. She must be far away.

She whispered to the horse, who stared at her from one white-edged eye. He knew she was afraid. She remembered Owain laughing. You must show your mount who's the knight, he'd said. She untied the reins. There was a huge log, of the sort cast up by the sea, so she pulled the horse to it and it came, snatching at the tall tips of grass. She flipped the reins over its head and slid onto the saddle. The horse stepped sideways and tossed his head and she swayed and clutched its mane.

Voices shouted on the far side of the house, more sailors. "Meet you in there," called one and he darted around the house, tunic already lifted. "Hey," he called out, "you look like someone I want to meet."

She slashed the horse with the reins. It jumped under her and she lurched to the side and nearly fell, but she wrapped the coarse mane around the palms of both hands and kicked the horse with both heels.

"Hey," the man called. "Wait for me, sweeting."

She kicked the trotting horse again, hard, and the horse put its head down and leaped ahead. She clung to its neck as they cantered across the wide field, hanging on, hoping he wouldn't stumble and throw her down, breaking her neck, because she had to find Bryn. The horse, spooked by shouts and shadows, by her weight flinging this way and that on its back, grabbed the bit in his teeth and ran. The reins ripped through her fingers. The ground fled by. Tears blurred her eyes, and the sailors' voices wavered and fell away. In her ears, wind roared.

CHAPTER FIFTEEN

Adpar

DARON TRIED NOT to gag. Behind her the kitchen maids giggled as they kneaded dough for the week's bread. The sour smell of the starter mingled with the greasy smoke of pork dripping over the fire. Daron wrinkled her nose and closed her eyes. When she opened them, George Fychan's cousin, the new cook, was in front of her, a frown drawing her bushy eyebrows together.

"Are ye ill?" she asked.

"No," said Daron. She forced a smile.

Cook grunted and went back to pounding the mutton with her thick fists.

Daron retied her apron strings. She had to be more careful. If it were true, no one, absolutely no one could know. Her eyes filled. She blinked the tears away and forced herself to finish stirring the batter to be poured atop the chopped apples and nuts. "Here it is," she said to one of the maids.

The maid grabbed the bowl with grimy fingers.

Daron sighed. If only Alica were still here in the kitchens. If only Tanwen were here. She edged out into the fresh morning air. The courtyard was empty, the slates black from last night's rain and it was very quiet. Owain and his men hadn't been back since summer, when he and Tanwen had fought and Tanwen had gone. Daron wandered out the gate and down the garden path. A few late roses bloomed, nearly smothered in the overgrown grass. She dipped her head to smell a rose, heavy with water drops. It smelled sweet. Too sweet. She let it drop and walked on.

Where was Tanwen now? Had she found Bryn? It had been the hardest thing she'd ever done, letting Tanwen go without confiding in her. Not that she'd been troubled then, it had only been a tiny worry, nothing to distress her cousin with, not when Tanwen had such terrible worries of her own. She knew Tanwen hoped she'd go with her to find Bryn. They were cousins after all, even if they never did see eye to eye. And Bryn was a sturdy child, but children were such fragile beings. Six had died of fever and a red itching rash in Adpar just this summer. And what if King Henry decided to hang his hostages? Though surely he wouldn't hang a boy?

Such dreadful thoughts. She touched her belly, then dropped her hand and gazed around her. But she was alone. The only sound in the garden was a lazy bee buzzing in the orange lilies, garish among the seedpods. The garden smelled, too strong, of mint. She walked to the end of the path, sat on Tanwen's bench, and massaged her damp forehead. She heard a cough.

Cook stood in the path, her apron glaring white in the sun. Her mouth was a thin straight line. "It's that Huw I warrant."

Daron clutched her skirts in her fists, but what was the use. Soon everyone would know. "Huw," she whispered, "yes, of course it is."

"If we get word to Owain…" said Cook, not unkindly.

"No!" said Daron. "He'll tell Huw. He must not know."

Cook frowned. "What are you saying? You must tell him."

Daron got to her feet. "I won't."

"No sense being stubborn. He can marry you." Cook crossed her big arms. "He should."

Daron stared at the ground, where a single ant lugged a huge breadcrumb. "It was a mistake, a terrible mistake."

Cook shrugged. "Mistake or not. Well, then, what will you do? Where will you go?"

"Go?" Daron echoed.

"You can't stay on here forever. Your cousin is gone. She'll not be back."

Daron felt her mouth fall open and she closed it, her teeth clacking.

Put that way, it was so stark. She looked around the garden. Fragrant, sheltered, buzzing with bees, it had come to seem like home. But this home was Owain's. "Tanwen will be back, any day now I believe."

Cook snorted and plucked a fistful of mint and trudged away.

Brave words. But what if Tanwen didn't return? What if Owain and Tanwen never reconciled? Daron twined her trembling fingers together. Whatever happened, she would never tell Huw about the child. Several weeks after Tanwen had left, Huw had returned. She'd thought he came to apologize for helping Owain take Bryn. But he hadn't apologized, nor mentioned Bryn at all. They'd walked and talked for hours, all night long it seemed. He'd used all sorts of words, grand words like duty and honor and promises. But they all meant nothing, because he'd gone back on his word. It seemed the only duty that mattered was his duty to Rhys. He couldn't marry her after all, he'd said, not with the war coming.

Daron felt a queer turning in her belly, deep inside, like the slow flutter of wings within water. She stopped breathing and waited, a palm on her stomach. The sun tinged the skin on her bare arm amber and her fingernails glowed with a soft pink light. She must try to act like Tanwen. Strong.

A month passed and another. One afternoon, as Daron wandered in the garden, a single yellow leaf drifted down from the sky and settled, like a sigh, on the grass near her feet. She kicked at it with her booted foot. It might be early, but it showed what was coming.

Whenever she tried to come up with a plan, she found herself buried in another daydream, adrift in longing for Huw. Decisions seemed beyond her. Tanwen should be here. Without her, she felt like a coracle, tossing in a wandering river. Daron picked one of Tanwen's roses and shredded the petals. Ever since they were children, it was always the same. Tanwen was always rushing off. Leaving her alone and stranded, far behind.

She walked on through the overgrown garden, blinking back tears. Could she return to Aberteifi and hope one of their old neighbors would take her in? But what then? She'd have the baby, and there she would be for life, beholden to near strangers. She might snatch a husband from one of the other girls, not one like Pennar, nor even a weaver as mother had planned. Rhodri had married and had a babe already of his own. Nothing so grand, a farmer perhaps, or a smith, someone who'd work her like a peasant.

At least once a day, George Fychan would stare down his long skinny nose and frown and she'd be terrified this was the moment he'd tell her she had to go. She avoided him, hid in her chamber, or in the rose garden, or stayed half the day in bed. A dozen times she'd started to pack her gowns, but as she smoothed the wrinkles from a mantle or folded her stockings, she'd sink to her feet and wake up from daydreams only hours later, whole afternoons passed as she wandered in her thoughts. She remembered lecturing Tanwen, as though love was so logical and easy.

"Daron." Elise hurried up the path.

"What is it? You look so hot."

Elise pushed her frizzing hair back from her pink face with two hands. "Have you had any news?"

"You ask me that every day."

"Surely she'll send for us. When she finds Bryn. She'll ask us to come and be with her." Elise stared at her, her fingers laced tight together.

"Be with her." Daron heard her own voice, loud and bitter. "Be with her where? She has no home now. Not if she leaves Owain for good."

"She could come back here. She might come any day."

"She won't." Daron snapped off the dead flower heads that topped the white daisies, so glorious only a week ago. "She's forgotten us. Forgotten you and me. We don't even know where to find her."

Elise blinked and twisted her apron string in an intricate knot around her fingers. "She could have come with me," she whispered.

"Where?" Daron asked.

But Elise had turned away. A tear slid down her cheek and dripped into the mass of overblown roses. "I'm going then."

"What do you mean?"

Elise's lips trembled. "I can't stay here longer. I'm going to the convent where my aunt shelters. They'll take me in."

"You are sure?" A convent. So final.

"I tried to get her to come with me. We should have been happy together. Why didn't she see?"

Daron frowned. "You're truly going?"

"Tomorrow." Elise's face crumpled and she walked away, her steps heavy.

Daron watched her go, a dark shadow against the bright grass of the field, until she merged with the shadows of Owain's manor and disappeared.

A cloud of dust puffed above the trees. Someone was coming, and since they didn't hide their approach, it could only be Owain. Daron crossed her arms over her chest. Her breasts were larger now and her gown stretched across her belly.

"You'd best go to your chamber," said Cook.

Daron took one last look at the glint of armor in the afternoon sun and followed Cook up the stairs.

"Pull this on, over your own gown." Cook handed Daron a thick wool gown of Tanwen's.

Daron wanted to push Cook out of the room and curl up on her pallet, but she dressed in Tanwen's gown and let Cook tie the laces. Putting on the gown made her feel sick, as though Tanwen had died and she'd inherited her clothes. She tugged at the neck.

Cook examined her waist. "That's better. I've got to get back to the kitchen."

Daron smoothed the dress over her hips. It was better. Tanwen was bigger than she and the gown reached around her without stretching.

Too soon, a kitchen maid kicked open the door. "Cook says you're to greet Lord Owain." She handed Daron the silver cup for welcoming the men. Daron picked up the cup with two hands and went down.

Male laughter echoed in the normally quiet hall. The stench of the men made her dizzy and she noticed how musty the old rushes were on the floor. She hadn't paid attention, not with Tanwen gone. Owain, in a chemise with billowing sleeves and a broad belt that gleamed even in the dim hall, lingered by the doors. Daron approached, the cup of wine in her outstretched hands. Once she would have reveled in acting the lady, especially in Tanwen's stead. Owain's eyes weren't friendly when they settled on her.

Owain rushed through the ceremony, then invited the men to table. After his speech of welcome, as the boys served the soup, he said in a low voice. "Why isn't Tanwen here to greet me properly? Fetch her." Steaming platters of caramelized onions and goose were being carried out by the kitchen boys. The men were excited, talking of how the English king had released Rhys, how he had returned to Wales and even now was planning new fighting to regain his castle from a Norman who'd thought to steal it away in his absence. "To Rhys, and Owain, his noble ally!" someone shouted.

Owain flushed and grabbed a cup from the nearest table and stood. "To Rhys! Back in Wales where he belongs!" Others leapt to their feet and emptied their ale.

Daron clutched her skirts with stiff fingers as she listened to the din. She wondered what Rhys home might mean for Huw. Then she felt ashamed. Rhys' return from captivity in England signaled more than her own gain or loss, it meant certain war and soon, men lost forever, blood pooling on the ground, bones crushed. And what would it mean for Bryn?

"Go fetch her, I tire of this game." Owain stalked away and she tried to call after him, but her voice failed her. She crept from the hall, catching one of the kitchen maids. "Give him plenty to drink Moira, wine will make things easier for all."

After a restless night, Daron rose early, stomach heaving. Out in the yard, she hung her head over a pail and tried to swallow down the bile. It had been weeks since she'd felt so bad; it couldn't be good for the child. Her cousin had made her own choices. It wasn't her responsibility to protect her from the consequences. Still, where was Tanwen now?

Someone must have told Owain that Tanwen was not at Adpar, for he didn't ask for her again. Daron worried; it was unnerving how totally he ignored her. Messengers rode in and out, men clustered in intense groups, sun on their red faces, arguing. Daron felt dread curl in her belly alongside the baby. She was run ragged from morning till late in the evening, filling requests for bread, ale, wine, ink or parchment. At night, she stared out the slit of a window in Cook's chamber, night sky lit by a blazing orange moon, tossing harsh light across the floor. The whispered conversations of the men always broke off when she approached. Still, she'd caught fragments. Rhys' name was on their lips always and furtive plans for renewed fighting against the Normans and English.

One evening, Owain sent for her. Eyes circled by dark shadows, he stretched out by the hearth, boots tumbled beside him on the straw. "Sit, Daron, you look quite pale."

She sat on the offered stool. "There have been some late nights."

Fingering his goblet, Owain looked suddenly uncertain. "Where is she?"

Daron watched his fingers twirl the goblet stem, round and round. "She is gone."

"I'm asking you. As her cousin. I know you know."

Daron swallowed and shook her head.

"Do you think I'd harm her? I have missed her."

"She will not be back."

Owain's head snapped up. "No?" He stared out the window, though it was black outside, the harvest moon hidden behind the hills. His fingers stroked the fat jewel on his dagger.

Daron twisted her hands together; she mustn't be afraid, it was just Owain. "I only know she went to find Bryn."

"What?" Owain got to his feet and loomed over her. "Foolish woman, she could ruin all!"

"Endanger Bryn?"

"No! Ruin our efforts, everything we're fighting for. How could she?" Owain flung himself onto his chair. "Rhys is this close to taking all of Deheubarth back again from Henry. A wondrous thing for Wales!"

"Wales?"

"No more Aberteifi and Dinefwr and Ceredigion, we'll be united against the Normans and English, don't you see it?"

"We'd be like them?"

Owain fiddled with the piles of parchment stacked on the table beside him, then swept them all onto the floor. "How could you understand, what a prince like Rhys sees, his vision?" He stared at the floor. "I must get out of here, back to the center of things."

"But you've only been home a few days, there are matters, so many, that need your attention." Daron thought of the farmers in the hills, and the cottagers down the valley by the river. It seemed Owain had little intention of helping feed them this winter, though their crops were destroyed these past months by the fighting.

"We need provisions. Wine, ale, oats, barley, as much as you can gather, we leave in a week's time. See to it." Owain drained the rest of his wine.

"But what about Tanwen," said Daron, wondering at her own bravery. "Will you find her? I'm so worried."

"She's made her choice. She stands against us, against me and Rhys." Owain's voice was flat as the leveled fields.

"No," protested Daron. "She thought only of saving Bryn." She paused at the grimace on his face, a twist of grief surely, but in a moment it was gone and the new hard Owain back.

"She was always half fey and now…" He stared into the fire, scowling.

Daron waited, but he seemed to have forgotten she was there, so she backed out the door. In the kitchen, she found Cook still at work.

"Did he notice your belly?" Cook asked.

Daron sat on a stool. "If he did, he didn't care enough to ask. I'm to gather food and supplies, everything, he said."

Cook narrowed her eyes as she thumped dough on the table. "What can be spared?"

"He said all." Daron stared at her fingers. "I thought he loved her. But he loves nothing now, or only this idea he has, Wales, and what is that?"

Cook shrugged. "We have to save enough food to last out the winter, Wales or no."

Daron brushed her hair out of her eyes. Her arm felt heavy, disconnected from her body. "If Huw loved me, he would never have gone."

Cook shaped the dough into a fat round and patted it with flour. "It's not so simple sometimes. Life and love, they don't always march by the rules."

Daron rubbed her eyes. "I hate this Rhys."

Cook looked up, her hands still. "Watch what you say. He's a prince and we all have to live."

CHAPTER SIXTEEN

The English Borders

NONE OF THEM COULD SWIM. The waters swirled in dark patterns around the open boat, which rocked low, heavy armor piled in a heap in the front. Bryn stopped on the high riverbank and stared down at the straggling row of boys below him, waiting to climb on board. The guards were pulling off hauberks and heaving wooden shields into the boat. The repeated clunk echoed through the forest.

One of the soldiers pointed. The first boy in line hesitated and another shoved him. He fell on his knees into the water and stumbled to his feet, coughing, tunic plastered to his thin chest and thighs in the wind. He climbed over the side rails and huddled, shivering, in the stern.

They loaded twelve boys on and then the soldiers argued, shouting curses Bryn had never heard before, but in the end they had to make two trips. Two pairs of oarsmen rowed the boat across, fighting the current, and beached it on the far side. They prodded the boys out of the boat with long oars and tossed the shields onto the grass and too soon, they were back. Bryn felt an arm shove him from behind and he stumbled down the gravel-strewn hill to the water's edge. It smelled of dead fish and the piled boulders were pitted from the water's rough handling.

"You, get over here," shouted a burly soldier. His greasy hair hung black and tangled past his shoulders and his large red nose dripped in the morning air. Bryn looked away, to the far side of the river.

"Little bastard," shouted the man, glaring. He shook the cudgel in his left hand.

Bryn hesitated. The soldier's eyes narrowed and he decided not to test his luck. Last night, one of the biggest boys had been beaten, punched and kicked as he lay on the ground until he cried aloud and wept. This morning he was silent, nose bent in his white face, his arm useless and dangling at his side.

Bryn splashed into the water, so icy he sucked in a breath. The current tugged at his knees, trying to pull him away and under.

"Get in," snarled the guard, squinting up the bank as a rider on a white horse pulled up. Bryn pushed down the surge of crazy hope that it might be Owain, come to get him back. That would not happen. His father had made that clear in their last conversation, their one conversation actually, while he was at Dinefwr. Huw had brought them together, then left them facing each other in the center of Rhys' great hall, cavernous and dim and smelling of old ashes and early morning cold.

Owain had stared down at him, fiddling with his green-jeweled dagger and Bryn wished Huw, big friendly Huw, had stayed. "You'll be fine," Owain said. "Henry might be a Norman king but he has his honor. Being a hostage, it's not the same as being a common prisoner. And no doubt you'll be exchanged for one of theirs in no time." Owain kicked at a half-burnt log in the hearth, sending a puff of grey ash in a plume into the air.

"Aren't you coming with me?"

Owain began to pace, gesturing in the air with his knife. "Rhys will prevail, you need not fear, by this time next year I'm sure you'll be back, one way or another. So learn what you can, you'll be in a fine big court, but never forget you're Welsh." He stopped pacing and stared at Bryn, his eyes wide, gold ringing the black center. "You're there for the glory of Wales, doing your part. I envy you that." He turned away and looked out the window where dawn tinged the sky a muddy grey. "I envy you that."

"Back to Adpar or here with you at Dinefwr?"

Owain blinked and frowned. "What?"

"When I come back, where will I go?"

"Learn how to fight, Wales needs her men. Learn those Norman tricks, they're good on the field, too good. Not that it will save them in the end." Owain shoved his dagger into its sheath. "You'll be back within the year, no doubt, Rhys will see to that."

Bryn had turned the likelihood of this over in his mind as he trudged along, through dark woods and hot fly-ridden meadows and along a high cliff above wind-beaten beaches. He'd had plenty of time to think. He concluded that Rhys was far likelier to get his own two sons back first. Even to the Norman soldiers they seemed important. They'd been mounted on frisky ponies with bells on their red bridles and rode in the front, while he trudged with the others on the muddy path in the back, prodded along by the soldiers' spears. It also seemed likely Rhys would go on fighting the Norman king, rather than forge another truce, soon to be broken like the rest. Which would hardly make Henry let the hostages go. Especially since all said Henry had a fierce temper. The soldiers joked that Henry frothed at the mouth, like a mad dog, when angered.

In the dripping woods, at the start of their journey, it had been cold at night and hot at noon and always the gnats buzzed around his nose and itched in his ears. His legs had ached and burned. Now they'd reached the coast the going was better. A fine breeze blew the swarming bugs away, but the soldiers were tense, wary and shouting, though there was nothing obvious to be seen. Owain didn't understand, Bryn decided. If he did, he would never have let him go to this mad English king. Owain was his father, after all. And it was easy to see who had duped Owain. It was Rhys. Without Rhys, Owain would yet be home at Adpar, hunting red deer in the mornings, eating pork pasties in the kitchen in the afternoons, sitting in the white rose garden lit with firebugs with his mother in the long summer evenings. As he'd always done, until he'd met Rhys. Then he'd been gone, gone so long Teilo grew grim-faced and he heard his mother weeping, sometimes, when he woke restless in the night.

Bryn felt hate for Rhys turn into a solid fist deep in his chest. His mother said hate was strong, so strong it took over your soul. Perhaps his soul was taken over but the hate he kept silent, within himself, for the other boys mimicked the young princes and idolized Rhys, but daily the hot solid feeling grew. He began to dream of how he'd make Rhys pay. Dreams of escaping, riding a white stallion to Dinefwr, striding right into Rhys' dining hall to make him grovel in the filthy ashes. How, he didn't know. But the dreams kept him warm and walking. Even when one of the boys fell off his horse and broke his leg and the soldier stabbed him through the neck with his dull sword, hacking twice. Even when one of the soldiers breathed and slobbered on his neck in the night and only went away when another soldier woke and shouted at him. Even when he was so tired he must think of Owain and knew that even if he stayed alive, his father might not want him back, ever.

Of his mother, he tried not to think at all. Some of the boys cried out in the night; he hoped he did not. But sometimes he'd wake, sure he smelled her lavender-scented hair on the night wind.

"Get going," snarled one of the guards and Bryn stepped further into the water. The guard shoved the boy in front of him. The boy fell in the water and stumbled to his feet, spitting and blinking water out of his eyes. He walked straight to the boat. He was small and had a hard time clambering over the side. The overloaded boat rocked and one of the oarsmen swore. The boy squatted on the bottom of the boat, despite the filthy water slopping back and forth.

Bryn climbed in, stepping by mistake on the boy's hand. He had to keep his wits about him, put thoughts of the past away. He inched closer to the boy and nodded. The boy, pale hair clinging wet to his head, gave him a crooked grin. Surprised, Bryn smiled back, then looked around fast, but no one seemed to have noticed.

The boatmen took up oars and the boys watched the bank recede. "Don't move or I'll toss you over," shouted one of the soldiers when a boy shifted and the boat rocked and swung around in the current. The oarsmen swore and sweated and the boat slowly swung back. The small boy ducked his head between his knees and grinned again. Bryn could see his fingers, white and wrinkled from the water, gripping his scraped-up ankles. They inched along, the men grunting and the water in the boat climbing up their shins, but finally the boat ground against rocks and Bryn leaped onto the shore. He waited for the boy and they climbed the steep bank together.

"Nick's my name," said the boy under his breath.

Bryn darted a look at the guard. "Mountains next," he said. "It'll be cold." They both stared at the mountains, topped with white, which could be rock but was probably snow. Bryn yanked off his dry tunic and handed it to Nick.

Nick hesitated, then shrugged it on over his wet clothes.

The guards yelled for silence and shoved them into a straggling line and marched them up a stony path winding into the mountains.

CHAPTER SEVENTEEN

The Mediterranean Sea

GETHIN SNIFFED THE AIR and frowned. It smelled musty, not fresh and salt. And the wind had set up a high keening around the top of the mast. Still, sun beamed down, catching the brass tips on the ship's wheel.

The captain approached, and the smell of sour wine floated with him. Gethin hid his distaste. The captain was a sot, but as a result, he was allowed above deck to guide the ship rather than laboring below heaving cargo. The captain wove past, saying nothing, and disappeared below deck. By noon, the waves were mounting into deep hills and troughs. The sun slipped behind blue clouds. The captain reappeared and Gethin thought he'd take the wheel, but he just stared out over the climbing water while the boat shuddered on.

"Perhaps we should alter course?"

"What's that? Who do you think you are?" The captain's nose reddened as he squinted at Gethin. "We'll make Marseilles today, storm or no. We've important cargo." He wiped his nose on his palm.

He'd mentioned the cargo before. Gethin had tried to find out what they packed. Back in Ilfracombe, it hadn't mattered. It was a ship; they let him sign on. Since then, he'd had plenty of time to wonder. "It won't matter if we hang offshore another day until this blows out," he said.

"Do as you're told," said the captain. "We're going in."

A tough hour passed. Wind howled through the masts and rattled the lines. They were plowing up and down, making little headway, winds pushing them towards shore, though not the port they aimed for. "You," Gethin yelled, "get the captain."

"Near passed out below, he is," said the man they called Arms, for his huge strong forearms. "And better so, I'm thinking."

"You know these waters?"

"No."

"I'm turning us out to deep water then."

Arms raised his black eyebrows and slapped his palms together. "I'll get some men."

They got the boat turned, with a fearful cracking of the sail, and she ran along with the waves, as though thrilled to be heading toward the deep. Gethin relaxed his grip on the wheel long enough to wipe his forehead with his tunic.

The captain emerged on the ladder from below, his face red. "I told you to hold course. Aim for the point there. You can see it with those wonderful eyes of yours I trust." He watched as Gethin turned the boat again and staggered back below.

A fog had come down and it was near impossible to see the swells. Gethin nearly lost his footing as a rogue wave tossed them. White foam crept higher with each wave and then roared across the deck. The boat creaked and groaned as though it would screech into separate logs again. Wind tore at his face. He focused on the waves, one at a time, cutting through each a victory. But he had no idea where rocks or sand bars might lurk. It was insanity to approach the shore this way.

"Give Pen the wheel." Arms thunked his meaty hand on Gethin's shoulder.

Gethin shook him off. "Lay off. You know I can't just leave now."

"Just do it."

Gethin unlocked his stiff fingers and let himself be pulled from the wheel. "This better be important." Pen was experienced, but the waves loomed huge as a cathedral.

Arms yanked him down the ladder below decks. Most of the crew clustered on some overturned crates. They were staring at the deck, covered in filthy sloshing water. "Where's the leak, have you found it yet?" Gethin demanded.

"Never mind that. Here's the thing." Arms seemed to be the spokesman. "Captain's gone overboard."

"What?"

Arms shrugged. The others said nothing. Water was bubbling up now between the floorboards.

"Who's second in command?"

"That would be me , by rank," said Arms, "and being the strongest." He shrugged. "But I don't want the job. Never been in charge, never want to be."

Gethin stared at Arms and the silent crew. The guttering light of the single smoking candle lit their faces orange and black. The ship screeched and shuddered through another wave. He had to get back on deck.

"We're thinking you're the one," said Arms. "You're best at the wheel and you're not liking the drink so much as the rest of us. Seems right." The ship gave a creaking shriek and tilted. Crates toppled and the candle flashed and flickered out. The men shouted and clambered over each other in the smothering dark.

"God's teeth," muttered Gethin. He cracked his elbow on a beam. The boat slowly righted. "Arms, find the leak and stopper it up, I don't care with what. The rest of you, tie this cargo down. What's in there anyway?" He climbed the ladder. "Never mind, just stow it and plug the leaks."

Wind and harsh rain lashed his hair as he hauled himself up the tilting ladder.

"I'm that glad to see you," said Pen, with a gap-toothed smile. He relinquished the wheel.

"Get below. Make sure those fools plug up those leaks proper. We're heading out to open water." Gethin gripped the wheel and hung on. The wind was moaning like some doomed wretch in a dungeon. Waves like a range of hills rose in front of him, grey and shifting and littered with seaweed, smelling dank, like earth in an opened grave. He'd have to think about the captain later.

Two days passed and the sea spread calm and oily beneath a yellow sky. The wind was silent and the ship listed, but it was floating. Pen appeared, a bowl of steaming broth in his red hands. "Here you go then, captain, and a fine job you done getting us through that squall."

Gethin unclenched his stiff hands and took the bowl. He smelled onions and pepper and he was suddenly starved.

"Found something below, whilst we were opening them crates."

"What's in them?" said Gethin. His voice sounded weary and far away to his ears.

"Furs and worked silver and cattle hides, trading goods." Pen shrugged. "Don't know why the captain wouldn't let us look before."

There was more to all this, but he couldn't think it through. He took another deep swallow and felt the hot liquid pour straight down to his stomach. He was so tired he was seeing two of Pen.

"Found something else." Pen laughed and ruffled his silver hair so it stood straight up in salty tufts. Pen led him to the stern of the ship. With a flourish, he tugged at a pile of heavy canvas. A small boy with wet hair was revealed, staring down at a knot in the deck planking.

Gethin blinked twice and leaned over. "Sam?" He hauled the boy to his feet. "What are you doing here?"

Sam stared at his bare feet.

He was filthy and skinny as a starved rat. It was well over a month since they'd shipped from Ilfracombe. "What have you been eating?"

"There's dried cod missing, and someone filched bread," said Pen. "He must be that hungry."

Gethin tugged at his hair and frowned at the boy. "Why did you hide?"

Sam continued staring at his feet, which were black with dirt and red with cold.

Gethin heard Pen grunt behind him. "All right, all right," he said, "take him below, give him something to eat, and scrub the bugs off him."

"What are you going to do with him?" asked Pen.

"I won't sell him to the Moors, though he deserves it." Gethin scratched his neck. "Enid's probably clear out of her mind with worry.

Did you even think to leave her any word?"

Sam made a small grunt but didn't lift his eyes.

Gethin rubbed his forehead with both hands and groaned. Pen snatched the boy and took him below. God's bones, this was a tangle. Enid would be searching everywhere. And the storm. The boy could have been swept overboard and no one ever the wiser.

Pen reappeared after a time. "Got him cleaned up and drinking hot broth now."

"Tell me now," Gethin said, "exactly how did the captain go over?"

Pen shifted his eyes to the mast. "I didn't see it. It was Jack and the twins. They were tying down the crates and a wave just came along and swept all three away. The twins and the captain that is."

"Why were they on deck fooling with crates in the middle of the storm?"

"Don't know. Something was in those three crates for sure. Captain was always keeping his eyes on them." Pen scratched his head. "Won't ever know now, I expect. At the bottom they are."

"I need sleep." Gethin felt himself sway, like someone drugged.

"Right," said Pen, "sleep away. I'll watch the boy. He's a hardy one, no mistake about that."

A week later, Gethin yawned and grinned up at the low ceiling. The captain's cabin was no bigger than a bed, but equipped with every-thing a man could need. Two wool blankets stretched over boards made a bed. Another plank formed a trestle table, which he'd piled with inks, quills, brushes, and parchment. Paradise compared to the hammock he'd occupied before his elevation to captain.

Mario, the ship's cook, barged in, banging the table and upsetting the ink. He set a steaming cup on the table.

Gethin grabbed a rag and wiped up the spill. "Ink's expensive and parchment even more."

Mario nodded, though he never seemed to get the point. "Never mind that, exciting things are happening," he said with a broad smile.

Gethin sighed. "What?" Enough had happened on this voyage already.

Mario beckoned, so Gethin followed. Up on deck, the sun was setting, and brilliant orange tipped the waves. Sam straddled a pile of fish, flopping and glinting silver chips of light.

"Nice work," said Gethin. Fresh fish would be tasty, grilled and seasoned with one of Mario's spicy mixes. But just seeing Sam made him uneasy. He frowned at the flopping fish. He kept thinking of the boy hiding under the reeking canvas. And that led to thoughts of what to do with him and what to do with the ship. Days, he kept busy repairing storm damage. Nights, it was like his mind was afire and he tossed, unable to sleep until dawn. He'd been working on a plan, a way to satisfy the ship's owners, sell their cargo and turn a profit.

Sam hoisted the huge fish under his nose.

Gethin snapped out of his thoughts. He admired the fish, fat and gleaming. Then he said, "you could have had schooling, Sam, and a good home."

Sam looked away and Mario jumped in. "Look at that beauty of a fish! He'll catch more. Think what I can cook with that!"

"Don't think you're going to get off with no learning," Gethin said to Sam.

Sam laid his fish carefully on the deck in front of Mario.

"He can stay then?" asked Mario.

Gethin put a hand on Sam's shoulder. These three way conversations were difficult. "I'll send word to Enid when we get into some port, though I doubt she'll get it."

Sam's nose turned pink and he fiddled with the gills of the fish. Mario grinned and headed back to his kitchen.

Gethin hesitated, then added, "You understand me, I know it, though you won't speak."

Sam stood up, wiping his hands on his tunic.

"I was alone too, as a boy," continued Gethin. "I knew my father's name, but he was a de Clare and never concerned himself with me or my mother. In the end, it can make you strong." Gethin pointed to the horizon. "But enough of that. We're headed to a grand port. And you're going to study, learn some Latin even, and work." Gethin stuck out a hand. "We'll be traveling hard, you'll have to take it and no whining, like a man."

Sam ignored the hand and picked up the fish.

Gethin sighed. "How about going down to the kitchens and help Mario clean this enormous fish. And Sam, nice catch. We'll eat well this night."

Sam shot down the ladder and Gethin stared out at the glinting sea. What might a boy see on such a voyage? He'd come back changed, for certain. It could be good for Sam to leave the bloody forests of Wales behind and start anew. And what might he himself discover?

At the next port, he'd send a missive to the ship's owners. Inform them he was taking the ship on to the city state of Venezia, where they'd load on wool embroideries, brocades, and Damascus silks. Venezia had the best cloth. But also the best maps, works of intricate accurate beauty, detailed in vermilion and cochineal inks. Maps that showed where the coast dipped and swelled, where mountains met the sea and sand beaches curved, cut by fast streams where fresh water could be taken on board. He'd find those silks the rich loved to flaunt and make coin for the ship owners but every moment he could tear away he'd make the secretive Venetians teach him what they knew. Ceredigion and Rhys, wet battles and blood, lurking and spying in service to other men's dreams and never his own, all that was behind him now. The ship rushed over copper-tipped waves and Gethin pulled out his notebook and sketched with sure, exuberant lines.

A fortnight later, Gethin sang under his breath as the wheel spun in his hands. The sea sparked, so bright it hurt to see. They'd stopped at a port yesterday and bought two baskets of aubergines and a cheese, white and round. Mario had been ecstatic. Gethin's mouth watered as he imagined what Mario might concoct.

Sam tugged at his sleeve.

Gethin looked where he pointed. He had good eyes, but he squinted into the light for a long time to be sure. Then he yelled a command and the sails sagged and flapped as the ship swung around. "Go below," he said quietly to the boy.

Sam's eyes opened wide.

"Now," said Gethin. The ship coming after them was fast and slim, not weighed down with cargo. She'd catch them in a few hours, or less. He almost wished the old captain were alive.

As dusk came down, the ship pulled alongside. Their captain babbled something in a language Gethin couldn't understand. "What is he saying?" Gethin called to Mario.

"Can't hardly catch it. Something about funds."

Gethin frowned. At least they weren't pirates, which was certainly possible in these waters. They seemed to be officials of some sort though, which could be worse. Their captain wore a red cloak crossed by a white band pinned with badges. He was pointing to a group of burly men armed with grappling hooks and axes. Undermanned as they were after the storm, they couldn't manage a fight. "Lower the sails." Gethin watched the canvas pile up on deck. The ship shuddered and bobbed, going nowhere. Their captain was still talking, his voice tossed about in the wind but his petulant tone clear enough.

Sam stood on the ladder, peeking up on deck.

"Pen," Gethin said softly, "if I don't come back I'm charging you with getting the boy home to Enid, wife of David the woodworker, in Ilfracombe."

Pen ruffled Sam's hair. "Won't come to that though," said Pen, "seen this before. They want coin and lots of it. Question is, do we have any?"

"Not as I know of," said Gethin. If there'd been any, it was at sea-bottom with the old captain and his heavy crates. He crossed over the plank they laid down between the ships and stood in front of the gesticulating official, who was thin and long-nosed. He couldn't understand him, but they were headed to shore until coin could be produced.

A week later, Gethin stood on a balcony, gripping the curled iron railing and staring at a flat silver sea, as he'd stood every morning. The sun was buried behind thick clouds. They wouldn't have got far anyway, he consoled himself, with no winds. He swatted a fly. The air was damp with the promise of more humid heat, and they were good as prisoners. They'd found a translator, but no solution. It seemed there was a hefty fee to be paid. The ship was known, the old captain had evaded the tax collectors before, and the sum they wanted now was beyond anything he'd be able to come up with.

There was only one way this could end and he'd known the exact moment the official had realized it. A smug smile had creased the man's thin lips and was quickly wiped away. All that was left now were the formalities. They would take the ship. And her cargo. He and his men would be freed, and he was given pennies enough to pay the men off.

Sam, hair standing on end and rubbing his eyes, was looking at him expectantly. If only the boy had stayed put with Enid.

"They'll let us go soon, maybe even today." Gethin didn't tell the boy that would be the start of their troubles. He'd figure that out, once they were cast out of these dirty but solid lodgings.

Two days later, a jovial youth unlocked the door and gestured them out onto the hot street. He handed them a sack with bread, water, and olives, grinned wildly, and waved them away. Apparently the officials were through with them.

"We'll be on our way then captain," said one of the men. They'd signed on with another ship already.

Gethin thanked them and the men shuffled off, joking and shoving, headed down to the docks. Pen shook his hand hard and long, his face gloomy.

"We'll be fine," said Gethin. Pen hugged Sam fiercely, then followed the other men.

"I'll stay on and cook," said Mario, not meeting his eyes.

"I can't pay you, nor is there much to cook."

Mario shrugged. "We can go to this Venezia you're talking about all the time."

Gethin stared at their former ship, bobbing on its anchor. He had no coin for passage, he couldn't take work as a crewman with Sam along, and Venezia was days of dangerous land travel away.

Sam and Mario waited in the noon sun for him to figure things out. "Come on," Gethin said. They should get out of this town anyway, and into the woods where they could hide and find some shade. Figure out what to do next.

CHAPTER EIGHTEEN

Pembrey Forest

TANWEN DEVOURED the bruised apple and tossed away the core. She'd been eating blackberries and hard pears found at the top of abandoned trees. She turned the last sour apple in her fingers, took a bite, and offered the rest to Horse. He sniffed with fluttering nostrils and returned to cropping grass. If only she could do the same. This journey was taking longer than she'd ever imagined.

And with fatigue and hunger her thoughts kept drifting. She couldn't seem to keep the past back where it belonged. The garden she'd kept so long ago, after her grandmother died, kept flashing into her mind. She would smell those malformed plants, beaten down by fierce sun, though she had lugged pails of water until her arms burned. Then the rains fell and fell, drowning the wispy stems, rotting the blackened fruits. In the end, under the dim November sun, there had been nothing to eat, only rows of icy mud. She'd choked down acorns from the forest, but when snow drifted down, sheeting the great meadow until all the world glowed white, she'd known she had to go or die. She had walked away from everything she knew, walked on stiff legs for three days as snow drifted down, hiding in frigid barns through long nights, and in the end, on a day of sleet slicing at her cheeks, she'd made it to Aberteifi and Agatha, her mother's estranged sister.

Tanwen got to her feet, her bad ankle aching. She fingered Ceridwen's amber charm at her neck. There was no sense reliving the past. She must go on, find a town, get food and ask directions, whatever the risk. She climbed onto the horse, feeling a moment of pride that she'd learned to control him. The moment faded too soon and though she cajoled the horse into walking well into the hours of half-light, she was clinging to its back, fatigue washing up her chest in waves, lost again in the past, which seemed to rise up and twine with the present as she traveled, as though time had left its firm footing back at Adpar. The horse slowed and she kicked him, but he pricked his ears and planted his feet.

Then she heard it too, hoofs clattering, hitting rocks. She twisted on the saddle, looking for a place to hide. To one side, spiky junipers grew thick as a wall. On the other, cedars draped their feathery branches. She whirled Horse toward the cedars and slammed his stomach with her feet. He reared, sending a flock of green finches bursting from the brush. He reared again and Tanwen lost her handful of mane. She slid to the ground, landing hard on her shoulder. Horse jerked his head and the reins ripped through her fingers. She reached out, palms burning, but Horse pounded away.

Around the twist in the path came a grey charger. The rider shouted and the giant horse slid to a stop and stood shivering, its four huge feet planted. Tanwen stared at the oiled black hoof closest to her hand, at the silvery hair curling where the beast's leg met the polished hoof. Dust spiraled up, gritty in her eyes.

"You there. Get out of the path," said an impatient voice.

Tanwen got to her knees, her shoulder stabbing, without meeting the man's eyes, hoping he'd just ride on.

He leaped down and dropped his reins. The horse waited in the path, its black eyes assessing her, glistening. "By the Lady, you're a woman."

Tanwen brushed gravel from her gown, trying to think.

The man, tall with blonde eyebrows that quirked upward, took a step toward her. "Are you harmed?" He looked around, with a puzzled frown. "Why are you here anyway?" He examined the woods, as though expecting men to leap out, but the finches had settled back onto their perches, chirping and chattering. "We must be twenty miles from the nearest village." He sounded angry, and he slapped dust off his tunic and wiped sweat from his forehead with his sleeve.

"I have a right to be here," Tanwen said cautiously.

"Surely you heard my horse."

She shrugged.

"Where do you live? I'll take you home." He noticed a long rip in her gown, and stared at her exposed ankle and calf.

"You were riding too fast," she said.

He took off his cap and scratched his head, then laughed. "I was at that. It's my job."

"Now my horse is gone. You must help me catch him."

"I'm sorry for it, but you've held me up too long as it is." His horse pawed at the ground as though it understood his words and he put a hand on its shining neck.

"Wait! I need news."

"News of what?"

He was examining her again, with suspicious eyes. "Of the hostages being taken to England, Rhys' sons, and all the others."

"What have you to do with them?" he said curtly.

"That's my business. Have you seen them?"

He gathered up his reins and leaped on his horse.

"Please," said Tanwen, putting out a hand. "Please, they have my son."

He looked away from her, into the forest for a long moment. Then he said, "You need food, and a fire, and dry clothes, if I'm not mistaken."

"I need information."

He fiddled with the reins. "I saw them, yes. Two days past, it was."

"You saw them, where?"

"Don't be so excited. I can travel far in two days. They were at Striguil, the king's castle on the border."

"How do I get to this Striguil?"

"You'd best return home and wait. Your son will return to you in good time."

"I am going on."

The youth, for she realized now that under his wispy beard he was young, barely a man yet himself, stared at the treetops as though he wished she'd disappear. "Striguil is huge and impenetrable and built all of stone. You cannot go there."

Suddenly he reached down and grabbed her with thin strong arms.

She tried to pull away, but his horse snorted and danced. "Where are you taking me?"

"There's a clearing back aways, and you need food."

"I have to go on to Striguil."

"Not tonight."

They rode for a short time, then he pulled her down from the giant beast and unsaddled the horse and rubbed it down with care. He built a fire and soon a hot mix of fruit and dried meat bubbled in an iron pot and the smell was so good she thought she might faint. But what would she have to pay for this luck?

He handed her a steaming bowl of stew. She gulped it down as he gathered more firewood and arranged it in a neat pile. He put a second pot on the fire filled with water and when it boiled, he handed her a cloth and disappeared. Tanwen felt herself blush in the dark, but she dunked the cloth in the hot water and washed and found her comb and worked the knots from her short hair. The youth returned and handed her a blanket.

"What is your name?" she said.

"You didn't see me here," he answered. "My master is Henry, king of all England and Normandy. I carry his missives. You didn't see me, and I didn't see you." He curled up in his blanket, his back to her.

Tanwen huddled by the dying fire, wondering if she should try to slip away, but the shine of eyes outside the firelight and the snorting of the horse made her think of wolves. She thought about the missives he carried for Henry, and wondered who they addressed and what they might say. His leather bag was tucked by his side, the strap looped around his arm. As though he sensed her thoughts, he stirred in his sleep, rolling so his arm covered the bag.

He had been kind to her, but there might be something in his bag that would help her get to Bryn. When he snored again, she slid toward him. She tugged at the bag and he shifted in his sleep, uncovering the opening. She waited, not breathing, until he drifted deeper, eyelids twitching. She thrust her hand in. Apples, a skin of water or wine, her fingers searched for parchment, or a rolled message, or a packet of some sort. A chunk of soft cheese, wrapped in cloth. She pulled the bag closer and peered in, but it was dark, a night of no moon.

"Hey, what are you doing?"

She was shoved back and sprawled onto the ground, the sack ripped from her hands. "Fool woman." He thrust the bag under his head and settled back into sleep.

Tanwen stared at his chest, rising and falling. She didn't dare try again, nor could she make herself leave the circle of light from the glowing coals. Her eyes grew heavy, and she listened to the in and out of his breath, and thought of watching Bryn sleep, firelight catching the gold shadows in his hair.

When she woke, confused at the bright light of morning, the fire had been stamped out and the smell of wet ashes filled the air. The youth was gone.

She never found Horse, though she searched a full day, calling and tramping through the brush, flies biting her neck and brambles raking at her ankles, her injured shoulder burning. But Henry's messenger had tossed a sack into the middle of the road. In it, two days measure of oats. He'd also sketched a rough map in the loose dirt, with three stones pointing east, and pebbles showing her how many days it would take to travel to Striguil. Seven. In only one week, she'd reach Henry's castle and she would find Bryn.

Twelve days of hill walking brought Tanwen to another high ridge. This time, she finally glimpsed ocean, flat and grey, through the streaky fog. She should have reached Striguil long ago. But she'd been turned around by a blow-down in the forest, and a path that dwindled to nothing. And in the end she didn't know if the king's messenger had been the kind youth he seemed, or he'd left her false directions. She'd turned it over in her mind as she trudged uphill, and come to no answer. He was her enemy, but he'd helped her. He was a boy, only a few years older than Bryn, yet he worked for Henry.

Round and round her anxious thoughts ran.

She watched the water crawl below, while her stomach ached and gnawed. She'd had but a few berries to eat yesterday and nothing at all today. Judging from the piling clouds on the horizon, the weather would turn nasty as evening came on.

At the foot of the hill, houses huddled around a rock-strewn bay. From here, the village looked tranquil, the people specks. Some clustered in the fields, some fished in boats that bobbed just beyond the mouth of the bay. Would they be Norman, Flemish, English? The only certainty was they wouldn't be Welsh, for the Welsh lived only in the high places. The lowlands had all been taken up by invaders, far in the past, though to hear Owain talk, you'd think it happened only yesterday.

"Are you a fairy woman?"

Tanwen whirled around. A child stared up at her. The girl's hair hung loose, silver in the dim light, her eyes bright blue.

"No," said Tanwen.

The girl rocked back on her heels. "I thought you might be, this seems a good spot. But I've yet to see one." She picked a few late daisies and twined them into a chain. "Still, I know they must be here, the food I leave is always gone."

Tanwen's stomach growled at the mention of food. The girl pulled a crust from her pouch and held it between slim fingers. She looked like she should eat the bread, not leave it to be carried off by birds or creatures of the forest. "What's it called, your village?" Tanwen asked.

"It's not mine, we've just been here since father died. A soldier killed him. With an arrow." The child's face creased, then smoothed out. "But there's lots to eat, though it's nearly all fish Tom brings from the sea."

"Who lives here? How do people make a living?"

"Tom's my brother. He goes out in the boats every day. My mother and me, we stay at home, it's not nearly so fun, but I slip away sometimes."

"Do you get lots of visitors in this place? Does it have a name?"

"It has no real name. Not like a person. The hollow, is all anyone calls it." The girl looked around expectantly, as though listening to someone. She tossed the crust in the air. "I have to go," she called and ran, her basket swinging wildly.

Tanwen slid and stumbled after the girl, down the steep hill. Her ankle stabbed and she slowed her steps. The child darted into an orchard. Tanwen followed, limping down a pruned aisle of magnificent trees, loaded with fruit. She breathed in the winey scent of apples and salt, carried on the sea fog. The child had disappeared and the orchard was silent. Tanwen almost wondered if she'd imagined the girl. She reached for an apple and ate it slowly. Eating made the band around her forehead feel less tight. It was just her mind, playing tricks. She was hungry and tired, that was all. She took another apple, examined its unusual stripes of red and green, and slipped it in her bag.

"You there, stop," called a gruff voice. An old man came striding across the high grass, waving a walking stick like a sword. His white eyebrows danced above glaring black eyes.

"I ate only one," Tanwen said, holding up both hands, "and took one more. I was very hungry. I can pay. I was hungry," she repeated, for he didn't stop frowning. How ridiculous to be caught for stealing an apple when she'd already stolen a horse. Still, she could hang for either offense.

"If I fed everyone who comes by I wouldn't have much for cider now, would I."

Suddenly Tanwen could see Teilo bent over the apple press and smell the bruised apples and crumpled leaves. She blinked back tears.

"I don't know all the village anymore and that's a pity, too many strangers. But you're not from here at all, if you don't know my cider." He yanked off her hood. "That's some head of hair you got. What're you doing here, alone? Speak quick now or I'll have you before the lord."

"Where's the nearest manor house?"

"Kidwelly. Near a day's journey."

"And Striguil, surely that's near?"

He squinted at her. "What would you want with a dread place like Striguil?"

"I'm not Norman, nor English, if that's what you think."

The old man tugged at his belt. "You should stay far from places like that. How do you think I lived to get these grey hairs?" He twirled the end of his beard around his thick forefinger. "I make cider and a goodly amount of silver and stay away from all that and live. Live," he repeated. "Take my word for it." He grabbed her elbow.

As he pulled her into the village, Tanwen kept her head high, as though she weren't a perfect stranger, with muddy hems and strange cut-off hair. She wondered if the old man meant to charge her with stealing his famed apples. They passed a row of tilted houses, doors jammed shut against the moaning sea wind. When they reached the last, he shoved the door open with his foot. Four women clustered around a central hearth, sewing. "Gertrude, see what I found in my orchard."

The women stared, their needles in the air, until one got up from her seat, a tall woman with iron hair in a tight bun on the top of her head.

The old man nudged Tanwen over the stoop. The chamber was over hot from the fire and close with the smells of wet wool and old women. "She took one of my apples," he added and went out.

The women started whispering. The tall woman looked at Tanwen with an annoyed wrinkle between her brows.

"I need your help." Tanwen could hear the ragged edge to her voice and swallowed. "Have Norman soldiers and their hostages come through here? They have my son."

"It's hard times we're in," said the tall woman, "for everyone. Travelers are common enough, but they don't like to be gossiped over." She gestured to the fire. "Warm yourself. I won't have it said I turned a guest away cold." Coals gleamed in the hearth, where a very old woman huddled, wrapped in a clean blanket. "That's my granny. She likes the warmth, like all old bones."

The old granny grinned, her long finger tapping the end of her chin. "Whose son is he?" she asked in a quavering voice.

"Mine," said Tanwen.

The granny sniffed, and her eyes scanned Tanwen's dusty boots and filthy skirts. "Yes, but who's the father? Why do they send him to the English?"

"He is son to Owain ap Macsen of Adpar."

The women exchanged glances and even the granny blinked and tugged the blanket around her shoulders.

Tanwen leaned forward. "You've seen them! You know of Owain? Which way did they go, when did they pass?"

The women were silent, their needles stabbing the cloth of the blanket they were making. "Tell her," said the granny.

Gertrude shook out her skirts with a snap and muttered, "A few weeks past, at least. Headed east to Striguil."

Tanwen took a deep breath.

"What do you mean to do?" Gertrude's voice was curt. "A woman alone."

"How do I get there? Just tell me that."

"You'll make things worse by chasing."

"And if not you, for sure his father will cause him harm," burst in one of the younger women. "I've heard this Owain joined Rhys' new revolt against the English. Heard it just yesterday, my man had it from the peddler passing through. Rhys has broken the truce, he's back to fighting. And that puts all the hostages in danger. They might make an example of one, or all." The woman shook her head, her eyes sparkling. "This Owain is with Rhys all the way. So I've heard. And be sure King Henry will hear too."

Tanwen put out a hand to steady herself against the wall.

"Be quiet Lise," said Gertrude.

The old granny put a veined hand over Tanwen's. "My two grandsons are off at sea, and I worry, but I wait for them and so should you."

"How could he," burst out Tanwen. "First he hands our son over to Henry, as though he's no more than a mule or a package of barley, then he joins Rhys in open rebellion? Henry would be in his rights to, to…"

The granny continued to pat her hand and the fire spat.

Tanwen snatched her hand away. "All the more, I must get to this Striguil. There is no time to waste. What way? You must tell me."

The granny jerked her chin toward a dark corner.

Gertrude beckoned to a back door nearly blocked by a sprawling honeysuckle. "Hurry then," she said. "Avoid the men, if you're set on this. They're pledged to Henry. This is Flemish country and it's our livelihood. We're weavers who trade our cloth with the English, and information too. And that's worth more than many ells of cloth." She pointed to the hills. "Head up. The highland Welsh know your language and perhaps they will help you." She dropped her arm. "Or perhaps not. Only turn south when you reach the river; that will take you to the castle. It will be longer that way, but you'd have no chance at all in the towns along the coast."

"I thank you," said Tanwen.

"Don't thank me. From what I've heard, this Striguil is a terrible place, if you make it so far. Think hard before you try this. Going home would be best."

Tanwen pushed past her and climbed the steep hill beyond the village as dusk fell. She climbed, breathing hard, until she could no longer hear the chink and clunk of the boats bumping against their docks, or the shouts of the children in the lane. At the top she rested, looking back. From up here the village seemed tranquil, candles lit, and dinner fires glowing. She turned her back on it, and climbed on into the dusk.

Four days later, Tanwen soaked her ankle in a pool formed by a trickling stream. It had swelled again with all the climbing and her shoulder stabbed with every step on the rock-strewn path. She'd found no food up here, and no people, and the cold water made her stomach ache. The midday woods hummed with frantic insects. She'd given up swatting them away.

She examined the ferns and grasses growing along the stream. The ferns were almost familiar and they'd likely taste bitter, but she had to eat something. Her head was swimming, so she gave up on the idea of kindling a fire to boil the greens and chewed the leaves off one long stem and then another. The feathery leaves stuck to the back of her mouth and she cupped her hands and washed them down with water. She didn't feel any better, but she got to her feet and walked on. At the top of the last hill she'd had a view and the landscape below her was all mountains, one folding onto the next, a few snow-topped though it was still summer, stretching as far as she could see. But there must be a pass through, somewhere.

As dark came on, she curled up to sleep, hoping the ferns would clear her head by morning. She woke in blackness, with her stomach clenching. She was ill, retching into the stream, and retching again, until nothing remained in her belly but still her body kept on, heaving. Between bouts, she lay in the wet leaves and tried not to think. She shivered so much she thought she'd break a tooth, drenched in sweat. Later, she heard rustles in the woods and once, the howl of a wolf on a far peak. When morning finally dawned, she dragged herself upright and stumbled on, along the barely visible path by the stream.

The path headed gradually upward and then turned steep. She forced herself to climb, using the trees to haul herself up. Her stomach was still clenched tight, but she'd stopped the terrible dry heaving. The ferns had looked like a variety she knew, but she'd been wrong. She was a stranger in this forest.

The air, as she climbed, grew less humid, and her head felt like it was clearing too, clouds thinning and thoughts coming through, but it seemed also that she could hear sounds now, whispers, as though the trees themselves were speaking with her, or about her, like the women of Agatha's village.

She dragged herself up, clinging to beech trees, then birches and finally to stunted firs, and at the top, she tottered, staring out over the mountains, rising like vicious teeth. She was on a steep cliff, faced with granite, and the treetops far below were spangled already with fall yellow. She wavered and stepped back, away from the edge. How long she'd been gone, so long, too long. Yet no one else would save Bryn now.

The path she found on the far side of the peak was barely wide enough for red deer, and it twined along the cliff face. She searched, but dusk was coming on, and she could find no other way to go. There was no choice, so she edged out along the path, both palms to the rock face, her back to the steep fall. She inched along, her wet skirts hindering. Why hadn't she tucked them in her belt? She dared a glance, and the path hugged the cliff, disappearing around the side of the mountain where mist trailed grey strands already. Soon the mist would cloak the cliff and hide the path. She took a deep breath. No way to go back now. She took one step, and another, and rested her forehead against the rough granite. After a time, she opened her eyes and moved her foot. One step and another. Her fingers traced the rough stone, her feet lifted over tumbled rocks, she tried to think only of the shine of mica in the rock in front of her eyes and not the endless space and wafting clouds behind her. She edged around a corner and the path widened and opened, left the cliff, and entered the woods.

Tanwen collapsed onto a patch of moss, her heart thumping. After a while, she realized the moss was wet and her skirts soaked and cold was seeping from her legs up into her chest. She got to her feet. As she stood, a group of men filed out silently from the woods. In a moment, their spears were in their fists, pointed at her neck, and they were shouting in a foreign tongue, one she had no hope of comprehending.

Tanwen was frightened by their weapons but she was glad to hear human voices. She waited as the men argued over her. One had a bloodstained tunic wrapped around his thigh. She gathered moss and pointed to his leg. The man eyed her but another of the group pushed him forward. She set about binding up his bleeding leg, ripping strips off her skirt to form a clean bandage. The men were silent, watching, and when she finished, they lowered their weapons and melted back into the woods, the injured one last and limping. After only a moment of hesitation, she followed.

She trailed them to their summer camp, high on the steep slopes, where they pastured cattle and goats and where she found women and children living in makeshift turf huts. The women crowded around her, fingering her shortened hair and her torn skirts, laughing and chattering. Too tired to wonder what they said, Tanwen lay down on the sheepskin they gave her and only woke late the next morning, sun full on her face.

The women merely tolerated her, but they fed her and the children helped search for parsley and cresses in the fields. When she'd recovered some and could be useful with the cooking and endless laundry, the women became curious too. She realized, after a few days, that the tongue they spoke was actually intelligible, merely Welsh pronounced in a melody that made the words unfamiliar unless she ran them through her mind again. Once she could speak with them, the women grew friendly, and their men were mostly gone, hunting or fishing or gathering wood for fuel, and ignored her. Three families lived in the settlement and others came and went from nearby hill villages and they all knew the woods and stones and springs of their mountain and followed paths she couldn't even see.

When the first day of clear blue skies arrived, with a snap in the air, they all readied to head down into the valleys for the winter, packing blankets and pots on strong ponies. Tanwen went to the oldest woman, whose eyes were milky and dim, and asked her help. The woman listened, saying nothing in response, but she told the men to guide her down to Striguil. What the old woman said to the men, to convince them, Tanwen didn't know, but three men came, strong men of middle years, with only Welsh on their tongues, men who hated Norman invaders. She traveled with the mostly silent men for an endless fortnight. They guided her down winding pathways through thick wooded stretches, places of perfect ambush between rock tumbled hills, and climbed with her over barren peaks, fighting fall winds and cold rain, and finally led her down the river valley, lush and green-lit with summer's bitter end.

When they approached Striguil, the men faded away. They were behind her one moment, then gone.

CHAPTER NINETEEN

Striguil

TANWEN'S BOOTS were cracked, her cloak had been ripped away by the wind, and she'd been five long weeks in the mountains, but she stood on the cliff, staring down at the tower and winding river below, and thought, I have made it to the English borders. That suddenly seemed so amazing and momentous that she reached out to the fir beside her and clutched its spiky branch to hold herself upright.

The mountains had been a fierce place. She'd been ill, coughing and feverish, and always hungry. Frightened she'd disappear up there, among the endless trees. Frightened she'd never make it to Bryn. But all that didn't matter now, for she had done it. She crept closer to the cliff edge and peered down.

Stone walls lifted straight from the riverbank toward the sky. Her eyes sketched the dizzy height of the main tower. The castle was alternately lit and pitched into shadow as purple clouds roiled across a pale sky. Rain would come soon. She should find a place for the night, but she crouched on, staring at the tower, daring it to disappear. But it did not. It was solid stone and real. She could make out soldiers patrolling the riverbank.

The last weeks she'd pushed so hard, climbing from early morning to last light. She'd pushed all her worries from her mind and simply walked. The evergreen forests they passed through, the hills shading lilac and purple to the horizon, the tumbling rills of blue-white water – she'd noted these. But no thoughts had she allowed in. Even on the highest peak when sleet had fallen in the night, she'd imitated her silent guides, ducked her head, waited it out, and walked on.

She ached to race down the steep hill to the grim tower, shouting out Bryn's name, but she must not. She could not be so rash. She pressed a fingernail into her palm. She should go down into the town. There would be some sort of inn and she had silver pennies. She could sleep deeply, safely, and when she'd awakened fresh, come up with a plan. But the dusk deepened into whispering shadows and a half moon rose and she couldn't find the courage. She wedged herself under the sweeping branches of a cedar and breathed in the dark aroma and tried to sleep.

Early morning altered the river's sluggish brown waters to a magical misty grey, sparkling with chips of light. A heron picked through the shallows, its silvery body barely visible against the gleaming river. Tanwen leaned against an ancient oak with sprawling limbs so heavy they arched back down to the ground. Acorns littered the ground and she rolled one between her fingers. She was thinking about Bryn and his silky baby skin, warm when she would lift him from his nap. Was he even alive? She dropped the acorn. She was so close, yet now it seemed like all her fears had thrust their way up to the surface, clamoring.

She straightened her clothing. The birds nearby stilled and the heron lifted his head and stared for a long moment before he resumed fishing. She frowned. She must move silently and secretly here. This close to Striguil. This close, finally, to Bryn.

She was a stranger, but Striguil was a port and they were used to strangers, welcomed them even. Still, her hair would draw attention. She made her way down to the river, keeping hidden in the cattails. When she reached the bank, she ducked her head in the water. It was freezing, fizzy, on her forehead. She slicked her hair back flat. The water would darken it from copper to nondescript brown. She wound a cloth around her head as a kind of cap. No one would recognize her now, leman of a Welsh lord though she was. She would get a job as a servant, one that let her stand silently by and hear what was said, and when she found out where they kept the hostages, she'd find a way in. And sneak Bryn out, one night, and soon. That was her plan, simple, but probably that was best.

She set off down the path and as she walked she examined the looming castle. She passed without incident through the town gates. It was early, the day dark with clouds, and people late to come from their doorways. She waited until a stream of people thronged the streets, heading to the market, and joined them, placing her feet with care on the mud-spattered cobbles.

By midday, the market was ending and Tanwen wandered the stalls, eavesdropping on the gossipers. It was true, she'd learned, the hostages were imprisoned here. She might see Bryn, even today, she might brush her hand on his soft boy skin, smell his unique smell. She took a deep breath and surveyed the thinning crowd. She must keep her wits about her. She turned her steps to the castle. She'd decided to go as a kitchen wench, for she did know how to cook and she'd heard they needed girls, with the extra mouths to feed. She reached the castle gate and passed inside, tagging behind a family with squabbling twins.

She found her way to the kitchens, sturdy wooden buildings on the east side of the walls. "Where will I find Cook?" she asked a boy carrying a brace of pheasants.

"In there."

She followed the boy's gesture into the largest building. It was dark, lit by fires at regular intervals along one wall. Smoke poured out holes high in the roof. Torches over three long worktables lit the faces of the cooks. She saw birds dressed for roasting, a haunch of venison, piles of onions and parsnips ready for peeling. She wandered along down the table, wondering who to ask, when a large man stepped in her path, his belly covered with a clean linen smock. "What are you doing here girl? You're filthy, you can't be in my kitchens!"

"I'm sorry," Tanwen said, her voice catching.

"Be off with you, there's no scraps here; come to the door at dusk, then they'll be plenty." He started to move off.

"Wait," she said. "Sir, I mean, please…"

"What is it?" He squinted at her, leaning close to peer into her face.

"I need work, I'm strong, and I can cook."

"Can you now." He laughed. "And can you make puddings for four score men? Do you have the measurements in your head? Can you cut up a hart and roast it and turn out breads for several hundreds? Can you make a swan out of sugar that looks like it could fly off the platter?"

"No," she stumbled out.

"Then you cannot cook." The sound of a cat yowling startled the man. He frowned as a tall woman entered, wiping her red hands on her apron. "We're to serve for fifty tonight," she said twisting the strings of her apron.

"Yes, yes, Hetta, don't panic. Just go chop those apples and be sure to put honey on them before they brown." He turned back to Tanwen. "You can't stay in here." He pulled her by the sleeve to the door and pointed to the corner of the courtyard. "The garden is there. Take a basket from the shed and pull onions. Eight rows." He gestured to a table piled with apples and lined with four girls, peeling. "I keep a clean kitchen. But I need a girl to weed." He frowned at her again, as though she'd defied him. "Maureen will show you where to wash. And you can sleep with her."

A plump girl with limp brown hair, her hands buried in greens, glared at Tanwen, and went back to work.

"I thank you," blurted Tanwen, but Cook was already gone.

Three long days passed. Then a whole week, then another. Tanwen stretched her swollen fingers and picked up the rusty trowel. She dug out another weed, its long root like a ghostly carrot. She'd finished four rows of leeks already and another seven left to go. The sun beat on her back and mud crusted on her face. And somewhere there was Bryn.

She'd had no chance to get into the central hall, where she was sure the hostages were held. She couldn't even see in, as the tall windows were shuttered, and guards stood by the double doors day and night. She'd hoped the hostages would be treated almost as guests, but they were prisoners in truth, constantly guarded. She didn't dare to ask anyone straight out. She was here at Striguil, yet no closer to knowing if Bryn were actually here, or somewhere else. The carved and locked doors mocked her. And all day and late into the evening she was trapped in the kitchen garden, weeding or lugging buckets of water.

Maureen bustled up and scowled down at her. "Cook wants a dozen leeks for soup."

Tanwen wiped the sweat trickling into her eyes. "Here." She held out a trowel.

Maureen rolled her eyes and crossed her arms.

Tanwen bit her lip. She wanted to throw the trowel at Maureen's smug face, but she must not. Maureen had a lover and hated sharing her pallet. She'd be glad to see her go. Tanwen grabbed a basket, dug the leeks, shook off the sandy soil, and handed them over. She couldn't help admiring how plump and healthy they looked. Maureen smiled unpleasantly and flounced away.

Tanwen wiped her hot face with her apron. This afternoon, she decided, this very afternoon, it had to be. She was so afraid of drawing suspicion, but she'd have to take a chance. It was market day again, and Cook had said they'd be free in the afternoon. Maureen would be happy to lose her, so she'd have a chance then, but how to get into the hall, surrounded by guards with swords strapped to their belts?

Afternoon arrived and though the clouds skirted low and a warm mist draped over the river and swirled up toward the town, there was no rain. The shouts of merchants crying their wares mixed with the squeals of children skipping rocks down on the riverbank. Tanwen trailed Maureen, wondering how she could circle back unseen, hoping the mist would deepen and rain pour down, pushing people indoors. Ignoring the vendors, Tanwen dropped behind and watched as Maureen met her lover, a tall man with the bushy beard of an Englishman and the black fingernails of a farmer.

She should turn around and walk back to the castle, as though she carried a message. She passed a cart on the corner and stopped. Heaped in piles were candles, tallow dips that would smoke and smell, and fine beeswax candles that would burn long with clear light and a fragrant whiff of summer. She'd buy some, say they were needed in the hall and she was to bring them. She didn't know what might come next, but she had to get into that hall.

In a rush, she purchased beeswax candles, using a precious penny, and waited, fingers tingling, as the merchant wrapped them in oiled cloth. As he pulled at some tangled twine to tie the packet, Tanwen grabbed the candles. "I'll take them as is."

The merchant looked like he wanted to argue, but another customer called to him. Tanwen backed off, clutching the packet. The mist had thickened. Droplets of water gathered on her cheeks like tears. Tanwen edged past the butcher, trying not to breathe in the stench of blood and lifted the candles with their reassuring scent to her nose, the scent of her garden tumbling with white roses and buzzing with August bees.

She left the noisy market behind. The street wound along, narrow and dark under jutting buildings. She stumbled over a basket of stones in the deep shadows. She rounded a corner, and another. Head down and walking fast, she turned a third corner into an alley and ran straight into a man, solid and tall, wrapped in a dark cape. Her packet tumbled to the ground, precious candles scattering.

"God's bones!" Tanwen said and bent to pick up the candles. So did the man. Their heads thumped together and she fell back, her hands splashing into a deep puddle. Her cap fell off and she scrabbled to cover her shorn hair.

The man was bending over her, stretching out a gloved hand. "Forgive me. Let me help you up."

Tanwen froze. It couldn't be. But she knew that voice. It belonged to Lyr Gethin. She ignored his hand, got to her feet, and pretended to brush off her skirts and pick up the candles. They were mud-streaked and two of the dozen were cracked.

He let her gather up the candles. She rolled them in the cloth and turned away. She felt his eyes resting on the center of her back, but he let her go. She turned at the first corner and rushed down the alley.

Then he was beside her, touching her sleeve. "Mistress Tanwen? It is you?"

"Don't use that name."

He watched her, saying nothing.

Tanwen shook her head and shoved past him.

But he followed. She could hear his boots, so she walked faster, and turned another corner into a calm wide square, where cream blankets on a line hung sagging in the mist. She crossed the square, hearing him call her name. The candles bumped against her breasts, but she couldn't drop them. She ran, down a winding path lined with closed doors, turning corners, heart beating fast, doors and whole lanes rushing past.

At last she halted, breathing hard. She was in an alley, deserted but for a black cat that hissed at her and stalked by, unhappy in the rain. She unwrapped the candles. She'd cracked one more clutching it too hard. But at least Gethin had stopped following. She brushed the mud from the candles. It was getting late. But still she had to try.

She had to ask directions three times, but she made it back to the castle, walked past the guards at the outside gate and stared at the double doors with their twirled iron handles. A guard waited, sword in his belt, under a banner of scarlet silk. When she told him her errand, he wouldn't even look in the sack. "No one to enter, that's what they said."

"But they asked for these candles. They'll be angered if I can't bring them."

The guard shrugged.

"Angered at you too."

"Away with you." He looked up, past her shoulder, dismissing her.

"You must let me bring them in."

His eyes snapped back to her, suddenly sharp.

She backed away, shaking her head.

In the end, she had been lucky. Cook had spent the afternoon preparing a feast of sugared walnuts and tiny songbirds cooked in a dark wine sauce, and he was pleased with the results. His good humor and hearty laugh and the smell of onions simmering in wine permeated the kitchens. No one noticed she was late. Even Maureen wore a smile on her pasty face.

Tanwen ate onions and broth with the others. The hot food made her feel better, though her ankle throbbed from the running and her head ached and she had failed, again, to see Bryn. She ate a slice of hot bread, dipped in gravy. She had failed, it was true, but only in one plan. She must just think up another. As for Gethin, he didn't matter at all. She wondered what he was doing here at Striguil, then shook her head. Whatever his reason for being here, he'd move on shortly.

She slipped from the overheated kitchen back out to the courtyard. It was empty and quiet, the kitchen staff done cooking and the soldiers at their evening posts. She strolled, studying the hall, its five arched windows looming in the dark. Chinks of light glittered around the edges of the heavy shutters. She could hear voices inside. Surely that was where they kept the hostages, why else so many armed guards? She'd been circumspect thus far. But where was that getting her? She stopped abruptly, the image of Bryn playing with his wooden marbles in the garden so sharp and strong she could smell the sun on the clipped grass and the earthy small boy smell of his hair. Perhaps she couldn't get in, but she could look in at least. She must look in. Her hands tingled and her stomach flipped over and she walked toward the doors.

The guards were eating, so she slipped along the wall, feeling the cold from the stones seep through her linen gown, but now she could hear music and fitful bursts of laughter. She looked around the courtyard, but it remained empty, and day was slipping into night. In her grey gown, she was near invisible. She glided along, stopping every few feet, her eyes scanning the courtyard, until she was near. Two guards were talking, facing away from her. A broad rectangle of light spilled across the slate pavings from one of the doors, which was ajar, and from inside, she could hear laughter. She stood, not breathing, listening. But she couldn't hear individual voices, only the roar of men talking. She hesitated in the shadows, hidden behind a stone pillar. Suddenly the door was flung open and two men strode out, shoulder to shoulder. She shrank back. Still, one saw her. He winked as he passed. She looked like any kitchen maid, she realized, going to greet a lover.

It grew dark again, and quiet. Even the two guards had disappeared inside the doors, now shut tight. Tanwen climbed the stone steps and reached toward the handle. She tried one door, then the other. She pulled, and then threw her weight against the doors, but neither would budge. Voices sounded, close by. She stepped back and the door banged open. A group of men pushed out, the smells of sweat and smoke strong. One followed behind the jostling group, a tall man, dressed in blue. It was him again, Gethin. What terrible luck. She tried to press back further, right into the stones of the wall.

Gethin laughed at someone's joke, laughed with her enemies, the men holding Bryn and all the other boys. The men lingered at the bottom of the stairs, guzzling wine from a bottle they passed around and talking. Tanwen stood, her back rigid against the wall. A cat wound between her legs and meowed. She reached a hand down blindly, trying to touch its head. "Quiet, quiet cat," she mouthed. The men had paused, then resumed their laughing and talking. Only Gethin was still turned toward the sound. She stood very still and dropped her eyes. He couldn't see her well, she was sure. It was dark and she was deep in shadows. She stared at the ground, her fingers in the purring cat's fur, feeling his gaze sit upon her. Finally, the men called farewells and ambled away, voices fading. She dared to straighten up. They were gone. The courtyard was silent and it was late. She should go, back to the kitchens.

Instead, she took a deep breath and ran up the stairs and tried the doors again. But still they wouldn't budge. She drifted past the door, to where the light leaked out from one of the arched windows. Could she climb high enough to peer inside? Ivy wound a tracery over the huge blocks of rose stone, the vines thick and ancient. Would they hold her weight? She placed a foot on the ivy, grimacing when her bad ankle stabbed, and climbed, trying not to rustle the leaves.

She climbed the height of a man, even with the bottom edge of the window. The smells of roasting meat and too many bodies mingled and flowed from the room. She couldn't see in, so she climbed higher, clutching at the vines and finding a foothold until she could peer in the top of the window, where a cracked and peeling shutter left a wide chink of light. She strained to see, eyes blinded by the brightness, so many candelabra lit along the walls, torches flaming by a central hearth and brightening the high table. Her candles were a pitiful ruse.

As her eyes adjusted, she saw a room crowded with men, arrayed in bright clothes, lifting sparkling goblets of wine. Her eyes darted from group to group, but these men were grey-bearded fighters; she didn't see Bryn, nor other youths that could be the hostages. Her fingers tightened around the ivy. She searched the room again, examining each table slowly and in turn.

Finally, in a far corner, deep in shadows, she found them. Surely it was them, a group of youths huddled around a low table, ignored by the servers. She stared at each. But one was too old, another too slim, another too big in the shoulders. She closed her eyes and opened them again. Bryn would have grown, in these weeks, and grown thin too. Would she know him? She studied the youths again. Suddenly dizzy, she tightened her fists around the vines. The bark bit into her palms. She couldn't be sure. She leaned against the wall, her forehead hitting the cold rough stones. Rhys' three sons were there, and some others she recognized from Dinefwr, but she could not see Bryn.

She climbed one foot higher and clung and stared in the window again, but it was true. He was not there. She started down, her legs stiff, her stomach aching. Halfway down, she missed her foothold and fell with a loud thump, crushing a bush of juniper, which sent its sharp smell into the air. She lay there, gasping, wanting to never get up. Just then the guards shoved back out the doors and took up their post, one still munching on a chicken leg. She sat up, slowly. She must stay in the shadows, circle back to the kitchen. The back of her head throbbed and smarted. She shuffled along the dark wall, stones scraping her knuckles, and then it seemed she just couldn't move any more. She could almost see Bryn, in front of her, that half smile on his face and brown eyes with gold near the center lit up; she could smell his soft hair. She swayed and when she put her hands to her forehead, it was strangely wet with drops of sweat.

"Keep walking, you must not stop here."

She turned and her shoulder stabbed. Gethin's dark eyes gleamed down at her. "Why not?" she said.

"Don't be a fool, they'll find you here. You're making way too much noise." When she didn't respond, he grasped her waist and hustled her away.

"Found yourself one," called a jovial voice. More men. Pale faces emerging out of the dark.

"I have," said Gethin, "I certainly have."

She stiffened.

His grip tightened. "Pretend if you value your life," he whispered.

I don't, she wanted to answer. But she said nothing.

The men veered towards them. Gethin yanked her to his chest. His lips glanced her cheek and then his lips touched hers and clung on.

One of the men laughed and said, "We'll leave you to it." Their boots thudded away on the stones.

Tanwen tried to push Gethin away, but his arm tightened around her and they stood, body to body. She could hear his heart beating, slow and steady, while her own skittered and her head ached and she could not breathe.

After long moments of silence, he backed away and said, "Come."

She followed. She couldn't see what else to do. Her injured shoulder hurt, perhaps she'd pulled it from its socket. She dragged behind Gethin, who was crossing toward the huge barn that housed the castle's horses.

The courtyard suddenly blazed with torchlight and filled with men, soldiers shouting, and she heard the scrape of metal. "What's happening?"

Gethin was looking over her shoulder. She followed his gaze. Two people were coming down the stairs, pointing their way. One was Maureen, eyes glittering, and the other Cook, looking extremely annoyed, his eyebrows flying.

"You see, it is as I've said," Maureen shouted, her face flushed, "she's meeting with one of them foreigners. She's naught but a slut, or worse, I say, she's a spy."

Tanwen felt all her fear turn into rage. "How can you say so, I've done nothing to you!"

"Enough," said Cook, "I'll not have quarreling in my kitchens. You both do good work, but I've no patience for women's arguments. Clear out your stuff, the both of you."

"Wait," cried Maureen. "You cannot mean that, I've done nothing. It's all her fault."

"You're a viper," said Cook, tugging at his apron, "and likely to spoil my soup with your rancor. I've told you so before, but you cannot change, it's your way." He shook his head, and settled his cap back into place. "I've made up my mind. Be off by morning, the both of you." He continued down the stairs.

Maureen turned on Tanwen. "You'll rue this day."

"I'll be sorry?" cried Tanwen, "you've lost me my position! I need this job, you cannot know." Her head swirled, she put a hand on the stone wall so she wouldn't fall into that void, black and endless. She wanted to curse Maureen with Ceridwen's strange verses, but her throat was clogged.

"Tanwen." Gethin was shaking her.

She shook her head, trying to clear the darkness away.

"She has gone. What is wrong? Are you ill?"

"No," she said. "Not ill."

He waited for her to speak.

She searched for the word, but despairing, desperate, doomed, those were nothing he needed to know. She remembered him joking with the men from the castle. He had been and probably still was Rhys' spy. She shook off his arm and tried to look composed. "I did not want to lose this position, but I will find another."

He took a step back.

She willed him to go further, but he didn't move away.

"Why are you here at all?" Gethin's voice held irritation.

She brushed grit off her hands, avoiding his gaze. The soldiers entered the barn and the stable boys took their horses and dust floated down onto the pavers and the courtyard fell back into silence. "I must go gather my things," she said, and he let her go.

Tanwen entered the attic where the servants slept. Maureen was not there. She had been though, for Tanwen's belongings were scattered across the floor. Her wooden comb was broken in two jagged pieces and her extra gown had dirt smeared across the bodice. Her tiny mirror, carefully wrapped, lay in shards. Owain had given that to her, when he first loved her. He'd laughed and said a comely woman needed a mirror, and his brown eyes had been warm with a light that he saved for her alone. She touched the broken mirror with a fingertip and left it, when she went, on the floor.

Gethin drank the last of his morning ale. The scrape of metal and shouts met his ears. He looked out the inn window, trying to hear what men were saying above the snorting of horses. Gold morning light glittered on the water in the horses' trough. "What's the commotion?" he asked the innkeeper.

The man pulled the shutters closed. "Word is the soldiers are off, with those hostages. Probably farther on into England, poor bastards. Seems things are heating up, there'll be real fighting soon." He gathered up a tray of last night's mugs and left for the kitchen.

Gethin took a last bite of the excellent toasted wheat loaf. He wandered to the door and observed the chaos of the soldiers' departure. Mules dug in their feet, pages lugged armor and shouted messages. In the center of the commotion, a knot of youths clustered, hands bound behind their backs, ringed by guards with swords drawn. Poor bastards indeed. But none of his affair.

He wondered what road the soldiers would travel. If they went north, he'd best press on ahead of them, or they'd clean out the villages of food and ale before he arrived. He climbed up to his room and packed a neat bundle, paid the innkeeper, and complimented his wife on her cooking. She smiled at him, a warm motherly smile that made him feel lonelier than ever.

He mounted Aeron, who skittered at the noises, but settled in. He'd had the horse only a week, but they were growing accustomed to each other, though he preferred a ship any day. He ran a hand through his tangled hair. That was an old and tired tune. There were no ships in his immediate future; he'd lost the chance he had. Now there was only the slim chance of finding good work. He was pinning his hopes on the border lord de Lacy. His castle at Ludelaue needed new walls, so the alehouse gossips in Ilfracombe said, and supposedly he had silver straight from the English king to pay for it.

Gethin urged the horse past the noisy crowd and left the commotion of the soldiers behind, choosing a wide path under the trees along the river. In the coolness, Aeron pricked his ears and pranced sideways, but he got the horse under control and they trotted along, the smells of waterweeds and cedar strong under the morning sun.

Behind them, back at the castle gate, the soldiers banged their swords on their shields, setting up a fearful sudden clamor. The horse tossed his head and shied, and Gethin grabbed at the saddle, but Aeron reared and then bucked him straight off. He hit the ground on his right arm and shoulder, hard. Aeron reared again above him, hoofs swooshing near. Gethin clutched at gravel and tried to roll away. Suddenly his head blazed and he smelled dust and the world went spinning red, then all went silent, slow-drifting white.

Tanwen crouched beside the man sprawled in the path. It was certainly Lyr Gethin. She rolled him onto his back and put two fingers near his mouth. He was breathing.

The soldiers had stopped hitting their shields and the sudden silence seemed to fill the humid air. Tanwen ran back down the path to peer down to the castle. If the soldiers were taking the hostages from Striguil, she had to follow. She could only hope Bryn was with them. She had no other lead. She ran back to Gethin. He could be trampled if she left him on the path. And this was her fault. The horse had seen her, trying to hide in the brush, had met her eyes and shied. He wasn't much of a horseman, she thought with resentment, he'd come off in an instant and now what was she to do?

She took a heavy leg in each hand and managed to drag him a body length off the pathway, behind a feathery bush with yellow flowers. Gethin groaned but he didn't move. Even his lips were pale and a dark bruise mottled his shoulder, where his tunic was torn away. She adjusted his cloak over him, trying to think. She ran down the path to catch the horse, but he cantered out of reach and slid down the steep muddy riverbank and dipped his head to drink. She stared at him and fanned away the midges swarming around her neck.

A rattle of rocks up on the path startled her. She darted into the trees. The advance scouts must be here already. She risked a look at Gethin, still out cold. She tried to silence her noisy breathing and hoped the horse would be quiet or wander further away.

The scouts passed and the path fell into silence again. Sun gleamed off the river and turned the path bleached and white. Tanwen backed further into some brush and hid her white hands with leaves. Soon she heard voices, boots scraping on rocks, marching men. She had to look. Bryn could be with them, he must be with them. Perhaps he'd been ill, or not hungry, that's why he was not seated with the rest last night. Her stomach felt tight and raw. She must know if he were safe, if he were alive.

The soldiers passed, the first few on horse, the rest walking. In the middle, the hostages. They sat on ponies, strung together, a dozen youths with arms roped behind their backs and two women riding together, their eyes glazed and expressionless. Tanwen searched the faces, her eyes darting from one to another as they rode past. But Bryn was not there. Another group must be coming. Or perhaps Bryn was still at Striguil. Or perhaps he'd never come here at all.

A groan interrupted her swirl of thoughts. Gethin was coming to. She thrust a hand over his mouth. He struggled at the feel of her palm. "Quiet," she whispered into his ear. "Danger!"

He opened his eyes and stared. He seemed to be having trouble focusing and then his lids fluttered shut. He slumped against her arm.

Where was Bryn? She sat beside Gethin, her mind flinging in endless anxious circles. The soldiers came on and on and then they were gone and the path glittered hot and silent. Gethin was silent too and horribly still and that was her fault. He might die here in the humid afternoon sun. And Bryn. Where was her child? Tanwen sat until the path darkened with evening and the birds quieted and cold seeped into her legs and up to her heart.

Morning came, a bright and brisk autumn morning when the grim thoughts of night seem impossible. Tanwen hadn't slept much. She felt like an old woman, stiff and aching in her ankles and hips. She turned to see how Gethin had fared. Underneath one barely open eye, a purple crescent loomed. "I see you're alive then." She felt a tiny splash of gladness.

He tried to sit up.

She pressed him back down. "Your head won't stand it."

"Where's my horse?"

"I'll fetch him." It took half a morning, but she found the foolish horse and it finally allowed her to sidle up and catch the reins, no longer amused at trotting away from her at the last moment. She tied him to an oak.

Gethin was sitting up when she returned, a hand on his forehead. If he wanted to kill himself, it was not her concern. She hadn't killed him at least.

"Thank you," he said. He sounded angry.

"For what?"

"It's obvious I required aid, and you seem to have been my physician."

She should tell him she was responsible, but she just shrugged her shoulders.

"If you check my saddlebag, there is food, some oatcakes and hot ale wouldn't come amiss right now."

She frowned at the order, but built a small fire, prepared the food and they ate in silence, the only sound the occasional pop from the fire.

He put his cup down and he did look better, his color more normal under the stubble of black beard. "Now, Mistress Tanwen, you will tell me what you're doing here so far from your home and alone."

"That cannot matter to you."

"Yet still I'm curious."

"My affairs are my own."

"An ungracious response," he said. "Still, when you've unseated me from my horse, I think you owe it to me to satisfy my curiosity."

She couldn't tell if he was amused or angry. "You're a worse rider than I am."

"Why are you afraid of the soldiers who passed?"

"I thought you were knocked out."

"Close enough." He shrugged and winced.

"Your head will pain you for some days."

"Why aren't you with Owain at Adpar? It's not safe for you here alone, surely you know that."

"Of course I know that." She got to her feet.

"You're very interested in Henry's soldiers. Have you a lover among them? Do you flee Owain?"

"I flee Owain, that is sure."

"The borders are dangerous."

Tanwen stared down at him. "So why are you here then? Are you back to working for Rhys? Ever the spy, prying out everyone's secrets?"

Gethin looked away from her, down to the river, flowing silver in the afternoon sun. "This was my home, once, a long time ago." The sentence dropped into the silence. Far above, a linnet trilled, and the sound echoed, melancholy, between the arching trees.

"I can't wait here with you any longer. I need to follow those soldiers. Do you know where they're going?"

He frowned. "They're taking hostages north."

"Taking them where? How do you know?"

"I have heard it rumored," he said, "they go north to Henry's castle at Ludelaue."

"Ludelaue," she repeated. "It's far, isn't it, so far. And I've come so far already." Tears stung the back of her eyes and she turned away.

"Why would you follow? You need to go home."

Tanwen stooped and picked up her bag. "Just tell me which way to go to find this Ludelaue."

"We'll travel on together."

She whirled around. He looked as surprised as she felt.

"You'll get there faster and safer with me." Gethin got to his feet slowly, hanging onto Aeron's reins and wincing. "I have to go anyway."

Tanwen watched him get up, but she didn't help. Why would he offer his aid to her? She didn't trust him. But with him, she would certainly reach this Ludelaue faster. A sudden wind tossed the branches over their heads, rushing through the leaves, turning them upside down and inside out, and sped down to ruffle the river.

CHAPTER TWENTY

G ETHIN CURSED as Aeron jumped and skittered under him. "Not again you blasted beast," he muttered and tightened the reins. Aeron subsided, having caused more than enough damage for the day, or the year, by God's feet. Gethin gripped the reins and frowned. He'd left Tanwen in the woods, well hidden, with stern orders to go nowhere and talk to no one. He was headed back to town to get more food for their journey. Now that he was away from her, he thought with gloom on all the problems traveling with a woman would cause. His head ached fiercely where Aeron's hoof had grazed him.

Returning from the market, Gethin had two sacks of food slung over Aeron's rump, and another packet tied on the saddle behind him. Inside was a cloak, blue-green in color, made of thick fuzzy wool. He'd found himself purchasing it, as though his hands belonged to another mind, the fingers counting out pennies. He shook his head, wondering at his own actions. Perhaps the blow to his head had addled him. But though the days were warm, the nights were dipping close to freezing. He couldn't let her shiver. He'd been the one who suggested they travel on together, but now he felt like spider webs entangled his feet.

When he reached the spot where he'd left Tanwen, he stopped Aeron and circled, then climbed off, stiff from his fall. He whistled into the dusk and heard only his own echo. God's teeth, she was an aggravating woman. He'd definitely told her not to move. He entered the woods and stumbled through the shadows, but he didn't find her. Back on the path, he called her name out loud. He walked in an expanding circle until full dark. His stomach growled and Aeron snorted and pawed the ground, wanting his feed. She definitely wasn't here. Gethin mounted again, head pounding, and headed north, the horse picking his way in dim moonlight.

He found her eventually, sitting on a boulder by the side of the path, rubbing her ankle. "I told you to stay put." She looked up at his grim tone and he saw the flash of her eyes before she shrugged.

"I decided it was best I went on alone, as I had planned," she said. "On reflection, I still think it best."

"Do you now?" He climbed off Aeron and rubbed the horse down with a hank of grass, then tied him to a stand of birches. "Show me that ankle."

"It's fine. Only a past injury." She pulled her foot under her skirts.

He opened his saddlebag and yanked out wine and fresh baked bread, which wasn't warm any more, but still smelled of yeast. He hacked off a chunk of cheese to go with the bread, tore into the food, and shoved a hunk towards her.

She stared at his fist full of bread.

"Don't be a fool, eat. I got enough for both of us."

"Why?" she said. But she reached for the bread. She ate fast. Color came to her cheeks even here in the dark.

With food, the pounding in Gethin's head lessened and his annoyance seeped away. He swallowed more wine and stretched out his legs. "Why leave Owain's cozy domain?"

She shook her head.

"There must be a reason. No sane woman would be out here wandering alone." She got to her feet and he saw a tear rolling down her cheek. He got up too, forgetting to hold his head still, and a groan slipped out.

She stepped towards him, hands raised.

He backed away. "Nothing a few days won't cure."

"Sit," she said.

"You can't travel this road alone, it's extremely dangerous," he said.

"You're the one injured." Her fingers parted his hair and probed, not gently.

"And whose fault is that?"

She studied his skull. "You need to rest." After a silence she added, "I have to go on. But you don't need to get involved. Probably, you shouldn't."

"Have to," said Gethin. "Why would that be?"

Tanwen shrugged. She spoke so low he hardly heard her. "I seek my son."

"Owain's son?"

"Mine."

"He is one of Henry's hostages?"

"Your head will make you dizzy and sick; you must take it easy and sleep." She moved away from him and the air felt suddenly sharp and empty.

Gethin followed her. "How did this happen? Owain couldn't prevent him being taken? I thought he was close to Rhys."

"Actually, he volunteered Bryn. He asked Rhys for the honor of sending his son to Henry."

Gethin hesitated. What kind of fool was this Owain? The silence stretched out, becoming one with the dark around them. Finally, Gethin rummaged in his pack and handed Tanwen the parcel.

"What is this?"

"I saw it in town. You need it. And now we'd best sleep. Tomorrow will be long." He grabbed his own cloak and lay down on the ground.

She sat for a long time with the package in her lap. Finally, she unrolled it and gazed at the cloak in her hands. He wished he could see her face, but he didn't dare open his eyes more than a crack. After another long time he heard her pull the cloak around her shoulders and lie down and eventually he heard her breathe the regular sighs of the sleeping. Only then did he move, to avoid the root grinding into his hip, and sleep himself.

Tanwen woke to the trilling of a yellow bird, swaying on a fir branch a few steps from where she lay. This bird was new to her, something that belonged in this strange border forest. Sun warmed her cheek and single exposed elbow and she felt rested, as though she'd slept deeper than she had in weeks. Perhaps it was a good omen, perhaps

Bryn was close. She smiled, almost hearing his laugh.

A pail clanked near her head.

Gethin stood over her. "You'd best rise if you intend to eat before we ride."

She sat up, breaking the spell. After splashing cold water on her face and neck and gulping the lukewarm oats he'd prepared, he pulled her up behind him on his horse. This horse had a smooth trot, and didn't seem to mind two riders, nor did it tire. The ground passed swiftly beneath them. She swayed as she watched and clutched Gethin's tunic. He grunted and she moved her hand to the saddle behind her. But she felt optimistic, for they'd catch up to the soldiers and hostages at this pace. Maybe even arrive when they did to Ludelaue, and she'd see Bryn, actually see him, after all these long weeks. The sky stretched blue overhead.

Gethin was quiet. Perhaps his head still ached. She felt some guilt thinking of his fall. But if he hadn't fallen, he'd never have taken her with him. The leaves whirring by were still green, but an occasional branch flaunted orange or gold, and the night had been chill. The soft folds of the cloak he'd given her wrapped around her shoulders, the wool tickling her chin. She hadn't thanked him. She had no words. She didn't know why he had he given her such a present, but it was beautiful and she didn't want to think on problems now.

They rode half a day, then Gethin halted the horse in a clearing. "Why stop?"

"We'll catch up to their backs if we continue," he said.

"We're so close?"

"To the second group, yes."

"There is another group then? You are sure?" Tanwen clutched his sleeve. "Tell me." Gethin stared at her hand and she felt herself flush and removed her fingers from his arm.

"There are two groups of soldiers, each with a dozen hostages, all traveling to Ludelaue. The first group left a day earlier and they were to meet up and travel on together, so I heard in the stables back at Striguil. But from their tracks, they're still going on separately."

"I see." She wondered why he hadn't told her all this before. She must remember to be careful.

"We'll rest here and ride again before dusk."

Tanwen looked down the path, smooth and wide. What if she just ran and ran ahead, would she see Bryn? "How long will it take us, to get to this Ludelaue?"

"Perhaps six days at this speed, if it does not rain."

Six long days. She felt for a moment like her chest would burst. But of course she could wait. She had waited so long already. "What will you do when you get there?"

Gethin shrugged and bent to gather wood.

Tanwen frowned. He could at least attempt to converse. "I shall try to get work as I did at Striguil."

He dumped an armload of wood on the ground, but he didn't ask her what sort of job. Or volunteer any more information about the soldiers and their movements. Instead, he pulled a blanket from his pack, lay down, and went to sleep.

Tanwen stared down at him. She couldn't nap, she felt like lightning sparked in her veins. They were so close. She could almost hear Bryn's voice. She paced, then sat on a rock, the dampness seeping into her skirts, and tried to concentrate on counting the different types of mosses surrounding her feet. She willed Gethin to wake.

When he did, he bridled the horse and pulled her up behind him. They rode, as before, through the afternoon stillness and camped when it grew dark. Gethin handed her a cold oatcake and a dried apple. She arranged them on her lap and considered him. "Where have you been since last I saw you?"

Gethin shrugged. "Here and there. Visiting family."

"You have a wife and children? That little boy Sam?"

"Sam isn't my son." He gazed into the woods. After awhile, he said, "His family is dead. I found him." He rubbed his hands through his hair. "I miss him, but he's best off where he is. He's settled. He'll be safe." He frowned and got to his feet. "Get some sleep." He walked off into the brush.

When he didn't return, Tanwen began to get nervous. Shadows had darkened to full night and there was no moon. "Gethin," she called softly. She tucked her skirts around her. The wind was rustling branches. She was only tired, that was all, it was dark and these woods were not her woods. And what did she truly know of Gethin, only that he could laugh with the Norman soldiers who held Bryn, and speak their language with perfect ease. Did he still work for Rhys? Did he spy for both sides?

Finally, her head aching, she slept, slumped against a tree and woke in the morning stiff and irritated, with Gethin tapping at her shoulder.

"You shouldn't sleep like that," he said. "Come, it's time."

"For what?" Her head felt fuzzy.

"Just come."

Her neck hurt and it was hot in the woods already, the sun high. They took a narrow path, barely visible, through the birches. Scrambling over fallen trees, they hiked up, until sweat trickled down her back, then followed a deer trail along the ridge. It was cooler up here, the air smelling of mossy earth. Gethin walked steadily, and the set of his back made her think twice about complaining. After a long time, they reached a flat place ringed with hemlocks. There was a round pool, a flat disk the pale color of the sky. "How did you know this was here?"

"I've been this way before. Hot weather, that means fall will come soon and sudden." He tossed off his leather vest and yanked off his chemise.

She stepped back. "What are you doing?"

"Swimming, of course."

"But…" She paused, annoyed to feel her face flush. He yanked off his boots and set them side by side under an oak draped with rust-tinged leaves.

"Come on. The water is especially fine here."

"We need to be on our way."

"We can't trail them too closely. There's time to catch them up later this afternoon, or tomorrow." He walked right into the water and dove under the surface, flinging white spray. A spatter of cold drops landed on her arm and burned. He rose to the surface, hair slicked to his head. "Come in, it's wonderful."

"I don't wish to."

"We've plenty of time."

She crossed her arms over her chest. "I can't swim."

"No?" He swam to the edge of the pond and stood up. He seemed suddenly so tall, wide-shouldered and muscled. Flustered, she looked away.

"Come in, I'll teach you."

"I cannot learn."

He laughed. "Why ever not?" He shoved his wet hair back. "You must know how to swim. You might drown otherwise, just walking by a stream, or pulling water from a well." He walked towards her, water dripping down his chest. "And what if you traveled in a boat?"

She examined the clear water. Her hair felt sticky and her head itched. "It must be hard?"

He smiled, but his eyes were serious. "You will find it easy."

She looked around the glade, but of course they were alone, the woods silent. The sun blazed on the water, and where a breeze ruffled the surface, gold light flickered. Hadn't she'd always wondered what it would be like, to slip into water, as though it were her world? "Can you teach me to swim on top, and underneath?"

Surprise crossed his face. "Absolutely."

Her feet moved toward the water. This was crazed but it was a magic she'd always imagined.

"You'll have to take off some of those clothes."

"My gown?" She tried to sound calm, but inside she felt shocked and somehow pleased.

"And those boots and stockings. The chemise is fine."

"It is truly necessary?"

"You must," he said, "or the water will pull at your clothing, make you sink."

She pulled off her sleeves and the air ruffled along her bare arms. Her hands reached for her laces and yanked them undone and she drew her gown over her head. He had turned away, pretending to watch a hawk in the trees. She tugged off her boots and tossed them aside, then stepped into the water. It was cold. Grainy sand slipped under her feet. She sucked in a breath and stepped in further. The water lapped around her calves and then her knees.

Gethin reached an arm toward her. She stepped out further, feeling the cold rise higher, up her thighs. His arm grasped hers and he pulled her out to him, keeping her head above the water. "Wait, I cannot feel the sand!"

"It's easier if you get wet all at once, you don't get cold. Don't worry, you can stand here." He set her upright and sand shifted and settled under her feet. The water swirled cold around her ankles and she thought of what might be down there, in the dark.

"I'll hold you and soon you'll hold yourself."

"Don't let go," she said. His arm was hard under her fingers, the skin radiating heat even in the cold water.

"I'll not let go." His cleared his throat and looked away.

She stared at his throat, the dark whiskers, the beat of blood in his neck.

"I'll show you. You stand very still." He let her go and floated up on his back, grinning at her surprise. Sun lit the water drops among the hairs on his chest. "Now your turn."

She bit her lip.

"Take a deep breath and hold it and just relax, let the water hold you up, it will. You have only to trust the water."

Her dream flashed in her mind, water, wavering light, golden ridges of sand. She took a deep breath and felt the water lift her.

"See, you can even breathe in and out."

She tried and started to sink. She flayed at the water, gulped in and choked.

He held her up and waited until she stopped coughing. "Try again, you nearly had it. Breathe calmly, as though you have no cares in the world." His gaze swept the treetops. "Right now, there is no world, only this pond, this water, holding you."

She closed her eyes and felt sun warm her lids and cheeks. Water slid over her throat and breasts and stomach. She floated like a cloud floats or a flower petal twirling along on a slow stream. His hand hovered under her waist, she could feel its heat. She floated and it was true, she had no cares and no worries, only sun and the slip of water over skin.

The screech of a sparrow hawk made her open her eyes. Her legs sank and sand bumped against her heels. Her head went under, but she stood up, unafraid. Water streamed off her shoulders. She touched her hair, slicked to her head like his. "How wonderful!"

Gethin was staring at her neck. He took a step toward her. Their eyes met and her breath caught.

He dove away from her, into the water.

She watched as he swam beneath the surface and broke up into the light on the far side of the pond. "Teach me that now."

"What?"

"To swim like that. Under the water."

He laughed, and for a moment, he looked like a boy and she thought of Bryn.

It took time. They stayed until shadows caught the edges of the pond and the water darkened and grew mysterious and green and colder. But she could swim several body lengths under the surface and break out into the golden air.

He strode out of the water and yanked his tunic on over his wet chest. She followed him, sand shifting under her heels, embarrassed as she realized her chemise was clinging to her hips and transparent. She threw her gown on.

The walk back was uncomfortable. Gethin said nothing and her chemise dripped and the wind had come up. The wet cloth chafed her thighs. And it was later than she'd realized.

In the evening, they traveled for only two hours. "It's too soon," she argued, but he just tied up Aeron and went to gather firewood. Once he built a fire, he disappeared, so she dried her gown, cooked them oats with apples, and shelled some nuts.

When he finally returned, he said, "Tomorrow we can leave with the sun. We're the right distance behind them now."

She nodded, uncertain what he'd seen, uncertain why his mood had changed.

She tried to thank him, before he went to sleep, but he just shrugged and said, "It was nothing."

"It was something to me."

Gethin stroked Aeron's velvet nose; the horse snorted warm air into his palm. The weather had shifted in the night, white frost would rim the leaves in another month.

"Gethin?"

"Yes." His tone made her face tighten, but God's bones, though the woman wore a wool gown, the gusting wind blasted the cloth to her curves. How silky her skin had been in the pond water. He dumped a pot of water on the fire, dousing the flames to a reeking mess. "I'd meant to be on the road long before this."

Thoughts flickered in her eyes, but she nodded. He felt a pinch of regret, but mostly relief.

A short time later they were on the road, the only sound Aeron's hoofs ringing against the occasional rock. The sun hid behind clouds of billowing violet, crowded like those spring flowers in masses across the sky. But the weather was sharp. Wind whirled under their cloaks and he felt her draw closer to his back, but she did not lean against him and he was glad.

By late afternoon a cold mist settled. Gethin pulled Aeron to a halt.

"We're stopping here?" asked Tanwen.

It wasn't a promising spot. Water oozed in the deep moss under his boots and gnats circled his face. He tugged Aeron through the swampy water to a spot under some oaks on higher ground. They cooked apples over a smoky fire and ate oats and onions. Gethin swallowed the hot stew in silence. Tanwen didn't question him about his mood, she seemed disinclined to converse. Just as well.

Later, in the dark of night, Gethin woke, disoriented. The wind was up, and mist dripped from the trees with an irregular plopping sound. But that hadn't disturbed him. Tanwen's pallet was empty. He threw off his blanket. Cold wind hit his belly. God's teeth, couldn't a man even sleep? Aeron whinnied and he crossed to the horse and stroked his neck. "Tanwen," he called, but there was no answer. He thought with longing of his pallet, but he couldn't leave the woman wandering in the night. He shoved on his wet boots, threw on a tunic, and circled, calling her name softly. He didn't need the king's soldiers on them.

When he found her, he nearly stumbled over her in the shadows. She looked like a still grey rock, her chemise just visible in the moonlight. "Tanwen," he said, fearful she was walking in her sleep. He'd done that, and it was terrifying to wake, no longer in one's bed, not in one's right mind, the world of nightmares and daytime merging. He touched her cheek, which was cold.

"Bryn has been gone so very long," she said. "Sometimes I fear…"

When she didn't finish, he carried her back, stumbling twice over roots stretching like snakes out of the half-frozen ground. He built up their fire. Her feet were bare and icy. He propped her up and faced her toward the fire. It was eerie how she let him manipulate her limbs, like she was a doll. The fire blazed up and he could see her eyes staring somewhere else.

"If I could only see him. He must be frightened. He's brave. But a man grown would be scared. And what if he's hungry, or hurt?"

"Tanwen." He grasped her chin and forced her to meet his eyes. "He's in no immediate danger."

Her eyes focused and flared with anger. "How can you know?" She struggled to her feet and he grabbed her shoulders before she could run. He held her tight, repeating her name, until she stopped shouting.

"I'm sorry," he said, "I'm sorry." He put her down on the pallet and covered her with his blanket and she turned away from him and stared into the black woods. Just before dawn, she fell asleep and he let her sleep on, though the sun mounted over the hills, a pale disk behind grey clouds, the day passing by.

CHAPTER TWENTY-ONE

T HE LAST THING he needed was complications, Gethin thought as they rode on two days later. What he needed was work, engrossing lucrative work, and for that he needed to convince the border lord Hugh de Lacy to take him on. He couldn't rely on Enid any longer. He wanted to send coin back for Sam's schooling. Securing employment must be his only goal.

Aeron tossed his head and chafed at the bit. When Gethin heard the gurgle of a stream, he turned toward it, Aeron stepping between the rocks, until they came to a clearing ringed by evergreens. They could strip off the lower boughs and make pallets more comfortable than they'd had in days. He pulled Tanwen down and tossed branches into thick pallets while Tanwen cooked the oats.

"Tell me more about that little boy Sam," said Tanwen. "Tell me where you traveled when you left Adpar."

"You don't want to hear all that," said Gethin.

Tanwen plucked a wet leaf out of the porridge. "I do want to hear. It will take my mind off this forest and everything else."

Gethin sighed. "I've told you already how Sam stowed away and how we were stranded on the isle called Corsica."

Tanwen gave the pot one more stir, dragged her cloak over her knees and looked at him expectantly.

"Here's the story then," said Gethin. "Mario, our ship cook, and Sam, and I hid in the forest. There were strange bright birds darting and tiny fast mosquitoes. They chased us back into the sun. We came out in an olive orchard on a steep hill. Mario pointed to a line of men, carrying scythes and climbing. There was nowhere to hide and besides, we needed water. So I pointed to the seedlings and mimed digging a hole. And we were hired."

Gethin smiled, his eyes watching that far off hillside. "I grew to like the sun beating and the cool water we buried in a flask in the earth and the leaves blowing silver in the breeze that raced up the hills from the sea each evening and cooled the mountain. Sam was given the job of running back and forth with jugs of watered wine and baskets of ham. The workers ruffled his hair and gave him slivers of green melon and told him jokes. At the end of a fortnight, we were given three pennies, three flasks of watered wine, and a long loaf of hard bread. I had already picked out the best land route to Venezia, talking with the men, but even the few who'd been off island had never ventured beyond the ports. Still, we set out. Sam running on ahead. I had to act the sober elder. But Venezia! Where men venture out to all the waters and lands of the earth, and return to set their memories on parchment. I'd heard of their new techniques." Gethin shook his head and tossed a birch log on the fire and watched it blaze up.

"And did you make it there, to Venezia?" asked Tanwen.

"Don't rush my story," said Gethin laughing. "It was a long journey and hard. Mario was always asking, how long will it take us? The first leg was on a fishing ship. We sat alongside a ripe pile of herring bait and rowed into the port. Genova was full of creaking ships and sailors, the bay ringed with multi-colored houses. Women drying grapes on the flat rooftops stared as we passed down the shadowy lanes and walked up the steep hill out of the village. Their suspicious glances made me itch to get Sam away."

Tanwen's fingers tightened on the spoon she was holding so he hurried on.

"We crossed endless hills of olive trees. Once we found ourselves in an orchard of apricots and Sam gorged on the fruit until his fingers dripped and his face was streaked orange."

"Did it give him a nightmare?" asked Tanwen.

"It did. I gave him a cup of water and sat by him until he slept. Mario was off at a tavern, meeting some travelers from his home village. When he returned, I said, we'll be in your home in two days, and he rubbed and rubbed at his long nose and finally said I'm heading south, to Rome. Don't you have family? I asked. I'll be gone in the morning. That's what he said. Tell the boy what you think best."

"How sad," said Tanwen. "I wonder why he couldn't go home."

"No use wondering," said Gethin. "In the morning, he was gone. We each of us have our past. Sam cried, then hid his tears. He watched me filling a pack with olives, ham, white cheese and wheat bread, running a finger along the feather of Mario's cap, ruffling it in the wrong direction. Sometimes I nearly forget the horrors Sam's been through. I realized maybe Sam thought I would leave him too." Gethin swallowed. "And that's enough."

"No, you must continue," Tanwen said, and scooped oats into two bowls. "Don't stop now. You still haven't told me about Venezia."

"Twenty-six days later we approached the city. Heat made the air shimmer and the marshy water of endless lagoons steamed and hummed with mosquitoes. I hardly saw the real place, just imagined everything I would learn there. It doesn't look like much from here, I told Sam, but once we're in the city gates, then you'll see. I'd been trying to speak more to the boy, to push away that darkness wedged inside him."

"Pilgrims were gathering in a long line, ready to enter the city gates, eager to see St. Mark's remains. Or San Marco as they called him. We'd go in amongst them, a boy and a man, nothing to draw attention. Children were rubbing sleep from their eyes and adults seemed cheerful now the line was moving. The sound of voices was good, after the long silence of the mountains with only Sam. We passed the gatehouse and came to the first canal. I swung Sam up on my shoulders and we passed over the bridge, edged with shops selling sparkling chains, and entered a market. Booths stretched in every direction, and everywhere the smell of roasting meat mixed with onions and apricot jam. The noise of shifting crates was overwhelming. We passed stalls hawking eggs, black and green olives, wheels of aged cheese, and plates piled with pink sweets in the shape of moons. I bought Sam a packet of moon confections and he ate one, then clutched the packet tight. Have another, I told him, no need to save them up. We crossed another bridge, with pillars carved into fantastical leaves and flowers, then entered an immense square, filled with brilliant light, so white we blinked and stared. San Marco. Pilgrims who had escaped the venders were hurrying toward the domed church. Across the dusty square the bell from a smaller church chimed. Behind its tower, an orchard stretched and beyond that, the gleam of water."

"That sounds so lovely. I wonder what fruits they grew in their orchard," said Tanwen.

"Is that porridge cooled enough?" asked Gethin.

"Yes, I suppose it is," she laughed, handing him a bowl and spoon, "but you don't get seconds unless you tell me everything about the city."

"We struck out down a winding lane, barely wide enough to walk abreast. When it ended, we turned down another, and another. Shadows and dank water everywhere. Light traveled across the buildings in shifting stripes of shadow and sun and whenever we turned a corner, we found another shadowy corridor, like a maze. Finally, we turned into a square along a narrow canal, green with sluggish water. Long black boats, decorated with bright silk streamers, floated at the bridge, and a cluster of men turned to stare. I greeted them, using Latin. Sam's pale hair and sugary mouth amused them and they brushed candy from his mouth and tugged at his ears. The men knew a widow with a room to let and a youth guided us to the house, with windows on three floors covered with latticework and white curtains swaying. The woman had her son show us the room. It looked right out onto the canal. Sam rushed to lean out over the water. I knew it would stink in the afternoon heat, but there was a bench for my drawings."

"And did Sam ever speak, with all those new sights?"

Gethin sighed. "No. Never. He had purple circles under his eyes. I told him to sleep. All that afternoon I stared out the tall window at the shifting water, murky and green. I remember a woman's ribbon, bright as new silver, floated by. And now I've talked enough."

"Go on, do," she said.

It was a good distraction for her, he decided, so he continued. "Sam was asleep the next morning, when the sun was already high. I paced, wild to get out into the city. When the widow knocked, I asked if she'd watch the boy and feed him when he woke. I got lost only once before finding the central square again. Doves darted in swooping circles overhead. A boy, with a tray piled with lemons, strolled by and I bought lemon juice mixed with honey. Is there a market again today? I asked. Always people are here, they come for the saint, the boy said, and pointed to the church."

"The crowd stank under the beating sun. Mothers sagged in their black gowns and heavy headscarves, and held whining babies on their knees, bouncing them. Children darted around the adults, playing a game and shrieking. Men clustered, faces dark. It seemed they'd been held up three days, no one gaining entrance into the saint's shrine at the church. No one knew why. Everyone speculated, except the exhausted mothers, who parceled out bread dry as crackers and sticky jam made of figs."

Gethin placed his empty dish by his boot. "I found men speaking French and Latin mixed. Merchants, selling wool and timber, buying silk and spices to carry home. They described the layout of the city, but they knew only the markets and places to tie boats. When I asked where I could find maps, they mumbled and found excuses to move away. Finally, one murmured the word arsenale under his breath, before he walked off."

"How strange," said Tanwen.

"This arsenale was a touchy subject. In the taverns, men grew close-mouthed when I asked. You can't keep asking about ship builders, one told me, they keep to themselves and prefer it that way. I wanted to ask more, but the fellow downed his wine and disappeared. After many awkward conversations, I learned the secrets of building Venezia's ships were closely guarded, handed down in families. The shipbuilders rarely came out of their quarter at all, they had their own port, markets, tools. A world unto themselves."

Tanwen looked up with a smile.

"One day I decided to go purchase more of those sweets Sam

loved. He was coughing again, the fever he had in the mountains as we traveled kept returning. As I walked I daydreamed. I'd find someone willing to let me enter this arsenale, someone who wanted to impart his knowledge of maps to someone else. I'd work hard and rent rooms nearby. We might stay a year, or three or four. Sam would need schooling, which could be arranged. Then the scream of a dying horse knocked me out of that dream." Gethin frowned. "Do you want me to go on?"

"Yes," said Tanwen. "You can't stop now."

Gethin swallowed. "A spear stuck out of a horse's hindquarters and pilgrims were scattering to the alleys ringing the square. The horse collapsed to the ground and soldiers, dressed in red and armed with bright-tipped spears, flowed into the square, forcing the crowd of people back, trapping them. I darted past a distracted soldier and down an alley, and another. I found the widow's house. Outside, I stood panting, holding myself up by the wall, covered in some mossy stuff, green and slimy. The widow's son cracked open the door. He called out, and the widow appeared. She put Sam's hand in mine and made a shooing motion with her hands. Her son shouted and threw the silver coin we'd paid onto the cobbles and slammed the door shut."

"Was Sam frightened? What happened then, where did you go?" said Tanwen.

"We walked down twisting roofed alleys. Impossible to keep track of direction without the sun. Sam dragged along. The lanes were too quiet, even for afternoon, and behind the closed shutters, eyes were watching. We came to a lane lined with shops, shuttered. From the painted signs, a street of glassblowers. There were candle-holders, lanterns, even glass creatures, pictured in glowing colors. I'll bring you back here to see the animals, I told Sam. He was pale and I could tell his throat hurt. We passed under an archway, carved with boats, some with oars and some with raised sails. The shutters were all closed tight here too and locked with brass clasps. We were stopped by a canal and had to turn around. It was silent, but on one street I heard a shutter creak and down another, there was a crash, as though a glass goblet fell from a table. We crossed a canal by stepping into a flat-bottomed boat, and then into another, and another. We passed through a second archway and wandered down a lane. At the end, a gate stood ajar. No soldiers stood guard, so we slipped in and kept walking, with damp stones underfoot. I hoisted Sam onto my shoulders. We crossed another canal and found ourselves in a winding lane between tall houses, silent and shuttered like the rest. But above the iron latticework of the shop doors, painted signs depicted scrolls and manuscripts and colorful opened volumes, complete with words and pictures. At one shop, the sign depicted a map of Venezia herself, with lagoons and canals and the big central square."

"You found it!" said Tanwen.

"Yes," said Gethin, grinning and shaking his head. "Deep inside the arsenale, the street of the mapmakers."

"But, why did you leave?" She was studying his face.

Gethin got to his feet and turned away. "All I had to do was wait, in a few hours the shutters would be flung open. But then, three soldiers rounded the corner at the end of the lane, yelling. I grabbed Sam and ducked behind a barrel of slimy water. The soldiers marched along, hitting their spears on the walls, shouting something at each house. They ventured halfway up the alley, then turned back and went on, around a corner and out of sight. I banged on the nearest door. Upstairs, a shutter creaked open and a man peered out. Why are the soldiers out? I asked. Fever, said the man. It comes off the ships or from the swamps. Some summers it comes and others not. It's late this year; we thought we were safe. He leaned further out his window. What's wrong with your boy? He's sick, I answered, but not with your fever. The man slammed the shutter tight."

"Oh," said Tanwen, and put a hand out toward him. Then she dropped it into her lap.

"Five shops down, a door opened a crack. Take this, said a woman. She placed a sack on her step. It's food and wine and an infusion of herbs, have the boy drink. We need a place to stay, I said. The woman shook her head and edged the door shut. I can't do that. Go to the harbor. Ships will be leaving. You should go too. It's no time for strangers in Venezia. Wait, I said, your shop, do you make maps here? Her eyebrows arched up and I saw she was older than she first appeared, with lively grey eyes. We make the very best maps here, she said, the best in the entire world. Everyone knows this. She examined my boots and Sam's flushed face. But what do you know of us? she asked. I'm here to learn, I said. Everything about how you make the maps. I'll work, I'll do whatever you need, anything. You need to go, she said, go now, and come back another time, when Venezia is calm. In winter. The canals flow blue and cold and the fevers are but a memory and then perhaps we will show our maps to you." Gethin tossed a stone at a tree trunk. It pinged as it hit the bark. "I told her, I come from so far away, you don't understand. But a man's voice sounded from deep inside the house and the woman just smiled, shook her head, and shut the carved door."

Tanwen waited, her eyes on him. Then she said, "That's it? That's the end of the story?"

"I found a ship, bought passage back, and brought the boy to Ilfracombe. He's there now, getting schooling." He went to brush the horse with swift strokes.

She came up behind him and touched his arm. "Thank you."

He turned around and stared at her. "Why did you do it? Cut your hair that way?"

She hesitated, then dragged her hood over her hair and walked away.

Gethin stepped after her, then stopped, and returned to his horse.

They ate oatcakes and hard pears in silence and went to their pallets. Tanwen fell asleep soon enough. He got up and paced and made himself think, not about Mario and Sam and the lagoons and canals of Venezia, and not about Tanwen and her silences and how he'd made a fool of himself telling his story to her. He thought about de Lacy and what he could do for him. Yanked parchment out of his bag and sketched. Putting it all down.

And then the plans for fortified walls, and gatehouses with trap doors, and crenellated towers for hiding bowman, transformed into lines and squiggles and shaded hexagons. He stared at the parchment covered with charcoal. It was all there. A sketch as of yet, that only he could decipher. The ridges they'd traveled along, the streams, the springs, the ravines perfect for ambush. He blew the charcoal dust away and rolled the parchment.

War was coming and a map of this borderland, that was something he could make and sell. He went to his pallet, and dreamed he was sinking in a black viscous sea that stuck to his thighs and rose, boiling and inexorable, over his head.

Two days later, the moan of an east wind woke Gethin. Swirling on the wind came the clank of armor and the jingle of horse bits. He moved toward the sounds, creeping from tree to tree. When he got close, he peered around an elm and saw ten armed men, and another ten or more, hands bound, sitting around a smoking fire. Fragments of their talk drifted to him whenever the fitful wind ceased. The bound men were silent, but the soldiers were joking.

"Roger, be quick with that porridge."

A tiny fellow in a green tunic waved his knife in the air. "I'm no cook," he said and the rest laughed. Soon cups were being handed round and even the bound men were given ale. These must be the Welsh hostages. He couldn't make out their faces from this distance, but he wondered if Tanwen's son were among them, or how he'd feel if it were Sam sitting there by the fire.

"Shut your mouth, have some respect for the king," said one of the soldiers. The rest looked up at the hope of a quarrel.

An older soldier got to his feet. "We've got to join up with the others before dark. So get busy." The soldiers scuffed out the fire and the bound men were prodded to their feet.

Gethin waited until they left, the hostages roped together on ponies, the soldiers on expensive chargers, before he returned to their camp. Tanwen was awake, her eyes wide and strained. When she saw him her face cleared. "Why didn't you tell me where you were going?"

"You were asleep."

"Next time, wake me."

Gethin went to feed Aeron, but he couldn't think of any other task that prevented their starting out. Tanwen was sitting on a log, her bundle by her feet. He'd hoped to reach Ludelaue by dusk tomorrow if they traveled hard, but with the soldiers so close, they'd have to wait again. Now it would take another whole day.

"Is something wrong?"

Gethin tossed the rag he was using on Aeron aside and faced her. As he tried to figure out what to say, he found himself thinking about her eyes, how they were not just grey, but flecked with green. And there were also rays of orange, darker than her hair, like sun scattered on a wide ocean. His finger reached out, as though it didn't belong to him, and touched her arm, the soft inside bend of her elbow. He leaned towards her, slowly, until he felt the stir of her breath on his neck. Her lips would be so warm and salty and soft, and he would want to sink ever farther into their depths.

She stepped back, and sharp air blew cold between them.

"I saw the soldiers taking the hostages to Ludelaue," he said.

Her hand moved to her throat, to the spot where her heart beat. She looked past him, into the woods, as though expecting the hostages to walk into their clearing. "Where are they, which way?"

"I heard soldiers before dawn. They had ten or twelve of the hostages, and no, I didn't see your son. But they were talking of meeting up with another group by dusk and going on to Ludelaue together."

"And when were you going to tell me all this?" She began to grab her the cooking pots and his things and toss them together into the center of his blanket. "We must go after them. Right away."

"Don't be crazy."

She stopped throwing his things in a jumble and stared at him. "We could get him away. He must be with that second group. We will get him away. Now, before they even reach the castle. Don't you see?"

"Don't be ridiculous," he said, "there are at least a dozen armed men."

"Bryn," she whispered. "Are you sure you didn't see him? He would be changed, he'd be dirty and thin. You might not recognize him. He must be with them. No, don't say no, not yet." Her eyes were silver-edged with tears.

Gethin felt his throat tighten. He looked away. "Some had no beards. They could have been boys. I couldn't get close enough to see."

"Yes," she said. "It could be him. It is him, I'm sure. Or he's with the other group, nearby." She threw the saddle blanket onto Aeron who snorted and tossed up his head. "Hurry, we must hurry."

Gethin kicked at a stump. "Remember the soldiers. De Lacy's men are notorious." He sat down on a stump.

"I'm going." She slung her bundle over her shoulder and walked away down the path.

Gethin watched her go. The soldiers would have moved on by now, she'd never catch them up on foot. She rounded a corner and disappeared. He decided to wash up in the stream. If he was to reach Ludelaue soon he'd best look competent. He scrubbed with sand and sluiced water over his head. Having spent enough time to sufficiently punish her, he felt a tug of conscience. She was a woman alone. Mounting Aeron, he nudged the horse to a trot. He'd catch her soon enough.

But by midmorning, Gethin still hadn't found her. Sun gleamed through interlaced branches, bare of leaves. A sifting of curled oak leaves covered the ground and rustled as Aeron trotted through. Gethin shifted on the saddle. He couldn't have passed her. Unless she'd deliberately hidden. Should he backtrack? Cursed woman. He should just go on to Ludelaue, she'd be fine, likely, and make it on her own in a few days.

But he wheeled the horse around. Aeron twitched his ears, as if wondering what in the Lady's name he was doing. By noon he was back where he'd started. He gulped some water and whirled Aeron back onto the path. He'd listened to his conscience long enough. She was no responsibility of his. He had a job to get to. His eyes scanned the path for any trace of Tanwen's passage. But she had vanished. He rode on, arguing with himself as night fell, deepening the woods from green to blue to gray. He would make Ludelaue tomorrow, he vowed, even if he rode through blackest night.

Tanwen clutched her cloak, the wool comforting and thick under her fingers. Purple shadows had chased the sun away and with them came her fears. She pictured Bryn's determined face, as he practiced sword thrusts with the other boys in the courtyard at Adpar. Surely that quality would serve him well. And he loved to laugh and joke. The others would like him, he'd find friends, he wouldn't be alone. She pressed her fingers to her aching forehead. How many times these same poor attempts at consolation had whirled in her head. They were losing their power to convince her. But she mustn't falter now; she was so close. Nearly to Ludelaue.

She crouched between two oaks as the wind gusted above her. Branches cracked and sharp acorns showered like winter hail. She hadn't caught up with the hostages, though the path was churned where their horses had passed through. On foot, she had no chance, unless they stopped again. It had all been easier with Gethin. She tugged her cloak tighter around her neck. He'd never said much that was comforting, but traveling with him she'd felt sure she'd reach Ludelaue. Now she'd lost the path. The borders were crisscrossed by trails cut by boar and home to bands of wild men who hid from the marcher lords and the honest merchants of the towns alike. But Bryn had seemed so very close. She could almost feel his shoulder, just where the bones moved under his soft skin. She stared at her fingertips, trying not to think. Later, she huddled in her cloak and waited, eyes open and burning. Finally, as the scrawny moon sank, she pillowed her head on her bunched up cloak and drifted off.

Just past dawn, voices woke her from a confused and anxious dream. She fluttered her eyes open. She didn't dare move; the dry leaves would rattle. Men's voices, shouting, coming closer. She caught a few words, enough to hear they were Normans. She knew some of their language from Owain's table, but wind mixed with their yelling, sending her some of their words and snatching up the rest.

Someone swearing. Clashing metal like crazed bells. Then a long shrill cry. She heard Welsh then, a man shouting, over and over, "Ye filth-ridden bastards." She pushed aside the branches, but she could see nothing save tree trunks and branches and leaves draped and wrapped and fallen over everything. The cry had been high pitched, as though from a boy. She tried to swallow the choking in her throat.

She must be silent. It was the only way to help Bryn.

But she had to see. She plucked the dry leaves from her gown and got to her feet. She drew the green cloak over her hair and hid her white face, parted the branches, and moved like a wood wraith from tree to tree, through the tangled undergrowth, toward the harsh voices. The shouting dropped to murmurs, then stopped. There was a clatter and clunk of hoofs against stones. They were moving on. She hadn't seen them yet. She didn't know yet if they even had Bryn.

She began to run, darting through the trees, desperate to catch a glimpse. A branch raked at her face, brambles dragged scratches across her arms, but she plunged on through thick branches, hearing them slap behind her, careless now of any sound, caring only to get to the voices. She ran until her breath came sobbing and fast and a stitch jabbed her rib, until she couldn't hear their shouts or clatter of hoofs or jingle of harness anymore. She stopped against a huge elm, her hands pressed flat on the ridges of bark, and strained to hear. But there were no sounds. As though they'd all disappeared. As though she'd imagined the soldiers, their sweating horses, the shouts and clanks and smell of smoke, imagined all. A woodpecker tapped above her head and water dribbled onto the flattened leaves and grey rocks and her uncovered head.

After a time, Tanwen walked toward the place where the voices had been. Her legs felt stiff, as though unconnected to her body, and she stumbled over a fallen log mushy with moss and orange decay.

She reached a clearing. Large and open to the pale grey sky, an empty open dome of light with billowing purple clouds piling on the hills to the west. The grass of the meadow grew tall and brilliant green. As she walked, her feet sank into the standing water underneath and it rose cold above her anklebones and drenched the hem of her skirts. When she reached the middle of the clearing, the grass was churned into a mess of ridged mud. It was absolutely quiet.

She walked on, following the path the horses had dug into the wet grass. Her feet made a sucking noise in the mud. She lost a boot and left it. She came to a granite boulder, flat-topped, not tall. Blood, dark and evil, splashed over the boulder top and dribbled into a pool below.

She touched a finger to the blood on the rock. It was not yet dry.

Her stomach heaved and her nose seemed full of the smell of blood mixed with the rot of black wet leaves. Not Bryn, it must not be so. Please to God and whatever spirits inhabited this evil place. She stared at the boulder, her breath coming fast and loud, until she realized, after a long time, that she was stiff with cold and the woods around her were growing darker. Soon it would rain, the deep pouring endless rain of autumn.

She wiped her finger on a tuft of tall grass, retraced her steps, and found her boot. She shoved it on, though it was full of water. In the shadows under the trees, she stumbled often, but she kept going. She didn't know how close she was to Ludelaue, nor if the soldiers she trailed would stop one more night, or press on in the dark. She didn't know if she was following one group, or the two bands had met and merged. She didn't know what she'd do when she found them.

"Stop. Wait."

Tanwen heard the voice and she picked up her skirts and ran. She darted off the path into a clump of evergreens and shoved through. Her skirt caught on a branch and whirled her around and she put up her arms, ready to fight.

Gethin thrust the branches aside. "It's me. Tanwen, it's only me. You're safe. Everything is alright." Though it wasn't, clearly. She was shivering, and blood was dripping from a scrape across her forehead. "Tanwen?" He sat on a rock and pulled her onto his lap and wrapped his cloak around her.

She put her face in her hands and sat there, for a terribly long time.

"What is it?" he said, as gently as he could manage, when he couldn't wait any longer. His leg was cramped. He shifted her weight off him onto the rock and he sat down nearby on the wet ground. Her soaked gown had drenched him anyway. "Did you lose your way? I shouldn't have let you go on alone."

"Blood. Blood on the rock," she said in a choked voice.

He frowned. "I saw it. The soldiers passed through here."

She pulled away from him and wiped her face with her sleeve.

"Owain has thrown in his lot with Rhys; he's more dedicated to Wales than Rhys himself now. He told me, to send our child, it was a kind of glory."

Gethin cast about in his mind, but there was nothing one could say. He cleared his throat and she looked up, but he shook his head, wishing he were anywhere but here. People lost their children all the time. That was life, and death.

"It's my fault," Tanwen whispered and got to her feet, ignoring his extended hand. "Being happy like that, for even one day. Forgetting." She met his eyes. "I need you to help me."

"Help you what."

"Save Bryn," she said. "I thought I could do it, alone, but I can't." Gethin got to his feet. "What you need is a fire."

Tanwen stared at him, eyes huge. She was shivering. He began to pile wood. "You're distraught. What mother wouldn't be? But Bryn is an official hostage, it's a matter of honor, he's Henry's now."

"How could he ever be Henry's? He is my son, and Owain's. But not Owain's to throw away into any danger."

Gethin lit the fire and pushed her to sit by the flames. "You can't get a hostage away from Henry. I'll make us soup, else you'll be ill." When the onions and mushrooms were hot, he ladled stew into a bowl and set it next to her hand. "Look, I'll get you to Ludelaue. Perhaps, once there, you can get some word to your son, maybe even see him…" He shrugged, his back toward her. "I'll get you there. I'll do that much, I promise."

CHAPTER TWENTY-TWO

Ludelaue

TANWEN LIFTED HER SKIRTS as she passed an open sewer. The town of Ludelaue bustled with farmers and merchants, hawking every manner of delight, but to her it seemed grim, and looming over the jovial market square towered de Lacy's castle, her son's prison.

The smell of bacon wafted by her nose, and her stomach rumbled. She was tired, her feet blistered, and her legs ached more than seemed possible. She pulled her cloak tighter around her neck and surveyed the crowds, jostling for a chance to buy legs of venison, game birds with feathers of bright rust and green, and solid wheels of white and yellow cheese. There was wheat bread too, its yeasty smell floating on the breeze and small pies that smelled enticingly of onion. In her pocket were two pennies, enough to buy food for today and tomorrow, but what of the tomorrows after that? She looked at the castle gatehouse, built of fitted stones, its crenellated top lit terra cotta in the morning sun.

"Hey mistress, meat pie?"

A lad with rusty hair and freckles grinned at her. "My mom makes them fresh each day and they're good."

Tanwen couldn't help but smile back. "Yes." She dug out her coin. He handed her a steaming pie and the crust burned her fingers in a heartening way. It was crunchy and bursting with spicy meat and raisins. When she finished, she licked gravy from each of her fingers and watched the castle towers gleam rose, then orange, framed by violet clouds. The colors were lovely. Hard to believe, in this merry town, that the castle served as a prison. The hot food brought her fingers and toes back to life. Her mind too. Gaining entry to the castle had to be her first goal, and finding work her next. She must focus on accomplishing this, though all she wanted to do was run past the guards, yelling Bryn's name.

A man passed on a horse, the shadow falling over her, and she felt the whip of the chilly wind. For a moment, she thought it was Lyr Gethin, but this man was older, and his horse a bay, and his hair simple brown and not dark as night. That she'd been attracted to Gethin was an unexpected complication. He'd been true to his word and brought her to Ludelaue, in record time, as though he couldn't wait to be rid of her. When they'd parted, he'd looked away from her, toward the river Teme, rushing in a foamy wash over piled grey rocks. His eyes had returned to her for a moment, in the barest form of civility, distant and unapproachable. Her words had died in her mouth and she had not watched as he walked away. Did he turn to see her as she disappeared into the jostling shoppers? What did it matter? Gethin was in the past. He'd helped her, for a time, then failed her.

In the afternoon, Tanwen loitered by a market stall piled with sheepskins, now closing. The crowds were thinning and people ambled by, children wailing and ready for naps, men lugging sacks of barley or rolls of thick wool cloth. She had a covered basket looped over her arm, crammed with the implements of her new trade.

She'd spent her last silver penny and it had frightened her. She'd clung to it before dropping it in the merchant's calloused palm. His fingers had closed over it tight, as though he sensed her reluctance. She took a breath, trying to slow her heart. If she failed to get in the castle gate, then she would fail Bryn.

She shifted the basket to her other arm. She'd bought a trowel, a hand-rake, stiff leather gloves, and ten clay pots. She'd come up with the plan back in the forest as she jounced behind a silent Gethin. It was an ambitious plan, wild even, but she'd considered it from every possible angle, and she thought she could do it. She would pass herself off as a master garden keeper.

She stopped in a doorway and tucked her hacked off hair inside a new linen cap, edged with green stitching, and shook the dust from her skirts. Straightening her shoulders, she gave a brisk nod as though to an acquaintance, and crossed the market square. She walked as though she had a right to the place, straight up to the castle gate where the people seeking entry formed a ragged line. Ahead of her two young maids, no more than twelve, giggled together. They wore the huge aprons of kitchen girls and their hands were red-calloused, from days in dishwater and cold air. The girls didn't seem to care, they were whispering together, and eyeing the young man who checked the packages for the head soldier questioning people at the gate. The boy sported a wicked-looking dagger hanging off a belt draped over narrow hips. His face was splotched red, as though he knew the girls talked about him. But his eyes were fixed on his superior, sporting de Lacy's colors with a tunic of yellow wool so fine it gleamed in the sun. The head soldier was questioning an old lady, a bag of embroidery wools over her arm, who seemed confused. His smile was intact but his dark eyes slid over the line of merchants behind her, sizing them up. Tanwen couldn't hear what he was saying, but she could hear annoyance in his voice. She didn't want him irritated, not now. She breathed in slowly and out again. She must not look agitated.

When her turn arrived, the boy rummaged through her basket, then gestured her through. As she started walking, the head soldier stepped into her path. His eyes scanned her torn gown and worn boots. "You're new around here."

"Yes."

He examined her for a long moment, then stepped out of her way. She hesitated, wondering what he might have glimpsed in her face, then went on, as though she knew where she was going. When she passed the gatehouse, she turned, and her eyes met his, still watching. She walked on, as though she hadn't a care. Her fingers trembled as she adjusted her basket higher onto her arm. But he didn't shout or follow. She fell in step with the kitchen girls until they emerged in the courtyard.

Ringed on three sides by timber walls and on the fourth, behind her, by the stone gatehouse, the courtyard seemed immense. Piles of stones along the walls at regular intervals told her they were converting the walls from timber to rock. Two towers rose high on the far side of the enclosure, built of stone and new timber, casting long shadows. Guards stood by the doors.

The kitchen girls disappeared into a wooden building ringed by sheds. Tanwen decided to walk the perimeter of the courtyard, near the walls, while she figured out what to do next. The stonework rose impressively high and solid, and unexpectedly beautiful, shading from apricot to a marbled mix of fawn and mist. The sun spilled light, gilding the puffy clouds overhead. Suddenly, despite the immense stones and the crowds of soldiers, she felt hopeful. She'd made it here, all the way to the English border and Bryn was here, surely, in this very place!

She scanned the twin towers and the gatehouse and the curtain walls, so thick they held rooms and rooms, cut here and there with narrow windows. He was here, in one of these many chambers. She would find out where. She would see him, soon. She pictured him stumbling on toddler chubby legs in the kitchen garden at Adpar, chasing the blue butterflies that fluttered among her white and pink flocks. But no, he'd look nothing like that, he'd be his new tall self, so hard to get used to, and taller still and thinner now, she guessed. He'd been gone from her so long, six wearing endless months. Her palm rested on the rock wall. Warm, it crumbled like beach sand, leaving a smear of orange across her hand.

A voice, someone scolding a servant, disturbed her. She resumed walking, trying to look as though she had a purpose. She studied the walls and the ground, stopping from time to time to assess the sun and shade, but in her head a voice kept singing a broken yet lilting tune… you're in, he's here.

She bent to rub the earth between her fingers and gazed across the dusty length and width of the courtyard. It would be a sea of mud if it rained, but now it was parched into cracked grey lines and pink dust swirled up in the gusts of wind. There were no gardens here. Not even slates to pave the courtyard. No hedges to define peaceful outdoor chambers. No benches to sit and linger in the dusk. Just dust and dry weeds and piled stone. Clearly Hugh de Lacy focused on his fighting. No wife lived here to soften the harsh reality of constant border fighting. Piles of weapons ready for cleaning were leaning against the east walls, with two boys set to watch sitting nearby and arguing. The worn away weeds in a large circle in the middle of the courtyard showed where the men loaded carts and tethered their horses. A few hardy wildflowers, like brilliant yellow stars, brightened the walls where thorn bushes flourished.

But something about the warm orange of the castle's stone made her feel tranquil. A beautiful garden could be created here. The yard was so desolate and dusty that any garden would seem a miracle. If de Lacy had a wife somewhere, or a mistress he wanted to please, she'd surely be in favor of a garden seat and some roses. Or, if she talked with the kitchen maids and cooks, they'd be thrilled to have a thriving kitchen garden. She'd seen only a small plot with wilting onions, struggling along. She could help them grow leeks, mustard greens, even watercress, for a stream crossed the courtyard, diverted from the coiling river outside. She could make a tiny Paradise here and while she did, she would be with Bryn, disguised in plain sight, devising a way to get him out.

"What are you doing?"

Tanwen started and almost dropped her basket. It was the head soldier from the gate, his eyes definitely suspicious now. His large feet, in polished leather boots, were planted in front of her, trampling the tender stem of a tiny onion.

"You're harming the shoots." She pointed to the ground.

He looked confused, but took a step to the left. "What are you doing?"

"I'm viewing the soil."

"Who are you?"

"My name is Tangwystyl," she said, giving him the alternative she'd planned on. "I come to work on the grounds and gardens, and I've seen enough here now." She looked at him expectantly. "Please take me to your lord now."

The soldier studied her, then slowly smiled, showing white even teeth. "De Lacy is a busy man."

"I'm sure he is." She turned her gaze to meet his, her eyes wide and innocent, she hoped. "I need to speak with him. I am an experienced gardener and I've journeyed here to work for him."

"He said nothing to me," said the soldier.

She smiled at him. "I'm sure you have so many important matters to discuss." She waved a hand at the courtyard, where men crowded outside the kitchen building. "Nonetheless, I am here now." She pitched her voice low, so he had to lean in to hear her.

He continued to frown.

She waited, willing herself to exude calmness, letting him think.

"Follow me," he said finally, and strode off.

She hurried after him and they passed through the huge double door of the keep. The sun was shut out here, the long windows shuttered tight. The hall was cavernous and empty and smelled dank.

"Wait here."

"Before you go. Please tell me your name?"

"Raoul." He gave an ironic bow.

"My thanks to you then, Master Raoul." She smiled again and he stared at her, longer than was necessary, then he was gone.

Tanwen shook the pink dust from her skirts and took a deep, shaky breath. Raoul did not return himself, but a boy with brown curls to his shoulders and eyes that matched his bright green tunic, entered the room. "My lord will see you now."

She followed the boy, who couldn't be older than seven, heart pounding and cheeks flushing hot. She must be clever, she must convince de Lacy, lord of this keep, and the king's key border lord, charged with securing and extending English power.

The chamber they entered was crowded and smelled of wet dogs and too many men. A large fire burned in a massive chimney on the side wall and men crowded together, talking loudly and laughing and eating hot cheese pastries the serving boys were bringing, heaped on wooden trays. She walked between the men, keeping her eyes down and trying to be inconspicuous, but this was impossible, for there were no women and she heard the loud silence in her wake.

The boy elbowed his way to the center of the room and Tanwen tried to ignore the grunts and heavy male bodies pressed too close, their bursts of rude laughter and the shoving noses of wet hounds. When the boy stopped, she nearly ran into his back.

"Lord de Lacy," the boy called out and ducked back into the crowd. The men around de Lacy looked up, but no one addressed her. They were joking about some incident with a horse earlier in the day. Hugh de Lacy sat on a wooden stool at their center, drinking ale, and eating a whole chicken, his red beard dripping with grease.

Tanwen felt her heart sink, but she lifted her chin. She'd made it here, to Ludelaue castle, and Hugh de Lacy himself sat before her. She must make him listen.

De Lacy ripped off a hunk of skin and tossed it to the dogs. He had a roughened face with a red scar on one cheek, but many men had scars. It was his eyes, ice blue slits, that made her wonder if she could do this. She curtsied to the floor.

He tossed the chicken carcass toward the fire and yanked her with a greasy hand through the boisterous crowd until they reached a window seat. He thrust her onto it and she sat, her back very straight. De Lacy threw himself across from her and slouched on the thick cushions. He waved away the cluster of men who would have followed. They backed off and it was as though they were alone in the bright light of the window, surrounded by a circle no one could enter.

"So you are the strange woman at the gate." De Lacy played with the ears of a large grey hound until the dog yelped and scooted away. "I hear you're interested in my walls."

Tanwen kept her face calm, but inside she was startled. So Raoul had reported on her.

De Lacy's hand shot out and gripped her chin, turning her face back and forth, scrutinizing it.

She fought to keep her face still and calm.

"You are comely enough, even in that nun's cap. Why are you alone?" He waved a hand and a boy ran up with a silver bowl that gleamed in the light from the window. De Lacy fumbled through the nuts in the bowl and selected a walnut. He cracked the nut open with his fist, ate the kernels and tossed the shells to the snarling dogs.

"I am a master gardener," Tanwen said.

He looked up.

Good, she'd managed to startle him.

"You grow onions and leeks?" He picked up her hand. Seeing the small scars and calloused palm, he dropped it.

"No," she said. "Not kitchen gardens, though I can help your cook grow three times the greens for your tables. I work for noblemen, such as yourself. I make them garden chambers, small outdoor places that are pleasant to sit within, small landscapes to ..."

"There's plenty of landscape out there," de Lacy interrupted her. He gestured to the window, where shaded purple hills climbed one after another toward the cloud-dappled sky. "Why would I need more?"

"It would please your lady wife, when she next joins you here," said Tanwen. "And those who visit you, important men you wish to please or impress, like the king." She saw the gleam in his eyes before the heavy lids dropped down. "It is the fashion in Aquitaine, where I have worked, to have such rooms formed in the outdoors, created from small trees and fragrant bushes and beds of flowers, a place where the air is soft and sweet, where councils can be held, where people can meet, and talk," she said, "intimately."

He raised his eyes to hers, amusement in them now, then examined her neck, where her chemise gathered in small pleats over her bare skin.

Tanwen swallowed. "They call them Paradises, lord. King Henry has need of such places, it is said."

"What do you know of the king?" De Lacy leaned forward and the dogs sat up and turned their blank eyes on her.

"It's common enough knowledge the king will spend his Yule weeks with Rosamund, daughter of de Clifford, this year." She'd heard this gossip in the market. "Clifford's castle is near, is it not?"

De Lacy frowned, his face reddening.

She nearly drew back. But she must show no fear.

The lad reappeared. "My lord," he gestured behind him, and a delegation of three messengers, their leggings muddied to the knees, knelt, breathing hard, crowding the barking dogs.

De Lacy jumped up, already turning away.

"Wait." She stood up.

"I have no more time for your odd notions."

"Let me create some gardens here. They will be useful to you, I promise." She knew better than to stress the beauty; this man would never notice or care.

He stared at her, leaving the messengers still kneeling. "Perhaps I shall," he said at last, a look on his face she couldn't interpret.

"I'm a master garden keeper," she said. "I'll need men to do the heavy work, but not many, two would do, men who can dig and carry."

He frowned, then laughed out loud. "Good then. Make me some beauteous rooms in the out of doors, Mistress Gardener, but you must make them perfection before summer rolls around next."

"Such a garden is the work of many seasons."

"There is no time. The waiting is over." He grinned, his teeth pointed and yellow. "Yes, some rooms of trees and flowers, that would be useful to me. Make it so." He grinned again, and she wondered what he could be planning. "Thomas," he called and a thin man appeared instantly, his fingers black with ink. "Mistress Gardener here will get a pallet in the upper chambers with the maids, her food, and two men to work for her through one year, saving the Yule." He laughed.

"And what of my pay?" She was elated, but a true master gardener would bargain.

He glared at her. "Don't try my patience woman. Oh, give her three silver pennies at each new moon, Thomas."

The man noted it down in a fine script. Already de Lacy had stalked away, his stocky body dwarfed by the tall messengers. She watched until the scribe touched her arm.

"This way." He guided her down a long curving hallway and handed her off to a maid.

She followed the silent girl to a chamber chipped out of the stone walls, high above the main hall and down a long corridor. The room was full of shadows and held six pallets. The girl pointed to one with a stained blanket and left without speaking.

Tanwen wondered who had slept there last and where that girl or woman had gone.

She went to the narrow window. Already it was evening, sun slanting in long gold rays to light only half the courtyard, leaving the rest in blue shadow. How tired she was of sleeping somewhere strange each night. She leaned out. Here and there, a candle lit one of the windows. She examined each in turn, listening to the swallows twittering as they darted over the high walls and the low roar of the river passing along below. The castle was dark and strange and full of strangers. But Bryn was here. She knew it; she could feel him.

PART III

CHAPTER TWENTY-THREE

The Borders, Ludelaue Castle, 1163

B RYN SHIFTED on his lumpy pallet. He could see his breath in the chilly morning air, but the close bodies of the other boys heated the room somewhat. Everyone slept but him. Some sound had awakened him, not the normal snorts and snores. He thought it was one of those water rats they'd seen in the moat, fierce and swimming fast. They had long naked tails and fur matted in soggy brown clumps. In the day, he and the other boys spent hours trying to hit them with rocks. The rats were clever and it was hard to kill one or knock it out. By night, the rats turned on him. He dreamed of their eyes, black and searching, and he lay awake, anxious he'd betray himself by crying out.

Nights were the worst. Bryn turned over and punched the pallet, though it was impossible to make the lumps go away. Somehow the other boys fell into what looked like deep dreamless sleeps, while he came awake. He thought of home, his lost hills with twisty brooks and fish hiding in green pools; his pony's serious eyes and soft muzzle brushing his palm; his falcon, with her sharp talons and striped feathers glinting silver as she plummeted from the sky. He did not think much about his lost birthright – although his mother always told him he would be lord of Adpar someday, he'd never truly believed it. Much could be learned by listening to servants' gossip. To the Welsh he was Owain's heir, but to the Normans, he was that harsh word--bastard.

Wind moaned down the chimney. Bryn heard the first stirrings of the servants. The master of this castle, Hugh de Lacy, demanded his household run like one of those perfect mill wheels the monks made that ground grain into flour with no uneven bits. Bryn threw off his blanket, picked his way around the sleeping boys and felt his way toward the privy. Cold timbers scraped his bare feet. Soon the kitchen fires would be roaring and he might get some food. One of the cooks said he looked like her grandson, but too skinny, and she fed him scraps and sometimes a whole slice of bread or an apple stewed with spices.

He found the privy down the dark corridor, and finished, turned to go. Someone blocked the doorway, a black shape darker than the shadows. Bryn hesitated, then called, "hello, I didn't see you there at first."

The man didn't reply. The shadow moved toward him. Bryn backed up a step, then another, but there was nowhere to go.

Pain shot through his belly. He was knocked to the ground. He tried to yell. A smothering hand came down on his face, grinding his cheek into the granite floor. He smelled the rank sharpness of old urine. He bit the hand and the man cursed, but didn't let him up; he was big, three times his weight. Bryn saw the fist descend and felt a flame of pain in his jaw and then a crack in his right shoulder. Shadows and lights danced before his eyes and he retched. He tried to roll away, but the man pinned him with a huge forearm and slammed a fist into his stomach. Darkness edged its way across his eyes, darkness mixed with sprays of green light. He must get away. This devil would kill him. Other boys had returned, limping, bleeding, unwilling to talk.

The floor was shifting and upending under his back, like a ship pitching. Now there were two men. Bryn shook his head, trying to clear it. A tall knight yanked the devil to his feet and spoke. The big man shook his head, like the black bull in the field at home, and bellowed, the sound ricocheting in the dank corridor. The knight said something more and the big man backed out the corridor. Then he was gone.

Bryn tried to sit up, but he couldn't seem to find his balance. "Merde," he heard the knight say, so he must be a Norman too. Why a Norman would save him from a Norman he couldn't figure out. He curled up on the floor and blackness swooped him up.

Bryn touched his head, which throbbed and seemed to be bandaged. He felt like vomiting but he couldn't even open his eyes. He slept again. And awoke again, and it was blacker than the chapel at home at midnight when the candles had all been snuffed out. He was lying on a pallet, a comfortable pallet that smelled like lavender and clean rushes. Like mother. He seemed to feel her hand stroking his forehead. When he woke a third time, it was day, and light streamed in bright beams that hurt his eyes and set his head pounding anew.

A soft voice said, "There, I'll close the shutters. I'm sure that head must ache so."

This woman had his mother's warm capable hands, but her voice was oddly accented. And her scent was of roses, the way they smelled in the garden when the sun shone hot upon them. He saw her by the window, a dark silhouette as she swung the wooden shutter closed. Her face was very white and her eyes big and very blue.

"Are you truly awake then?"

"I think so." His voice cracked, and he felt himself blush.

She regarded him seriously and came to sit by his pallet, which was raised off the ground on a platform.

"Where am I?" He tried to sit up, embarrassed to be lying down in front of her.

"Don't injure yourself further." She pressed him down. "You're in Sir Geoffrey's chambers. This is where his pages and squire sleep. They're down in the courtyard practicing now." Her voice was lilting and he didn't catch every word. But who was Geoffrey? He was too tired to ask.

He was awakened later by a gruff voice. "Is he ever going to wake up?"

"He already has, but his head will take some days to heal."

"Is he addled?"

"Just tired. He sleeps much of the time."

Bryn stared up into the stern eyes of a knight in leather armor and tried to raise himself to a sitting position. He heard the woman clucking with disapproval. "You stopped the devil," said Bryn.

The knight looked surprised, then laughed. "He is a devil I'll admit, but Nevil is only a man."

"I thank you," said Bryn, "and wish to offer you my services in recompense for your aid." The formal words seemed the only way to offer something valuable to this knight.

The knight stopped laughing and regarded him. "We'll see what can be done. You're Owain of Adpar's natural son."

Bryn frowned but nodded. The woman muttered something he couldn't catch.

"Show some discretion Mariel," said the knight.

She said no more but her agitation showed in her noisy rearrangement of the herbs and medicines on the tray by his bed.

"De Lacy has crossed the channel from France; he's due in a sennight," the knight said.

Bryn felt his insides clutch. So far, he'd not met the dreaded de Lacy, but stories of his beatings had been nightly fare among the soldiers as they'd journeyed.

"I hear de Lacy is coming to escape the king's anger at that archbishop," said Mariel. "Is it true?"

"True enough, though you must not talk of such things, what am I to do with you?"

The woman smiled.

Geoffrey's mouth twitched as Mariel swished out of the room. He gave Bryn a nod and went after her.

Bryn tried to get up off his pallet, anxiety shooting though him, but he couldn't move without setting off a pounding in his head and a stabbing in his shoulder.

A few days later, Bryn perched on the edge of his bed and tied his leggings. His head only ached if he moved too fast. He hadn't seen Mariel today and the knight hadn't reappeared at all. But down in the courtyard he could hear the commotion that signaled travel. He was bored with lying in bed and he wanted some real food. He peered out into an empty corridor and slipped out.

The floor was rough timbers, uneven, and he stumbled. The jolt brought a sharp pain to his temples. He walked more carefully and found himself on a wall looking down on an immense courtyard. A few chickens rooted in the grass near the kitchens, and a horse was tied to the far gate, but the travelers were gone. As he scanned the dusty courtyard, he felt a moment of dread. Was he alone in this enormous place? Then he thought, what if he could slip out the gate, maybe take that horse, and make his way home? He thought of the summer sun slipping down, lighting his special hills orange. He had no idea which way to go, but he could ask. He could find streams for water. Food was a problem. What if he took some food, just enough to last him? That wasn't true stealing.

The only way to the kitchens was straight across the courtyard. He raced down the steps and darted across the trampled grass. It felt like eyes were on him from all the dark windows. The chickens ruffled their feathers and squawked, scattering.

He shoved open the kitchen door, his head pounding oddly. Inside, it was cool and dark and empty. On the enormous table there was a wheel of cheese, covered with a white cloth. He found a carving knife and hacked off several chunks and wrapped them in the cloth. There were pots and goblets and knives but no more food. He noticed a door at the dark end of the kitchen and went through. This room was also empty, but he smelled the sour aroma of warm bread. He edged down the corridor to a chamber lined with shelves. Loaves and loaves were cooling. But what to put them in? He found a discarded apron, spattered with grease like a kitchen boy had worn it turning the spit, but Bryn grabbed four loaves and wrapped them up.

He retraced his steps. The chapel bells were ringing and people were streaming out of the opened doors of a strange round chapel at one end of the courtyard, ladies in brilliant silks, serving girls holding their skirts out of the mud, and knights sporting silver belts. The roar of their conversations mixed with the clanging and spiraled up the tower walls. More and more people came out and three robed priests, lit by the glare and flash of jewels. Bryn stared at the chapel from his spot behind the kitchen door. How did that round chapel manage to stand up? He'd never seen a building like it.

A page dropped a shield with a crash that reminded him he must get away. The crowd was enjoying the respite from smoky rooms and the bright sun shining. They wouldn't disperse soon and already a string of kitchen boys headed his way. He dumped his parcels behind a barrel and tried to look like he belonged.

Two tall boys, brothers maybe, entered first. "Hey, who're you?"

"Sir Geoffrey's page. Who're you then?"

The boys exchanged glances. "Why're you dressed like that?"

"You'd better go get Cook," said one to the other. "He's stealing food, I wager."

Bryn held up empty hands, but the smaller one ran off. Bryn eyed the remaining brother and tried to push past him.

The boy shoved him and said, "you wait for Cook…"

"No," said Bryn and launched himself at the boy. They went down together, toppling a pottery crock off the table. Full of sugar, it dusted the floor and sifted crystals into their hair.

"Now you've done it." The boy struggled to his feet, his eyes huge.

Bryn was already past him, out the door. He squirmed through the crowd, his shoulder stabbing, and barreled into a tall man. "Please sir," he stammered not looking up. "I didn't take anything, just let me out, my mam needs me home."

"Perhaps," said a grim voice and a hand grasped his tunic. "What are you doing out of bed?"

Bryn looked up, into the brown eyes of the knight.

"It doesn't seem like much of a way to thank Mariel. She's had me searching this past hour."

"I'm sorry," Bryn murmured, returning his eyes to his bare feet.

"You will be if you worry Mariel."

"You could just send me home." There was a silence. Bryn looked up. The knight's eyes weren't laughing anymore.

"I wish I could. But there's no help for it, you're a hostage to King Henry, and I'm pledged to him these days, sadly." Geoffrey scowled and spat in the dust. "Hugh de Lacy is back from Normandy." He waved an arm at the throng. "You'd best stay far from his sight. Matters aren't going so well over there. I must return you to the chamber with the rest of the hostages. I had permission to keep you only until you recovered. You could use another few days, but with de Lacy, they'll be no more concessions."

"You're going to take me back?"

"I must. Don't think of escaping. The king's men would hunt you down, with hounds, and shoot you with their bows like a hart in the woods. Then they'd send your chopped off hands as a message to your father."

"That wouldn't matter much to him."

Geoffrey was silent. Then he sighed. He pulled a long gold and black feather from his sleeve. It dangled on the end of a worn string. "Look here. If you have need, find a way to slip this to me. I will try to help, though I can make no promises, nor will I go against my pledged word."

Bryn took the feather. He touched the fringed curling tip and wondered at the brilliant bird that had carried it. Where was that strange bird now?

He followed Geoffrey across the courtyard and back down a long corridor to the dim chamber that formed their prison. Doves cooed up in the beams and dust drifted in the light from the single window near the ceiling. Nevil lurked by the door. Bryn hesitated, but Geoffrey put an arm over his shoulders and walked with him past the guard, past Nevil, and into the room.

Nick ran up. "Where have you been? It's been days." Smiling widely, he handed Bryn a piece of mashed cheese. "Saved it for you."

Geoffrey leaned over the boys. "Keep your heads down and stick together."

Bryn watched Geoffrey walk out. He tucked the feather inside his sleeve and eyed Nevil. He stayed put, by the door, for now.

A month later, Bryn loped along behind Geoffrey, a dulled sword gripped in two hands, as they left the noisy clanging of the practice area behind. "I can swing it faster than yesterday."

"Maybe," Geoffrey said, as he trudged, two oak shields slung over his back. "But accuracy matters more."

"I wish we could stay out longer."

"You know well I must return you by noon."

Bryn lowered the sword. "I know. But tomorrow, we can practice again? And can Nick come too?"

"I'll do what I can." Geoffrey's face was stern but his eyes smiled.

Bryn whirled, swinging the sword. His wrists stuck out from his sleeves and his legs had grown. He felt new muscles moving.

"Enough." Geoffrey took a step back as the wild swinging ranged close.

Bryn flushed and shoved the sword in its scabbard.

Geoffrey just shrugged. He didn't even look mad. Bryn thought of Owain, how his eyes were always distant. They walked along, Bryn trying to match his stride to Geoffrey's. "Why do you help me?" he asked.

Geoffrey shrugged. "I don't know." He walked more slowly. "I had a brother, a small brother, your age about."

"What happened to him?"

"He died."

"How? Was he your page?"

"You ask too many questions," said Geoffrey. He picked up the pace and Bryn had to jog to keep up. "I could eat two sheep, how about you?" asked Geoffrey after a while.

"Ten!" Bryn leaped up to rip the leaves from an apple tree. For the last three days, he'd been allowed out to practice with de Lacy's pages outside the castle walls. He didn't know how Geoffrey had managed it, but getting out of the smoky crowded room where the hostages lay around, playing chess and strumming lutes and arguing over any trifle seemed a miracle of freedom. Bryn sucked in air, bright and sharp. He jumped over a log and yanked the last yellow birch leaves from a dangling branch.

Geoffrey laughed and cuffed him on the shoulder. They reached the kitchens, where smoke seeped from the thatched roof along with the delicious smell of sizzling fat. They'd slaughtered the pigs last week and even the hostages had feasted one night on fresh meat, the first in weeks. Geoffrey stopped to talk to the grooms and Bryn ran ahead and set the sword in the rack by the door. He raced up the steps.

"Bryn!" a voice whispered.

He stopped, his hand on the door. A woman moved from the blue shadows into the light.

Bryn's blinked twice, but it was true, she was there, real, holding back tears, her hands on her cheeks, her face thin and very white. "Mother!" He hugged her and the familiar lavender scent of her hair made his eyes smart and water. She felt thin and fragile in his arms. He blinked hard and stepped back.

She was smiling now, laughing, more her real self. "Bryn! It is you. You've grown so very tall. How glad I am." She took his two hands and examined him, smiling and shaking tears away at the same time, as though he was exactly as she'd hoped. Suddenly she stopped smiling and her eyes searched the courtyard and she dropped his hands. "No one must know who I am Bryn, or that I'm even here."

Bryn looked around, but even Geoffrey was still talking to the grooms. He put his fingers through the belt Geoffrey had given him to hold up his sword. "Don't worry. I'm very glad you're here."

"It could be dangerous, if anyone knew." But she reached out again, as though she couldn't help herself, and touched his cheek.

He felt hot color flood his face. "But what are you doing here? How did you come? Is my father here? Am I to be released?"

"No. No." She withdrew her hand. "I came alone."

"Alone…" Bryn stopped, thinking of his own trek through the swampy woods and across the flooding streams and over the wild mountains. "How…"

Geoffrey's yelled over to him. "We need to get you back Bryn."

"Coming." Bryn leaned over to hug her, then remembered he shouldn't. He took an awkward step back.

"Tell him nothing, do you understand?" whispered his mother. "I'm here, but you must pretend not to know me, and Bryn…"

"I'm glad you're here. Very glad." He picked up the heavy sword. "I have to go now. Will you be here tomorrow? They'll let me out every day until it snows, Geoffrey says. For two hours at midday. Don't be sad."

Tanwen bit her lip as Bryn walked away. The knight, the one he called Geoffrey, looked over, but she turned aside and watched out of the corner of her eye as they entered one of the two towers, where she could not follow.

She walked off in the opposite direction, blindly. Bryn, her boy, her lost child. She'd found him. Yet how old he'd seemed, almost a stranger, with dark wary eyes. She could feel the trembling of his cheek under her fingers. She longed to hug him and never ever let him go. But she must not show she knew him; no one must know. How thin he'd grown! How long she'd waited for this exact moment and now it had come and passed again so very quickly. She stopped walking. It was hard to draw a breath. She felt she'd imagined it all. She put her fingers to her eyelids and pressed, willing the tears away.

"Mistress Gardener, are you well?"

Raoul, de Lacy's captain, stood in front of her on the path. She let her hands drop and wrenched her mind away from Bryn. "Yes, I'm well, just something, dust perhaps, has blown in my eye."

When she said nothing more, he pointed toward the stables. "I've brought you two men for your gardens. They can work for you days and sleep in the barns."

"Thank you. And perhaps you'll know also where I might find a ready source of seeds?"

"The men will know." He started to walk toward the stables and she followed. "You were talking with that boy."

Tanwen felt her breath stop but forced herself to keep walking. "Yes?" She hoped she sounded unconcerned. "Who is the tall man he was with?"

Raoul glanced her way. "Geoffrey. A landless knight. A younger son from the north country. He should have gone into the church." He entered the barn.

Tanwen followed, hoping she'd distracted him. Perhaps she had; he'd sounded chagrined.

Her two men turned out to be a father and son. The older man was strong looking, with sparse hair and one hand missing fingers. He saw her glance. "Lost it in the fighting, but I can still work," he said. The son was young, but tall, with thick hair tucked under a strap of leather round his head.

Raoul observed her too closely.

"Do you require anything else?" she asked, hoping he'd go on his way.

He snapped his finger to a passing boy, who ran off to fetch a horse. "I look forward to seeing your creations. Mistress Gardener." He gave her an ironic smile and leaped on his horse.

She watched him ride away, then turned back to the two men.

The father said, "If it's seeds you're after, it's a wise woman you want. Helori, she's the one. She lives in the woods. If we go now, we can return before dark."

They rode short ponies, their feet trailing near the ground. On the road through the village, and the path through the birches and down through an oak forest, rust leaves rustling in the sharp breezes, the man and his son were silent. Tanwen was glad, as it let her think. She went over and over the moment of meeting Bryn. He'd had bruises on his arms. He was too thin. She'd have to find a way to get him food. But he was alive. He was alive. She'd seen him. She would see him again.

The men led her to a clearing, watered by a fast running brook, and under a tall oak hung with maroon leaves was a house. "She's in there." The old man sat down on a log and his son dropped to sit at his feet. "Helori doesn't like menfolk. You'd best go in alone."

Tanwen gazed at the cottage, its roof of golden thatch reaching to the ground, its door shut. She threaded through the waist high grass and before she reached the door, a tall woman emerged, dark-haired and barely older than her.

The woman drew her inside the house, filled with the smell of warm bread. Tanwen's eyes adjusted to the dim light. Charts and brushes and papery bulbs were heaped everywhere. Rushes piled on the floor smelled of fresh hay and mint, and a large book was open on a chest in the light of the only window.

The woman waited until Tanwen took in the room's contents. "It's not often I'm privileged to meet a stranger. Where are you from? So discourteous of me, but I'm curious."

Tanwen sat on the offered stool by the fire and watched the woman move some bowls off the only other seat. Like Ceridwen, she seemed calm and sure. Even the smell of the cottage was the same. Tanwen smiled at the fire, and felt something tight in her relax. Where was she from? Where was her home? In truth, she was in limbo, suspended between her past life and whatever was to come.

Helori was watching her face. "Well, I see you like my home," she said, stirring up the fire and bringing over two steaming bowls. "I'm glad." The broth was full of beans and leeks, and spicy with pepper.

Tanwen ate, then set the bowl down. "I've sought you out because I must create a garden, not an ordinary garden, something unique."

"Ah," said Helori, her spoon in the air. "Where are you making this garden?"

"At Ludelaue."

"Not an auspicious place."

"No, but I must change that." Tanwen noticed her fingers twisting her skirts and relaxed her hands. "It's important."

Helori picked up their bowls and rinsed them out. "Ludelaue is a place of danger."

"Is that why you live here, so far away?"

"In part."

"I need seeds. I can get them in the woods, but it would take more time than I have. And I don't know when the snow will fall. De Lacy has set a deadline. The gardens must be ready next summer."

"He is a hard man. He will hold you to it."

"And gardens do not always follow a timeline. Nor do I know the weather here, in your hills. Nor am I even a gardener, if the truth be told." Tanwen bit her lip, thinking she'd said too much.

Helori put a hand on her arm and stared away out the window. After awhile she said, "Why did de Lacy agree to an ornamental garden at all, that's what I'm wondering. He has no eye for beauty, nor cares about anything but power."

Tanwen hesitated. "I think his captain, Raoul, had something to do with it."

"Ah." Helori stood up. She opened a small door, hidden by a curtain of patterned wool, and murmured, "Come then."

Tanwen entered another chamber, even smaller, more a large cupboard. There were jars of pottery and thick green glass, labeled with flowing brown-inked script. The room was dark, but Helori picked jars from the shelves without hesitation. "You're not frightened."

"My grandmother, she had a chamber of herbs like this."

Helori handed her a heavy jar. Together, they sorted the seeds on her table and labeled the packets.

"It is quiet here," said Tanwen.

Helori's hands paused and then resumed packaging the seeds. "Generally that is good."

"It can be lonely among people too. Perhaps I could return?"

"I would welcome you."

"De Lacy has given me funds for the gardens." Tanwen took a few coins from her gown.

Helori paused in filling the last jar. "I'll accept some payment, if it comes from him."

Tanwen wondered what she meant. She placed the coins in a small stack on the table and ran a finger over the waxed surface, smelling of summer and honey.

"You must take care," Helori said, as Tanwen put on her cloak. "De Lacy is like all the border lords, a dangerous man, full of temper, and certain he is always right." She plucked a sprig of rosemary.

"Perhaps when you return, you'll want to tell me more."

CHAPTER TWENTY-FOUR

GETHIN LINGERED by the narrow window in the chamber he shared with a dozen others, mostly masons working on the walls, and one nervous priest, who spent hours each night fingering his beads. The day was gray and an early dry snow sifted down. Two months had passed since he'd reached Ludelaue and he was no closer to his goal of convincing de Lacy to take him on. Down in the courtyard, he could hear de Lacy bellow. Gethin muttered a curse and the priest looked up.

"It's nothing," said Gethin, turning away from the priest's avid stare. He surveyed the hills, half-obscured with snow, his fingers drumming on the windowsill. November was just difficult, and last November had been so very different, out on the Mediterranean with small Sam, the aqua sky swirled with fat rosy clouds. Out there, enveloped in clear air, there had been whole days when he'd thought of Julianna not at all. Was he being punished, for forgetting?

Gethin headed for the door. He needed to lose himself in work, and since he had none that paid, he'd devised some of his own. He'd wheedled permission from de Lacy's clerk Thomas to check the ancient chests, looted from an unfortunate abbey, and he'd pulled out eight maps of the surrounding area, of varying size and quality. He'd set to work with high hopes, but they were contradictory and flawed. He could do better, if de Lacy would just give him the funds.

Outside, Gethin took a narrow path shoveled through the drifts. Half way along, he was startled from his thoughts.

"So we meet once more," said Raoul, genial as though they were still drinking ale in that tavern in western Wales. "You've been wondering, I'll wager, if I recognized you."

Of course he had recognized Raoul right away. Gethin thought again of that Welsh guide, dead in the woods, and tried to keep the thought from his face. He nodded silently and stepped into the snow to go around Raoul.

"A moment," said Raoul, blocking his path. "Your work can wait that long." His sword clunked against a polished boot.

"It can't, actually," said Gethin.

"And what is so urgent?"

A boy with a red nose ran up and spit out his message, interspersed with coughs. "A scout has arrived, captain. He awaits in the great hall."

Raoul looked annoyed, then put on a smile. "As you see, I'm busy. But we'll converse again, soon. Seeing as neither of us is exactly what we seemed."

Gethin watched him go, disquieted in spite of himself. Perhaps he should abandon this castle, try somewhere else. De Lacy had the most coin on the borders, it was said, but others could use his services surely. He could even go to London, as he'd first planned. He started walking again, thinking about the risks, kicking at the snow. But soon, he was thinking about de Lacy's maps again. He hated to leave before finishing with them. They'd been stored in a dank corner of de Lacy's seldom used library, above the chamber housing the hostages. He hadn't been able to persuade Thomas to move them somewhere dry, much less admit him to de Lacy's presence. He had no coin for a bribe and anyway, the clerk seemed to live only for de Lacy's approval.

Up in the musty chamber, Gethin lit a candle and pulled out one of the maps and untied the leather strings. This particular map was old, perhaps drawn two centuries ago. He wondered about the hand that had inked the wavering brown lines. Had it belonged to a monk, or a knight, to someone young or old? He spread the map before him on the table and weighted down the corners with four brass orbs. The map was square and quite detailed, but limited to the castle and burgh, even the hills represented with simple mounds and named "the dark and endless forests." De Lacy would never be moved by curiosity or seek out knowledge of places far away, but a map of the mountain passes and the route to the southern coast, now that was strategic knowledge, useful to a border lord, especially with war looming. He took out another smaller map and frowned over it. He found it sloppy, badly drawn, lines of ink wandering on the parchment in a pattern neither beautiful nor useful.

"You'll not find what you seek that way."

A woman, dark-haired and sleek, walked toward him. He hadn't heard her slippers on the stairs.

"You've been staring at these maps for a very long time." She traced a finger along the edge of the map, making him notice the large aquamarine on her white finger.

"Yes." Impatient as he was to keep working, he'd better be polite; she was probably wife to someone important and he was here, after all, to secure work. "My name is Lyr Gethin," he said and bowed.

She gave him an amused glance. "I know that, of course. What is it you look for?" She slid around, so his view of the map was blocked by her hips.

He pointed to another of the maps and unrolled it for her. "This map portrays the coast of Brittany, but with many mistakes, places badly detailed or in outright error."

"And badly drawn I see." She pointed to a blot and smiled, tipping her head back.

"Yes." He turned his eyes away from her white neck. "Badly drawn. Though perhaps it was done by a sailor, with little experience of pens and inks, or the roll of waves to contend with."

"Why does he make a map then? It's work for monks, is it not?"

"Usually," said Gethin, his attention caught by an arrow drawn to a cove near the farthest tip of land, pointing towards England. He longed to flip the map over, see the explanations.

The woman tapped her fingernail on the table and pulled up a stool. "You haven't asked my name, and I'm hurt. But I'll tell you. It's Isolde."

De Lacy's natural sister, and only recently come to live at his newly acquired castle. So Gethin pushed the map aside and chatted with her for an eternity, until she stood up, still smiling that cat-like grin. She was regarded as a beauty, but he didn't like those brilliant eyes, so black they seemed to have no center.

Yet when she'd gone, he couldn't settle back into his work. An hour passed unproductively and the winter light failed. Gethin put the maps back in the chest, shut the creaking lid and went out into the cold. The bulk of the snow had stopped, though a few flakes fluttered down.

As he scuffed along, his eye caught a flash of green in the white and grey. A woman in a green gown was standing, very still, staring up at the castle walls. Gethin hesitated, but found his legs heading towards her. Green, like spring waves rolling, or lush summer in the hills. He'd told himself to avoid her, and he hadn't spoken with her since the day they'd arrived at the castle and gone their separate ways. But somehow, she'd managed to get in to de Lacy. He needed to swallow his pride and find out how, that was all.

The wind carried the crunch of his footsteps away. Tanwen's eyes remained fixed on the walls. He stopped a man's length behind her. Ice crystals formed fantastic stars on her dark cloak. He was glad he'd bought it for her. He cleared his throat.

She whirled around. "Oh, it's you."

"What are you looking at? Haven't you noticed it's snowing?"

"You've decided to speak with me then? I find that strange."

He shrugged. "You're looking at a blank wall. I'm curious, that's all."

She turned her eyes back to the wall. "Perhaps I see something else."

"Do you? What?"

She blinked, her eyelashes catching snowflakes. "I don't see why I should tell you, but I will. I see summer."

He considered that. "Were you happy then, in summer?"

She looked at him so long, her brows drawn together, that he thought she wouldn't answer. Then she said, "Once."

"So?"

She brushed the snow from her sleeves. "So I've taken on work as a master gardener. Hortolanus to be precise. I'll be making a garden right here, and I'm thinking of what it must look like by next summer."

"Must?"

She hesitated. "There's a necessity to it."

Gethin kicked at the snow, exposing the pile of dark earth she'd had carted in. He didn't wish to know her problems. He'd feel responsible, like he had to fix things. He'd heard she was hired as a garden keeper, and he'd seen her fiddling with ferns and herbs in the forest, so probably she could fool de Lacy for long enough. "So what will this garden look like, by next summer?"

Tanwen turned, surprised at the odd catch in his voice. He sounded annoyed, even angry. He was staring at her, ignoring the sharp wind, his eyes like a dark night, empty of stars. She shook the image away, annoyed that it made her care, and pointed. "Here, cypresses. They grow as tall spires reaching upward and their green is very dark and mysterious."

"I've seen them."

Tanwen wondered if he had and where. Owain had bought her two to plant at Adpar, from some passing crusaders, burnt dark by sun and limping with old wounds. "At their feet will be beds of ivy, sprinkled with white periwinkles. Also, jonquils scattered throughout, of a variety that is palest yellow, like sparks of sunshine."

He nodded, and half smiled.

She cleared her throat, embarrassed, but he seemed interested. "And over here," her arms traced a wide half circle, "I'll plant a wall of spiky holly and it will form a secret chamber, out of doors. There will be seats of turf and moss, and around the perimeter will be white roses and iris, so their mingled scent will float and linger on the air." A gust of wind whipped her hood off. She pulled it back on and laughed. "I've learned a great deal from Helori, a wise woman who lives in the forest."

He smiled then, a true smile. He was handsome when he wasn't scowling, though his nose was long and thin, and his brows so very dark. He must have been a carefree boy once, like Bryn once, before all this happened. Her eyes went to the tall windows, shuttered tight, where Bryn and the other hostages were held. She'd managed to speak with him a few times. It was wonderful to know he was alive, but nearly impossible not to grab him and run. She was working on a plan. They needed a way to get out, but also a way to get home, and a place to hide while she worked on convincing Owain.

"Tanwen." Gethin had an odd way of hesitating on the last syllable of her name. "Thank you."

She blinked and looked at him. "For what?"

He just nodded and walked away.

She sighed. He had the unwelcome power to unsettle her with a few words. She grabbed her shovel and started spreading out the pile of earth streaked with aged manure.

A week passed and Tanwen knelt in her plot, arranging smoothed stones carted up from the river, inventing patterns, wondering which would look best. She loved these morning hours in the garden. It felt like she entered another world, where time didn't pass nor worries accumulate and she could ponder and dream and entice something to emerge from nothing. It was a kind of enchantment. But when the morning hours fled and she trudged in to the midday meal, all the worries came flooding back. The hostages were guarded well, and though she rejoiced that Bryn was fed and housed, she hadn't come up with a way to get him out.

"This might help."

Tanwen looked up. Gethin was standing just beyond the rectangle of turned earth, holding out a packet. His ears gleamed red in the cold wind. "What is it?" she asked.

"Parchment and charcoal. I thought you might use it to draw your designs," he said, not meeting her eyes. "It might be warmer than doing it out here, on the ground." He shrugged. "I divided the parchment with ruled lines, in a grid, so you can make a correspondence, you see, an inch for a foot perhaps."

Tanwen hesitated, then took the packet from him. She unrolled the parchment and examined the straight inked lines. She could try out different ideas and get a sense of how they'd look together, an idea of balance. She had a thought of translating the intertwining pattern of her silver brooch into plants and paths. She smiled. "Indeed, this will be useful."

He turned away, then turned back, kicking at the ground. "I've been meaning to ask you, how did you manage to get an audience with de Lacy?"

So that's why he spoke with her. "De Lacy's captain arranged it. His name is Raoul. I believe he oversees everything for de Lacy."

Gethin frowned. "You should have nothing to do with him."

"That's not your concern." Tanwen rolled up the parchment and held it out to him.

"It was a gift," he said, and walked away.

That night, when the other women slept and she lay awake as always, Tanwen lit a candle. She picked up a stick of charcoal and began to sketch. The lines crossed and linked and locked in intertwining knots, like her life and Bryn's, as though there existed a pattern, waiting somehow in her fingers to be drawn out and made real, a way out.

CHAPTER TWENTY-FIVE

DARON THRUST her last coin into the grimy hand of the boy selling biscuits. Her stomach rumbled as he opened his basket. She almost grabbed the fat biscuit and he gave her a disapproving look before shouting for more customers. It had been frightening and exhausting, traveling for days with only Owain's two men for company, the creeping dark woods enveloping them in ice and silence. As soon as they'd reached Ludelaue town, the soldiers had left her. Orders from Lord Owain, they'd said, when she protested and cried. So here she was, in a doorway overlooking the market. How much trouble Tanwen had cost her. But the biscuit was hot on her fingers and left a delightful smear of melted butter on her palm. Encouraged, she left the doorway and strolled, admiring the cloth and deep baskets sold in the market stalls. Soon, after a quick look around, she'd find Tanwen, and then her troubles would be over.

She stumbled over a loose cobble and landed against the hard arm of a soldier.

"Watch your step. I mean, pardon, mistress," said the soldier, seeing first her face and then her stomach. He backed away.

She snatched her cloak around her belly.

"Wait," he said, but she hurried on, heart pounding. Every soldier looked like Huw. But he'd never leave Rhys. He had his duty, as he'd said, so many times. She need have no worry of meeting him, nor hope.

Ludelaue's towers loomed above the square. Norman soldiers swarmed at the gate and Daron hesitated, but of course there were soldiers guarding the gate. She crossed the crowded square, picking her way through icy puddles. A guard assessed her with lazy eyes, and gestured her through. But when she reached the bottom step, a second soldier stopped her and asked her business.

"I seek my cousin."

"Name?" He slapped a glove against a hard thigh.

"Her name is Tanwen. I have a message for her."

"Tanwen. You are sure." The soldier waited, expressionless.

Daron picked at the strings on her cloak and willed him to let her through. "Of course. She's expecting me," she added, worried suddenly he wouldn't let her in.

"You come from Ceredigion?"

"Yes," said Daron. "How do you know?"

The soldier's eyes flicked over her. "This Tanwen, what does she look like?"

"She is tall and red-haired."

"There is no one here by that name. But we won't put you out, perhaps this cousin of yours will arrive soon."

"I thank you." Daron pressed her trembling lips together. She picked up her bag and followed him into the huge keep, feeling small and overwhelmed.

He pointed to a dark winding stair. "You can sleep up there for the time being."

She climbed and found a dark chamber, crammed with pallets. She placed her things on one of the beds and when no one came, lay down. She was tired and her swollen legs ached and she'd expected to see Tanwen right away. Tears seeped from her eyes.

When Daron woke later, in the dark, a woman crouched beside her. "You are here!"

"Hush." Tanwen looked around, but the women on the other pallets slept on. "Don't cry, whatever is wrong? How do you come to be here Daron? Imagine my surprise when I saw you here in my chamber!" She hugged her cousin. "It's so very good to see you."

Daron clung to her and sniffed and they both laughed. "I'm so glad I've found you, that man at the gate was frightening and he said you weren't here."

"Which man?"

"He had dark eyes and a very disapproving way. But he let me in even though he claimed he didn't know you."

Tanwen gripped her hand. "Did you ask for me, by name?"

"Of course."

Tanwen dropped her arm.

"Did I do wrong?"

"It's done now," said Tanwen. "I've been using the name Tangwystyl here. They know I'm Welsh, for I can't conceal my way of speaking, but I didn't want them to connect me with Owain or the hostages." She rubbed her forehead. "Actually they call me Mistress Gardener."

Daron pulled the blanket around her neck as wind rattled through the room. "Have you found Bryn?" she whispered.

Tanwen nodded. "We'll talk more later. But you must call me Tangwystyl."

"I'll try, but I'm likely to forget."

"This is no game."

"I know that, I'm not a child."

"No," said Tanwen, her gaze going to Daron's round belly. "Huw?"

Daron flushed. "I can explain." The woman on the next pallet muttered in her sleep.

"You should have told me."

"You had your own troubles. I didn't dare. I wasn't sure."

Tanwen pushed Daron's hair back from her face. A stick knocked on the door and a boy called out, "Rise all, time to be stirring." Tanwen whispered, "Tell me one thing, did Owain send you?"

"Of course he did. He says he'll take you back. He wants you to come home."

"And Bryn?" Tanwen whispered.

Daron looked away and chewed at her fingernail. "He says you must leave Bryn here."

The other women were waking. Tanwen handed Daron a cloak. They went down and after a breakfast of hot oats, left the hall arm in arm. "Tell me now, what did Owain say exactly?" said Tanwen.

"He said I'll give you silver and two men to travel with. Go direct to Ludelaue on the English border, that's where she'll be. I asked, then what? He said, then you bring her back here. With Bryn? I asked. He grew very angry. No, he said, she'll ruin everything, she'll endanger all. He was very angry." Daron shot a look at Tanwen. "I said, there will be war, and already there is no food in the village and no meat to last out the winter. He said I didn't understand; I didn't see what he saw." Daron shrugged. "I'm with child, Tanwen. I'm sorry, but I didn't wish to journey all this distance."

Tanwen sighed. "War unsettles us all."

Just then Raoul fell into step with them. "Have you found your cousin?" he said to Daron.

"No," stammered Daron, hesitating too long. "No, this is another acquaintance though. Mistress Tangwystyl, she is a gardener and has worked on my aunt's lands."

Raoul smiled, bowed to them both, and turned away toward the weapons room.

December's dark days wore on. Tanwen sorted seeds, sketched plans for flowerbeds, checked soil, water, and light, as though she would still be here in spring, as though the gardens would be overflowing with blossoms by midsummer. Yet the work was unexpectedly absorbing and she found herself wistful that her plans would never come to fruition.

The rest of the castle prepared for the Yule. The cooks worked deep into the nights, baking pear tarts and honey-walnut sweets. Tanwen watched as they created fantastical flowers out of pink sugar until the busy head cook shooed her out of the kitchens. Alica would have been amazed and disapproving of such elaborate food. She talked with the kitchen girls and the boys who groomed the horses, trying to learn whatever she could about the patterns of rain, sun, and thawing here. From them she also heard rumors. That King Henry wasn't heading back to Normandy for the holidays, as had been his custom, to celebrate with Queen Eleanor. He would be nearby, in the castle of de Lacy's rival Clifford. The thought of the king so close was disturbing.

Daron heard the most distressing rumor. That Henry might actually come to Ludelaue over the Yule. Tanwen fretted and slept less each night. That Owain expected her to come back, without Bryn, weighed on her. She felt the cut of his betrayal as though it happened all over again. Through this whole nightmare journey, she'd always imagined bringing Bryn home. The truth that they could never return was frightening. The world was so enormous. They had to get away from here, but now they had to have somewhere definite to go, and a way to live once there. And Daron was here now too, depending on her. She'd have to get them all away, and soon, before Daron's time.

The festive preparations grated on her nerves and she had to bite her tongue not to argue with Daron, who chattered and made friends with the soldiers and the servants alike and seemed to believe the fiction that the hostages were guests rather than prisoners. "The kitchen girls gave them the leftover honey cakes yesterday," Daron said.

Tanwen jabbed at her mending. Bryn was thinner each time she saw him, a growing boy needed meat and fresh greens, not onions and left over oats day after day.

"When will we head back to Adpar?" Daron asked, yawning. "After the Yule? I wish Owain's men had stayed. How will we travel by ourselves? We'll have to hire men. How much coin do you have Tanwen?"

"We're not going back. Or I'm not. And I have only a few pennies."

Daron put down her mending and stared. "You can't mean that. If you don't go back, Owain will turn you out forever. And what will I do?"

"You know I'll never return without Bryn," said Tanwen.

"Owain said I must bring you back. Otherwise, I can't stay there. He'll turn me away. You know that, and I'm having a baby." Daron burst into tears and ran from the room.

Tanwen watched her go, but she had no energy left to comfort her cousin. She stared out the window instead and went over the plan she'd devised. She and Daron would meet up with Bryn, when he went out to sword practice at noon with Geoffrey, and they'd slip into the woods and with the two hours lead time, she hoped Raoul and his men would decide they weren't important enough to chase. She could only hope that Geoffrey, who seemed fond of Bryn, would agree and perhaps cover for them. She'd decided it was best to surprise the knight, not ask him earlier and give him too much time to think. With his help, they might gain a few more precious hours, even an entire night. She'd already collected food. It remained only to watch for a break in this early winter weather, pick a day when the snow thawed to slush, and begin.

The very next day, Tanwen chanced speaking with Bryn when he set out for his practice with Geoffrey. "King Henry himself may come to Ludelaue."

"I know! If he comes he'll bring his best knights and there might even be a tourney, as they have in Normandy!" Bryn laughed, and swung his empty hand as though he held a sword.

"Bryn," she said, too sharply. "Henry is a dangerous man, absolutely no one will stand in his way. He has a terrible temper, he might do anything. You must call no attention to yourself."

"Of course." He stared at her, eyes bright, waiting to run after the others toward the playing fields.

"It's important Bryn."

Bryn glanced away. "There's Geoffrey!" A gladness rang in his voice that was not for her. "I must ask him something, Mother," he said, waiting for permission to go.

She forced a smile. "Be ready."

He looked puzzled, but he was in a hurry to catch up. Take care, she wanted to call after him as he ran off, but she did not. She watched him greet Geoffrey and then she tramped through the snow toward her gardens, head aching. She should be glad he had Geoffrey to look out for him, and she was. But she felt resentment too. He spent far more time with Bryn than she could. And in truth, when she spoke with Bryn now, he was often touchy, polite but impatient. A boy on his way to being a man.

She picked up her shovel, feeling every ounce of its weight. Under the frost-hard surface the ground could yet be worked. She dug until her arms ached and the sun warmed her shoulders, until she began to smell again the cold earth and rotted leaves, and see the bones of her planned garden emerge from flattened leaves and dead grass. She imagined grape vines winding up four tall posts, making a room out of doors, with ceiling and walls draped in living green, decorated with swathes of climbing white roses, a room where a person could sit and be at peace, hearing only the flutter of wind and the sleepy sound of bees. In such a room a person could forget, just for a time, and be content.

Tanwen woke in the blackness of night. A heavy quiet enshrouded the room. She lay still, wondering why she was awake, staring out the slit of window, where darker clouds raced over a black-violet sky. Rather than thawing, the weather had turned bitter cold. She pulled her thin blanket up over her ears. Beside her, Daron groaned and thrust off her blanket.

Tanwen put a hand on Daron's shoulder, which was hot.

Daron bit back another moan. "I'm so hot and I've pain." She placed Tanwen's hand on her rounded belly.

Tanwen felt the child twitch under her palm. "For how long?"

"For a time, each night this week."

"Why didn't you tell me?" Tanwen found a candle end and struck a light.

Emma, the gruff kitchen maid who slept on the next pallet, rolled over. "What are you doing? Douse that light." She turned over with a flounce and went back to snoring, mouth gaping.

Tanwen rubbed Daron's back until she drifted off into a fitful slumber.

When Daron woke, she seemed her normal self. "I'm sorry I woke you."

"Of course you should wake me, you should have told me sooner."

"You have your own concerns."

"You're here, aren't you? It's better if I know."

Daron flinched. "It's not the normal way then, for a child?"

Tanwen sighed and pulled on her boots. "I don't know, I don't think so. But I'll ask Helori, or bring you to her, even better."

"Who?"

"I met her when I first arrived. She gave me the seeds. I've been meaning to find a reason to go see her again. She's very skilled at herbs. No doubt she'll have a tea that will ease your pains."

Daron nodded uncertainly. "Can we get there today?"

"Yes," said Tanwen, peering out the window. Though she wasn't sure. Her workmen knew the way, but they were gone for the winter months, building walls for de Lacy. "I'll ask Raoul."

"That dreadful soldier?"

"Who better to ask than de Lacy's captain? And he wants to do me a favor."

Daron held her gaze. "Don't put yourself in danger for me."

Tanwen bit back her reply. That Daron's coming had already put her in danger, and worse, endangered Bryn, and she was frantic with worry about how to get them all away.

For three days the wind blew gusts that shook the kitchens and dry snow dusted through the cracks in the roof to coat the platters of food with a lace of cold flakes. Tanwen stood at the kitchen door, peering out at drifted snow and more swirling down, until Tess, one of the serving girls, shouted at her. She slammed the door shut and opened her mouth to speak, but closed it again as Tess gave her a sour look. The girl's capable hands gutted the chicken, warm from the butcher; her efficiency robbed Tanwen of the urge to ask if she might know what was wrong with Daron, still curled up in their cold chamber. Tanwen tugged at the knot in her apron strings, remembering Daron's pinched nose and the blue crescents under her eyes.

She left the kitchen, trudged through the snow and stamped her boots as she entered the great hall. De Lacy's men lounged by the fire, but de Lacy himself was away at Clifford's castle. Lyr Gethin poked at the coals with a long stick, a black look on his face. More than once, she'd seen him turn on his heel and walk the other way just to avoid her. Raoul, in a maroon tunic closed with a bronze brooch, sat on a stool examining an arrow, his eyes already on her.

She reached the men, and stretched her hands to the blazing fire at their feet, as though she sought only the heat. Her hands were cold in truth, and she wished she could lift her heavy skirt and warm her feet and ankles. "Master Raoul, have you a moment?"

Raoul looked surprised, but waved aside the serving boy bringing a steaming bowl of stew. She drew him away to a private window seat. He sat down opposite her, his eyes watchful, the cold eyes of a soldier, or a turtle, or a snake. She glanced back at the hearth. But Gethin had turned away. "I have a favor to ask."

"If it's in my power."

"You've realized that Daron is my cousin."

"I've realized you are not exactly as you seem," agreed Raoul.

Tanwen swallowed, feeling a moment of racing fear. She met his gaze. "Is anyone?"

Raoul glanced down, where her gown caught on her thighs.

"I need to go to Helori once more, she has herbs that will help my cousin."

"The king may come soon. No one can leave or come to the castle."

"Exactly why I have come directly to you." Tanwen smoothed her dress over her knees and looked up at him. "I know the times are unusual."

He hesitated so long she thought he'd deny her, but then he said, "Why not? The next day travel is possible, that is."

Tanwen left him sitting by the windows, staring at the snow sifting down. She climbed the stairs. Outside the door she stopped, leaned her forehead against the rough wood, and let her breathing slow.

In return? She hadn't promised him anything, exactly. He'd taken off his glove and reached across the space between them, run a finger from her earlobe, past her collarbone, stopping only at the edge of her bodice. She'd swallowed hard, but she hadn't stopped him.

Four days later, Tanwen rode through the snowy woods, a glass vial filled with an orange liquid kept warm next to her breasts. Cold air sliced against her cheeks and flooded the valley with an icy blue light. The herbalist had listened to her description of Daron's symptoms and said she must rest, do nothing active at all until the baby was born.

"But she can travel surely, if she had a horse, or perhaps a litter?" asked Tanwen.

Helori regarded her silently. "No."

There'd been no chance for further conversation. Raoul had insisted on coming with her and he waited outside, mounted on his grey horse, muffled against the cold in black wool. Helori had glanced out, and blinked twice, her hands still. Yet she'd promised to come to Daron when her time arrived.

The woods were absolutely silent but for the creak of their saddles and the muffled thud of their horses' hoofs. Tanwen felt Raoul's gaze between her shoulder blades. She closed her eyes and thought of Helori's instructions. Icicles hung from the tree branches and behind her Raoul whacked one off with a startling crack.

When they reached the castle, Tanwen slid off the tired pony and thanked Raoul without meeting his eyes. She hurried inside, her frozen boots clunking up the stairs. She found Daron alone, huddled in blankets, her back to the wall. Tanwen pulled out the glass vial. "It's going to be fine," she said, her voice radiating confidence she hadn't been able to fake before.

Daron burst into tears. "I do want this child."

"Then rest up and don't worry." Tanwen poured the contents into a cup. "Drink."

"What about you, and Bryn? I'm in your way. What about Owain?"

Tanwen shook her head. "I'll think of something." She took Daron's hand. "You can't travel, that's what Helori says; you're not even to leave your bed. You must rest here quiet on your pallet until the child comes." She tried to smile. "And besides, it's a frozen world out there. We can none of us go anywhere now, not until spring arrives."

CHAPTER TWENTY-SIX

G ETHIN IDLED IN THE COURTYARD, his boots leaking water in the unexpectedly warm February sun. Everywhere snow melted and water dripped from icicles and the kitchen girls were outside flirting with the stable boys. Warm wind feathered his hair, but he felt only gloom. He'd reached the end of his coin. He couldn't stay here longer and he couldn't go back to Enid and Sam empty handed. De Lacy had finally returned from his long stay at Clifford's castle yesterday. But Raoul controlled who got an audience with de Lacy and who did not, and Raoul was never going to let him through.

He noticed Tanwen shoveling earth in her garden, sunlight flashing on her uncovered hair. She flung her cloak on the ground and he thought about her eyes, grey like the sea on a cloudy day. She started doing something with sticks and a length of twine, measuring off ground. He should tell her he was leaving, at least.

She raised her dark brows at his approach.

For a moment he said nothing, his eyes drawn to her legs, where wind wrapped her gown around the curve of her thigh. But then she smiled up at him and said, "It's a truly lovely day, is it not?"

He glanced at the high clouds scudding by on the wind. "I've seen the famous gardens in Firenze," he found himself saying, instead of bringing up his plans.

She stopped her measuring and sat on a bale of straw, pushing up her sleeves, her eyes. "On your way to Venezia? Tell me."

He focused on the picture in his head. "There are long walkways, perhaps four feet wide, very straight, and patterned in a pleasing geometry, which can be viewed from the balconies above. The paths are softened by lush greenery, vines and shrubs, arching overhead at precise intervals, so that it's like walking through a living green cave. Everywhere, water gurgles and fountains run over marble stones, with a delicate splashing, like intricate music. The flowers are pink and canary yellow, large as a man's hand, or tiny like blue butterflies and massed in tangled vines, draping over the walls, doubled by the pools. Songbirds of lime and yellow and blue sing and dart. The sun beats down, but in these gardens the light is muted, everything becomes dappled and glimmering, and the scents of jasmine and earth and water mingle."

"Ah," she said, and her face held pleased surprise, as though she actually felt that soft wind brush her cheeks. "How fortunate you are."

He thought about tossing white pebbles into the pools with Sam, and taking a nap while Sam trained the tiny birds to sing on his finger, luring them with breadcrumbs. They'd been on their way to Venezia, he and Sam and Mario the cook. But like a shell gleaming in seawater, that future had been farther away than it seemed. Gethin pointed. "So what are you doing with those sticks?"

"This will be a garden room, with small bushes making a wall," her arm sketched a wide semi-circle, "which will block that wind that blows often from the north, and there will be seats here," she pointed at the ground near her feet, "arranged in a square so people can sit and quietly dream, or converse, as they like."

She continued, and he thought how he liked the sound of this voice, confident and dreaming of making something beautiful, a world of ordered harmony in the midst of de Lacy's dusty chaos.

She was looking at him, expectant. He felt his face warm. Surprisingly, she laughed. It reminded him of finches rising in a cheerful chatter of lime and yellow. He felt his lips twist in a grin too, like an idiot.

"You are not listening to me, not a word."

"Of course I am."

"What flowers then, will be planted here?" She pointed to his left at a clump of soggy grass.

"I heard what you meant." His voice came out too serious. He cleared his throat and looked away. There was only the rustle of wind in the bare elms over the wall and the single clang of the town bell.

She stood with her arms folded, a vertical wrinkle between her brows. "I see." Pink splotched her cheeks.

He wanted to say something more, but he didn't know what.

"Mother," a voice called.

The rose faded from her cheeks and her eyes took on that desperate look as her boy ran up.

"Bryn, hush, don't call me that, not so loud." She almost touched him, then laced her fingers behind her back. They stared at each other.

"I'm sorry, I forgot." Bryn nodded a greeting to Gethin. "But look!" He held out a parchment with a sketch of a cart, a strange cart with six doubled wheels instead of two. "I've been thinking about how a cart could go faster over rough roads. It's a present for you."

Tanwen took the sketch and studied it. "I love it."

"Thank you for giving me the parchment and charcoal," said Bryn, turning to Gethin with a shy smile. "It's wonderful to have enough. I have so many ideas."

Gethin smiled. "I'll find you a wax tablet, when I can."

Bryn turned back to Tanwen. "We're going out to practice sword work now too! First time we're let out since last month's storm!" He leaned in to give her a hug, thought better of it, and smiled, shifting from one leg to another. "I missed you," he said and ran off.

Tanwen stared after him as he strode out the gate with Geoffrey, then down at the convoluted sketch. "You gave him drawing supplies," she said, "thank you."

A stable boy tugged at Gethin's sleeve. "You're wanted."

"By who?"

"Lord de Lacy," said the boy.

De Lacy? Gethin shook his head. Why would he suddenly see him now?

"You must go, right away, haven't you waited weeks to meet with him?" Tanwen asked.

Gethin hesitated; he had more he wanted to say to her, but of course he had to go, this was his chance. "You should leave here," he blurted out.

She blinked and thrust Bryn's sketch in her sleeve. He followed her gaze and saw Raoul watching, as he leaned against the weapons shed.

De Lacy was thick bodied, chunky with muscles, and a long scar raced down his cheekbone, raw against his red-brown stubble. His hands were square and blunt-fingered and right now without gloves as he stared down at the table and the map before him. "Why would you bring this to me?"

Gethin swallowed. Though he'd waited for weeks for this meeting, he wouldn't have long, he could see. He drew in a long breath, his mind alarmingly blank. This was no Rhys, ready for a philosophical discussion of the past and future of maps and man's conception of his world and the heavens. De Lacy would care only about military practicalities and immediate ones at that. "This map," he began.

"Yes, yes, I see it's a map, something for monks to fool with in their monasteries, lovely to look at, but what do I care for that? Why are you here anyway?" De Lacy gulped his wine. "Thomas." His eyes searched for his secretary. "Why have you brought him to me?"

Thomas, across the chamber, raised an eyebrow at Gethin.

His chance and he was ruining it. He had to focus. "I can promise you wealth and power."

De Lacy turned back. "Now you're talking like a man. Yet many say that. What do you have that they do not? Besides your name." De Lacy sat down on a bench and leaned back. "Gethin, the dark. You are dark, in apparel and face and mood too I think." He chuckled at his own wit and grabbed a wing of chicken from the trencher.

"I have what's in my head. I can make maps." Gethin spoke fast. "Maps that guarantee wealth and power and military control, because they bring you knowledge. You will know where each river, each hill and each camping clearing will be. Each fording place. Each field of wheat. You won't need guides or scouts or spies. I can make you maps that show not the celestial heavens, or far off Jerusalem, but this world around your castle. The borderlands. In every detail."

De Lacy narrowed his eyes and chewed, spitting a bone onto the floor. "And how can you do such a thing?"

Gethin noted Thomas, pretending to examine a parchment on the table. "I need to speak in private with you."

De Lacy tossed another chicken wing to the hounds. He waved his men away. They glared and took their time.

"Your secretary too."

Thomas stood up, his back stiff. De Lacy laughed. "Go away Thomas, I can listen well enough on my own." Thomas bowed and exited. A key grated in the lock and the logs shifted on the fire, showering sparks. De Lacy glared at the sparks as if daring them to spring into flames, and they sputtered out on the bleached wood floor. "Now," he said. "We are alone."

Gethin pulled the precious leather case from under his tunic, where he always carried it. He pulled from the oiled cloth the sketches he'd drawn in the Mediterranean, and spread them out on the table. He launched into explaining the idea behind the maps to de Lacy, and showed him the directions, the colors used to indicate topography, the circles designating rough size of population, the contours showing coves for hiding a ship, the sources of water, the placement of castles. He was too passionate, and talking too fast. But it all came pouring out.

De Lacy let him talk, and when he was done, he examined the maps for a long time. "Where is this place?"

"The Mediterranean sea, near Venezia, a huge port where ships enter from all parts of the world." Gethin pointed. "And over here is where Queen Eleanor holds her lands."

"Perhaps you intend me to challenge the Queen, or even ally myself with her, against the King?" asked de Lacy with a grin full of food-flecked teeth.

Gethin felt the color drain from his face. The quarrels of Henry and Eleanor were fierce and known to all. "Of course not. As a good subject of Henry, you would have no need of this map, though Henry would see its use." He felt distress roiling in his stomach. "But here, in the borders and on the coasts of England and Wales there is much to be learned, of great use to a powerful lord like you, and consistent with your charge from the king."

"Yet Henry wouldn't like it anyway, this mapmaking of yours. Me, knowing so much. Having so much power." De Lacy traced a blunt forefinger along the bulge of coast as though it were a woman's breast.

"I don't know what this king will or will not like." Gethin shrugged. "I just want to know what is out there in the world, and I want to set it down. Pay me what it's worth to you, just enough that I can do the project. The results are yours."

"And copies?"

Gethin frowned. "I can make several, or only one copy."

"I don't want this map in anyone else's hands. Even..." de Lacy's fingers curled into a fist, "Henry's."

Gethin hesitated, but it was his dream. He wouldn't have another chance. "I'll make just one copy," he said, "but the project must be secret. Even from your knights, and your secretary. From your captain."

De Lacy drank the rest of the wine and put the goblet down. "Agreed. How much will you need, in time and in funds and goods?"

"I have a list prepared." Gethin handed him the accounting of provisions and funds, enough to cover two years of work.

De Lacy tossed it on the table. He walked to the window and looked out, over the hills toward Wales. "You must finish sooner. Before next summer."

Gethin opened his mouth.

De Lacy grinned again. "Choose, my friend. My dungeon for treason, or your work at the end of one year. It's useless to me otherwise."

Gethin rolled up the maps. De Lacy was clever, and obviously planning something, which was worrisome. Still, as Gethin bowed and backed away, his mind racing over the risks, the silver bowl by de Lacy's arm gleamed in a beam of sunlight and the apples within shone brilliantly red. Gethin burst out the oak door, surprising Thomas. He bounded down the steps three at a time, into the bright noonday sun.

Tanwen pressed her forehead to the cold stone in the snaking corridor beside the great hall. She'd convinced herself she must wait for

Daron to have her child, that in spring's warmer weather, they'd all be the safer. But sometimes unease would leap up and lodge in her throat. She'd be overwhelmed with the feeling she'd made the wrong choice, that no one and nothing should come before saving Bryn. That perhaps she couldn't save them both and she was wrong even to try.

She scrubbed the sudden tears off her cheeks with her apron and went outdoors to her garden, hoping to distract herself with work. The turned rectangle of earth was still nothing but a dark gash in the ground, despite all the visions in her mind. What had made her think she could pass herself off as a master garden keeper? She dropped to her knees and began to dig. The earth was warmed on top, but ice crystals lurked underneath.

"You should use a spade for that surely."

It was Gethin, decked out in his usual dark clothing, his hair tied back for once with a black ribbon. "I know that much."

He crouched down and fingered the earth. "Can you make a garden here, the sort de Lacy expects?" he asked, examining her face.

"I don't know." Tanwen rubbed her temples. "In truth I never expected to be here still."

"You do know about plants. I've watched you, in the woods. You'll find a way. You have a feeling, a companionship or something I mean."

She felt a rush of tears and blinked them away. "With the plants?" She laughed, but inside she was waiting for his answer.

"Yes, with the plants. Is that so strange?" He extended a hand. "Come."

"Where?"

"You ask so many questions."

She shrugged, but she was curious and in need of distraction. She brushed at the dirt clinging to her knees as Gethin strode away, expecting her to follow. Serve him right if she didn't. Except, what did he want to show her? She trailed him to the stables, where he saddled his horse and jumped on. He gave her his arm and she clambered on behind.

He didn't say where they were going, and she found she didn't want to ask. They rode through the gate and headed toward the hills.

Gradually, she relaxed, enjoying the bumping motion of the horse beneath her and the lack of responsibility to guide him or even notice where they went. Sun poured golden on her cheek and she closed her eyes for the pleasure of seeing the warm red haze through her eyelids. She began to hum, then stopped, remembering Gethin's presence.

"Don't stop," he said. "You have a lovely voice."

She shook her head, and did not continue. They'd been traveling on a wide road, but they headed along a path that disappeared from time to time as it wound through oaks with branches that would block the sun completely once the new leaves came. Now light dappled the ground and winter's dried ferns rustled, but she could see new shoots curling from the wet earth.

After a time, Gethin stopped the horse and she swung off, though she couldn't see any reason to stop here. The sun disappeared behind violet clouds. "What are we looking at exactly?"

He grinned. "No need to be so short."

She lifted her eyebrows, but he just tied the horse to a tree. He started to walk, so she followed again, wondering what she was doing out here. She needed to be working on the garden.

Gethin turned, his eyes glinting blue light. "Never mind," he said. "There will be time."

He had a knack of guessing what she was thinking and she didn't like it. "It was a lovely ride, but shouldn't we be heading back?" she said.

"I didn't bring you out here just for a ride."

"What are we looking at?"

"We're finding ink." He searched the ground around her feet and retrieved a small oak gall.

"Why don't you just purchase some at the market? Or get some from that horrible secretary of de Lacy's. You seem to know him well enough."

"Good ink is expensive, and rarely made well."

"Do you plan to write a letter?" He was searching the low branches and gathering the galls. He didn't answer, just sorted them into green and brown piles and tossed some rotted ones back onto the leaves.

She wanted to probe more, but knew he wouldn't answer. "What makes a good oak gall for ink?"

"It's the wrong time of year for the best," he said. He showed her a good one and she bent to help. They gathered a small sack full, as Aeron tossed his head and munched the pale grass poking through the wet leaves.

She straightened up, her back creaking. "So, what is the ink for?"

He almost spoke, but turned away.

"You needn't tell me." Her voice came out shrill. She could hear the chagrin and he did too. Their eyes met and held.

He looked away. "If I tell you, you must keep the secret."

"And haven't I told you everything I hold most secret and dear?"

He tied the sack onto Aeron's saddle and turned back. "I would not add to your danger," he said quietly.

"I know already it's for your drawings, or perhaps a map. You have a new project?"

He gave a short laugh. "You are too clever."

"Indeed, I can be." She smiled and loosened her cloak in the warm sun. "Like the monks make, a scheme of paradise and earth?"

"You have seen such?"

"I saw one at Rhys' Dinefwr. Drawn as large as a man and embellished with gilt and colors. It showed all the world, divided in four quadrants and Jerusalem floated on a cloud at the very center, with a king's crown on the top of her towers. Such a map is valuable beyond price he said. He intended it for the new abbey at Ystrad Fflur, where his brother resides."

"Ah, Cadell." Gethin looked troubled suddenly and far away.

She touched his arm. "I'd like to hear about your map."

"It will be a different kind of map. Something I heard of en route to Venezia. A map not for monks or kings, but of use to merchants and those who trade on the sea. A map that shows the lay of the land, mountains, water sources, the pattern of coves, as though one were a bird flying overhead and looking down. As one does from a very high hill, seeing the fields and villages below as tiny squares and triangles of land."

"Yes." She knew he loved to draw, trees mostly, tangles of branches, mysterious patterns of black and grey, old trees against pale skies.

"Such a map," he said dreamily, "that every detail will be accurate and together it becomes something..." He shrugged his shoulders and jingled Aeron's bridle in his fingers.

He was embarrassed, she realized. "Something beautiful?" She went to where he leaned against a tree, stripping a pine branch of its needles. "Like a garden, such a map needs colors too."

"I hope to use some, though colors are expensive." He reached out and flicked the cap off her head. "Your hair is gold and copper, like evening sun on the bay in Ilfracombe."

She felt her face flush, and she wished, for the first time, her hair would grow in faster. It clustered still in loose curls around her ears.

The woods were silent, the birds resting and the sun starting its slow descent. Shafts of gold light split the shadows and Gethin's eyes were on her. He brushed a finger along one of her curls and stopped just as he reached her throat. For a moment, it seemed hard to breathe. The world narrowed to his dark brows and deep blue eyes and the exact place where his black hair sprang from his white forehead. She swallowed, and he drew back.

She reached for him, placed her palms on his shoulders and sent her mouth into his. He froze, then gathered her tight in his arms and she felt the length of him, chest and stomach and thighs. Felt lips and hands and hot sun on her head and closed eyelids, hard kisses down the side of her neck.

"Tanwen," he said between kisses, three times as though memorizing her name.

She opened her eyes. She felt dizzy, her throat tight, her heart leaping. Dazzled, and suddenly afraid. "We should head back," she said quietly.

He was silent for a long moment. "As you wish."

"Is it of Ludelaue then, this map you'll make?" Tanwen bent to pick up her fallen cloak and wished her voice would come out as steady and normal as his.

He swung into the saddle and hauled her up behind him. She

tugged on his tunic, but he didn't answer. They wound through the trees and when they reached the road, it was empty, but he pulled to a stop. He didn't turn to look at her, just spoke into the air. "I'll be at Ludelaue another fortnight, perhaps a month. But then I go away."

She felt that like a blow to her stomach. "Back to Ilfracombe? Or to your Venezia again?"

"De Lacy doesn't have pockets deep enough for that."

"What does de Lacy have to do with it?"

"He will pay."

They rode in silence after that, through the forest, back through the arched gate, and up to the stables.

"How long will you be gone then?"

"Long," he answered.

"Fare well, then," she said, but her voice came out sharp-edged, and her chest hurt, even to breathe.

CHAPTER TWENTY-SEVEN

T HE OTHER WOMEN HAD GATHERED their bedding and shuffled
out of the bedchamber, yawning, at Daron's first moans near
midnight. Tanwen shivered in a draft and pulled the thin blanket
over her cousin's shoulder. Daron pushed it away. Her eyes fluttered.
Tanwen waited, her hand poised, but Daron drifted away somewhere,
not to normal restful sleep. The dull light of a bitter afternoon barely
lit the room. Tanwen eyed her rumpled pallet in the corner. If only
she could just lie down and sleep, forget everything for a time.

An hour passed and Daron opened her eyes. She studied the
beamed ceiling and oak door, as though she didn't know where she
was. "I'm going to die." Her fingers searched for Tanwen's wrist.

"No. I won't let that happen. Here, I'll straighten your blankets."

"It's so warm. Can't you open the window?"

The unshuttered slit of a window was already open to the raw
air. "I'll find you some water, that will cool you," Tanwen said. She
ran down the stairs and banged out the door. The air was sharp and
burned her throat. At least it was untainted by sweat and fear. She
wiped her forehead with her sleeve and thought of the day she'd
birthed Bryn in the forest, the leaves smelling rich and lush with
promising summer. She must not fail her cousin now.

Helori had promised to be here for the delivery. She'd sent a
message with a stable boy, but with this storm, it would be at least
a day before Helori could arrive. The sky was flat with dull clouds,
pressing down on the walls de Lacy was building and on the tower
where Bryn was held. Despite the bitter weather, no fire smoked
from their chimney. She picked her way past puddles edged with

ice and paused in the center of the deserted courtyard. Overhead, two grey swallows winged right over de Lacy's high walls and sped away toward the far off hills. She watched the pair soar, wings nearly touching. When had she come to be so alone?

Tears welled up in her eyes and she shook them away and walked on.

She lifted her skirts to avoid tripping over the ruts of frozen mud and hurried to the kitchens. Inside, the steamy scent of cooking oats made her stomach growl. At the table, Gethin spooned porridge from a blue bowl. He stopped with the spoon nearly to his mouth, and gestured to a platter of venison dotted with plums in vinegar sauce. "I've never had such a meal from Cook before, nor has de Lacy, I'd warrant. Nothing like leaving to merit a good dinner."

"I thought you were gone already."

"Nearly." Gethin glanced at the two kitchen maids, peeling apples and yawning by the fire. He spun a heavy cup between his fingers. "I had some matters to ready. And, of course, this blasted weather."

She sat down across from him. "I need your help."

He put down his knife. "You know I can do nothing for Bryn," he said quietly.

"I know you will do nothing. For that, I have made my own plan." She poured water into a pitcher and found a cup. "It's Daron. I'm worried."

"Why?"

"She's with child, as you might have noticed if you looked up from your maps. In fact, she's having her child, now. Gethin, something's not right and I don't know what to do."

"You should get a midwife. What makes you think I could help?"

"I've sent for Helori, but with the storm...and there's no midwife closer by." She picked a spoon off the table and put it back down. "It's a border castle, not a home. Even the town lives only for war. Perhaps you'll think of something I've missed. I have no one else to ask."

"You don't know what you're asking me."

"Surely you can delay your leaving by a day or two. It might mean her life."

"I'm the last one to save her."

"Whatever do you mean?" She leaned towards him. "Gethin, please."

He pushed his bowl away. They crossed to the hall and climbed the stairs without speaking and found Daron huddled under her blanket, her dark hair clinging to her neck. "Tanwen, thanks be to the Lady. Where did you go?" Her voice was strained and weak. "Don't leave me."

Tanwen pushed the soaked hair off Daron's forehead. "I've brought water sweetened with honey."

Daron drank two sips and fell back on the pillow. "I feel terrible."

"It is always so."

"Don't lie," said Daron. "I watched you have your child. Something isn't right with me."

Tanwen turned to Gethin, who waited in the doorway, sweat in oval beads on his forehead.

"There's nothing I can do here," he said.

"Huw?" Daron tossed and turned over on the bed. "Is that Huw?"

"It's not Huw. And I thought you didn't want him," said Tanwen.

"I want him now." Daron thrust her fist in her mouth and moaned.

"I'll find him." Gethin flung himself back down the stairs.

"Gethin? Wait!" Tanwen jumped up, but he was already gone.

Daron clutched at her hand. "It's true," she said, "you have your child, but I'm going to die."

"No, you're not. You must rouse yourself, try." Tanwen knelt beside her cousin. But Daron did seem so frail suddenly, like a curled and faded leaf. Tanwen breathed a prayer. Who to, she wasn't sure, the world seemed a haphazard place, people scattered and lives tossed about, nothing like the world of Gethin's maps, everything accounted for and in its place. Maps were like a wondrous dream, all order and symmetry, but life wasn't like that. It was more a dark tangle.

Evening came on, with Daron sleeping and waking. Tanwen bathed her face, stroked her hair, and gave her sips of watered wine. Wind howled around the tower and sleet sheeted against the walls, with a sound like precious glass breaking. As midnight approached again, Daron seemed to awaken. Her gaze darted around the room, to a crack in the wall, or a trickle where snow melted on the windowsill. Her lovely dark hair was plastered to her neck. Surely the pains should be coming fast and even now.

Someone pounded on the door. Tanwen flung the door open. Gethin stood there, his fist raised to bang again. He glanced at Daron and swayed. She thought he might fall over. "I've sent word. Huw will get the message but with the storm he can't get here in time."

Tanwen nodded, wondering how he'd known where to search.

"What can I do now? The snow is letting up."

"Find Helori, if you can. She must come quickly."

The morning hours arrived and passed, and neither Gethin nor Helori arrived. Wet snow still gusted in the window and crusted on the sill. Daron clung to Tanwen. Her eyes stared and didn't see. She was exhausted and grey and slipping somewhere far away.

The winds halted and the first stars were coming out when the door swung open and Helori entered, straight backed and swathed in a purple shawl. She pulled it off calmly and shook away the snow. A progression of kitchen girls paraded up the stairs and entered, carrying linens and pots of steaming water. Helori issued instructions and bent over Daron's pallet.

Gethin's hand gripped Tanwen's elbow. He tugged her away. "You're exhausted. You've done what you can." He led her downstairs and out into the fresh air and wrapped his damp warm cloak around her shoulders. He pulled out a flask and she took a gulp of spirits, sweet with cherries, and hot. He drank the rest.

"I don't like the sickroom," she said.

"Not so unusual." Gethin stuck the flask back in his pouch.

"In a healer it is." Tanwen touched her forehead. "My grandmother taught me. But I've always hated it. The healing part I mean. It's the herbs I love." She thought with longing of her garden at Adpar, the spires of lavender, buzzing with bees in the July sun, the spiky rosemary, and the carpet of silvery white-blossomed thyme. How had it come to be, that she and Owain were apart and Adpar closed to her forever?

Gethin was staring at her with a frown. "Each person has their own way," he said.

"Daron is dear as a sister to me." Her own words surprised her. She began to cry.

Gethin drew her into the circle of his arms. "Hush. You're tired. All will be well now."

She pushed him. "Hush? As though a child is of no importance."

"I never said that." His face was white and strained.

Tanwen tried to step back, but Gethin gripped her shoulders tight. "She left me," he said. "She took the child and went away and there was nothing any man could do." His eyes were staring over her shoulder to somewhere far away, watching her, whoever she was, go. "My fault," he whispered.

"Gethin?" Tanwen cleared her throat. "When did she leave you? Who? Do you have a child somewhere?"

His eyes turned on her, unseeing, and his grip tightened until she almost cried out. "What are you saying? She's gone, dead, where no man can follow. Haven't I said so?" He released her and stalked away, so suddenly she nearly fell.

Toward noon that same day, Gethin threw a saddle on Aeron. The horse sidled, trying to step on his foot. He flung the reins over the horse's neck. Fine snow sifted down, melting as it hit the black ground. His head ached from lack of sleep. But he'd had one good idea as he rode to fetch Helori in the night. He'd go to the abbey and find Cynan, his boyhood friend. His inks were the best and besides, it would be good to be with a true friend for a night and drink ale and laugh.

Loud boot steps crunched on the ice and shadows stretched across the stable floor. Two men rounded the corner, followed by two more. Aeron took advantage of his distraction and tried to bite his knee. It was Raoul, and that bent back secretary.

Raoul grabbed Aeron's reins. "Where are you headed?" His mouth twisted as though at a secret joke.

"What business is that of yours?" asked Gethin.

"Everything that happens in this castle is my affair," said Raoul. The two burly men behind him exchanged grins. Aeron tossed his head, nearly toppling Raoul.

"It's a waste of de Lacy's funds, which come from the king," said the secretary in a squeaky voice.

"What is, exactly?" Gethin stared down at the secretary, who stepped back, closer to the guards.

"We haven't spoken much, since you arrived, have we?" Raoul said. "Though I think we have common interests."

"I would disagree and at any rate, I'm leaving," said Gethin, "and thus no longer your concern."

The secretary tugged at Raoul's sleeve and whispered something Gethin couldn't catch. Then he marched away, slipping on the ice, but not quite falling.

Raoul watched him go, with an amused look, and brushed a wisp of straw from his sleeve. "He thinks you will replace him with de Lacy. I know there is more than that at stake."

Gethin grabbed Aeron's reins back. "Your master has given me a charge and I mean to see it fulfilled."

"Yet I know, as de Lacy doesn't, you've worked for Rhys in the past. Perhaps you work for him still, as his spy."

"So why haven't you told him then? He is your lord."

"Perhaps I will yet." Raoul smiled. "Or perhaps I'll wait, and tell King Henry, when he arrives. Either way, I could see you cut, in four pieces, as a traitor. You should leave here, that's my advice, and not come back." Raoul slapped Aeron's rump and the horse jumped.

Gethin mounted, but hesitated, the horse circling, eyes ringed with white. Finally, cursing, he rode out the gate, pushing Aeron to a reckless canter, though the path into the hills glared with melting ice.

A week later, on a warm bench in a smoke filled inn, Cynan told another joke, and Gethin laughed out loud and took a drink from his mug. The ale was frothy and tasted of autumn.

Cynan clapped him on the back. "I knew you remembered how. Now you tell one."

"What, a joke?"

"You know some, don't you? You're the one living in the lord's castle. I'm just a monk."

Gethin felt his mouth form another unfamiliar grin. "You'll stay another night?" asked a kitchen maid. "Cook is wanting to know should she prepare a chicken?" Gethin shook his head. He'd been enjoying himself, conversing with Cynan each evening after his friend finished his labor of sketching and painting for the day. They'd talked late into each night, about maps Cynan had seen. He'd learned a great deal, though Cynan remembered best the embellishments around the borders, rather than the technical details of how the map was constructed. He missed this kind of conversation. But lists were compiling in another part of his mind. He had inks and parchments wrapped in oiled sacks, charcoal sticks, soft brushes, and even some of Cynan's brilliant precious colors. It was time to push on.

"He'll stay for the midday meal." Cynan shoved his long sleeves up his arms. "I must hear more of these fabulous maps, for it's sure I'll never see Venezia myself." He didn't sound sorry, he hated to travel anywhere far from his own pallet.

"Do you truly never wish to see the world?"

"I'll see it whether I will or no."

"What do you mean?"

"I'm being sent away."

Gethin swallowed. "You didn't tell me that." He'd never thought of Cynan leaving the borders. He'd been in the abbey since they were boys learning to read together.

"It's not so bad." Cynan tugged at his ear. "I've just learned myself. Clairvaux is where they're sending me, across the channel. They have a huge farm there and the food is said to be spectacular." Cynan started talking about the text he was illustrating with goats and pigs, scenes of farming in all the seasons. Gethin let him change the subject and drained his ale and imagined the tiny sheep Cynan painted, lost and wandering far from home.

In the late afternoon, while the monks were at their prayers, Gethin climbed back on Aeron and rode out of the abbey town. The day was full of gusty wind and clouds rolling across a blue sky. The week had been warm and the snow had melted and the meadows were green with sprouts. Aeron shied at every bent blade of grass, but calmed when they reached the woods, trotting on and letting Gethin think. He imagined Cynan on a sailing ship, and traveling on a fat pony to the abbey in far off Clairvaux. He hoped he would be safe. Most men left a cleric alone, but the roads were never free of thieves. Still, the church took care of its own. With King Henry feuding with his archbishop, perhaps it was safer for Cynan over the channel. Probably his abbot thought so too. He was a kindly man, with a long nose and a love of art that passed his love of God and certainly his love of fellow sinners. He'd want Cynan secure, well stocked with paints, able to concentrate on his intricate miniatures, for the glory of God, of course.

As twilight came on, Gethin pulled Aeron to a stop. He had some miles to go, but he'd sighted a cluster of huts hunkered against the hill. He could just make out a keep looming above them, even higher up. He gazed at the square house with its symmetrical timber walls covered with vines and ancient shade trees placed at each of the four corners. As he watched, gold light sparked from a tall window on the top floor. Gethin tried to imagine the chamber and the woman who had lit that candle. What he really envied, he realized, was that even Cynan had a home to leave.

Gethin cantered back through Ludelaue's gate past midnight. Despite the hour, servants rushed from kitchens to hall, torches burned and smoked, and grooms were missing from the stables. Men gathered in the doorway to the great hall, blocking his way. Boys hurried back and forth with bread, turnips, and apples piled in baskets. Gethin snagged some flat bread and a venison slice as a boy careened by. "Who's the feast for?"

The boy turned, eyes huge. "The king!"

God's bones, Henry? The English king was famed for these flying visits, arriving unexpected, tossing everyone onto the wrong foot. Gethin retreated to Aeron's stall and munched on the venison, raw in the middle and blackened outside. Henry travelled with dozens of spies and de Lacy's servants would betray him easily for a penny. He decided to finish the few remaining tasks for his journey in the night, hoping to avoid Henry's men and Raoul. As Gethin worked, the servants rustled back and forth on their endless errands, sweeping, gathering rushes, bringing candles, and they gossiped. Of Henry's mistress, Rosamund, daughter of the border lord de Clifford. Of Clifford, lording it over de Lacy, right here in his own castle. Of the king, a man besotted, as a man is when past his prime and a young girl eyes him for his coin and power. This Rosamund was soft and rounded as a spring wren, her skin that unblemished cream of youngsters a grown man could only halt and wonder at. Clifford was busy selling her too, thrilled with the riches Henry showered on him.

By morning, the last winter ice had melted into pools of sparkling water. Gethin lingered by the kitchen, eating bacon. He licked the grease from his fingers, regretting he'd spent so long in the tranquil abbey, and wondering how Tanwen fared with the king here. He went to the stable and fed Aeron, delaying his departure, wishing he could speak with Tanwen before he left.

A boy tugged on Gethin's sleeve. "Sir, I've been searching for you everywhere. You're wanted in the solar." Gethin put down the brush and stared at Aeron's glistening neck. The horse nipped at his sleeve. In the private solar above the great hall, he'd certainly find de Lacy, and probably also the English king. He should have been gone with the dawn. But he couldn't refuse to go now. He brushed hay wisps off his tunic and polished his boots, then tossed the rag in a corner with a curse. He was no refined courtier from Normandy, he was a maker of maps. But what did Henry know of that? Nothing, he hoped.

Gethin mounted the stairs. He saw de Lacy first, oddly dressed in a tunic embroidered with swirling flowers. The old soldier stood stiff by the hearth. Near the window, on the far side of the large room, sat the king, ensconced on a low chair plumped with emerald cushions, surrounded by gleaming courtiers. Gethin bowed.

Henry was frowning, his ruddy brows drawn together, a goblet of wine already in his hand, and he ignored Gethin. The famed

Rosamund was there, dressed in fluffy pink, hair loose down her back. Beside her Isolde laughed and ate sweetened chunks of venison with her fingers, jewels flashing on her white neck. She flung Gethin a triumphant glance. Rosamund's father lurked behind the three, in the shadows.

Gethin wanted to fade into the shadows too, but de Lacy beckoned him to the hearth, where the hounds slept in a pile at his feet. Gethin watched the king from the corner of his eye. It was a fine bright day, when work should be done and down in the hall men were milling around waiting, but Henry was here nuzzling Rosamund's breast.

"No need to look at me so sour," muttered de Lacy. "It's not as though I want you here."

"What does he want?" asked Gethin.

De Lacy grimaced. "He couldn't possibly know." He cast a worried glance around.

Gethin sighed. De Lacy was certainly no actor. Isolde leaned toward the king, distracting him for a moment from Rosamund, and whispered. A moment later a boy darted over. "The king desires your presence."

Gethin crossed the room, his boots silent on the thick carpet laid on the old timbers. De Lacy trailed behind. Gethin bowed low again. Henry had a hand on one of Rosamund's breasts. She appeared not to notice, just smiled at him in a pretty way. Was she truly so mindless, or grasping as her father? Or did she have any choice in this business at all? Gethin jerked his eyes from her breast to Henry, who smiled, knowing exactly how uncomfortable he was. Isolde was smiling too, staring down at her white hands smoothing the silk of her gown across her thighs.

"So, your project, how goes it?" said the King.

Gethin tried not to choke. "My project, sire?" Beside him, de Lacy grunted and his fingers twitched.

Henry tweaked Rosamund's breast and took his hand away. "Where will you begin?"

Gethin hesitated. De Lacy coughed beside him.

Henry grinned, a thoroughly unpleasant grin. "Just so," he said.

He pointed to a servant, who carried a bag over on a tray. "To aid in your work." The sack was thrust in Gethin's hands. He felt the slipping of coins inside. "No secrets here. We're all on the same side here, are we not?"

De Lacy coughed again and muttered, "Yes, sire, of course."

The king ignored him and said to Gethin, "You'll bring your work to me, directly, to Normandy even, if needs be." He turned his gaze back to Rosamund, and Gethin, dismissed, walked out, his mind awhirl and his stomach churning. Who had known, and who had told the king?

He blundered down the stairs and into the great hall, thinking. Tanwen called out to him as he entered and hurried over. "I must speak with you," she said.

Gethin led her to a bench, hoping she would tell him she was planning to leave the castle. She arranged her skirts and handed him a cup of wine. It was far too sweet. De Lacy hadn't brought out his best, even for the king.

"I wish to thank you," she was saying. "I've heard, that is Geoffrey told me you're teaching Bryn to draw." She smiled. "Actually what he says is that Bryn draws strange contraptions that can never work, draws for hours and only stops to practice sword work and even then, he talks of whatever device he's planning until he drives Geoffrey half mad." She took a sip of the wine. "It's very kind."

"I enjoy it," said Gethin. "His mind turns to understanding how things work and inventing new solutions."

Tanwen's brows came together. "That's good, I know, but he's different; he doesn't blend in. You know people don't like something strange or new."

"Some people," said Gethin. "But he has a talent, you can't stop it."

"Still," she whispered, so that he had to bend closer to hear. "In this place." She shook her head. "I believe you are traveling very soon."

"Yes, as I told you. I've done what I can here. Indeed, I leave this very day."

"We could come with you," Tanwen whispered, staring into the wine.

"That's your plan?"

"That was not my plan. But things have changed. I must get Bryn away right now. Even you can see that. And there's Daron."

"Daron can't travel yet, not where I'm going. She's much too weak. I can't take you, Tanwen. And certainly not Bryn."

"I must get Bryn away. He calls too much attention on himself. Drawing these pictures and talking incessantly about them. He stands out. I fear for him, every moment he is here."

"He is Henry's captive, and Henry himself is here, right now."

"That's why the time is perfect. No one will expect it. Nor will they want to call attention to one missing boy, not while the king himself is here."

Gethin frowned. He ran a hand through his hair. She was perhaps right about that. But why did she always push at him, wanting more? "I'll speak with Geoffrey," he said. "I have some coin, I'll leave some for Bryn. Enough to ..."

"I don't want your money. And Geoffrey has been kind, but he's not Bryn's father. He helps Bryn, but he doesn't understand him."

"I cannot," Gethin said.

"You want to do de Lacy's work, too much," she said. "These maps you're making, you'll give them to him." She looked up at the high table where two silver goblets stood side by side. "You'll give them to de Lacy, or even to the King."

Men were coming in for the morning meal. Isolde entered and passed by on her way to the high table, her perfume of sandalwood and jasmine trailing behind her dark skirts. She gave Gethin a sharp glance and her eyes rested, too long, on Tanwen.

"You should take care," Gethin said softly, when Isolde had passed on, "you must trust no one, especially de Lacy's captain."

Tanwen frowned. "He's helped me at times."

"He's dangerous. More than you know."

"So tell me." Tanwen was interrupted by a blare from three horns. The king entered, de Lacy behind him, and both kissed Isolde and sat in matched high-backed chairs. The servants passed, bringing stewed fruits and roast chickens.

Gethin watched Isolde, de Lacy, and the king, laughing and downing goblets of wine. He didn't understand the game himself, the chess match between de Lacy and the king over the borders. But with war looming, his maps had turned into a coveted weapon, better than a longbow or a new lance tip. Tanwen had no idea how he was watched, how dangerous just talking with him might be to her. "You should leave here, just as soon as you can," he repeated softly and watched her frown.

Isolde glanced his way again.

Gethin stood up abruptly. He was not the one to help Tanwen. He couldn't be the one to help her, now.

"You're going then." De Lacy's hand rapped a tattoo on his shield. "Good. Thought you might weasel out."

Gethin stiffened, then returned to tying his packs on Aeron's saddle. They were in the half-light of the stable and shadow split de Lacy's face in two halves.

"Don't take offense, it would be reasonable, given the way things are playing out."

"What do you mean?"

"Henry is fair purple in the face with the Welsh. I've heard it said he's eaten straw once, being so angry, and I've not seen a man get so mad and live through it. Still," de Lacy sighed, "he's a king and not a real man at all. Something else."

Gethin frowned. Philosophical ruminating was not de Lacy's style. "Henry has a truce with the Welsh, does he not?"

"That's it, in a nutshell." De Lacy yelled out the stable door to his men, "Back to the fields, you gluttons." The men grabbed bread from the serving girls and raced each other as de Lacy watched. "It's one of Clifford's castles Rhys is after now winter's done. And Henry's new darling is Clifford's daughter." De Lacy slapped his leather glove on the wall. "You do these maps, but I won't help you, if it comes to it. King or not, his head is addled from that woman. He promised Rhys justice for the murder of his nephew Einion, and Rhys has a right to it. But Rhys won't get justice, not unless he gets it for himself, so what kind of justice is that?" De Lacy shrugged. "The truce means nothing anymore."

Gethin thought about Henry, and the way a woman was swerving him from his life's purpose.

"Rhys won't stop, once he's got the bit in his teeth. Mark my words, there's war coming." De Lacy shoved on his stiff glove. "Good luck. Don't get caught, by either side. They'll both be after you now. And remember, those maps you'll make, those are mine, king or no."

CHAPTER TWENTY-EIGHT

HUW RUBBED HIS PALMS on his tunic. He felt jittery, like the night before a battle, when you stared into the fire and thought whether you'd see, ever again, afternoon sunlight slant through the willows. Lush July enveloped him. He waited for dawn in Tanwen's garden, where beds of yellow flowers smelled sweet, like Daron.

He had a son. He'd left his post in Rhys' encampment near Llandovery as soon as he got the message. He hadn't told anyone he was leaving, as he knew Rhys wouldn't let him go. When he arrived, he'd lurked outside Ludelaue's gates until one morning he glimpsed Tanwen. She told him he had a healthy son and told him also that Daron did not wish to see him, after all.

His son was named Hefin. A fine name. He'd done what Daron wanted, and left her and the baby, the river, and the castle behind. He'd thought to go back to Rhys and the fighting that would come. Instead he'd wandered the hills in a circle, slow and purposeless, watching the hills transition from chilly spring into the fullness of summer, admiring the dark solitude and the bright furry stars. He hadn't thought it out, but here he was, back again, revolving like those stars.

This time, he'd vaulted over the half-built walls in the early morning dark and walked across the courtyard to Tanwen's garden. He'd snapped off a white lily and waited as dawn crept over the hills, fingering the waxy petals and inhaling the faint disturbing scent.

When full morning came, he took a deep breath and walked across the courtyard, through the doors, and up the winding stairs. At the chamber, he stopped, but it felt odd to knock, so he pushed the door open with his boot. Daron was there, standing at the window, a creamy shawl draped over her arms. When she turned, he noticed her nose was red. He crossed the room and for a moment she stiffened, but when he took her in his arms, she pressed her face into his chest. They stood that way, for a long time, together.

"Do you wish to see him, your son?" Daron said finally.

Huw cleared his throat. "Of course. And you, how do you fare?"

"Helori came and in the end, it was not so very bad." Daron knelt beside the pallet and pulled the fuzzy blanket back.

Huw saw a tiny face. The baby's eyes were shut in a perfect sleep and his fist moved as though swaying in a silent breeze.

Daron pulled the cover back over the sleeping child, and got to her feet. She went to the window and stared out. "There was another child. I named her Agatha. But she didn't live past a day."

Huw thought about that and cleared his throat again. "Tanwen didn't tell me. I should have been here. But Daron, why didn't you tell me you were with child?"

"What difference would it have made?" She sighed. "I used to understand everything, it seemed. I was so sure. Now I think nothing is certain in this world."

Huw stared at the baby breathing, blowing tiny bubbles. "I haven't been back to Rhys or the fighting. I've been here, waiting." He touched Daron's shoulder, willing her to smile.

"Take us back Huw, to the village near Adpar. I have friends there." Daron put her palm on his chest. "We're a family now. You and me and this baby."

Huw thought of the difficulties of riding through the forest with a newborn.

Daron turned back to the window, where the first light streamed in across her face. "Helori took our daughter. Back to her house in the woods, to bury her. She said it was lovely there and peaceful in the sun. But I'll never see that place." Daron's face crumpled and then smoothed out again.

Huw took in a deep breath, but he couldn't think of anything more to say.

At noon, Tanwen walked in the door, stripping off her work gloves. "Huw! What are you doing here?" She touched the baby's cheek with a fingertip. "You must leave, right now. What if de Lacy's men see you?"

"I'm going, tonight," said Huw.

"And I'm going with him," said Daron.

"What do you mean?" Tanwen asked. "Where would you go?"

"Back to Adpar. We'll get a cottage in the village there," said Daron.

"You're not strong enough to travel yet."

"We'll take it slow. I'll care for her," said Huw. "I'll care for them both. Come with us. Our home will be yours."

Tanwen turned away, shaking her head. "You know I can't." She felt her teeth clench together with the longing to go back, to be home again.

"I know you won't," said Daron evenly, "but I am going." She returned to rocking the baby, singing a soft tune.

Later that afternoon, Huw and Daron hid in the stables, in an empty stall surrounded by bales of hay, waiting until it was dark enough to go. Huw told Daron Rhys was fighting for his castle at Dinefwr, and when he regained it, he had every intention of fighting on, for all the other castles along the winding Towy near his home. When he finished talking, Daron said nothing. Huw frowned. "I don't make the times."

"No." Daron nodded, but edged her fingers out of his grip.

"It's the turning point." Huw said. "Rhys will not stand alone this time. He's allied with all the other princes of Wales, united for the first time against Henry. It cannot fail."

"And you will want to go with him and join the fighting," said Daron.

Huw shrugged.

"Fine words, but not words of yours I think," said Daron, "and what is all that to us, if you are harmed?"

"So many are already dead."

She knew he thought of the dead sister he'd told her about one night, but still she couldn't leave it alone. "Will you go back to the fighting then?"

"Christ's bones, Daron."

She shook her head, sifting the hay through her fingers. "You go for revenge. That matters more to you, more than our future, more than us. Leave it behind, Huw, in the past. Stay with us." The baby woke and started a thin wailing cry.

Tanwen watched Daron and Huw go into the summer dusk, merging into the fields, and then she watched mist drift across the tips of ripe grass. Daron had talked only once of the child Helori had taken away. She had her son, but her daughter was lost to her forever. Tanwen wondered if Huw would settle down to village life, or return once more to the fighting. She wondered what it would be like, to have a husband, to be able to go home. She had waved until they were gone from her sight, but she hadn't called out I'll see you soon, for when would she see them again? She hoped at most for a letter, some day.

Tanwen slipped back through the small doorway she'd chiseled into the curtain wall at the back of her garden. It had taken days and days, but she'd chipped out the hardened wood splinter by splinter with her shovel until she'd made an opening, just large enough to shove through, and well hidden by thick vines and a hedge of shadowy cypress. She'd fashioned a wood door and leather hinges. She pulled the door back into place and pushed a flat rock against it to keep it shut. From inside her garden, she examined the tower, as she always did, arrow loops rimming the chamber where Bryn and the others slept.

She'd pretended to be confident when she'd talked to Gethin, but each day that went by, she'd been more and more frightened. One night, Henry had motioned with a flick of his fingers and one of the hostages, daughter of a minor lord, was carted off to his room. The court had pretended it hadn't happened, but she'd heard the girl weeping. She was over young and not pretty, but she was Welsh and there for the taking. Everyone was naked and unprotected before this king. And like all kings, Henry was a man with no soul.

Yet summer was proving warm and kind this year, in opposition to her mood, her plants strong, lush spills of heart-shaped leaves and fragrant blossoms. How amazing that she'd managed to grow such lovely plants and create this secret garden room. She touched a serrated leaf and ran a finger along a silvery lamb's ear. She'd never thought to be still here, and yet she'd never have made this garden if they hadn't been delayed by Daron and the child. She must not fall into fear now. She had made a new plan. She'd worked it out, over and over in her head until she'd thought she'd scream, for it must be perfect. How could she risk him, her perfect child? But he was at risk here, every day that she did nothing.

She touched the arching cane of a white rose. How sad she wouldn't see her work finished, this garden chamber years from now, clematis and roses climbing fragrant past the height of a man. But she would use this garden. Persuade Hugh de Lacy to invite Henry for a formal dinner, a long evening with food and much wine and musicians playing in the dusky summer night. While the courtiers drank and ate, jousting with words, all together in this one place, she would lure the soldiers guarding the tower away with ale and promises. She would have horses waiting at the gate. She would ask this much of Geoffrey. They would ride out, Bryn disguised as one of her garden helpers, carrying her tools. And they'd ride to Helori, who would help them with food, and then they'd go on. To the coast, to the continent, to Bruges, and further. Far as they must. She had silver pennies from her earnings for the ship passage. She would find work as a garden keeper when they got there, wherever there might be, and they would survive. More she couldn't imagine. She knelt down and pulled weeds. Her gardens must be perfection if she would persuade de Lacy of her plan.

The news arrived with three messengers, disheveled, mud-spattered, panting with thirst. They were given ale as they knelt on the rushes in the great hall. Then they blurted out their news. The Welsh were gathering in the mountains to the west.

Henry overturned his goblet. "Rebellion?" He stalked from the chamber. De Lacy followed.

There was a hush and then a roar of talk. Henry had concluded his great council at Woodstock just last year. He'd made the Welsh leaders plead for their lives and forced oaths of allegiance to the English crown. Even Rhys had sworn, his hands enclosed in Henry's, before he'd gone home, his escape from hanging a miracle, most said. And now Rhys had formed a new alliance with the Northmen and the mountain Welsh. They were a crazy people, murmured the Norman secretaries and lawyers, and even the knights, standing around the edges of the chamber, looked uneasy. The Welsh were strong fighters who flung themselves on you in ambush in the dead of night and then faded away into the mist before you could ever strike back and it was said they had women who rode with them in the hills, who could see into the past and into the future and who told them when to strike and where.

Tanwen, listening at the edge of the crowd, could almost have laughed as the tales grew more elaborate. But it was frightening, listening to the malevolent hum of the enthralled courtiers. A warm sickly wind blew in the open doors and made the torches smoke and the great banners flutter.

That evening, her head aching with a hot afternoon of wondering how this news would affect her planning, Tanwen resolved that there was nothing to do but wait a week or a fortnight and let matters settle. She left the hall, where men were yawning, and slipped up the stairs to her chamber. In the corner, gazing out the window, was Raoul.

He slapped a glove on the windowsill. "Shut the door."

She swung the heavy door shut, closing in the stale air.

"Latch it."

She pulled in the latch, noticing the tremble in her hand. She was glad her back hid this weakness from him.

"Summer has peaked, soon the dark will come down again." Raoul peered out the window. "De Lacy has asked me about your gardens."

"They will be perfect in another fortnight. I did not expect the king to come to Ludelaue so soon."

Raoul laughed. "Henry is not predictable, to you or me or least of all to de Lacy. A king makes his own seasons."

"Perhaps."

"Tanwen verch Sorcha, leman of Owain ap Macsen, traitor to the crown." Raoul eyed her and lingered over the words. "I've known since you first walked through the outer gates you were not what you seemed, and it needed only time and coin to find out what I wanted to know. Owain's leman here, right under Henry's nose. What would Henry do if he knew Rhys had sent you here, to listen, for him?"

"That's not true! I'm not a spy. Certainly not Rhys' spy." Tanwen swallowed. She must not let him goad her. Perhaps he still didn't know. "I'm in no one's pay."

"And then there's the young cub of course." He circled round behind her.

Her skin prickled and she felt his finger trace a line down the nape of her neck.

"Yes," he said, "exactly." He walked out.

Tanwen listened to his boots thud down the stairs and the slam of the outside door, her breath coming fast. She stared at the wide oak planks of the floor, at the dust gathered in the cracks between the boards. He was unpredictable to her and that was a very great danger. Rebellion or no, the time to act had come. She must persuade de Lacy, lure him in with promises of power, advantages to be gained. Convince him this dinner was no diversion but essential now the Welsh rebellion had come. She went to the window and gazed out into the dark, wishing she could see what lay ahead.

CHAPTER TWENTY-NINE

F OR THREE DAYS, Tanwen planned every detail and avoided Raoul, which was easy as he was occupied with drilling his men or in council with de Lacy. On the third night, Tanwen lingered in the great hall, hoping for a chance to approach de Lacy, but his sister Isolde was always at his side and they left together. Tanwen trailed after them, but when Isolde curtsied to her brother and went to her chamber, de Lacy went directly to the weapons shed, where Raoul stood at the door. Tanwen felt a chill on the back of her neck as she stared at them across the dark courtyard. Her gardens were as close to perfect as she could make them, the roses at their peak, white petals flung open and gold centers gleaming. Even the weather was warm and the air soft and as the darkness finally came, the moon and stars danced above the flowers just as she had imagined. She felt a moment of wonder that she had made this beauty. She climbed to her room, wondering if she could approach de Lacy in the morning, though he was gruffer in the early hours.

On the landing, she passed Henry's manservant, locking a massive chest, his ring of keys jangling. He was arguing with another servant. She couldn't understand their Norman words entirely, but he wanted the chest carried somewhere. There was a crash outside and the servants rattled down the stairs. Tanwen hurried to the window. A line of donkeys hitched to carts stretched across the paved area by the gate and a swarm of boys carrying baskets of cheeses had gathered at the kitchen doors. Tanwen's breath caught as she watched. Henry and his advisors hadn't seemed to sleep since news of the Welsh rebellion had come. And now the king, it seemed, was leaving. Leaving Ludelaue, as suddenly as he'd come.

Tanwen flew down the stairs and stepped out into the moonlight. She stopped one of the servants. "Where is the king going?"

"Normandy, but what's that to you?" The man pushed past her, a heavy chest on his shoulder that jingled with the sound of coin.

All the way to France. Tanwen stepped back into the shadows. If the king left, what would happen then? And what of her plan? De Lacy would never agree to the dinner if the king weren't here to impress. She thought of Raoul's threat, his finger on her neck.

She dodged between the loaded barrows and annoyed donkeys and reached the cedars by the tower door. With all this commotion, perhaps she could just sneak in and somehow get Bryn out. The courtyard was chaos, the servants tired and preoccupied. What if they could get out through her secret door, this very night? No, she'd have to get horses first, they'd never evade capture without horses, but what if they could leave at first light? The servants and guards would be exhausted and abed after getting Henry packed and away. A hot wind gusted, sending the smell of roses mixed with dust. A storm was coming. They'd get wet, but even that was more luck for it would slow anyone chasing.

The guard at the tower door stretched and surveyed the commotion and cursed under his breath. He wandered off around the corner to relieve himself. Tanwen ran up the three steps and slipped through the heavy door. Inside, she hesitated in the airless dark.

Men were talking, above her, on the stairs. Slowly, she felt her way up the dim uneven steps, her fingers tracing over the rough stone blocks. On the first landing, an arrow loop let in a breath of humid air. The spiral stairs turned to creaky timber, and the guard's voices grew louder. She climbed to the next landing and one of the guards shouted. She flattened against the wall and held her breath. But then they all laughed. She heard the clank of a tin cup and more loud laughter. They were just above her, she could see their long jagged shadows reaching out around the turn of the stair. She edged upwards, climbing three more steps.

Suddenly, just above her, a door swung open, a gaping orange wedge of light, and two men hurried side by side down the stairs. She froze, but there was nowhere to hide.

"What's this?" whispered one.

"Mother," the other blurted out.

"What?" said his companion, and Bryn grabbed his arm. "You will say nothing," he whispered, his voice menacing and he shoved the youth back up the stairs. Above them, the guards burst out laughing again and Tanwen realized they were playing some sort of drinking game.

Bryn took her elbow and rushed her down one flight of stairs. He opened a small half-hidden door and pulled her into a low-ceilinged room. It was even darker than the stairs and smelled of mouse droppings. Already the storm had arrived and rain slanted in the window and puddled on the uneven stone floor. "Mother, whatever are you doing here? It's not safe for you."

Tanwen shook her head, tears welling, unable to speak. It was so wonderful to see him, thin and pale as he was.

He went to the window and stuck an arm out into the rain, letting water splash off his open palm.

"Is it safe to talk here?" she asked, when she could speak.

"Safe as it gets with the king here."

"I have a way out for us."

He blinked and pulled his arm in. "A way out?"

She moved closer, until she could feel the rain on her face. He didn't move away, but she felt him shift his weight. "Listen. Henry is leaving, this very night, or just at dawn most likely. It's chaos outside, everyone milling around, that's what the noise is all about and by dawn the servants will have been up all night packing and lugging boxes and drinking ale. When Henry goes, they'll seek their beds."

"I don't see," he said.

"Even the guards will be abed. This is our time."

"For what?"

"To leave here, of course."

He folded his arms over his chest.

Tanwen sneezed and held her breath. No sound came from the

stairs. "We'll go to the coast by horse, then catch a ship."

"A ship. You cannot even swim Mama." Bryn grinned at her.

"This is no joke. A ship will take us to Bruges or somewhere in the low countries."

"And what would we do there?" He pressed his mouth against the iron bar and breathed in the rain soaked air.

"What does it matter? We'll find work. We'll be free, and you'll be away from Henry, from all this."

"Free," he said softly. "Sometimes I think..." He frowned and shook his head, then stepped to the door.

Tanwen blinked back her tears. "It's raining, I'll bring warm clothing. And Bryn, you must tell no one." Cold wind rushed in and ruffled her skirts.

Bryn leaned out the door and beckoned to someone. "I'd have to tell Nick," he said. "We'd have to bring Nick along. I won't go anywhere without Nick."

Tanwen shrank back as a man stepped into the room.

"It's just Geoffrey," said Bryn.

The knight bowed to her. "Madame, my apologies for disturbing your conversation." He frowned at Bryn.

"We were nearly done," said Bryn. "Tell me, have you shown him my sketches?"

"Yes, but do not show such impatience in front of your mother. We can talk later." Geoffrey handed a packet to Bryn. "Sword practice at noon, the king is going before dawn," he said, giving Tanwen another assessing look, and left.

"We haven't been allowed out once since Henry arrived. Cooped up like chickens destined for the block always," Bryn said.

"You must not say anything, not to anyone, even Geoffrey," Tanwen said. "I'll find us a horse some other way. We can't trust him, or anyone. Bryn, are you listening? In the back of my garden, behind the tall cypresses, is a secret door I've made. You can slip out in the confusion when Henry goes."

The tramp of boots sounded, men coming down the stairs. "You need to go," Bryn said, taking her arm. "We'll speak more, later." He

pushed her, gently, out the door and disappeared, like the thin ghost
he now resembled, back up the dim stairs.

Dawn came, but the donkey carts still trailed across the courtyard.
The day passed like a strange time-slowed dream. The king did not
go, but stayed closeted in the solar above the hall with messengers
running in and out, while rain drummed down. Tanwen waited and
worried, and swiped a round cheese, fat as a harvest moon, from the
storage room when the cook was scolding one of the kitchen girls.
It was stolen, but it would bring them good fortune. She'd sewn the
pennies she'd earned tight into the bodice of her gown. She felt taut,
vibrating like a lute string, going nowhere.

She spent the endless afternoon in her rain-soaked garden, worried that Bryn might try to slip out and she wouldn't be there. She
wished she could tell someone how to care for the roses and trim
the cedars. She weeded in the watery earth around the marguerites
and snapped off some stems of lavender to tuck in her pack and after
that she pretended to work but mostly she touched her plants and
memorized the shape of their leaves and inhaled their scents, trying to
lodge each one's special fragrance in her memory. This garden room
had sprung from pictures in her mind. Even so, it went its own way,
ivy wandering away from the path instead of blanketing the spaces
between the wet stones, marigolds crowding toward the afternoon sun,
not sending gold blossoms straight into the air. Yet it was beautiful
in its waywardness. She dug up three fat bulbs and slipped them into
her pouch. Perhaps they would survive in a new land?

The torches were lit early. Still the donkeys waited, ears twitching,
soaked and matted in the driving rain. Tanwen hovered by de Lacy's
half-built walls and thought of home. What would it be like to see
the silver underside of the birch leaves, and the bright river winding
through the ferns, to be near Adpar? Perhaps she would never see
home again. Where was home for her and Bryn now?

At dusk, when the distracted grooms went to the kitchens for their
dinner, Tanwen slipped into the barn and threw a bridle onto the
horse she'd picked out. He was old and tame and let her put the bit

in his mouth without trouble. She led him out into the rain, waiting for shouts, but in the confusion and driving rain, no one seemed to care. She passed out the back gate along with three farmers with empty wagons and once they reached the turn-off for the village, Tanwen let the farmers walk on ahead. She tied the horse to a bush and went to sit on a flat rock, wrapped in her cloak. The rain was slowing and the patter on the leaves high above her sounded bright like dancing music. Now they were truly going, she felt sudden excitement race through her, surprising, like a sparkling drink of French wine. Clouds were sliding away, leaving bright stars shining, and the clean scent of wet grass blew past her on a fresh wind. The weather had shifted, surely Henry would leave now, and Bryn would come.

Did she doze? She wasn't sure. It was dark, with no moon. She heard the crack of a stick under someone's foot. A man's shadow, too big to be Bryn. She jumped up and hit her head on a tree branch. Footsteps thudded and too late she ducked behind a clump of hazel, dragging her skirts behind her. A long silence. Then an arm grabbed her waist from behind.

"What are you doing here?"

Tanwen stopped struggling, recognizing the voice. It was Gethin, though that made no sense. She looked past him, searching the shadows for Bryn.

Gethin jerked his chin toward the castle walls, where two men patrolled, bows cocked. "Quiet," he mouthed, and yanked her along, timing their darting from tree to tree with the pacing of the guards. At the river's edge he picked her up.

"Gethin!" Her yell was smothered in his tunic. Already they were in the water. He had taught her to swim, but this was a torrent of frothing water, surging around his thighs. He crossed on the flat rocks arranged as a hidden path beneath the water's dark surface, slipping once. She clutched at his neck. At the far side he carried her through sopping ferns to the line of young birches, and dumped her down, breathing hard.

She examined the far bank, but she could see no sign of Bryn.

But it was definitely growing lighter. It was dawn. "I slept. I should never have slept."

Gethin stared at her. "What?"

"Bryn. He was to meet me. What if I've missed him?"

"You tied your horse in plain sight. He could not have missed you." Gethin ran his hand through his hair. "Who are you actually meeting?"

"My lover, is that what you think?"

He frowned at the river. "Perhaps you meet Raoul."

She felt herself flush. "And perhaps you meet Isolde? I'm going back." She walked down to the water, but hesitated as the fast current caught her ankles.

"Do you want to be seen?" He yanked her to a stand of high ferns and pushed her down. The ferns crushed beneath them, smelling of green darkness and water.

"I will get Bryn away from here. However I can. You know that."

"Even that?"

She looked away. The ferns curled and arched and twined, suffocating her with their spicy humid smell. They sat there, silent. Then she said, "I'm leaving here, with Bryn, today."

"How? Bryn is with the other hostages."

"No." She swallowed. "He will slip out. In the confusion with Henry leaving. I told him to meet me here."

"The king is just coming now." The iron portcullis screeched open as Gethin spoke and the earth shuddered with the hoofs of dozens of horses. "Henry was held up, waiting for messages from France," said Gethin. A trumpet sounded and a heron squawked as it flew low over the river. The first horses and their flashing riders thundered past, and then the long sleepy train of carts began to trundle by, donkeys braying and men shouting. Tanwen and Gethin watched from their hiding place. Finally, the clatter ceased and only the deep ruts in the mud showed that the king had passed by.

"Bryn must have come in the night. I've missed him," said Tanwen, staring at the castle towers.

"Bryn will go to the practice fields with Geoffrey, now the king's not here, as they have done many mornings. Perhaps you can chance speaking with him."

"This was not as most mornings." She curled away from him and hid her face.

"Geoffrey is a good man." Gethin stared at Tanwen's back, at the nape of her neck where the skin was so white. Many mornings he'd watched the knight with the boy, and felt a loneliness for something he'd never had, nor would.

"He steals my son from me," Tanwen said, turning around and glaring.

"No, he takes an interest. A boy needs that, a man to take an interest." He waited, but she didn't answer. Now the king's party was gone, the strange silence of the forest ceased and the normal hum and chitter started up again. Down in the shallows, the geese and ducks began their honking. In the birches, Aeron stamped a hoof. "I must be going," said Gethin. Sun lit the trees and glistened on the cobwebs stretched over the grass. Like small hammocks, a shimmering web to hold one up.

She didn't look at him. "Go then."

"I can't leave you this way."

"Why not?" She shredded a fern and tossed it aside. "You've left before. What are you even doing here? Never mind, don't tell me, not that you would. Go back to your maps, they're calling you. De Lacy and even Henry will pay you well. You are their creature." She turned back to the river and covered her eyes with her palm as though the light off the water was too bright.

"He's just a boy, he doesn't think."

"Aren't you supposed to be on the south coast drawing these maps of yours?"

"I decided these mountains would be a better place to start."

"The passes are to the north and south."

"Nonetheless, I've been working here."

Tanwen said nothing more, her eyes still resting on the castle gate.

The sun grew hot on the back of his neck. At noon, a stream of black figures walked back from the practice field and filed into the castle. He couldn't see if Bryn or Geoffrey were among them. The gate screeched shut.

There was a loud splash in the river. Tanwen parted the ferns. Two swans settled into the water, leaving a v-shaped wake as they swam, arching their necks, admiring their own blue-white beauty. Steam hovered above the river and a hum of insects sang. Tanwen sank back and touched her temples with her fingers. "I was going to take him away. To the lowlands, where he could be free. Where we could be as we were."

Gethin watched the swans touch their beaks to the black water. "Time only rolls forward."

"That's a hard truth." Her eyes met his.

He leaned toward her, until her breath warmed his neck, and he picked up a strand of her bright hair and twirled it around his finger. He thought about her body, pale as foam on a gleaming beach when a wave sweeps and falls back, leaving gold sand sparkling. Spangled with seaweed.

Tanwen cleared her throat. "Tell me again," she whispered, "about this sea you've been to. This Mediterranean sea."

He looked away from her, to the river. "The water there is green, and yet, not green. There is blue in it, and gold, and it is clear like the finest glass. The sands underneath are alive. Tiny fish flash and play, silver and blue."

She nodded, tears gathering in her eyes.

He spoke faster. "Sometimes, a storm blows up so sudden you sink to the deck of the ship, and splinters grind into your knees. You only find them later. The waves toss you so high and so deep you know you could never swim to land and the water is spraying like a greedy rain on your face. Then the squall blows over and the water spreads calm and flat and blue, and fantastical fish fly above the surface, keeping pace with your racing ship."

Tanwen felt his fingers tighten on her arm. She thought of Bryn, and it was as if she saw him on that ship with pale gold sails, racing away from her, the gap between them ever wider, and the water wasn't icy green but these warmer seas, rich with wondrous fish who could fly, flowing with water so clear that though he was far, far away, she could still see him, perfectly.

CHAPTER THIRTY

The Berwyn Mountains

GETHIN TUCKED THE QUILL PENS into his oiled bag. He'd camped in the mountains northwest of Ludelaue through the humid months and into the last breath of summer, mapping ravines, hills, and streams. It was past time to head south to the coast as he'd planned. He would stay with Enid, David, and Sam for the cold months, setting down all he'd learned of the borders, then head along the southern coast as he'd promised de Lacy. But for three days now he'd packed and unpacked his bag and fiddled with building a box for his inks. He wanted to go back to Ludelaue, to say something, he wasn't sure what, to Tanwen, if she were still there.

The next morning he set out. He hadn't heard much news, but he knew the English king planned to teach the Welsh rebels a permanent lesson, which meant certain war in the spring. But when he reached the castle, a stiff wind cracked the banners above the gatehouse and the guards huddled over a brazier, waiting for their midday replacements. They waved him through with no inspection or interest. No one lingered in the courtyard, dismal with early morning frost.

And Tanwen was not in her garden. Gethin hesitated as Aeron pawed at the ground. He'd imagined her there always, crouched beside the mint in the sun, late roses dropping petals onto the clipped grass. Why had he come? But he had, so he tied the horse by the stable. Inside the barn, three boys argued over a hot meat pie. They looked up, with guilty eyes, when he entered.

Gethin sniffed the spices and his stomach rumbled. He beckoned to the youngest, a pale lad of about seven, and handed him a penny. "For a pie all your own." He reached back into his pouch and found the rounded river rock he'd picked up that day by the river, after she'd gone, smooth and soft as a woman's breast, and veined with lines of pink on grey. He turned it slowly in his fingers. "Do you know de Lacy's garden keeper?" he asked the boy. "Is she still here, working on the gardens by the walls?" When the boy nodded yes, fist closed around the coin, Gethin said, "Take this stone to her when she comes out to work, and you must put it directly into her hands and no other. Don't forget. Do it as soon as she comes."

"And tell her what?"

Gethin hesitated. "Tell her, remember."

"Remember what?" said the boy.

"Nothing else," said Gethin irritably. "Just that, remember." He hesitated a moment longer, then climbed back on Aeron and cantered out the gate.

Weeks later, after following the Wye, camping in icy rain and then in sleet and snow, still sketching and writing notes in crabbed coded script, Gethin reached Ilfracombe. He arrived as the stars shone out in a twilight sky edged with pink. He hugged Enid, welcoming her smell of cinnamon and pepper.

"Wherever have you been," she cried. "We had no thought of you turning up for the Yule."

"Nor I," said Gethin, "but with the weather so foul, I had to hole up somewhere for a few weeks." He smiled and handed her a package. "Besides, I wanted to come. Where's Sam?"

"Learning his letters. The monks have started a school here for the boys in the winter months." Enid set the package in the center of the table. "We'll wait until Sam's home. Won't he be surprised!"

"How is he?" Gethin pulled off his wet cloak and hung it on the hook.

Enid smiled and reached for a bowl and two eggs. "Much better, most days. It's been good for him here, with David. They're peas in a pod, both working the wood and Sam livening things up. He's made pets of the chickens and that dog you gave him never leaves his side."

"Does he speak?"

Enid cracked the eggs into the bowl and dribbled in honey. "No." She put a hand on his arm. "Who knows what horrors yet lie sleeping in his mind? It's not something that can be forced." She went back to stirring her cake. "It matters little. We get along fine."

Sam and David filed in later and Sam pulled Gethin back out to the woodshop to see the stool he was building. He picked up Gethin's hand and ran it along the smooth grain of the quarter-sawn oak. Later, after a stew of simmered chicken and onions, and a dessert of custard and the sugar doves Gethin had brought, Enid dragged Sam away to help her feed the hens.

David cleared his throat and sat down by the hearth. "You've been traveling far."

"Along the Berwyn Mountains. I've figured a system for recording the landscape, a kind of short hand so I can set it down accurately, even months later. I can accomplish so much more. I have pages of notes." Gethin picked up David's carving knife and tested the blade. "But you're right. I had to travel with care. The woods crawl with soldiers. And there will be more come spring."

"Dangerous times. Good the boy stays here. He's settling in," said David.

"I'm glad of that." Gethin shrugged. "I am. Though it turns out I miss him."

David took back his knife and began to work at the head an owl, carved of maple. After a time, he said, "Heard you'll be fitting out a ship; how'd you manage that?"

"A long story. I've got funds for just one season and I'll be taking her west, mapping the coast."

"Any news from Wales, of the rebellion I mean?"

"Nothing you haven't heard. Rhys took back all of Ceredigion before the snow. Henry won't rein in the border lords, or can't. There will be full out war, it's sure now."

"And de Lacy?"

"He's paying for these maps."

David paused in his carving. "You'll give them to him?"

Gethin stood up and threw a chestnut into the fire. "I've not decided." He rubbed his hand through his hair as he paced. "I don't know what's right and that's the truth. With war coming. These maps, all the details of the borderlands. They'll give the advantage to whoever has them. And there's more than one who wants them."

David polished the small owl with an oiled cloth until it gleamed. "You'll know what's right," he said, "when the time comes."

A few days past the Yule, Gethin strolled by the Ilfracombe docks. Three ships that might serve his purpose floated in the harbor. He passed barrels of fish bait, piles of rope, men lugging nets and casks. This was the future, this trading and travelling, something beyond and above the endless squabbling of border lords over glory and honor and land. The water rippled and ran silver-pink, the whole tidy bay rimmed by rosy hills. As Gethin gazed at the bright water, something shifted, deep in his chest. The tightness he'd held so long, since Julianna and the baby died, seemed to drift away into the frosty air. He was living again, that's what it was. He wouldn't be going back, not to de Lacy or Rhys or any of their kind, not again. That dark wandering life, it was all behind him.

Sam and some other boys raced among the bait barrels. They'd found rope and were tying each other up in intricate knots. Enid told him the boy still woke with half-recalled nightmares. But not so often. He'd come with a thought of taking Sam along with him, but here the boy could learn to write and read, learn to work the elm and oak in David's shop. He'd play with other boys. He could maybe bury his own past deep and move on.

Gethin gazed at the chips of light on the dancing water and his thoughts drifted to Tanwen. He'd tried to keep her out of his mind as he'd journeyed, evergreen branches crowding his path and oak boughs threatening to swipe him from his saddle. Always there was one more turn in the river bed, one more hill to climb, one more stream wandering off to be followed, and here in Ilfracombe, the pleasure of sharp smelling ink as he transferred sketches and notes into an intricate and beautiful pattern. He could only work a few flying hours in a winter day, then the light failed and his eyes blurred. He feared ruining the maps with a line that couldn't be sanded away. Still, joy stole through him as dusk fell and he contemplated the lines wandering over the page, each an intricate symbol of a place he'd been and seen. But no one to tell.

Winter passed and spring came, with the smell of green growing drifting over the land. One morning, Gethin descended the hill from Enid's home and entered the alleys by the harbor. A whiff of bacon smoke from the tavern reminded him he'd had no breakfast. He'd chartered a ship a week past and yesterday they'd seen to the final loading and even the early greens and spring onions were aboard.

Gethin caught up to Sam and two friends, rolling barrels along the uneven pier. "Don't grow too tall this summer. I wish to recognize you when I return." He gave the boy a hug and a gentle shove. Sam clutched him tight around the waist, then he was off. Gethin watched him leap over a piled net. He'd asked Sam if he was planning to stow away again and Sam had laughed, shaking his head. Gethin put a foot in the skiff and grabbed the oars, wondering why that made him sad. Sam, at least, had found his place.

On board, Gethin went below deck, bending his head beneath the low oak beams and found the dark closet that would be his home. He stumbled over something on the floor. Groping around, he lit a candle and swore under his breath. The table was upended, the straw mattress overturned and tipped against the wall. Lamp glass lay smashed across the floor.

The first mate poked his head down. "All settled?" His smile faded. "Seems you have something someone wants."

"Nothing I know of."

"They've left your coin, there on the floor. Strange, don't you think?" The sailor stared, forehead creased, and seemed to reach a decision. He called over his shoulder as he left. "Your brother is come to bid you well away, he's on deck and you'd best be quick, we're sailing within the hour."

Gethin surveyed the mess. He knew what the searchers had been after. He touched the quiver hung diagonally over his chest. Inside were rolled parchments, his entire fall and winter's work. Three large maps, and together they showed the entire border realm, from the mountains in the north down to the sea near Striguil. Spring had come, and war, with Henry invading through an unprecedented land route through the border mountains. The maps were beyond valuable.

Up on deck, wind tossed his hair and he shoved it out of his eyes. Gulls screamed and men shouted and the ship creaked. Gethin saw Cynan arguing with a sailor who was trying to get him back into a skiff.

"There you are," said Cynan. "I've been trying to tell this good fellow I couldn't leave without blessing you for your voyage."

The sailor rolled his eyes. "Be quick about it then, no long winded blathering. We've got to catch this wind and if he's aboard, he's coming."

Gethin put a hand on Cynan's shoulder. "I didn't expect you."

"I'm headed to Calais. My ship was to sail yesterday, but we're delayed for a week with repairs, and then I heard you were here."

"A good thing too," said Gethin. He dropped to his knees in front of Cynan and bent his head as though for a blessing. "I've something you must take ashore for me and hide it well."

Cynan made the sign of the cross on his forehead. "Do you now, well, that's interesting. What?"

"My maps. Someone is after them."

"I see," said Cynan. "You want me to take them to David and Enid?"

"No," said Gethin. "Too dangerous for them. It's the first place they'll search."

"If not there? I can't take them to Clairvaux. That won't be convenient when you wish to retrieve them."

"No, take them to Ludelaue."

"You'll sell them to de Lacy then?"

"We're casting off," said a sailor, running by.

"Not to de Lacy. Take them there in full secret, and give them privately to de Lacy's garden keeper, a woman, known as Tangwystl, but her real name is Tanwen."

"You're sure? To a woman?"

"Tell her guard them well. She must on no account let de Lacy or anyone know they exist."

Cynan slung the quiver over his neck. "Fare well my friend."

"And you." Gethin stopped, his voice hoarse.

"Don't get maudlin on me." Cynan laughed. "Now that it's started, I'm beginning to enjoy my small adventure." He was gone over the side into the skiff, bobbing toward shore.

Gethin watched Cynan land at the pier and he waved, though he knew he had disappeared into the brilliant white light off the water. The ship rocked out of the harbor, hit the winds, and raced away from land. Soon the smell of musty leaves and the stench of the harbor fell away and there was only salt and endless rushing water.

CHAPTER THIRTY-ONE

Ludelaue, 1165

Tanwen felt she'd never seen such loveliness. Spring flung itself on them in a flurry of soft breezes and sprouting crocus, white ramsons and feathery piling clouds. She was out in the warm air, digging and pruning and transplanting, perfecting her garden.

Despite all the beauty in nature, the world of men felt awry. Henry had called a war council at Northampton last fall. Raoul and all the men had ridden out, but for a skeleton crew, their horses jangling with bells, the men flaunting bright tunics and the boys hoisting fluttering banners. They'd returned a fortnight later, gleeful as boys playing, with plans for a massive summer invasion, direct into the deep heart of Wales. It seemed the Welsh had lit a bonfire with their rebellion, and it had smoldered on through the dark winter months, and now it was bursting into flames. An irate de Lacy rode out each morning to drill his men and returned fuming at twilight with news of traitorous vassals already joining the Welsh bands in the mountains. Tanwen swatted at a horsefly buzzing around her head and wondered where Owain might be in this chaos of shifting alliances. That she wondered at all made her angry.

Raoul had put foreign guards at the door to the hostages' chamber. Bryn was no longer allowed out to practice with Geoffrey. Yet despite the gangs of soldiers gathering, practicing spear throws in a ceaseless clatter, her garden grew lush and fragrant, tossing white blossoms of feverfew over the rock walls. Tanwen ran her palm over the grass, sprinkled with bluets and buttercups. Tiny lime butterflies danced over the grassy turf. She found their stilled wings sometimes, draped over the rose heads or caught on rose thorns. In her fingers, the fragile papery wings disappeared into soft dust.

One hot day, Tanwen yanked weeds, her hands soaked with sweat inside her gloves. The orange afternoon sun seemed to press against her shoulders. She wiped her forehead, sitting on the turf bench. An image of that cool pond where Gethin taught her to swim swirled into her mind. How icy the water, dripping from her legs and pouring off Gethin's chest. She shook her head. She wouldn't think of that, or of him. He'd left Ludelaue, without a word. Or a word she could understand. Remember. She had the stone. But remember what exactly? She remembered all too well his shoulders under her fingers, the cool dampness of moss, and the crushed green scent of ferns.

"You're mad if you think it," shouted a boy with a red hat, interrupting her thoughts. The hostages were being paraded around the courtyard, the one time each day they were allowed out of their crowded room high in the tower. She stared, hungry to see Bryn.

"It's Henry who is mad." That was Rhys' son.

"Quiet you fools," hushed an older youth, glancing at the soldiers.

"We will prevail in this war, I tell you," said Rhys' son.

"But will it matter, to us?" said the first.

"Of course it will, we'll be free then."

"They will never let us go," said the older youth.

Tanwen's eyes flew back to Bryn. He'd just passed his twelfth birthday, here in this dread place. He was ignoring the prince's sons, and talking to his friend Nick, a sheaf of parchments in his hands. He was always drawing. Detailed designs for contraptions to plant wheat and move stones and bridge streams. Sometimes, he held the sketches up to show her as he passed. She'd had no chance to talk with him, no chance even to find out why he hadn't come to meet her, that day the king had gone to France. She'd thought about it endlessly, concocting reasons in her head. She'd even tried to ask Geoffrey, who shook his head and said, "You must ask him, when you can. Perhaps there's another future waiting for him."

Even if Bryn wouldn't come to the lowlands, she needed to get him out of here. For now, Henry simply planned his great invasion. His men fletched arrows and gathered stones. But the snow had melted early off the mountains. Any day now, Henry would sail back across the channel. She'd resurrected her old plan of an evening party in the largest garden chamber, rimmed by cedar and promising to be fragrant with white roses. She doubted sometimes she could convince de Lacy, doubted she could carry it off, but she told herself over and over that she must not lose heart.

Summer came on early, with De Lacy turning the castle inside out with his demands for men, men to be scrounged from the neighboring farms and hamlets, whether they could be spared from the planting or not. He paced in the great hall, issuing orders for arrows, horseshoes, wood shields, apples to be dried, oats to be stolen and stockpiled. Rumor was the Welsh forces had wintered in the hills and were gathered already, ready to begin the fight. Henry had invaded Wales once from the north by sea, and triumphed, and another time from the south coasts, and won again. Sure of victory, he planned this coming invasion to strike deep into the central mountains, so destructively they'd never manage to fight again. Men crowded into the castle. Most were farmers, some merchants or artisans; few were soldiers. They stepped on Tanwen's flowerbeds and pissed behind the hedge. The real soldiers, the mercenaries, camped outside the walls, speaking their guttural language that no one could understand. So many would be injured or die, but Tanwen felt her heart close against them. She had no emotion left for others, only for Bryn.

One afternoon, as she clipped the turf edging her garden, trying to avoid her grim thoughts, the castle gate screeched and she watched Raoul ride through and pause to look around. Seeing her, he tossed his reins to a boy. She got to her feet, her heart speeding. He'd been gone since midwinter, gathering men for de Lacy and the king. "I didn't realize you were back," she said, when he approached. "Does this mean you'll be riding into Wales soon? Has the king returned from France?"

"You know I can't answer that." Raoul stepped closer. "It's time for plain talking between us. You know we go to war."

"All Wales and England know that."

"Yet I have not betrayed you. I've kept your secrets."

Tanwen swallowed. But she knew this could happen. She could smell the soldier smell of him, see the dark shadows under his eyes. She turned her head aside.

"Your son, bastard though he is, is heir to Owain ap Macsen, Rhys' most ardent supporter. Owain will do anything for his master. Was he a real man to you?" Raoul laughed. "I think not. But I am. I make no secret of it. I want you."

"Why?" she whispered.

He put his hands on her shoulders. "I could have you now, right here against the stable wall. Or tonight in my chamber, or any night or day."

She shook off his hands.

"But I have not. Don't you wonder why, Tanwen?"

She looked into his eyes. "Perhaps you are a better man that that."

"Perhaps. But you must not count on that."

Just then a score of mercenaries marched by, tramping in the dust with new leather boots. "Where are they going? Who are those men?"

"A precaution. They go to guard the hostages. It's full out war now, my Tanwen. Henry will stop at nothing this time."

The morning sun was harsh, gleaming off hauberks. The courtyard was muddy after three days of rain and crowded with soldiers. People from the town were pouring in the gate. Merchants threaded through the jostling crowd selling pies. Tanwen stared, dazed by the horde of people, many in their best bright tunics and gowns, joking and laughing, sure of victory. She examined the soldiers lining up to march into the mountains, clad in metal, hoisting long swords, sweating in the sun.

Raoul was in the center, calling orders, black hair gleaming. He wore bright yellow and his horse had blue ribbons braided in his tail. She saw him glance toward her, and she quickly looked away.

"There they come, filthy Welsh dogs," muttered a man near her, his breath sour with last night's ale. His wife pointed with muscled arms. Tanwen felt her stomach lurch as the hostages were paraded out of their tower in two rows, prodded to the center of the courtyard with long tasseled spears. She threaded her way through the crowd. There was Bryn, tall and thin, his arms bound with thick cord. "Welsh bastards!" someone shouted and someone else threw an apple. It splattered on the ground.

People were pushing, trying to get closer. Tanwen shoved through the crowd, her limbs slow as though she waded through knee-deep water. More shouts, and a rain of thudding apples. The hostages ducked and turned away, trying to shield their heads with bound arms. Apples hit the ground, rolled, and smashed into faces and backs.

Tanwen flung herself against the man in front of her, ducked under elbows, and reached the front as a stone flew up, dark against the sky. All watched it lift and hesitate, as though it floated, and then it arced down. "No," Tanwen screamed, and the crowd was screaming too. She was thrown to the ground. Her palms scraped against rough stones. She scrabbled among leather boots and filthy bare feet, spat out gravel, and scrambled to her feet.

The hostages huddled together, backs to the crowd. One slumped on the ground, blood puddled under his blonde head. She ran toward them. Raoul, mounted on his grey stallion, tore into the crowd. "What's this," he shouted, his voice harsh.

The crowd was silenced. Rocks clenched in men's hands dropped to the ground. He glared over their heads. "It is not time, not yet. Get back to your work."

The men grumbled and hesitated, but they dispersed. Women hurried children away, and a few youths backed off slow, swearing. Raoul barked to the guards who hoisted the injured boy and herded the rest of the hostages back into the tower and slammed shut the solid door.

The portcullis creaked open, with a lengthy screech of iron. Raoul trotted his stallion up to Tanwen and leaned down. He spoke in a low voice, to her alone. "I can save him for you Tanwen. Your choice, now." He spurred the horse and the grey leaped, red drops

flying from its sides. The soldiers followed, clattering out the gate in
a welter of color and banners flapping bright.

He'd saved the hostages, saved Bryn. What did she owe him, for that?
Tanwen paced in her garden after the men left. Yet if she gave Raoul
what he wanted, what then? What guarantee did she have he would
truly let Bryn go? Did he truly have the power to do so? The king
had returned to the borders and gone straight on to the mountains
with his endless rows of soldiers marching, seeking the spot where
the rebels from all of north and south Wales gathered. She had no
idea how long Raoul would be gone, or how much time she had to
get Bryn away before they all returned, triumphant. And the foreign
mercenaries Raoul had brought in guarded the tower day and night.

Tanwen heard steps crunching on the gravel path and turned, glad
to have her dire thoughts interrupted. Geoffrey crossed towards her.

"I've just seen Bryn. I thought you should know."

"How did you get in? How did you find him? Is he well?" She
stopped, her tight throat making it hard to speak.

"He's had a fever. Many in there are ill. They need better food,
fresh air. Time grows short."

"I know that, I'm not ignorant."

"I never said so, nor implied it, I hope. But the day is coming
soon when I will leave here, go back to the north of England. This
is not my war."

"I see," Tanwen said, dismayed. She hadn't realized how much
she'd counted on him to watch over Bryn.

Geoffrey's eyes scanned the courtyard and returned to her. "You
don't know this, but I was a hostage once. For two years, over in
France. The life of a hostage is complicated. It's hard to know who
to trust. One has to make judgments, take risks." He shrugged. "It's
not safe here anymore for these boys. This war has come and when
it's over, the hostages will be at even greater risk."

Tanwen bent down and yanked out a handful of weeds. "Or
things will be better then, as they were. I'll be able to get him out of
here. I have a plan."

Geoffrey frowned at the castle walls. "This war will not be quick and easy, if any war can be called so. I only speak the unpleasant truth, which I think you know full well." He hesitated. "And Bryn is not a child anymore."

"What are you saying?"

"Only this. No child stays a child in captivity." Geoffrey stared at her, as though he expected an answer.

A fortnight later, a troop of men headed by Raoul, galloped into the dusty courtyard and stalked into the great hall. Tanwen watched from her garden, dread in the pit of her stomach. In the evening, as the men wolfed down greasy pork and last fall's wrinkled apples, Raoul came to sit by her and said in a low voice, "I have news." His hand groped and found hers. "Times are bad, and likely to become much worse. You know this." He cleared his throat. "You're not safe here."

"What do you know?"

"Nothing," he said. "Or nothing certain. I will protect you, if I can. But I will be gone a great deal, and de Lacy's men are tired of waiting for the battle to begin. He's losing control." He dropped his voice. "Times will grow worse, I can take care of you. Let me."

She felt her bones creak in his grip. Did he mean the king might not win? She swallowed and resisted her urge to pull her hand away.

"I will let it be known that you are mine. Under my protection. I'm asking you to be my wife."

Tanwen blinked and her mouth fell open. "But I have no lands, nothing to offer." She shook her head. "I have a son who is a hostage. I'm Welsh. I'm rumored to be granddaughter to a witch."

"I've heard all of this," he said. He looked away, as though his eyes could be seen into, though she had not mastered that trick. "Think on it Tanwen, but not long."

Several strange and uneasy weeks passed. Raoul and his men stayed away and Tanwen worked in her garden, trying to still her disturbing thoughts. Heat lingered into the long dusky evenings, drooping the leaves in the row of white roses and dampening the tables in the great hall so they dripped, mildewing the rushes on the floor. Once she heard voices from the hostages' tower, raised in anger, but otherwise the hostages were silenced, as they all were, by the heat and the violence. She thought often of Raoul's proposal, wondering if he could truly get her and Bryn away. Or if he only meant to save her. She couldn't trust him, but perhaps she must. Still, nothing could be decided until the war ended and the men returned.

Tanwen weeded a bed of lilies, scoured her palms with sand, and splashed them clean in a pail of water. She couldn't remove all the stains from her roughened skin. She picked at the dirt under her thumbnail. Still, she liked how her hands looked now. Capable.

"Mistress Tanwen."

A brother, in the long cream robe of his order, dusty at the hem from travel, had come up behind her. He thrust back his hood. "I've been a long time on the road. You should have had this weeks past."

"Had what? Who are you?"

The monk dropped his voice. "I have something, something precious, from Lyr Gethin. He said I am to put it in your hands and yours only and asks would you keep it safe for him, until his return."

Tanwen raised her brows. "That's unlikely. What do you want truly?"

"I would have been here sooner. But the mountains are full of soldiers. And this weather." He shrugged.

It had been raining for weeks and the roads, she knew, were impassable with deep sticky mud, the fields a mess of rotting barley. "Where did you see Gethin?"

"In Ilfracombe. He was setting out."

Tanwen bit her lip, wondering if it were true. He was gone then.

"I have his maps."

"Gethin would never give up his maps."

The monk looked impatient. "I have little time. I've been delayed too long already. My abbot thinks I'm in France." He wiped sweat from his forehead, leaving a ragged streak of dirt. "They are fighting everywhere."

"They say this strange weather is a sign," she said. The weather

347

had been odd, heavy fogs and mists in the mornings, storms with streaming rains in the afternoons, lightning and thunder rumbling into the night, and always this pressing heat.

"Everything is a sign."

"Why send them to me? Why don't you keep them for him, if you're truly his friend."

"I am for Clairvaux, I cannot take them with me. You must keep them safe, and hidden." The monk frowned. "He trusted you."

Tanwen rubbed her hands on her apron. She knew how precious they were, months and months of work and artistry. But she hardly needed more trouble.

"Was he wrong?" The monk stared at her, eyes demanding.

"I will keep them." She reached out a hand.

The monk hesitated. "It would kill him if they were lost, or worse," he paused, "if they fell into the wrong hands."

"What are the wrong hands? Has he decided what side he's on then?"

"Sometimes neither side is right."

The next afternoon, Tanwen found Gethin's maps where the monk told her he had left them, in an oiled leather quiver, buried in the hay on the second floor of the barn. She sat, thinking, the hay scratchy and clinging to her damp legs.

At twilight, she slipped out the hidden door she'd placed behind her garden and walked in the summer dusk until her legs ached and she came to a place where two strange tall stones leaned against each other, surrounded by moss and climbing pale blue flowers. She unrolled the maps and examined them as best she could in the dusk. She placed them back in their case and put the quiver in a cleft between the stones and covered them with earth and a large flat stone.

For a long while she sat on the stone, listening to the breezes swish through the high leaves, wondering what she might do and who she would be when all was over and done.

CHAPTER THIRTY-TWO

The days continued heavy with muggy heat and rain. They ate only oats for the wheat was ruined. The peddlers never arrived with news or bright ribbons. The minstrels were silenced by the oppressive air and the empty hall. Tanwen spent her days in the garden, trying to still her fears through work. But the flowers drooped and the leaves were spotted with black mildew.

With King Henry's arrival, the two armies were expected to fight, but somehow they did not. Camped in cramped soaked tents only a few miles from each other, the soldiers fired volleys of arrows, sending back bloody men, and ambushed each other's scouts in narrow valleys, but never joined in decisive battle.

Tanwen wondered what to wish for. If the Welsh lost, Henry would have conquered Wales. And if the Welsh won, Henry would fall into a vindictive rage, and what might he do then? Raoul came and went, appearing unexpectedly in the garden, or at breakfast or dinner, throwing her off balance. He set a dozen soldiers patrolling on top of the new walls. He drilled his men and scoured the countryside for provisions and brought them back in case of siege. Every evening he was in the castle, he sat beside her in the great hall. He gave her snippets of news about Bryn. She found herself waiting for this, but when she tried to question him about the hostages, or convince him to let Bryn out, or ask him how he planned to free her son and get them all away, he always halted the conversation.

This night, Raoul vibrated with nerves or excitement, his fingers tapping his goblet, and his eyes darting around the room. "I want you to come with me, tomorrow."

"Come where?" Tanwen shook her head, which felt full of water. It was so hot in the crowded hall and so close with the smells of goose fat and sweating men. Or perhaps she was ill.

"You know something of healing."

"A little," she said.

"Let me show you something," he said and he led her up the outside stairs that climbed to the top of the newly built walls. She'd never been up here; it was reserved for the guards. Below, spreading out in the dim light of summer evening, she could see everything. The town of Ludelaue, its market square, its grid of streets. The fields, where a mist glowed over flattened barley stalks, and finally, the forests. Trees dark, and thick; they spread up and over the rounded hills right to the farthest horizon. Directly below, the river wound, black, steaming, birch trees bent over the slow water, dangling their ghost twigs and pale limp leaves.

A breath of a cool breeze fanned her flaming cheeks and she could breathe again. "It's beautiful up here," she said, "above everything, even the heat."

"Look," said Raoul.

He was pointing, but she couldn't see anything but trees and more trees, then she saw a thin stream of smoke.

"That's where they are."

"Who? You're being so mysterious."

Raoul's lips tightened.

She shouldn't tease him; he had no sense of humor she could find. "Who?" she repeated.

"Henry's men, those that need your help." He straightened up, shoulders square. "You can take Jeremy and Jake, you'll leave at first light. No need to bring your things, you'll return here when the need is over."

She looked down at the river, her mind whirling. Bryn was here, she couldn't possibly go anywhere else. And she had no wish to help Henry. "I'm no healer. What about Helori?"

"She is gone."

"What do you mean gone?" Surely Helori would never leave her lovely clearing. She looked into his face, unfamiliar in the dim light.

"It's war, Tanwen. She helped. Then she was in the way." He grasped her chin. "You too have secrets, many secrets."

"Surely not so many." She forced a smile and took a step back. She depended on his good will, but she did not understand him. "No more than any woman."

"I'll keep them for you." He did not smile as he took her arm, but his face resumed its normal expression. "It will be better this way, better if you're not here. And when this is all over, we'll plan our future. There has been delay, but now time will favor us."

A wind rose from the forest below, tossing her hair, raising bumps on her arms. She shivered and pulled away, but there was nothing, after all, to say.

Tanwen rode a fat donkey, hitched to Jake's pony in front of her. Raoul's men had come for her at dawn. She'd argued, but they told her she could come with them, or leave Ludelaue. The castle was being secured, only the essential could stay on, the rest prodded out the gates by nightfall to survive as they could. She'd managed to get a half hour stay and found Geoffrey grooming his stallion. She'd hated asking, but he'd agreed to watch over Bryn until she returned. "We must talk then," he'd said, "about Bryn's future." He'd wanted to say more, she could tell, but there had been no time. It felt wrong, terribly wrong, to be riding away from Ludelaue, leaving Bryn locked up behind.

The forest air was clammy; her gown stuck to her back. The donkey was fractious too, and the flies buzzed incessantly. It was dusk when they pulled to a stop. The donkey shook his head and brayed and then she smelled it too. A hot blood smell, sharp and full of iron.

They entered a clearing, where the soldiers had hacked the underbrush away from tall graceful elms. Now she heard the sounds--groans, mutterings, shouts of soldiers. Dozens of injured men lay strewn on the ground, their clothes muddy rags, the earth soaked black and heat and flies a noisome blanket over them all. Her stomach lurched and she swallowed the sharp bile. Climbing down from the donkey, she saw that Jeremy and Jake looked shocked too, their faces white. "How long have these men been here?" she asked.

"Don't know, haven't been here before myself." Jeremy's voice trailed off. He swallowed and his Adam's apple bobbed in his thin neck.

"I see." No one seemed to be about to welcome her or assign her duties. "Jake, I need water, hot water, as much as you can heat, and any cloth at all you can find for bandages."

"The captain sent cloth and such he said you'd be needing." Jake tugged the pack off the donkey, and let it tumble to the ground. He grabbed Jeremy, still staring, and dragged him off toward the center of the clearing, where a fire flickered and smoke snaked up to wander in the leaves.

Trying to ignore the sweet stench hovering in the still air, Tanwen unwrapped herbs and bandages, her fingers shaking. When Jake returned, she said, "Arrange the men in rows, if you can." She stared out over the clearing at the tall trees, hearing the men's moans and above them, the sound of birds crying.

She bent over the first man. He groaned when she touched his shoulder. Under the filthy beard and dried blood, he was so young, barely a man at all. She swallowed the lump in her throat and went to work.

A fortnight later, Tanwen was still in the clearing, ringed by trees flaunting fall colors early, eerie orange when the sun filtered through. The field was cut by a fast stream, flooding its usual banks, making deep puddles where green scum gathered and clouds of gnats hummed. The grass was trampled, the ground churned to rusty mud, and injured men kept coming day and night.

It was early morning. The boy she'd been tending would die today. There was nothing she could do with her limited skills. She stared at the sunlight slanting over the eastern hills, casting gold down onto the steaming trees. If only she had some real skill or hope to offer. It seemed she just delayed their pain and death. So useless, this endless skirmishing between the two armies, and never a true battle, never an end. Yet for too many the end was here already.

She brushed a spider from her arm and scratched a red bite. Thoughts of Bryn circled and swam; she had contemplated walking away from this bloody field so many times each day. But the soldiers watched her, she was unsure of the way back, and war raged around them. They often heard the clash of swords or the strange whirring of arrows flying, or an ominous birdless silence. It seemed the forest itself had been ruined by men, hacking each other to jagged bits and dying in the rain.

By the next morning, Tanwen was staggering on her feet. She'd slept not at all, for a cartload of men, chests pierced by long arrows, legs and arms bloody shreds, had arrived. Nothing to be done but try to staunch their blood and murmur comfort. She'd dealt with the easier cases first, the ones wearing some sort of leather or metal armor, for they had the best chance to survive. Now she saw the next to last man, stretched out at the end of the groaning row, had already died, his face a snarl of pain.

She draped a blanket over his face and turned to the last, expecting another corpse. But this one, covered in dark blood, was alive, his eyes watching her with a gleam of something like hope. She could hardly bear it.

The face was bloody from a deep cut on his forehead, the hair black with sweat. "It's my arm." His eyes met hers.

"Gethin!" She bit her tongue. "God's bones," she whispered but no one was near, except the dead man on the next pallet.

"Tanwen? Is that truly you? I thought I was dreaming."

She bent over him, ripping at the front of his tunic. The cloth was stiff with dried blood and she yanked out her knife and cut the tunic away. Shattered bone poked from the skin above his elbow and a long slash seeped blood along his ribs.

"I know my arm's broken." He reached out with his good hand and touched her fingers. "Do what you can."

She ripped off the rest of his filthy tunic and prodded him, but though he was covered in blood and dirt, he had no other injuries. She washed his forehead and ribs and dabbed the wounds with honey, then turned to the arm. "I must get herbs, pretend to be unconscious if anyone comes near." She yanked the blanket off the dead man and covered him. "How did you come to be here?"

Gethin shrugged and grimaced as he moved his shoulder. "I was on my ship," he whispered, "my room had been searched. You know this. You've seen Cynan." His eyes searched hers.

"Yes, yes, he came," said Tanwen.

"Men were trailing me, I knew it. They followed, they set my ship adrift and captured me when I went ashore in a town of strangers seeking water. They took me straight through the high mountains, so I knew they were Rhys' men." He fell silent.

"Rhys had you captured? For what?"

"We played chess. We talked. He wanted it to be like old times. I was right in Rhys' encampment, in the middle of the fighting. One day, I left." He shook his head and winced again.

"Never mind that now," said Tanwen, unsure if any of this were truth or a hazy dream caused by his wounds. "How did they come to load you on the cart?"

"I don't know. I was hit; I heard groans. I groaned too."

"I'll be back as soon as I can." She rushed to her sack and yanked packets of herbs out, but she didn't have any comfrey, she knew that already.

"What is it?" said Jeremy, coming up behind her.

"I need comfrey to set bones." She sat back on her heels. "I'm sure some grows downstream."

He stepped in her path. "You're not to leave the clearing."

"Don't be ridiculous, I must. De Lacy won't thank you for interfering with the saving of a good foot soldier."

"I can't let you go."

"Come with me if you must, but I am going." She let her temper loose for a moment and he stepped back. She knew they called her a witch at night, around the fire. No one talked of it, but Helori had been here before her, serving in this clearing. She seemed to hover over her shoulder sometimes, adrift in the humid air.

Tanwen shivered and let more anger flare into her eyes. She didn't give him any more time to think but strode away into the forest. It took half the morning, but she returned with an apronful of comfrey and set to work mashing it into a paste. She was glad Gethin was sleeping, it would strengthen him for what must come. When she'd first come to the clearing, she'd gathered all the herbs she could find in the forest nearby, but the dark herbs, henbane and hemlock and poppy, herbs to make a man sleep like death, of these she'd had hardly any. If a man must lose a limb, she had only ale left to lessen the pain. When the boneset was ready, she knelt beside Gethin.

His eyes opened. "You were gone a long time."

"Can you drink this ale, it will help."

He managed half a cup and fell back on the pallet. "Do what you must."

"I'll get a man to hold you down." She touched his chest. "You must not speak my name, nor speak any words in Welsh."

"I will not speak."

She found William, an incurious fellow with hefty arms and had him straddle Gethin and grip him by the shoulders. "You'll keep the arm," she said, and hoped it was true. It was his right arm, the one he used to draw. She hesitated, knife in hand, and it seemed Ceridwen and Helori's faces swam before her, one solemn, one laughing.

The bone was broken in two places. She picked out the fragments and pushed the bones back into place and washed the blood and dirt away, then bound the arm with cloths dipped in comfrey and honey. Gethin groaned once and then was quiet. If William noticed she used more of their precious honey than normal, he didn't protest. Finally it was done. She stared at a squawking cloud of rooks at the edge of the clearing.

"There's the captain, I've got to go," said William, jumping to his feet.

Raoul and three others, important by the silk gleaming on their fresh tunics, rode up to the fire, scattering foot soldiers before them.

Tanwen looked down at Gethin, grey-faced and shivering. What terrible luck Raoul chose this day to appear. She wanted to cradle Gethin's head so he'd sleep, but she walked to the fire, cleaned her hands and took some lukewarm stew. It was greasy and little more than gristle, but she ate the whole bowl, determined to appear unconcerned. Raoul conferred with his highborn visitors and only when darkness had fallen did he suddenly cross the clearing and stand in front of her. She hadn't dared check on Gethin more than twice, as she would for any man.

Raoul pulled her hand into his. "You are cold."

"I am tired. Exhausted. Tell me only, how is Bryn?"

He shrugged. His finger traced the circles under her eyes.

She turned her head aside.

Raoul took his gloves from his belt and pulled one on. "Your son's idol, Geoffrey, isn't that his name? He's gone."

"What do you mean, gone?"

"Evidently, he's a younger son no longer." Raoul laughed. "His older brother has died, and now he's heir to lands in the north country. He's gone there, taking his sister and mother from the nunnery at Hereford."

"You sound jealous."

His fingers paused, then he tugged on the second glove. "Perhaps I am. Though I shouldn't wish death on my older brothers, it's hard to have no place."

Tanwen looked over his head, at the treetops swaying, birds darting in the branches, and thought of Adpar, lost to her and to Bryn. "De Lacy is not an easy master."

"Yet the harder tasks bring greater gains."

"I don't think that's what you care for, truly."

He studied her, fingering the brooch at his neck. "That's why you must marry me, Tanwen." He looked with distaste at the rows of groaning men on the ground. "After this? Where would you have us go?"

She ran a tongue over her dry lips and shook her head. She was dizzy with tiredness and bantering with Raoul was too hard. Any future seemed impossible. "I must go to my pallet. We can talk on the morrow."

She could see his dark eyes gleam and knew he wanted to argue. He would find Gethin; it was inevitable, he was too clever. But nothing would happen until morning and now, she had to sleep. She stumbled to her pallet and he didn't follow, except with his too curious eyes. She lay, stiff and aching, thinking of Bryn alone at Ludelaue, with no one now to watch over him at all. On the morrow she must convince Raoul to take her back. But how? How? Her thoughts whirled, fastening on nothing sure and her eyes felt hard and burned in their sockets. But then she heard the birds settling for the night and their soft twittering swelled and filled her ears, like the sea roaring in a shell, and she slept.

When she awoke, she felt familiar dread before opening her eyes. The sun was strangely high; the men had let her sleep late. "Captain said we're working you too hard," said one.

She got up, her shoulder sore from sleeping without moving all night, and checked on Gethin. He was hot, but not burning up with fever, and he was conscious. She must get more honey, dress the arm again and the slash over his ribs, where the skin had grown pink and tight. "Where's Raoul?" she asked one of the soldiers.

"He went back to Ludelaue, at dawn."

"There were messengers," said another, "seems the king wants more men, the Welsh alliance is holding, they're not quarreling as they always do." He hoisted a body over his shoulder. "He'll come for you again, so he said, in a sennight."

A whole week. And Bryn alone. Her stomach ached and her throat was so tight she could hardly swallow the brackish water they called soup. She made her rounds, tending the men, wondering how she could escape the soldier's eyes and somehow find her way back to Ludelaue, wondering if she could leave Gethin behind, wondering if she should and must. Wondering what might be happening at Ludelaue again and again and again. Like time had wrapped around itself in a circle and she was trapped, back where she'd begun, a girl in the forest, deciding what she might do, who she would be.

By late afternoon, flat clouds raced in and stalled over the mountains. Tanwen had the men who could be moved placed under the shelter of some fir trees and put cloaks and blankets over the rest as it started to sprinkle.

For the next three days, the dull sky poured rain and wind whipped leaves from the rocking trees. Branches creaked and cracked, and some fell in the night. Six men died. Rain soaked the blankets and doused the fires and they could not be warmed. Impossible to know if they would have died anyway. The others shivered and burned and coughed with fevers she could not quench. Gethin was feverish like the rest, his broken arm hot to the shoulder and the knife wound rimmed and streaked with red. "You got them," he whispered to her, "Cynan brought them to you? You know how important they'd be now, de Lacy or Henry himself would murder for them. Whoever has them would set on the rest; they'd know the secrets of the passes," he gasped out and coughed. "All would be murdered as they slept. Not dozens like this." His eyes swept the miserable clearing. "By the hundreds."

"Yes," she tried to soothe him, "I know, don't worry, they're safe. I've hidden them away." She gave him water and had him moved under a hemlock, at the end of one row, but he shivered and shook and when she returned next he was lost in delirium, tossing and muttering nonsense, some English and some in Welsh. The soldiers, luckily, were huddled by the tiny coals of the only fire and didn't venture close enough to hear. She felt feverish herself, cold and aching, knowing she alone held the secret of the maps, knowing, if she must, however he trusted her, whatever it meant, that she would barter them for Bryn. The maps lurked and glimmered at the shadowed edge of her mind. So many might die. But she was a mother, and who could say in the end what was truly right or wrong?

She saved her ale for Gethin, drinking water from the stream herself, though she knew it was risky, and hoped it warmed him enough to survive.

"You'll keep them well hidden. And you'll tell Enid what's happened to me. She'll hear it from you," he said, in a spell of consciousness, as she bent over him on the fourth morning of rain. He clutched her fingers with sudden strength. "And Sam, you'll tell Sam?"

"You'll tell them yourself," she said fiercely.

"But if not."

"Think only of surviving; that is how to beat back the fever."

He studied her face, then nodded.

But the rain showed no sign of stopping. It would slow, and resume, and the winds blew strangely forceful and warm. Smells rose from the forest floor and mushrooms and fungi sprouted in terrifying colors, orange and blue against the urgent green of the soaked mosses. Tanwen bent over each man, her back aching, her fingers bandaging, her voice soothing, her mind racing. Raoul would return, in only a day or two at most.

Next time she knelt over Gethin, she said, "You must ready yourself. You must go, soon." She wasn't sure he even understood her, but he nodded.

Clouds pressed down on the clearing, concentrating the smells. Blood, urine, pus. Black mildew grew on her blankets and the hems of her skirts. Her hair seemed to crawl. She dreamed of a hot bath and the sharp scent of lavender soap. She stumbled from bed to bed, changing bloody dressings, and thought of Bryn, imagined him as he was now, tall, and as he would be, free. Together they would walk away from this cursed border and its humid hills and go somewhere new, where the air cut fresh and smelled only of cedar and water.

Toward evening, wind whipped up until branches creaked and leaves whirled down. The horses stamped and snorted and left off grazing. The clouds grew purple, edged with ugly yellow and towered upward. Lightning flashed and a sharp crack sounded; the rumble growled among the rocks, echoing.

"Help me," Tanwen called. The soldiers lugged the patients into a circle where tree branches were less likely to fall, though they were more exposed to the rain. When she reached Gethin, he shook his head.

"Leave me, this is the time to get away, I'm half hidden as it is."

So she passed on, as though she didn't see him. Lightning lit the clearing, startling the men, turning their faces ghoulish, with black eyes and gaping holes for mouths. Thunder crashed and cracked, shuddering the ground and raining sharp pinecones down. Tanwen heard a giant crack, and felt the earth shake; she lost her footing and fell, bruising her hip. The horses screamed. Soldiers were shouting and cowering and then the rain came, whipping sideways on the wind, slashing their faces. The soldiers clustered together, arguing and shoving.

Tanwen stumbled around the edge of the clearing, her hip needling, waiting for the dark between lightning flashes. The horses were wild-eyed, stamping in their makeshift pen. It was hard to stay on her feet. She touched the shivering neck of one and slipped past the soaked flank of another. She picked a gelding with a wide back and tugged him free of the rest.

The soldiers were gathered around two men, wrestling and grunting in the mud. She tugged the horse after her, hoofs crashing in the underbrush, but thunder and pounding rain covered their noise. "Gethin," she called.

"Yes." He stood beside her, startling her so she almost dropped the rope. Sweat and rain dripped off his grey face.

"You can't, you're not ready."

"You know it's now or never." He glanced at the men, still absorbed in the fight. "Help me on." She wheeled the horse alongside a log. He got himself half up and she swung his leg over the other side. He groaned, hunched over the horse's neck, and gripped the saddle with his good hand. "Come with me, Tanwen. You cannot stay here."

"I must go back for Bryn."

"I'll stay with you then."

"No, you must go. You're speaking Welsh when the fever comes on."

He shook his head.

"Just hold on. The horse will carry you. Go to Enid." She looked behind her, the men were still cheering the fighters. "Go." When he hesitated, she shouted at him. "Go! You're putting me in danger here, can't you see?"

"Yes." His eyes locked on hers. "But Tanwen, you must come when you can." Lightning lit his face white.

Tanwen brought her hand down, hard, on the horse's rump. The horse tossed its head, nearly unseating him, and plunged off into the woods. She thought of ambushes, fever, and fierce wolves and she reached out her arms to call him back, but he was gone.

CHAPTER THIRTY-THREE

R AOUL RODE INTO THE CLEARING, tossed Tanwen on the back of his horse and brought her back to Ludelaue the day after Gethin rode into the forest. He answered no questions and rode out again immediately.

Tanwen waited in the empty hall until the clunk of his horse's hoofs faded, then she ran straight to the tower. The door was closed tight and bolted as always, but no guard sat outside. Perhaps there weren't enough men left. She stared at the rough oak, at the long split running down the right side, as though someone had tried to break the door down and failed. When one of the kitchen girls came by with a pail of soup, she grabbed her sleeve. "The hostages, how do they fare?"

"They're all skinny and white in there. Like mushrooms in the dark. Shouldn't like to be penned up myself," the girl said, and shifted her pail to the other hand. The soup, a greasy broth with cubes of stale bread floating, sloshed over the sides of the pail.

"Let me take the soup in," said Tanwen.

"I'd lose my job. And what do you want with them in there anyway?" She eyed Tanwen and knocked on the door. It gaped open and the kitchen girl was swallowed up in the shadows.

Tanwen managed to hold herself back from rushing in behind the girl. She rubbed her cold fingers. She hadn't eaten. She needed sleep. Already she'd heard the whispers, frightening gossip which swirled through the castle, of bodies piled in ditches, of great lords deserting with their men, of thieves cutting fingers off bodies for their rings, but who could tell what was even true? She should go sleep, but she couldn't make herself move away from the tower steps, so she sat in the shade of a struggling hathorne and tried to distract herself by imagining a home, a real home, enveloped in ivy, ringed with a wall of roses and spikes of blue delphinium, where even the breezes carried beguiling scents of thyme and rosemary. Like Ceridwen's cottage, before she died and grandfather turned his eyes away from the living. Like Helori's cottage. But now Helori was gone too. Disappeared. Nowhere, it seemed, not even the past, was safe.

As dusk fell around her, the clatter of plates and goblets finally drew Tanwen to the hall, where men gathered, drinking their ale. Perhaps she could find out how the hostages fared from their talk. She nearly collided with Raoul. Usually so finely dressed, he wore a stained tunic and muddy sweat dribbled down his temples. "Come," he said. "I've wasted time looking for you already."

Tanwen trailed him up to his solar, her mind blank. The time had come for whatever would be required of her. Raoul yanked off his tunic and told the servant to leave. The door banged shut. In only a sweat-soaked chemise and leather leggings, Raoul sat down opposite her and stared.

"Have I three eyes?" she asked.

"Hardly, my beautiful Tanwen." He reached over and pulled her headscarf off and her thick hair tumbled down, brushing her shoulders. He wound a hand in her hair and forced her head back.

She could smell his sharp sweat and a drop trickled from his chin and fell in the hollow of her neck.

Abruptly, he released her.

She walked to the window and threw open the shutter, letting in fresh but humid air.

"Where are they, Tanwen?"

Fear tingled in her, but she kept her face turned toward the window. "Who?"

"Did you think me a fool? Or maybe you thought I was so ensnared I'd overlook all else?" He crossed the room and shoved her against the rough wall, his eyes unreadable, but lit with a strangeness that made her recall Gethin's warnings. "The maps, where are they?"

The door slammed open. "Captain! Sir, your pardon."

Raoul released her and went to the door where the soldier whispered in his ear. Her arm burned where he'd gripped her. Two guards with empty faces and muscled arms arrived to fill the doorway.

"As you see, I have urgent business. But I will deal with you, soon."

They locked her in. She pounded on the thick door and called, but no one answered. Cradling her bruised fist, she studied the dark chamber, a long rectangle with a high timbered ceiling laced with cobwebs. Through the arrow loop she could hear Raoul shouting down in the courtyard, his words garbled. The room held a soldier's bed, a folded grey blanket, a chest, open, against the wall. How had he found out about the maps? Who could have told him? It didn't matter; he could ferret out any information. She rifled through the chest, but there was only a tunic, a pair of leggings, a silver cup, and a lovely book of hours, richly illustrated and bound in soft green leather. No hangings on the wall, or furs on the floor, nothing of the luxury she'd thought would surround him.

Through the open window, she heard shouts and the buzz of people gathering. Townspeople were crowding into the courtyard far below. She could hear the laughs and screams of children, despite the late hour. Had the war been lost then, or won?

She banged on the door again and shouted to the guards. Bryn would be hearing the same shouts; that he'd feel the same fear was like a stab in her throat. She slumped onto the floor. The shadows in the corners, and gathering near the high ceiling, seemed to waver and shift and quake. Her hair clung to her neck. She must be ready, prepared for what would come, but she was so tired. She had misjudged Raoul, underestimated him. The day had started with birds singing, but now she thought of the darkness of birds, black crows and screaming owls, fierce shadows that flew, taking souls.

Sometime later, the bolt on the door scraped and Raoul entered, his face white in the dim light.

She scrambled to her feet. "What is happening out there?"

"Ah Tanwen," he sighed. He dropped on the bench and pulled a cup towards him and filled it from a skin of wine he'd brought.

She could feel her throat ache, so dry it was hard to swallow.

"This room is like a bread oven," he said.

"What is going on? Why are the townspeople gathered?"

He downed another cup of wine, then stripped off his chemise. She took a step back and then stopped. She'd do what she must, to save Bryn. But she must be clever, ensure that after, he'd do as he promised. She put a hand on his arm. But he just sank down on the stool and put his head in his hands. "What has happened? You must tell me."

He stared up at her with a strange half smile. "How beautiful you are, like a star." He touched her hair, so gently she couldn't quite feel his finger. "The king is withdrawing."

The humid air weighed her down, making her gown sag heavy on her shoulders, and her mind ponder along. "What do you mean?"

"It is over, for now at least, for this year. This weather has finished it, these freakish storms. Lightning struck the field two days past and twenty men were killed at once, in a flash of yellow and purple light. Rain, rain and more rain, and hail stones pounding, the fields are turned to ponds and tree trunks mired in murky lakes and the men have no clothes left, they've rotted away, and their feet are green with mold and the food is full of worms and still the air crackles with thunder and the rains fall every God forsaken day." His voice was low. "It's over," he repeated. "The men won't fight. They say white spirits rise from the muck and scream in the night. Foolish, of course. But the king is retreating from the mountains. Back to England." His voice fell to a whisper. "He is angry. In a rage, as only he can rage. Someone must pay."

Tanwen felt her stomach clench before the words penetrated her brain. "No," she said.

"No, you say." His eyes held a queer green gleam in the darkened room. "But he's Henry, King of Normandy and England, Lord of Eleanor's Aquitaine, ruler of half of Europe." He shrugged.

"Henry is not," Tanwen paused and swallowed the lump stopping her speech, "not coming here, to Ludelaue?"

"Not yet. He's summoned de Lacy to meet with him at Chester.

He hopes to rally the Dublin Norsemen there and return to fight again in the spring."

Relief raced through her veins, and she sat down. "Ah, that's good."

"Yes," he said, "I suppose it is."

"Why are the townspeople gathered then? Have you announced the end of the war?"

"Do you think they'll hear that with pleasure?"

"Perhaps not entirely. But surely they'll be glad the war is done. They can salvage some of the harvest, what's not rotted away." She touched his sleeve. "And you can let them out, the hostages. It must be so hot in that tower room." She picked at the bodice of her gown, which clung to her with the sticky dampness. His sharp eyes swung to her breasts. She dropped her hand.

"No," he said absently, "the hostages must stay imprisoned."

"But the war is done for now. Over, you say. There is no more point."

Raoul got to his feet, sighing. "You should go, return to your village."

"What village? I have nowhere to go."

"Owain, he would take you back, would he not?"

Tanwen swallowed. "You would send me back to Owain? I thought you wished to marry me?"

"There are dreams we speak that should be kept silent." He sighed. "He would want you back. You could go home, away from this place. You should."

"Not without Bryn, you know I cannot. I will never leave him."

"Bryn is a man, and must live his own life."

"He's a boy, and I won't abandon him, though his father did."

Raoul flung himself on the bed, eyes closed.

"Let us go, Raoul. You can do it, you hold the keys."

"I could have loved you well," he said, turning his back to her. "Life is miserable at times."

"What do you mean? Are the hostages in danger?"

"They're hostages," he said, "they're always in danger. Have you not said so to me time and again?"

"But not," she whispered, "from you?"

"You ask too much of me, lovely Tanwen." He got up and flung open the door. "Isn't it enough I let you go?"

Four stifling days passed. The servants were grumpy and the soldiers fractious and even the horses seemed overset. Tanwen learned from one of the kitchen girls that the hostages had been moved the afternoon she'd spent locked in Raoul's room, paraded before the townspeople, hands bound and barefoot, and shoved into an empty stable.

Tanwen sat on a turf seat in the ruins of her garden, under a drooping arch of ivy, hands pressed to her temples. The time for evil choice had come around. Raoul knew she had Gethin's maps. How, she didn't know, but Raoul or de Lacy would give much to be the one to offer such a valuable prize to the king. She could even think of going to King Henry herself. But what consequences might come to Gethin, to everyone she knew, if she gave them up? Gethin had pleaded with her. How terrible if his maps would be the weapon to kill so many. Her head stabbed and her eyes were sore and burning. But time had run out.

She sat on, in the still heat, surrounded by the dusty leaves and wilted stems, the white roses blown open and eaten by black beetles. She took her knife from her belt and smoothed the blade between her fingers. She thought of Geoffrey and how she should have thanked him graciously for helping Bryn, how she should have been grateful, not full of resentment. She thought of Gethin and wondered if he'd managed to stay atop the grey horse, whether his arm had festered, and if he'd made it to Sam and safety. She thought of Daron and Huw, and wondered if they'd made it through the violent men in the forests and what sort of life they made for themselves together, or apart. And she thought of Owain, who had started it all, and wondered if he ever remembered her or Bryn or the peace of evening in the moon garden at Adpar.

She sighed and pushed her hair off her forehead. As she got to her feet, Raoul rode up and loomed over her, his horse stepping into her garden, a giant grey hoof smashing a late rose and crushing the hedge, sending the smell of bay leaves to mix with horse sweat in the air. He leaned over and snapped his fingers near her face. "Where are they Tanwen? The king has failed at Chester. There will be no Irish bowmen in the spring. The war is well and truly lost." He laughed wildly and swung down from the horse and grabbed her shoulders. "Henry is coming here. Now. I must have something to give him. Something to distract him. Even now, whoever holds those maps will hold the borders. They are the key."

"To what?"

"Power. And what comes with it. Coin. Respect. A future."

"A piece of parchment can offer all that?" She tried to speak with scorn but heard her voice tremble.

"You should have gone, Tanwen. I told you to go. Why didn't you heed me?" He ground a boot onto the wilting marguerites. "I'll find them if I must, but it would save time if you would give them to me. Time, and much more perhaps. If it can be managed." He looked over at the stable, where the hostages were penned, guards circling day and night.

Tanwen swallowed. "I am Welsh."

"You're from nowhere. What have the Welsh ever done for you? Or your Owain?"

"So many would die."

"They will die anyway. And what is that to you, Bryn would be safe."

"How?" she whispered.

"I could manage, if I had the maps."

She stared into his eyes, unable to see whether she could truly trust him.

A messenger ran up, panting. "The king's scouts arrive!"

Raoul thrust her aside. The king's advance guard rode in, arrayed alike in burgundy, but their fine clothes were filthy, and their horses drooping, necks darkened with sweat.

That evening, Tanwen waited until the boy Raoul had set to spy on her was distracted, eating his stew and laughing with a maid. She slipped out her hidden door and emerged outside the walls. She slid down the banking, darted behind a hedge of willow, and waited. When no one shouted, she flitted from tree to tree, losing her way twice in the lengthening shadows. Finally, she reached the standing stones, looming askew in the gathering darkness. She would use Gethin's maps. She must use them, no matter the costs, to bargain for Bryn.

She listened to the forest, a breeze tickling her cheek, and when the wrens resumed their chattering, she got down on her knees and tugged the heavy flat stone aside. Her fingers dug in the earth and groped in the dark hole, and groped again, finding wet acorns and slimed oak leaves. She shoved aside the ferns and dug out the black leaves and dirt, dug until her fingers scraped granite. She felt everywhere, all around, until her fingertips stung and bled. But the maps were gone.

Tanwen staggered to her feet. Wind swept like a dread spirit wail through the tree branches. She had nothing now, nothing to trade for Bryn. She grabbed the heavy stone with both hands and whirled it through the air. It whacked into the trunk of an ancient elm, leaving a jagged white gash. She pounded the standing stones with her fists, her voice so loud and eerie it frightened even her, echoing. Behind her, the damaged tree wept sap.

CHAPTER THIRTY-FOUR

The Berwyn Mountains

OWAIN TWIRLED HIS SILVER DAGGER, spinning it on the polished table, until Rhys stilled his hands with a silent glare.

Owain sighed, but not aloud. Rhys was a great leader, that's why they were in this forsaken village after all, penned up in a wealthy merchant's house, dirtying his solar with the mud from their boots. At least they weren't out with the rest of the foot soldiers in the rebel camp, their tents of rotted canvas pitched in the streaming rain. But Rhys could be imperious, and sometimes Owain longed for the careless peace of Adpar, before he'd taken to the cause and dedicated his honor to Rhys and to Wales. That didn't mean anything though. Anyone could long for a thing in the dark of night. If sometimes he did think of Tanwen with longing, he couldn't help it.

Wind rattled the shutters and dampened the air, even by the hearth, not overly filled with wood. Owain frowned and rubbed his hands together. The merchant was reputed to be rich, but he wasn't generous. Rhys wouldn't care, he never stood on ceremony, but a few comforts weren't out of order for leaders dedicated to Wales' future.

Voices murmured from the other end of the room. Rhys' lawyers, he brought them with him everywhere. But this wasn't an ordinary evening. For tonight, if the news the scouts brought was accurate, the last of Henry's great army would slip away, back over the border into England.

Rhys was quiet, not betraying tension, unless you knew him well. Owain did, now, and he was proud of it. He observed the stiff back and the way Rhys' index finger tapped against his cheekbone as he stared out into the night.

A door slammed below and everyone in the room started. Rhys dropped his hand and leaned against the wall. Footsteps thudded up the stairs. A sweating red-faced soldier swayed in the entryway, and dropped to his knees. "They are gone, lord."

The words, though expected, stunned the room. Even Rhys said nothing. That they'd defeated the English king was so fabulous, though they'd longed and worked and fought, it seemed to all a waking dream.

Rhys tossed a pouch of clinking coins into the soldier's hand. "Let's dine then," he said quietly.

They sat at the polished table and ate thin mutton soup and Rhys drank red wine from the silver goblet he carried with him always, a ferocious dragon climbing up the stem. When they were done eating, Rhys stood, goblet raised. "We have chased the Norman invaders back over the border. We have fought with honor and valor and we have done what seemed impossible to lesser men."

The dozen men around the table cheered and Rhys let them, his face solemn, then he motioned them to sit. "Soon the English King Henry will sail back over the channel to Normandy. He will not return, I think, not for many years. So we have it now, the freedom we have long sought." Rhys walked away from them, to stand at the window and look out into the night. "What will we do with it?"

Owain frowned at the table and took a gulp of wine. Rhys could get melancholy at odd moments, thinking of his parents and brothers no doubt, all murdered or blinded or maimed. Still, this wasn't the time. Around the table, the men studied their clasped hands.

"We must do something worthy," said Rhys softly, so they had to lean towards him to hear, "something true and grand. We have recovered my grandfather's kingdom, but the world is not as it was then. A new season has come round and we must meet it as new men." Rhys spun back to them, his eyes intent as though looking down an open road. "I will move my caput. Dinefwr is a symbol of the past. We'll go now to Aberteifi, to take the last castle there from the Normans, and in that tower, looking west over the endless sea, that's where our future will begin. I will gather those who value our ancient stories and the new learning alike, and we will be a people living in peace, untroubled and free in our own lands."

Owain looked around the table. Some men nodded, approving the taking of Aberteifi, but most looked confused, even embarrassed, eyes on their trencher. They'd follow Rhys anywhere, when he spoke of glory and revenge, but they didn't understand him. Owain wasn't sure he understood entirely either, but he'd glimpsed the gleaming vision that enticed Rhys on. When Rhys spoke, it was like a great window swung open in his mind, and sharp air and bright light flowed in. When he was away from Rhys, he could never recapture that feeling or sense that light. It was why he stayed on with him, and would stay on, no matter the costs.

Dinner wound down; the men filed out to their pallets in the merchant's stone storeroom.

"You go too," said Rhys, "I want to be alone."

Owain nodded, but he wasn't tired and he didn't want to leave. As he walked out the door he turned back to look at Rhys, alone in the dark, goblet in hand. One couldn't understand him, but it was enough to be in his orbit. Part of something monumental, something that would stand once time had flowed on and away.

In the morning, the woods were searched and revealed as empty and stripped, the Normans flown, leaving only pattering rain and the endless wash of water over rocks.

CHAPTER THIRTY-FIVE

Ludelaue

THE KITCHEN MAIDS SLEPT on the stone-flagged floor, tumbled in a corner like puppies. In the hall, the men bellowed and drank, and out in the courtyard Raoul circled, alert, waiting for the English king. After the arrival of the advance scouts, the king's long line of loaded wagons had creaked into the courtyard, but hours had passed and Henry himself had not yet come.

Past midnight, the roasted meats were stored away and the grumbling cooks went to their beds, but still the men drank. The torches flickered and smoked in the great hall, casting light and dark across men's faces, as though demons within had been set free. Tanwen hid in the shadows, wrapped in a dark shawl, deciphering the clang and clunk of metal and the shouts of the guards, trying to think where Gethin's maps could possibly be. But as the hours passed she was only waiting like the rest, looking out for any desperate chance to get to Bryn.

Raoul shoved through the door and shouted to his men. Trailed by a dozen soldiers, he slammed out to the courtyard and she heard more shouting and the ring of metal weapons dumped on stone. She edged out of the hall into the gloomy stairwell. Keeping an eye out for Raoul's men, drunk and dangerous, she climbed up to his private chamber. Would there be a guard? As she wondered, she stumbled over one in the dark. He slept on, his breath rank with ale. She held her breath and stepped over him and shoved at the door. It opened and she slipped inside.

She examined Raoul's shadowy room. The maps must be here; where else? Somehow Raoul had found her hiding place in the forest, or perhaps he'd just been playing some disturbing game with her all along. She flung the grey blanket aside and searched the straw mattress. She tore down the wool hanging on the wall. She crossed to the chest. From the courtyard below rose a confused clamor. Tanwen ran to the window and leaned out. Men were chanting and cheering. She watched for a moment, then returned to the chest. Fingers shaking, Tanwen tossed the pewter pitcher off and propped up the heavy lid. She yanked out tunics and boots and the book of hours she'd seen before and stared at the empty bottom of the chest. She ran her hand over the chestnut wood; there must be a clasp, or something. She tossed through Raoul's tunics, shaking them out. A packet fell to the floor. She snatched it and yanked open the ribbon tie. No emerald seas or burgundy castles or rampaging dragons. Only the cramped script of a clerk, a record of funds spent, perhaps household rolls, or some accounting for de Lacy.

The door swung open and the guard stood in the doorway, swaying. Confusion spread on his wide forehead. "Here now, what're you doing? Stop that."

Tanwen dodged away. "Leave me be!"

"You're not allowed in here."

"Take me straight to the captain then. I'll tell him how I got in, walked right over your drunken self."

The guard paused, and she dashed around him and down the stairs.

The next morning, the castle slept late and the smells of sour ale and vomit lurked in all the dank corners. Tanwen had only dozed for an hour and her head ached behind her eyes. She questioned the sleepy boy at the hall door, who said the king had still not come, only a dozen of his lords. Tanwen crossed the silent courtyard and entered the kitchen. A new plan had crept into her mind, deep in the night, while all the others slept. Crept in, fully formed, as though it had waited there, for this time of need. It was dangerous, and most dangerous of all to her. But what choice had she now, with even the maps gone?

A man stood by the kitchen hearth, eating a hunk of dark bread with honey swirled on top.

Tanwen halted in the doorway. "George Fychan, is that truly you?"

Owain's steward put the bread down on the table and rubbed his sticky fingers on his tunic. "Is there somewhere private we can talk?"

Tanwen led him to the buttery, where the empty shelves were coated with dust and mouse droppings.

"I bring greetings from Adpar," said George.

"Owain, he is in good health?" Tanwen felt concern tug at her and she resented it.

"He is well, though seldom in residence. Adpar has changed, since you were among us."

"Much has happened," Tanwen agreed, wondering why he could be here. Perhaps Owain sent him to help get Bryn away?

"Adpar has changed, and not for the better," George repeated, "with you gone."

Tanwen felt the annoying tug of concern again. George would have done anything for Owain, once. "You have a message for me?"

George pulled a packet from his sleeve and extracted a parchment, rolled.

Tanwen hesitated. It was tied with a green ribbon, her favorite color.

"I'm to wait for a reply." George cleared his throat and extended the parchment closer to her hand. "I'll wait in the courtyard."

"Yes," Tanwen murmured and clutching the letter, she walked to her garden. She sat on the rounded stone she'd had carted in, surrounded by her trampled lavender. For so many weeks after she'd left Adpar, she'd imagined just this. Some message to say he was sorry, he didn't mean any of it. Come home.

She untangled the ribbon and smoothed the thick parchment against her thighs. Her fingers were stiff. The letter was not in Owain's own hand, of course. The elaborate calligraphaphy of a scribe danced in front of her eyes.

To Tanwen verch Sorcha, all gracious greetings,

*It having come in recent weeks to my attention that you reside
in the de Lacy castle at Ludelaue, and serve as garden keeper to
his lordship, so I write to you now. Truly, I find myself amazed
to think you have accomplished this, though I know your
talents for coaxing greenery and such from bare earth. You've
been able, no doubt, to assure yourself by now of our son's
welfare. Thus I pray and request at this juncture, that you will
return to your true home at Adpar. Matters are reaching such
a successful conclusion in this war, beyond our wildest dreams,
that it is only a short term, surely, before I myself will return
to Adpar, and all the hostages will be returned to Wales. Rhys
assures me we have not long to wait. And I desire greatly your
presence, having missed you and indeed longed for you. I think
often of our beginning, darling Tanwen, when you danced
in the woods. Let us begin anew. Rhys has such plans. I send
George for you, with coin and a horse and such for your return
journey.*

Owain, Lord of Adpar, Ceredigion, Wales

Tanwen's eyes raced over the lines again, trying to gather in the
meaning beyond the curled black letters. Boots crunched on gravel
as George came up behind her. She rolled the scroll up tight. "There
is no answer," she said.

"I was to wait," George said.

"Tomorrow then, I will give you an answer tomorrow." Her voice
sounded faint and full of echoes to her own ears.

"I'll meet you outside the west wall. But if you're not there, it's
back I go. I can't stay longer. Not with the English king himself here
any time." George frowned at his worn boots. "Still, I'll say it again.
It hasn't gone well, with you gone. There is sickness in the village.
The fields are mired. There will be no harvest again."

Tanwen watched him go, walking heavily through the dusty courtyard. Then she sat on in her garden, the letter on her lap, feeling unable to move or even think. George thought it her duty, to go back. Back to managing the fields as well as the manor, filling in for Owain each time he left. And how very much she longed to go back, back to her own dappled forests and bee-filled garden. She felt her throat close up as she thought of the white roses leaning over the winding pathway of her garden at home. Owain had made a dread mistake, surely this letter showed he realized now the immensity of his betrayal.

She scanned the lines again, searching for his voice beyond the stranger's hand and the flatness of the page. If only she could climb to the top of Ludelaue's walls once more and peer out, over the dark forests and endless hills waving toward Adpar and the sea. Look away from this castle, from Henry, from boys penned up like beasts and men crazed with blood. She dropped the parchment and it slid to the ground.

She couldn't, of course. Couldn't see Adpar from this cursed castle and couldn't go back. Owain called to her to sink with him into some dream of the past, but no erasure could be possible. She bent over and picked up the parchment and read it again. In the end, he hadn't even apologized. As though he hadn't realized the dangers he'd put Bryn in, hadn't realized, or didn't want to know, even now. He spun a lovely daydream of them all returned and together again. But whatever Rhys said, it would not turn out that way. The world could not be reassembled, like a child's game, to be played over and over again. That time was gone, and only the future remained, stretching unfamiliar and uncertain before her.

Another endless day dragged on, and still the king had not come, throwing his advisors and the great lords into a frenzy of speculation. Servants rushed up and down the stairs, soldiers argued and shoved each other in the courtyard, lawyers gathered around the tables in the great hall, debating in low urgent voices. Tanwen pretended to work in her garden, then gave up and sat with her arms wrapped around her knees, dizzy from lack of sleep. If she couldn't use the maps, she had only this one other option. One she'd sworn many long years past never to use. Sworn with her hands within her grandmothers' hands, before she'd received any teaching. She could see her grandmother's alarmed and angry face each time her eyes closed and yet it seemed there was no other way and she must do what she could to get Bryn away, whatever the cost.

Tanwen lifted her head, realizing the hum in her ears came from people. Crowds from the town were gathering, people streaming through the opened castle gate. The morning sky was beautiful as the fairest pearl, glowing with a creamy pinkish light that made her chest ache.

She left her garden through the arch of ivy and plunged into the gathering crowd, which carried her, like a river current. She was swept among merchants and housewives and past shouting boys; the smells of sweat and piss were overpowering. She fought her way to the side, and a big man in a blacksmith apron lifted her up onto the wall, laughing. She peered out over the cheering crowd, over the children on men's shoulders, and realized they were all staring at one man. At the king. Henry. He had come.

He was arrayed in burgundy and bright gold and the light picked out jewels on the sash over his hips and sparked off the pointed gold crown on his head. He was mounted on a white stallion with a rippling mane and fierce eyes. Even the horse was clad in scarlet silk and when it tossed its head, green jewels flashed on a silver bridle.

Henry raised his arm and the crowds cheered and then slowly the sounds fell away and everyone was staring at this one man and the world under the pearly sky fell silent.

And then Tanwen saw the hostages. Soldiers herded and prodded them out of the stables in a straggling line and pushed them into a semicircle twenty paces from the mounted king. The youths stood up straight and the younger boys clung to each other and the two women were crying. She could see their pale faces and dark frantic eyes. Her eyes searched, but she couldn't see Bryn. She felt her stomach heave and forced it down and shook her head to clear it. If she had the maps. Even now. She could save him, perhaps save all of them.

But her hands were empty.

The king's arm sliced through the air and the crowd roared and the hostages were seized from behind. Her throat closed and she jumped down from the wall, but her way was blocked by wide backs and huge thighs. The guards were dragging seven of the boys up to a raised platform and the crowd was screaming, a roar like the wildest wind.

Someone snaked an arm around her waist. She tried to claw free, but a strong arm looped around her neck. The man threw her over his shoulder. She struggled but he held her tighter and ran, breathing hard, and they shoved through a door, her knees banging the timbers, and he dropped her to the ground and her head hit the granite wall.

"Be quiet," he said, breathing hard.

It was Geoffrey. "When did you get here? What are you doing?" Her head was swimming and she felt a trickle of blood on her temple. "Bryn," she said in a low voice.

"I have him." He shook his head so she'd say no more and pulled her to her feet and through a snaking dark hall and out a door, hidden behind barrels of flour. They rushed down an overgrown path and she stumbled over the roots, clumsy and panting. They scrambled up a rock-strewn hill, underbrush scratching her cheeks. Finally they reached the top. Tanwen swayed, her head splitting, and blinked to clear her eyes. They looked down on the practice field, where the men swung swords at each other every morning. Geoffrey was gazing back to the castle and she saw his lips whiten.

She twisted back to stare.

"Don't," he said, but she had seen. Already four youths dangled, their long legs kicking in the air, tiny black figures from this distance, hardly real. The guards had a woman now, surely they wouldn't harm her, then she heard the scream as a soldier hit her and the woman dropped. They hung her too, but she was already dead.

"By the Lady," said Geoffrey, crossing himself. "They've gone mad."

Tanwen stared at the pearly sky, stretching bright and terrible, until Geoffrey yanked her away. He had a horse, tied to a tree. "We can't leave Bryn," she shouted.

He threw her on and they galloped, trees whipping by, her eyes blurred.

They reached a clearing. Helori's clearing, Tanwen realized. The tiny house sat silent under the oak tree, everything the same and nothing the same, with Helori gone. Geoffrey swung her down and kicked open the door and carried her inside. He kindled a fire in the cold hearth. The house was silent and smelled of dust.

"Where is Bryn. I want to talk to Bryn. Is he here?" Her head seemed to be splitting open and she was seeing two doors and two fires.

Geoffrey shook his head. "I've got to go back."

"I'm coming." She tried to stand up, but her legs wouldn't work.

"You hit your head too hard. You must rest."

She wanted to protest, but the ground was swirling around her feet, like the lazy currents of the river by Adpar.

He built up the fire and said, speaking fast, "I came back to Ludelaue this week to see the king. To have him free me from my oath, so I can remain in the northlands I've inherited. I heard the king's guards talking, about what would come. I managed to get Bryn out, as one of the mercenaries knew me well from when we fought in Normandy. I've hidden him in an abandoned root cellar."

"He's safe?"

"As can be, in this madness. I'm going back for him now. I won't chance a return until full dark. Bar the door."

Silence grew to fill the hut once the hoof beats faded. Tanwen lay down on the floor, distressed at the musty leaves under the bench in Helori's once neat chamber. She closed her eyes and thought of Bryn, a child in this border world of duplicity and violence, and willed him safe.

Early stars glittered, eventually, above the trees. She roused herself to put a few logs on the fire and drink some water from the bucket Geoffrey had left by the door. She was shivering, despite the fire, as though a fever had set in with the blow to her head. For the first time, she wondered what would happen to Bryn if she died, or she was too weak to save him. She stared into the flames and wished. Wished for Helori to be back in her storeroom and Ceridwen not to be dead. For Owain to be as he had seemed that first day in the summer forest. For Bryn to be beloved by his father, beloved and safe and free.

She woke to light, comforted by some wisp of a happy dream. She felt stronger and her head pounded less. She crawled out, into the morning's soft sun, and staggered to her feet and slowly circled the clearing until she found the tiny grave of Daron's daughter. It was covered with a flat stone of grey marble, veined in pink, and around it tumbled white violets. The marble felt smooth and cold, and yet alive under her palm. A hummingbird, green and gold, hovered drinking from the violets and flew on. Something to tell Daron, one day.

Geoffrey rode into the clearing alone, sometime past noon. "Bryn's still hidden. I've got the only key. I couldn't get him out, not with all the guards on watch. He's safe enough for the time being. But the king is in a fearsome rage. He's hanged seven hostages and maimed others, even the girls. Ears and noses cut away, hands chopped off. He blinded Rhys' son himself, with a stick through the eyes. He feasts even now in the great hall, the eyes beside him on a white napkin on the table."

"How terrible," Tanwen whispered.

"It's war." Geoffrey looked pale and angry. "Rhys knew it. Owain knew it. They sent their sons, even knowing they meant to rebel, knowing it would be their own sons' deaths." Geoffrey spat on the ground.

"Who is dead?"

He told her and the names flowed by and he said more, but she couldn't hear it, seeing only the fine tall boys in the sunlight on a happier day.

At dusk, they argued. "You must wait here," Geoffrey said. "The king means to execute more."

"I cannot just wait," said Tanwen. "You must see that." She got to her feet. "I'm strong enough. And I can help. I can distract Raoul, while you get Bryn."

Geoffrey frowned, but pulled her up behind him on his horse.

Tanwen said, as they started out, "You have broken your word to the king."

Geoffrey tightened his fingers on the reins. "I never thought to break my oath. But some things are not meant to be stomached."

They rode the rest of the way in silence. When they reached the castle, Geoffrey shouted to the guard at the gate and rode in.

Tanwen watched two kitchen maids hurry across the moonless courtyard, their faces averted from the black bodies still dangling.

Tanwen left Geoffrey rubbing down his stallion and walked to her garden. Her steps felt uncertain, the ground wavering beneath her and her head throbbed. She sank down onto the grass and fingered the petals of a gold-eyed aster. Even half ruined, her garden was lovely and a tiny pale night moth drank and danced. She thought about its life, so short and frantic.

She sighed and went to find Raoul. He sat alone in the great hall, still wearing armor, his eyes hidden by a dented helmet.

"Have you brought the maps?" he said.

"You have them! Why do you pretend to me still?"

Raoul stood up and leaned over the table. "He will kill them all on the morrow. All. Do you understand?"

"No," she gasped. "He could not."

"Even now, you could tell me."

"But I don't know," she whispered.

Raoul straightened and stepped back. "Your son is back in the stables with the other hostages." He watched her, like a snake. "If Geoffrey takes him away again, I'll have his balls chopped off as a common thief, even if he has inherited endless lands in the North."

"Raoul. Save Bryn. Save them all."

"You mistake me, Tanwen. I am de Lacy's man and de Lacy serves the king."

She stumbled around the table towards him. "You wanted me once. Save them. I'll do anything. Whatever you wish."

He gave a bark of laughter and turned away. "It's far too late for that."

CHAPTER THIRTY-SIX

Tanwen found Geoffrey by the kitchen woodpile, saddling his horse. He had a dark bruise on one cheek. "Raoul knows you took Bryn," she said. "He has him again."

"I know." Geoffrey tightened the girth and avoided her eyes. " But I can't stay here any longer. I have Mariel to think of and my mother and sister too. They all depend on me now. There is no one else."

"You've already done so much," whispered Tanwen.

"Not enough. Yet I've just come from the market. There is a rumor that may be hopeful. The king is leaving too, they say, sailing back to Normandy immediately. His men have been buying up all the foodstuffs in the market and the wagons are already loaded."

Tanwen looked over at the stables where the hostages were held, watched by foreign soldiers. "Leaving? The rest will be safe then?" She said it, but she knew it wasn't true.

"You can profit from the confusion. I've slipped a chisel in to the captives through a soldier I know. Come." She followed him around the back of the kitchens, slipping along behind the bushes after the guard passed by and before the next came around the corner. "You'll have just a few minutes, it's all I could manage." Geoffrey pointed to a jagged hole in the wall behind a holly bush, where a timber had been broken and pried away. He hesitated, as though he would say more, then turned away.

Tanwen crouched down. A hand reached out and grasped hers. "Bryn!" Her throat closed and she couldn't manage to say anything else.

Bryn squeezed her hand tight. "The king is going! I wanted to say good bye."

"What?"

"I'm going, Mama. The guard Geoffrey knows owes him a great favor, his life indeed, and he has promised to look the other way. I'm going, this very night, with Geoffrey."

"But," she said, "how can that be, you're not a Norman." A pain knifed her forehead. How could he prefer Northumberland, prefer Geoffrey, to her? Horrified at her own wicked jealousy she clutched Bryn's hand tighter.

"Nor is Geoffrey," Bryn was saying. "In the north country, the Normans are far away and the people live free. Life will be simpler there. Clear. And Nick is coming too."

"Yet it's not your home," she whispered.

"I can't go home, you know that."

Tanwen gripped his wrist, as though she could pull him from his prison. She imagined them stealing horses and riding away together, toward the bright sea. "We could still sail to Bruges."

"I must make my own way as best I can. The Lowlands are far away, there's nothing for me there." Bryn's voice was impatient. "An old man lives on Geoffrey's estate, a builder of cathedrals. Geoffrey took my sketches to him when he went north. Mother! He says my sketches show promise."

"Bryn, I've had a letter. From your father."

There was silence on the other side of the boards. He pulled his hand from her grasp.

"He asks us to come back Bryn. You might yet be his heir."

There was a long silence. "I'll never go back. He does not love us."

Tears burned the back of her eyes and spilled down her cheeks. She covered her mouth with her hand.

"It will not work out that way," Bryn said.

It would not work out as she had imagined or planned or hoped for all these long months. Bryn had said it, and perhaps she had known, but now she heard the words repeated over and over in her head and along with the words came an image of blue night, a pale round moon encircled, nearly drowned in clouds, and silvery light on an empty field, cold and white with new snow. Tanwen lay on her pallet in the stifling chamber, with the other women sleeping and mumbling uneasy, blankets tossed aside in the heat. There had been no time for more conversation between them. A new guard had come on duty and Geoffrey had yanked her away and through the long dusk the king's soldiers had shouted and stomped about in the courtyard, preparing the carts and horses for the royal journey on the morrow.

Geoffrey had started to say that she must come with them to the north country, but Tanwen had stopped him mid-sentence. She would slow them, her absence would be noted by Raoul, she would endanger Bryn. She knew these things, all too well. Geoffrey had looked uncomfortable, but relieved. "You will come after a time, when it is safe. You will visit or even live among us, as you wish. Mariel and my mother and sister, they will welcome you." Tanwen had nodded, though such a journey to the far north seemed impossible, as though having come this far, she had no strength left in her legs to carry her further.

In the warm darkness, Tanwen blinked, her eyes dry and hot. She imagined Geoffrey and Bryn and Nick stealing out the stable door, running to the hidden door behind her garden, and fleeing down the steep hill to the river. They'd mount their fast horses, hidden at the edge of the forest, and ride away. She took a quick ragged breath. How relieved, how elated she was that he would be free, perhaps was already free, at long last. And yet how strangely frightened and alone she felt, as though the humid night pressed the very air from her chest. It would be better, in the morning, with the light, surely.

Long hours passed by. Tanwen strained her ears but she heard no commotion or shouts as the dim moonlight moved across the stone walls. And finally dawn came. She dressed quietly. The day was hot and the air heavy already, with no hint of freshness or breeze.

She walked to the kitchens, thinking how strange it was that Bryn was no longer within the castle walls. She should feel jubilant, but what she felt was exhausted and blank. It was done, he was free, and she was glad, of course she was glad. But she needed time to accustom her mind to his dreams and plans in which she had no part. In the kitchen, a pot of oats bubbled over the glowing coals in the hearth. She spooned some into a bowl and sat at the table, thinking that if she willed it hard enough, she must surely know if he'd made it away, if he were truly safe and free once more.

One of the house maids burst in. "It's awful what they're doing out there, horrible." Her eyes glittered and her voice was shrill. Tanwen shoved her bowl aside and followed her out into the courtyard. Sun glared off the damp stones. One of the hostages was being shoved along by a group of four soldiers. Tanwen put a hand on the walls to steady herself, her head swimming. It was not Bryn. She was horrified at her relief.

The soldiers prodded the tall youth up the three stairs of the dismal platform in the center of the courtyard. The townspeople were gathering, running through the opened gate, screeching and waving arms. Tanwen heard her own breath coming fast. Sun gleamed off the boy's pale hair. She covered her eyes, and opened them again, her stomach tightening into a painful knot. The boy on the platform, it couldn't be, but it was. Nick. Tanwen ran to the center of the courtyard and stopped, looking around. The king's soldiers and the lines of loaded carts, they were all gone. The king himself was gone. Gone with his scouts and courtiers and even de Lacy, all of them gone and by now en route to the channel and Normandy. The hostages should be safe, Henry's killing rage appeased. Nick should be on a horse, galloping through the mountain passes with Geoffrey and Bryn.

The blonde boy stared at the sky and the soldier looped a stiff rope around his neck.

Raoul strode out of the hall, on his head a tall conical hat with flying black ribbons. He snapped his finger to the soldiers, waited a moment, then went back into the hall. Tanwen took a step after him.

The soldier shoved the boy off the platform. There was silence, a loud clunk, and a gasping choked off scream. The crowd watched, intent, until the kicking slowed. The boy's body, dark against the white sky, twitched once more and hung still. Tanwen swayed, the noise of the jeering crowd rushing in her ears, her stomach heaving.

She took a deep shaky breath, and ran into the dark hall.

Raoul stood by the high table, where de Lacy's sister Isolde sat eating honey pastries. She looked composed and cool, despite the glaring heat, in an inky dress that showed her white breasts and long neck. Raoul took a pastry from her plate and bit into it. Tanwen waited, until he looked up and their eyes met.

"It's too late, Tanwen, don't even ask. Henry has left his orders and I'll see them carried out."

"What orders?"

Raoul shrugged. "I told you to leave here."

"But the King is gone to France. De Lacy isn't even here. You could say you never got the order. Say you weren't sure de Lacy would want you to obey."

"Risky." He glanced back at Isolde, who smiled, her white teeth gleaming.

"Not so great a risk as killing that boy."

Isolde twined her fingers in Raoul's.

Tanwen stared at their linked hands, Isolde's aquamarine ring winking. "I meant the risk to you Raoul, to your soul." She stepped closer, trying to look into his eyes.

Isolde fingered and jingled her twin gold bracelets until Raoul looked her way. She took his arm, laughing, as though at a fine joke.

Tanwen turned back to Raoul. "Whatever it is that Henry has ordered you to do, you must not harm the rest of the hostages. They're just innocent boys."

Isolde looked at Raoul. "Didn't you say one would hang each morning? On my brother's orders?"

Raoul shrugged and adjusted the sword hanging off his thick belt. A gold armband gleamed above his elbow. "I'll do my duty."

Tanwen watched as they went out together, Isolde smiling back over her shoulder. The door gaped behind them, white light glaring, dust floating in shafts of light above the disturbed rushes. She turned away from the bright door and blinded, bumped into de Lacy's secretary Thomas. "He won't do it, will he?"

Thomas tugged at the neck of his tunic with inky fingers. "He will do as de Lacy orders, of course."

A crash of metal startled them both. Thomas shrank back into the hall, muttering, and disappeared up the stairs. Tanwen rushed to the door. Soldiers gathered under the raised portcullis, pointing at something outside the gates. Two of the king's Norman guards marched across the courtyard, dragging a knight between them. They halted and the knight stumbled to his feet, cursing. Tanwen glimpsed his face.

"Geoffrey!" she yelled, and ran down the steps towards them. One of the soldiers dropped Geoffrey's arm. The knight shoved the other away and ran. The soldiers shouted at the men at the gate, who couldn't hear, and shouted back. Geoffrey threw himself at the two soldiers at the gate and they all tumbled to the ground, rolling in the dust. He grabbed one of their horses and leaped on. The horse tossed his head and reared, then galloped away at his command. They pounded across the sward and into the river, spray flying, hardly slowing as they crossed the secret underwater path. The soldiers argued and ran half-hearted up to the water and let him ride on across and escape.

There was a shout then, from above, high up on the stone walls de Lacy had built. One of the bowmen, black against the bright sky, drew his longbow and shot. Across the foaming river, Geoffrey faltered, and his horse spun in a frenzied circle, and he fell, face down into the river. He lay still, water frothing over his body.

Tanwen clutched at the wall, as people flowed past her and shoved her aside, crowding out the gate to see.

She ran in the opposite direction, shouldering people aside, until she reached the corner of the stables and stopped to look around. Everyone still gathered at the gate. She darted behind the holly bush and found the hole in the stable wall. She banged on the timbers and stuck her arm in. "Bryn! Bryn!"

She felt his hand grasp hers. "We have to get out of here," she said, "now."

"It was Nick they hung this morning. Nick, Mama." Bryn gripped tighter. "He was always laughing. Sure we'd be free. He always talked of what it would be like, when we got out of here."

"I know. God's bones, they will answer for this," she said.

"He liked to fish and hunt in the woods. We planned how we'd go to a lake he knew, in the mountains by his home. He was going to come with me, to the North."

"I know. I know. But we must go now. Right away. Which one is the guard Geoffrey knows? You must get him to let you out, right now." Around the corner, she heard the loud voices of men shouting and swearing.

"He's not on duty now."

"What? Then use the chisel Geoffrey left for you. I'll get a shovel. Pry these timbers loose." Tanwen turned around, at a crash from the gatehouse. She crept to the corner and peered around. At the gate, soldiers gathered, shoving back the townspeople and shouting. The portcullis had been lowered and they were closing the giant doors. She crawled back to Bryn. "Do it now. The guards are distracted, something's happening at the gate."

"I can't leave here," said Bryn. "Not without Nick. I won't go, not without his body, he was my friend. It wouldn't be right. Where's Geoffrey? He was supposed to come last night."

Voices shouted, nearby, coming closer. "We've got him," shouted one of the younger soldiers, so excited his voice squeaked.

"I have to go," Tanwen said. "Be ready Bryn, I will come, as soon as I can."

Tanwen thrust out through the holly, ignoring the scratches along her arms, and peered around the corner of the stable. Three women lingered by the huge laundry tubs, pretending to load muddy clothes into the vats, watching the commotion at the gatehouse and gossiping. The harsh smell of soap floated over the steaming vats. Tanwen tried to see behind the women and beyond the crowd of soldiers, circled tight around a captive. If only it were Geoffrey. Perhaps he'd only knocked his head and he was unconscious, not truly dead.

A chunky woman with strong shoulders dumped a heap of soiled leggings into the tub. She whirled the filthy water around with a thick board, her dark hair falling from her bun and sticking to her sweating neck. "It's not that knight at all. That one's stark dead, more's the shame. It's the dark haired fellow with the sad eyes."

"You sound like a minstrel," said her companion. "Who are you talking about then?"

"Lyr Garth or Geth or some such Welsh folly is his name," the first woman said. "Maybe he'll be hanged on the morrow with another of those poor hostage boys."

"Fine looking he is," said a third, "but he's got no friends and what's that about? I think he's a spy, just like they say."

"You believe everything your soldier boy says," laughed the third.

The first woman stopped stirring the water in the vat and noticed Tanwen. She glared and shouldered her wooden paddle. "What are you looking at?"

Tanwen backed away. The women couldn't be right. Gethin was in Ilfracombe with Enid and small Sam. Or had he come back then, for his maps? And she had lost them. Who knew who had them, or what use they'd put them to. She put a hand to the stabbing pain in her forehead. She couldn't think about Gethin now, nor of kind brave Geoffrey. She walked to her garden and picked up the shovel. But the courtyard was full of soldiers and gawking servants. She thrust the shovel under a sprawling rose bush.

Soldiers blocked the hall door, so Tanwen crept around to the back and entered the dim hall through an unshuttered window. A man was seated in the center of a circle of soldiers, near the cold fire pit. His face was covered with a dark growth of beard and his hair tangled. But one arm was bound in a filthy sling and one hand rested on his thigh; those were certainly Gethin's long fingers. Raoul was there too, his hands linked behind his back and a satisfied smile on his face.

A kitchen girl passed by and Tanwen grabbed at her tray. The cups of ale sloshed over the girl's wrist. "You take it then," she said and flounced away. Tanwen steadied the tray and carried it toward the men.

Gethin looked up, and she met his eyes for the briefest moment. She served the men ale and slices of cheese. She even served Gethin, who hesitated, then took the cheese with his good left hand and gulped it down. She offered ale to Raoul. He took the cup, sipped, then pointed to the door. One of his soldiers took her elbow. He hurried her toward the door and when she tried to turn around, he said, "It's not smart to cross the captain. Word to the wise."

"I was just bringing refreshment to that poor fellow. He's a guest."

The soldier laughed. "You could say so."

"Why is he being questioned?"

"A spy, so they say. Wouldn't like to be in his boots."

Tanwen wanted to protest, but she just nodded and the soldier, mollified, went back in the hall. She retreated to her garden. After a time, soldiers dragged Gethin, bleeding from a cut on his forehead, across the courtyard. They dragged him past the laundry women who watched with huge eyes and tittered, soapy water dripping from their thick wet arms. They lugged him to the dungeon under the gatehouse, threw him down and shut the heavy trap door. Two men shoved an enormous flat stone over the top.

Tanwen imagined rats and silence and unending dark.

A cool breeze blew up and the afternoon wore away. Golden light spilled across the courtyard and meadow pipets sang in the hedge. The foreign soldiers stayed at their posts, alert at the stable door. Raoul remained cloistered in the hall, surrounded by lawyers. Tanwen waited in her garden, unable to take the shovel to Bryn, unable to help Gethin, heartsick about Geoffrey and Nick. She willed Raoul to ascend to his private chamber. She had only hours. And much to prepare.

Gethin pressed his fingers to his temples and tried not to groan. He was sweating, his forehead beaded, though it was cold. The granite floor hadn't seen sunlight for years, or maybe ever. His hands shook and he decided he was still in shock from the fall. His right arm burned when he moved. Not broken once more, but close to useless. His legs were intact. That was good. He closed his eyes and slowed his breath. He'd always hated to be boxed in; he felt like he might beat his fists on the rock ceiling. He must stay calm. They would drag off that rock, sooner or later, and he must take whatever chance came his way. He'd come back to get his maps and to help Tanwen.

Much good he'd do her in here. But he hadn't expected those soldiers fanning out through the woods, searching for someone. They'd found him, instead. He stretched his legs out one at a time and focused on what he'd do to Raoul and de Lacy and Henry himself, if ever he saw them again.

Time passed, days it seemed, or maybe it was hours. He grew hungry and then the hunger disappeared. He was stiff with cold and his ribs ached and more alarming, his arm didn't hurt at all. Once, he let himself think about Tanwen. The light sparking on her hair. He hoped she'd get away with her son. He turned his mind from her, but the light stayed with him.

He was shaking when they pulled the rock away. The scraping filled his ears like a sea-roar and he tried to leap up but his legs wouldn't hold. They yanked him out and it was night, scented with fresh wind and roses and smoky air. Soft clouds flitted across a moon-drenched sky and it seemed no one was awake in this dark world at all.

Tanwen heard the scrape and grind of the giant stone. She had remained in her garden, watching and waiting for a chance to get to Bryn. She strained her eyes in the darkness, as two men dragged Gethin from the pit, while a third looked on, barking orders. Gethin was bent over and he clutched at his arm. They lugged him to the shed behind the kitchen and locked him in.

But there was nothing she could do for Gethin now. She fingered the vial she carried. She had gathered the dark herbs from her garden as dusk fell, from the secret garden hidden in plain sight in the center of the flowerbeds, where each plant had a doubled purpose. She'd made the solution in the kitchen by moonlight, when cook was gone to bed and the kitchen boy sprawled asleep and Raoul, finally, had gone to his chamber. She must slip some drops into Raoul's drink, and into the ale of the foreign soldiers outside the stables. Her heart was tripping over itself, but she must appear calm. Using the dark herbs was full of danger, for those she drugged, and even more for her, if they found her out. They would stone her, or burn her, or drown her, as a witch. But the even greater danger lay within, the danger to her own self, to who she was and what she might become. She could almost hear Ceridwen whispering, but what she was saying, that she couldn't make out. In truth, it no longer mattered, it was for her now to decide.

Tanwen brought the ale laced with henbane and poppy to the stable doors first, giving a skin to the kitchen girls to share with the soldiers. She waited and watched them all laughing and drinking together, then she entered the hall and beckoned to one of the guards. He winked at his fellow and came over. She handed him a mug and lifted a second heavy skin of ale. "I'll do that for you mistress," he said.

She tried not to mind that he was amiable and so young. The drops wouldn't kill him, only make him sleep, and when they were all fallen into that sleep like death, she would go to Bryn and they would escape. She could have drugged them so they never awoke and she and Bryn would be the safer. But she'd added the exact amount to make them sleep deep and long, but wake again to life. Yet all herbs were unpredictable, the dark herbs most of all. Some slumbered and never awoke. Ceridwen's first rule hummed and buzzed in her head. Never do harm. But who else would save Bryn now, and all the others?

She waited as the soldiers guzzled the ale and waited longer, until they stumbled and slumped to the floor. She dragged the young one first, gripping a leg and tugging, until she had him behind a bench. She draped a tablecloth over him, leaving space for him to breathe. She went back for the second guard, a hefty man of middle years. He was harder to lug. Breathing hard, she left him under a table nearer the door. She went for the third soldier and got him rolled under the table just as two of the grooms came in, their dinner in their hands. They sat at a table by the door and ate. Without them seeing, she tried to rearrange the disturbed rushes on the floor as best she could.

Hoping the grooms would finish quickly and leave the hall, hoping the guards wouldn't snore in their drugged sleep, she slipped out and climbed the stairs to Raoul's room. "I have a message for the captain."

"He sleeps," said the soldier at the door. "He'll not want to see you now."

"I think he will." She pushed the door open and went in. The soldier swore but let her go.

Raoul was not in the bed. But he was alone at least, sitting on a bench by the fire.

"Have you wine?" she asked. After a moment, he gestured to a table in the corner. From the three squat bottles, she selected a ruby wine, poured a full goblet and drank.

"You should go slower with that."

She took a deeper drink. "You can share the bottle if you like."

He frowned at her, but he took the goblet and emptied it.

She laughed and went back to the table and splashed more into the cup.

"You've had enough."

"Not nearly," she said, but handed him the bottle. "On the morrow, it will be someone's child."

He shrugged. "They are fools, these Welsh nobles, to send their sons and daughters to Henry."

"Perhaps they believe in honor?"

"Or maybe all they care for is themselves."

That was true enough and silenced her.

A soft knock sounded. Raoul set the bottle on the floor and went to the door.

Quickly, Tanwen drew out the vial and dumped the contents into the bottle. She swished it around, listening to the woman's voice murmuring at the door. One of Isolde's maids. The woman laughed and Raoul shut the door. She thrust the vial back into her bodice, her heart pounding. She poured more wine and handed him the goblet.

"After you," he said.

She turned away and pretended to swallow.

Raoul came up behind her and put a heavy hand on her hip. He took the goblet, drank, and set it on the bench. "De Lacy has given me Isolde's hand in marriage and her extensive lands. For doing what needs to be done." His fingers moved up over her waist and shoulder, to the bare skin at the nape of her neck. "One has to be sensible in this world, accept things as they come."

"Is that what Isolde tells you?"

"That's what life tells me. Beggars can't choose. I won't be a beggar now."

She slipped out from his hand and filled his goblet once more. He emptied it, his eyes locked on hers, then swiped a trickle from his chin with his sleeve. "You probably think you can make life what you want. As though life were a garden, growing according to your plan."

"Nature has her part," said Tanwen.

Raoul frowned and passed a hand over his forehead. He glanced at the empty goblet and tossed it on the bed.

Tanwen took a step back and he followed her, placing his hands on her arms. His eyes bored down into hers, as though she must agree, as if her opinion mattered. Or had he realized what she'd done? His breath was coming hard and fast. The herbs weren't working; surely he'd drunk enough by now. As she wondered, his hands slipped up from her shoulders to gently encircle her neck, his thumbs meeting at the soft spot in the front of her throat.

She tried to back away, but he gripped her neck. She tried to say his name, but he was squeezing tighter. She shoved at him and he laughed. His laughter was strange and high, blending with the humming sound rising in her ears. She pushed him again; he couldn't know about the vial, he should be stumbling and falling now.

"I wanted…" he said. His eyes sought hers.

She tried to speak and couldn't. She struggled and shoved at him. His hands loosened and she pushed him away, gasping.

"My head…" he said, clutching at his hair with two hands. He swayed and gagged and pulled at her skirts so hard she fell to her knees. The vial tumbled out from her bodice to the floor. She saw his eyes focus on the shattered glass. She scrambled to her feet and shoved him again. He stumbled back this time and fell, heavily, to the floor.

Tanwen stood over him, holding her throat. He did not move and there was no sound from him, nor from outside the chamber. She opened the door a crack. The guard yawned at the top of the stairs. "Your master will sleep now," she croaked. "Do not disturb him." She handed him the last of the wine and hoped he'd drink it down. She made her way down the steps.

Outside, all was dark and still. She shook her head, trying to clear the dizziness away. Perhaps she'd swallowed some of the herbs, or it was lack of air. She walked to her garden, using the walls to stay upright, and found her shovel where she'd hidden it, under the red rose.

The soldiers at the stable door slept, propped against the walls, pillowed on the sleeping kitchen maids. They slept as though enchanted, as in a magical tale of maidens and youths deep in a witch's forest. Tanwen passed them, carefully, but they did not stir and she went round to the back of the stable, thrust her way through the thick bushes, and stuck her shovel into the hole in the boards. She pried at the timber. The wood plank squealed and screeched. She froze, then shoved the shovel in again. "Bryn," she called softly. The plank gave a notch. "Bryn," she called out, louder. Inside, she heard people stirring. She pried the board again, and it splintered with a loud crack, but held. She grabbed at the board and tried to yank it away.

Hands reached from inside. "Give us the shovel," called a youth. "Here, use this chisel." She heard Bryn's voice. They pounded away at one board, and pried off another. "Where are the guards?" said someone. "Hurry," called a second.

A torch was lit by the great hall, sending up smoke and throwing long wavering rectangles of light across the courtyard. "Yes, hurry," Tanwen called. "You must hurry." A thin boy wriggled out, and another followed behind. They huddled in the fresh wind, as though confused or waiting for direction. "Run," she said, "run, all of you, run, just go." She pointed out her door standing open beyond the garden.

Another torch was lit in the hall. Men were spilling out the door, milling around, shouting. Perhaps they'd found their captain, or the drugged guards. Perhaps she hadn't given them enough of the wine and they were waking early. The tenth boy out was Bryn. Tanwen grabbed him, hugging him to her tight.

"Mama." He stopped, seeing the commotion at the hall door. "Mother. You know what I am going to say. I go with Geoffrey, tonight. I want your blessing."

"Come away from here, there's something I must tell you." She tried to tug him along, toward her garden, but he planted his feet.

"Tell me now."

"It's Geoffrey. He's gone, dead." So bald it sounded. Was there no way to shield him from this awfulness? Death circling everywhere, stealing loved ones, stealing a future. Night wind slid cold around her ankles.

"I see." She heard the last of his childhood drop away. The future rushing up, surf climbing a golden beach.

She clasped his hand. "We must go now, we must go on."

"He said I would always have a place at his hearth. Like a nephew. Northumberland is a different world, he said that often, far from the duplicity of this place." He squeezed his eyes shut. "We'd be happy there, he said, where everything is clear."

Tanwen nodded. Geoffrey had been right; Bryn would have flourished there. "He was a good man and generous," she whispered. "We will keep him and Nick always in our hearts."

The doors to the hall were flung open with a crash. Bryn grabbed her; she could feel his heart racing.

"We must get out of here. We must get you safe," he said.

CHAPTER THIRTY-SEVEN

Gethin leaned against the wall in the dark shed, surrounded by empty shelves, though he could swear he smelled the cheese and sausages once stored here. He felt like he hadn't eaten for a week, though it must be only three days. His hands were tied with tangled cord, wrenching his bad arm. But he was out of that wretched dungeon. Above ground again, he could breathe and think. He'd come back to get his maps, and to get Tanwen and her son, and so far, he'd bungled all.

The grey horse Tanwen stole for him had bolted in that lightning storm, veering off the path and taking him deep into the forest. He'd managed to stay on its back, but too late, he'd realized the horse was taking him in great wandering circles. The rain had streamed off the leaves and steam floated between the trees and his arm had swelled, oozing. But on the fourth day, he'd found a stream and with water his head cleared enough that he could head the horse east. He'd reached the river and traded the horse for a boat. Floated mostly, as he couldn't paddle. Drifting in and out of fever, his mind drifting over old sorrows, the child who might have been, the wife he'd hardly known, the life that had vanished in just one night. But it seemed the time had come to leave guilt and sorrow back there, in the past. He'd let himself drift in life too long, guided always by someone else's dreams. Rhys. De Lacy. Never his own.

When the boat ground onto the sands north of Ilfracombe, he'd got himself up the hill to Enid's. He scared Sam, when he shoved open the gate and limped in, bloody and filthy, but the boy ran for Enid who dressed his arm and fed him mutton soup. A long fortnight passed but as soon as he could mount a horse he was off, his arm bound in linen, heading back to Ludelaue.

Loud footsteps crunched in the gravel outside the shed. Gethin shook his thoughts away and waited for the door to be kicked open. But it swung open soundlessly, and Raoul entered.

"What do you want?" said Gethin. "Get it over with."

Raoul shrugged. "No hurry." With a swish of silk skirts, Isolde squeezed in behind the captain. "I've work to do here, Isolde," said Raoul.

"You must be quite special, Lyr Gethin," Isolde said. "When my brother Hugh puts someone in the hole, we don't usually see them again." She handed Raoul a bottle and left, and the heavy door slammed shut.

"So, the maker of maps returns. The hostages have escaped. You'll pay, in their stead, on the morrow. But before that, you'll tell me where those maps are."

When Gethin said nothing, Raoul shrugged. "My men will get it out of you." He stuck the bottle on a high shelf and went out whistling.

Hours slid by. Gethin watched light gleam through the wide gap under the door and tried to loosen his bonds, but with one arm useless, he couldn't get a hand free. He managed to get to his feet and kick the door, but it was solid and locked and though he could hear servants passing, none answered his shouts. Eventually, he sat by the door, watching the light fade. He wondered if all the hostages had gotten away and if that meant that Tanwen, too, was gone. He wondered how Raoul knew about the maps and he was glad that somehow, Tanwen had kept them safe. How ironic that now he'd decided to live, he might die on the morrow.

He waited, but Raoul's soldiers did not come to question him. He was thirsty, his throat scratchy as gravel. The bottle Raoul had left loomed out of reach. He imagined clear water or sour wine. Dusk deepened and the sounds of bustling servants fell away and he was enveloped in the silence of night.

He got to his feet again. He got a boot behind the shelf and shoved, but they were built of heavy timber and merely shuddered, puffing old dust into his face. He shoved harder and the bottle toppled and fell with a thump. He felt about in the dark with a foot and found it. The fall had loosened the cork and most of the wine had leaked out, but he managed to gulp a mouthful. The liquid burned his dry tongue. Sighing, head aching, he leaned against the wall and wondered what morning would bring.

A thump outside startled him from a doze, and a muttered curse, as though someone stubbed a toe. Gethin, slumped on the floor, sat up, his head spinning. A cold wind swirled around him. The door must have opened. He couldn't see anyone in the blackness. "Who is there?"

"Quiet," said a female voice. A knife sawed though the bindings at his wrists.

He recognized Tanwen from the irritation in her voice. The knife nicked his good hand. "Have a care," he said, his voice sounding like he spoke from twenty paces away.

"Follow me," she said.

He stumbled after her, clumsy on his feet, head throbbing, one arm hanging down useless. She pulled him outside, around the shed, and through another door. He found walking hard and had to lean against the walls. Tanwen took his arm. They shuffled down a long corridor lined with small rooms, a wine cellar by its acrid smell. He let her pull him along, as life flowed back into his fingers. He wondered if he'd be able to hold a pen again. They edged their way down another long passage with a low ceiling. The air was black and thick against his face and it seemed the ground was an endless swirling river.

"Quiet," she whispered. "The great hall is just above us." Finally she opened a door and the quality of the darkness altered. It was black outside too, with no moon, but the sky was brilliant with a sweep of stars and the air blew fresh and chill. He gulped it in like water and shook his aching head. They were near her garden. He could smell the overturned earth. She led him to a door in the walls, hidden behind thick ivy, and she opened it a crack.

A tall youth loomed up in the darkness and examined his face. "He's in bad shape," the youth said.

"Gethin, listen to me," said Tanwen, stepping close.

Gethin reached out for her. He wanted to touch her skin, the soft looking spot under her ear. There was something he needed to say, about why he was here, but everything was jumbled, what he must say lurked in his mind and he couldn't find it. "Where are the maps?" he said instead. "I can't go without them. They're a danger to everyone in the wrong hands."

"Don't worry about that now." She took his hand and placed it in the boy's. Bryn, he realized.

"Go now," Tanwen whispered to Bryn. "Stay together. I'll meet you by dusk tomorrow. Wait near Helori's for me, not in her cottage. Hide in the woods."

"He can go on alone. I'll stay with you," said Bryn.

"No! It's you they'll search for at first light. We have two horses, thanks be to Geoffrey. But we must have a third," Tanwen said urgently. "I can manage it. The guard who owes his life to Geoffrey, he'll help me. I'll use the last of the silver. And he can't go alone, look at him."

Gethin swayed on his feet, his face white in the dark. "There must have been something in the wine," he said.

"How much wine did you drink?" Tanwen clutched his hand.

"I wanted to drink a river," said Gethin.

Bryn reached over and hugged her tight. "I'll take care of him. Just get the horse and come as soon as you can." He hoisted Gethin's arm over his shoulder and they disappeared into the night.

Tanwen and Bryn had seen Gethin thrust in the shed, as they huddled deep in her garden, toward the edge of her unfinished maze. They'd been hiding there since they'd run from the stables, hand in hand. Tanwen had wanted to go with the other hostages, out the door, down the hill, away. But Bryn had refused to go without burying Nick and Geoffrey.

"But how can we get their bodies?" Tanwen had cried. "I know you want to honor them, but Bryn, we cannot."

"It's dangerous, but I have to try. I can't let them stay here, picked at by crows, as though they meant nothing."

They'd seen Raoul and Isolde enter and leave the shed. As though Bryn could hear her worried thoughts, he'd said, "And we can't leave Master Gethin in there. He brought me parchment and pens and ink."

"I know," Tanwen had said, her fingers shredding the feathery fronds of a tansy plant.

They'd crept from their hiding place only when it was completely silent and dark, their clothes smelling of wet earth and flowers. Bryn had argued with her again, but she'd convinced him to wait by the hidden door while she went back for Gethin alone.

Now Tanwen stared into the blackness framed by her door, but Gethin and Bryn were gone. She couldn't see them or hear them any longer. For a moment more, she lingered, feeling the new season's brisk wind on her face. She closed the door, replaced the stones and moss that hid it, and sat one last time on the turf seat in the gloriet in the center of her garden. She had done what she set out to do. And though she had used the dark herbs, fate had been kind to her so far. She had only one task left. She would ask the guard for the bodies. She thought he would grant that, for Geoffrey's sake, and she had silver to pay for a horse. So, it was done.

Yet strangely, she felt bereft and unsettled, like a leaf in the oak trees they would pass through on the morrow, torn whirling from its branch to settle at long last on the ground, but finding the ground to be fast flowing water, slipping away and away. Her mind lurched from one garish image to another, faces and places she'd been, and as she turned her eyes up to calm herself and watched the night sky, even the stars seemed to leap from their settled places and arc away, trailing streamers of bright light.

Tanwen slept in her garden maze for a few hours and woke chilled and hungry. She brushed the straw from her skirts and seeing the courtyard still deserted, and no tapers lit in the great hall, decided it was safe to go to the kitchens for food and then search out the guard Geoffrey had known. A fire snapped in the hearth and onion soup was already steaming in a big iron pot. Tanwen greeted the kitchen maids and ladled up a bowl of soup.

The door slammed open and one of the kitchen girls squealed.

"Quiet," said a fierce voice and soldiers crowded in. "Which one of you is Tanwen, leman to Owain ap Macsen."

The girls backed away, dropping their bread.

"I am," Tanwen said.

"Then you'll come with us," said the soldier.

"Where do you take me?"

"De Lacy will see you, that's all I know," said the soldier.

"De Lacy's not even here; he's in France with the king."

"No more," said the soldier. He grasped her elbow and dragged her out the door. She stumbled over the stoop and past a line of soldiers, watching with cold eyes. "Witch!" one called and a few laughed but most looked uneasy.

They locked her in the round chapel, and Tanwen smelled Isolde's jasmine perfume mixed with the incense burning. It was cold and the candles were not lit. Damp from the stone floor seeped through her skirts. The sounds of the soldiers and servants outside were muffled and indistinct, as though she'd already passed on to some other realm.

Long hours passed. Perhaps she deserved this, for daring to use the dark herbs. Ceridwen said there would always be a cost. But she would do it again, she would do it again and again, whatever the gods thought or did, to save Bryn.

In the quiet of late afternoon, Hugh de Lacy entered with three men and the cringing clerk Thomas. De Lacy loomed over her, in a black traveling cloak and fox fur collar. He eyed her with cold distaste. "So, not a garden keeper, after all," he said. "Just another witch. Or another Welsh spy."

Beside him, Isolde waited with folded hands and downcast eyes.

"Stay with her," said de Lacy to Isolde. "I'll deal with her later this evening."

"And I will have something for you then, brother," said Isolde. "A present of sorts."

De Lacy grunted and swept out the door.

Isolde seated herself on one of the benches, arranged her skirts and drew her furs around her neck. "He will be more interested, later," she said calmly. "They will be so very useful to him, in the next stage of this war. How chilly it is in here, to be sure." She examined Tanwen's damp skirts and red hands, and finally met her eyes and smiled.

"It's you," said Tanwen. "You have the maps. You took them from Raoul."

Isolde tossed her black hair over her shoulder and laughed. "What harm is there now? Yes," she said. "Yes and no. I knew Lyr Gethin had made them from the start. I overheard his conversations with my brother and I knew how valuable the men thought them in this war. Then, when I saw you with that monk, I was curious. I followed you, into the forest. It was easy. They never think to worry about me listening." She went to the window and peered through the thick green glass. "They are gone now. Come."

They left the chapel by the priest's door. Outside, Isolde tugged her along, beside the stone walls, until they came to her garden. Wind rustled the ivy. There were alone, de Lacy's men eating in the hall. Tanwen thought of screaming or shoving Isolde aside and running, but Isolde was tall and strong and her chances might be better with de Lacy's sister than with the border lord himself.

"Dig there," said Isolde, pointing to the bed of pink asters beside the arbor and seating herself on Tanwen's bench.

Tanwen dug, her bound hands making her clumsy, until her trowel clunked against some object made of wood. She pulled out a long box fashioned of rough wood with a brass clasp.

Isolde went right to her hidden door and opened it.

Tanwen smelled the cold river coiling below the walls. "I didn't think of you," she said.

"No one does," said Isolde. "Until now." She pulled a dagger from her boot and gestured to the door.

Tanwen hesitated. Isolde's dagger pricked her waist and Tanwen felt the dribble of blood. "Why?" she whispered.

"I needed them. My brother planned to marry me off to that captain of his, or one of his wretched friends. I'm nothing to him but another purse full of coin or more acres of land on this cursed border. You've seen how they all use Rosamund; it's shameful. She is my friend." Isolde shook her hair off her face. "My friend, do you see?" Her forehead wrinkled and she smoothed it with the back of her hand. "With those maps, I would be free. I could look higher, much higher, than my brother's crazed captain."

"But the cost, in lives," said Tanwen. "To you."

"Move on," said Isolde, and pricked her again with the dagger.

Tanwen stumbled down the grassy bank to the river and stared at the black water. Isolde laughed behind her and Tanwen wished anyone, even de Lacy, would find them. They reached the slippery bank and Isolde pushed her forward. Water surged icy around her ankles. She slid on a rounded stone and almost fell.

Isolde laughed again. "Go, go," she said. "This is no place for you any longer. You see how generous I am, how I let you go free. We could have been friends, you and I, in some other time or place."

Tanwen stared up at Isolde and backed away. She stumbled over a slippery log, wedged between rocks and fell. Cold water rushed up over her mouth and nose. She struggled upright, gasping, her wet skirts dragging, her hair clinging to her face, covering her eyes. She looked up and down the river, but they were far from the underwater pathway, and even on the secret path, water had climbed to Gethin's thighs. The river was swollen now, huge with the summer's endless drenching rains. She crouched in the icy water.

Above her, Isolde stood on the bank, the maps cradled in one arm like a baby. "Go! Make it across and away if you can, and if not, the river god will take you. It's up to you now." She held up the dagger and the point caught the light and sparked like a malign star.

"Isolde, what are you doing?" Raoul hurried and slid down the bank. Isolde dropped the dagger to the ground and stepped back to hide it under her skirts. She handed the box to him, ceremoniously, with two hands, and smiled.

Raoul hesitated, then took the box from her and shook it. The rolled maps clunked inside the wood. "You had them?" he said. "You? All along?"

"I found them," Isolde said, "for you."

Tanwen thrust her soaked skirts into her belt and slowly rose to her feet. Water rushed against the backs of her knees, icy and bubbling.

She ran toward the pair, stumbling and sliding on the slippery rocks and mud. Absorbed in each other, they didn't see her coming.

Raoul looked up first. His eyes met hers and he yanked his knife from his belt.

Tanwen, eyes blinded by the red ball of sun, reached for the maps.

She heard the whoosh and thump and the odd high scream. She looked away from the sun and blinked, unable still to see. Slowly, the world came into focus, the blur of green resolving back into grass blades and granite and pale sky laced with clouds and lit with a garish setting sun. It was Isolde who had screamed and who stood silent, her hand over her mouth. Raoul lay in a sprawled heap at their feet, a black arrow stuck through his throat.

Tanwen felt her knees give out. Then Gethin was sawing the ropes from her wrists and Bryn was bending over Raoul, a dark longbow in his hand. Isolde was running up the hill toward the gate.

"Let's get out of here," said Gethin. He thrust the maps back into the wooden box and handed it to Bryn, then picked Tanwen up with his good arm and headed into the river.

Tanwen turned her head to yell, "Bryn!" The water climbed and dragged at her skirts and the stones slid and tipped under his feet and at one point, Gethin had to swim, tugging her along by her skirts. Bryn swam alongside. Tanwen pictured the green pool deep in the border forest where she had learned to swim and wondered when and where her son had learned to survive. They were all silent, the river tugging and pulling at them, until they squelched out through the ferns and mud on the far side.

Gethin cut the straps binding her hands. Bryn grabbed the reins of two horses. Tanwen turned to look back. Raoul's body merged with the darkness of the grass. The castle walls loomed purple against the dusky sky. A nightjar churred and called.

CHAPTER THIRTY-EIGHT

TANWEN WOKE TO BRIGHT MORNING, sunshine and clouds flitting across a brilliant sky. She shrugged off a heavy wool blanket. She was in a real bed, sun beating on fluffy clean pillows. She shook out her wrinkled gown and tried to smooth her snarled hair with her fingers. A bee hummed in the asters outside the open window.

No one was outside in the kitchen garden either. Feeling like she'd dropped into some enchanted cottage, she gazed out over a clearing wide enough that a strip of barley had been planted and ripe seed heads swayed and shimmered gold in the sun.

Gethin, followed by Bryn, came around the corner of the cottage, pails and long sticks in their hands.

"I'm going fishing," said Bryn, "there's a stream just over there." He pointed with the pole and was gone before she could say anything.

Gethin's right arm was wound with clean linen. "Let me look at that," she said.

"It's fine. I don't need you as a healer."

She studied his face, then nodded. She swung around and looked at the cottage. "Where are we? Whose house is this?"

"Some people I knew lived here, once."

"They won't mind us in their home?"

"No."

"Is there any food? How long have I been sleeping?"

Gethin fetched some early apples and a pear and a wedge of aged cheese. "Nearly a night and a day," he said. "It's well into the afternoon."

"Don't you want some of this?" She held out a slice of apple.

He shook his head and fiddled with his knife while she ate, drawing lines and symbols in the dirt beneath his feet. The moment she finished, he said, "I've thought it all out. I can bring you to the river, and we'll find a fisherman there. I've silver enough to pay him to take you and Bryn to the coast and find you a guide to take you on to Adpar. There you can wait until Owain returns."

"Owain?"

Gethin tossed the dagger so the point stuck into the ground. "He's with Rhys. I saw him only weeks ago in the rebel camp in the mountains. He asked about you."

Tanwen looked away. A flock of chittering finches swooped in the apple trees. "Owain will never leave Rhys. There's no room in that life for me or for Bryn." She thought a moment. "Why were you in the rebel camp?"

Gethin laughed uncomfortably and started to pace. "Rhys wanted to talk."

"What about?"

Gethin shrugged. "He's fought his whole life. But now he's won, he intends to start something new. A different kind of kingdom on the west coast of Wales."

"Is there a place for a mapmaker in this new kingdom?"

"He offered it. Actually he had me hauled off my ship and brought to his camp. Just to talk, so he said." Gethin sighed. "He's lonely, I think. We used to be able to talk, once, he and I." He looked away, at the shadows shifting over the grass and one blue butterfly wandering.

They said nothing more, until the day lengthened into summer evening. Bryn returned, with three fat trout. They roasted the fish on long sticks and ate crumbly yellow cheese and honey and drank water from the spring. Bryn told her how he and Gethin had decided, both at the same time, that they must go back for her. "I should be very angry with you," Tanwen said to Bryn. "I told you to stay at Helori's clearing, safe."

"I made my own choice," Bryn said calmly, and crunched an apple he'd found at the top of an old tree. He tossed the core away. "Where will we go now?"

"Where would you wish to go?" asked Tanwen. How unfamiliar and grown up he seemed.

"I've been thinking," said Bryn, "that it would be sad to go to Geoffrey's house without him, with him gone, I mean." He stared away, into the woods, slender birches here, with pale fluttering leaves and sun dappling the ferns and mosses on the ground. "His sister came with her abbess and they gave her the body," he said, "we saw as we watched for you from the woods. But we couldn't get Nick, they had buried him already in the pit with the others." He swallowed and tossed another log on the fire.

Tanwen put her hand on his arm. He let it rest there a moment, then shifted away. "I suppose I could still learn from the castle builder there, but…"

"Is that what you want?" asked Gethin.

"More than anything," said Bryn. "I want to build things, I want to know how to turn these pictures in my mind into working designs. It's all I thought of, caged up in there."

"Where does one go to learn such things? Where did you learn?" Tanwen asked Gethin.

"Some at the abbey, and more from a builder who worked for a time in Ilfracombe, and more again when I worked for Rhys. But I never learned enough, that's why I wanted to go on to Venezia…" Gethin paused and thought a moment. "Cynan would know."

"That monk?" said Tanwen.

"Cynan is my good friend. He's also a great artist. He would know where to get such learning, if anyone does."

"But the church?" said Tanwen.

"He wouldn't have to enter the church," said Gethin. "The only problem is that Cynan is at Clairvaux."

"Let's go there," said Bryn, leaping to his feet. "Clairvaux, isn't that in France? Let's go, now."

Gethin laughed and looked at Tanwen. She was staring at Bryn's face, fired with excitement. Perhaps these years of misfortune could be, if not erased, somehow eased?

They left the mountains and journeyed down into the valleys, avoiding the worn path by the river for fear of meeting de Lacy's men, and traveling the trails Gethin had mapped, some created by men and some trodden down by deer or other creatures. The autumn days were bright, the sun golden and the air sharp. At times Tanwen felt like a girl again, wandering in the forest, and at other moments, seeing Bryn ahead of her on his horse, she felt breathless with the flight of time.

Late in the third day, at the hour when light slanted through the low branches, they came out of the woods and dismounted above the river. "Are we safe now?" asked Bryn.

"I think we're far enough away," said Gethin. "They'll search to the west; they'll think we headed back towards Adpar." Sun shimmered off the ribbon of water below them, ruffled by lazy waves.

"Did you map this river too?" asked Tanwen.

"Most of it," Gethin said.

"What will you do with your maps now?" Tanwen asked. "Will you sell them to de Lacy or to Henry, or give them to Rhys?"

Gethin was silent for a long time. "I have been thinking," he said. "They could make me wealthy, no doubt. They might make me famous, or better yet, give me the funds to do more exploring. But the dangers are too great. I made them with joy, but they would be turned to something evil."

Bryn said, "You can't just keep them. De Lacy knows of their existence. They've been stolen and hidden and lost and recovered, and it could all happen again."

"Yes," agreed Gethin. "I'm thinking I'll give them to Cynan's bishop, or to Cynan himself in Clairvaux. They will value them and preserve them, for the knowledge they contain, not the battles they might win."

Bryn unsaddled the horses and Gethin started a fire. Tanwen sat on a dry rock and watched the setting sun turn the water bright gold. She thought about the glorious colors of Gethin's maps, and the heart shaped leaves of the sleeping herbs from her gardens, and how a thing of beauty could be turned this way or that, glinting dark or light. Later, they ate pears hot, roasted on long sticks.

"After we reach Clairvaux, will you go to your sea once more, your Mediterranean?" Tanwen asked Gethin, when Bryn had gone to feed the horses.

"I hope so." Gethin cleared his throat. "Perhaps you'll want to see the world too."

"Perhaps," she said, and in the dusk their fingers met and linked.

After that day, once they left the shadows and mystery of the forest, time resumed its normal march. They boarded a ship a week later and as they left the Severn the sea tossed choppy waves and purple clouds skidded along against a backdrop of flat grey sky. In two days, they would reach France.

Tanwen lay under a blanket in a protected corner of the ship's deck, with Bryn sleeping by her side, an arm flung over his head, and Gethin standing at the rail staring out at the sea. After a time, he lay down on her other side and fell into sleep. Overhead, the night had begun with clouds, but when she looked up, they had streaked away in the fast winds, and the sky stretched out violet-black and soft as the fur of a cat. Stars were flung wide and they glimmered and sparked in great wheeling patterns over their heads. Tanwen imagined glowing flowers and sparkling vines and she thought of all the wondrous gardens and novel lands she might see. She put one hand on Bryn and another on Gethin. Neither stirred nor woke, but she felt their warmth and as she watched the stars glow she felt comforted by something fragile and new, something like hope.

Days of travel would pass. She and Bryn would talk of what he hoped for and what he'd learn. Away from England, she would watch the cautious hunch in his shoulders disappear and his infectious laughter flow back. They traveled to Clairvaux and on to the university in Paris, tracing Cynan, and they had time, walking along the wooded paths together, to speak of the oaks and elms and multitudes of late wildflowers, and when they entered Paris, to gape at the crowded lanes and connected houses and the stone walls rising for the great cathedral. When they finally left Bryn, living with the master builder

Cynan knew well, Tanwen knew he would thrive. They made a plan to meet in Paris after two summers time, when the first stage of his apprenticeship would be over.

Bryn hugged her tightly, crushing her shoulders. "I will make you proud," he said.

"You are perfect as you are," she answered.

Nothing had gone as she'd expected or planned. He hadn't wished to be saved in any way she knew. She'd never imagined this for him, but seeing his intent face as he bent over his intricate drawings, she felt amazed and glad.

"I want to go to the sea," Tanwen said to Gethin, after they left Bryn in his new lodgings. So in the still warm days of November, they traveled on ponies until at last the Mediterranean stretched out before them. They reached a crescent of coarse gold sand, and Tanwen pulled off her boots and dug in her toes and let the sand sift and trickle through her fingers. She thought of Bryn, seated at his desk or sketching Saint-Germain, learning the secrets of numbers and proportions, arches and doorways and windows opening out. She thought of the long uselessness of the border war, the endless quarrel over who controlled the land, as though forests or flowing water could ever be owned. She thought of Gethin, standing at the edge of the water, waves lapping over his toes, and what he might learn and do when he finally reached Venezia. And what might she herself learn and create, in that land of flourishing gardens and warm winds? The water before her was moving light, flowing under an immense sky, the world a perfect silver orb, and she felt content. Consoled with nature's patterns.

She shrugged off her gown. Gethin grabbed her up in his good arm and rushed them into the sea. Icy bubbles fizzed past her face and she gasped and flailed, but then she remembered, and floated up, and swam. She broke the surface and laughed out loud. Gethin laughed too and reached for her. She twined her leg around his and his leg was warm and solid and strong and they floated together, buoyed up by the salty water, lapping cold around their shoulders.

They swam out, side by side and slow, into the flat silvery bay toward the unknown horizon, the water billowy and fragrant with salt, something decided without words. They swam as wild geese fly, nudging, calling out one to the other, exclaiming in wonder at it all. Tanwen imagined feathery hemlocks and ferns laden with snow, falling suns, glittering waves tossing and rolling and smelling of salt, and hope, that stranger, nudged her again. The future opened wide, as it had when first she set out.

ACKNOWLEDGMENTS

Dafydd ap Gwilym's luminous ode to summer lodged deep in my mind when I first read it in Richard Morgan Loomis' translation in *Dafydd ap Gwilym: the Poems*. Tanwen was the eventual result. But her journey only emerged when I also came across the account of Henry II's maiming and hanging of 22 young hostages on the Welsh/English border in 1165, in *The Chronicle of the Princes of Wales*. In the gap between these two fragments, a poem and a historical account, a story and a woman and a world came into being. As a reader, I love to fall into an imagined land so completely that it replaces my own and haunts me. I hoped to create such a world here, at the edges and in the silences beyond what the historical chronicles say. In attempting to do so, I've had the wonderful chance to live in this world myself. As I prepare to go into exile, I imagine Tanwen and her story going on.

As this is a novel, Tanwen, Owain, Bryn, and Gethin are fictional beings, but the historical frame around them is generally accurate. Many of the characters are "real" people: Lord Rhys, Henry II, Eleanor of Aquitaine, and the border lord Hugh de Lacy. With the exception of Adpar, the places and timing of events are real as well. Rhys' rise to power in south-west Wales, his battles and truces with Henry II, and his dream of a united polity are historical events. Interested readers can find a list of books I consulted and enjoyed on my website. I am absolutely indebted to the early historians who recorded events in chronicles and later scholars who researched the persons, events, and places found in this novel. I also want to thank the historical preservation societies which keep up the castles and historical sites in Wales and England, where I spent some wonderful days imagining away car parks and train tracks and soaking in the mist and marvelous moving clouds.

To my fellow writers in the many workshops I've attended while working on this novel, thank you so much for your encouragement and suggestions. I'm especially delighted to thank my wonderful fellow writers Jenn Stroud Rossmann, Siri Chateaubriand, Mary Edelson, and Harley Mazuk; I couldn't have finished Tanwen's journey without our group and your weekly attention. Thank you also to Jill Reich, who understood, and gave me the immense and crucial gift of time. And to Malena Watrous, thank you for inspiration as a wonderful writer, and for being the most thoughtful and generous teacher I can imagine; your encouragement, insight, and tough tasks took me from the dreaded middle to the end.

A huge thank you and hug to all my extended family, for cheerfully asking over and over when the novel would be done. To my grandmother, Clara Phinney Eaton, who first told me I could and should tell a story. To my mother, Carol Eaton Elowe, for the music within and beyond language. To Hannah, my first reader, for greeting my words with enthusiasm and care. And to Morgan, for teaching me about nature and art and love; I've learned absolutely everything I know about being a mother from you. Last, to Bruce, for always believing, and for InDesign therapy; without you and all we have together, there could be no novel.

I should have the right words to properly thank you all, but words are always just a glimpse and never tell the entire story.

ABOUT THE AUTHOR

Arlene MacLeod was born in Massachusetts and grew up in New England. She earned her A.B. in government and history from Bowdoin College, and she holds a Ph.D in Political Science from Yale University. She teaches comparative politics and political theory at Bates College. She lives with her husband near the coast in Maine, where she enjoys walking, swimming, and painting. She has always loved to read, especially books that transport the reader to a new time and place. *A Necessary Garden* is her first novel.

www.arlenemacleod.com

Author Photo: Morgan MacLeod

www.ingramcontent.com/pod-product-compliance
Lightning Source LLC
Chambersburg PA
CBHW051208120726
47905CB00004B/1027

* 9 7 8 0 9 9 7 8 0 1 0 1 9 *